MW00532669

THE QUIRK

Also from Alyson
by Gordon Merrick

THE LORD WON'T MIND

ONE FOR THE GODS

FORTH INTO LIGHT

NOW LET'S TALK ABOUT MUSIC

AN IDOL FOR OTHERS

THE GOOD LIFE (WITH CHARLES G. HULSE)

THE QUIRK

GORDON MERRICK

alyson
books

LOS ANGELES •NEW YORK

MANUFACTURED IN THE UNITED STATES OF AMERICA.

THIS TRADE PAPERBACK IS PUBLISHED BY ALYSON PUBLICATIONS INC.,
P.O. BOX 4371, LOS ANGELES, CALIFORNIA 90078-4371.
DISTRIBUTION IN THE UNITED KINGDOM BY TURNAROUND PUBLISHER SERVICES LTD.,
UNIT 3 OLYMPIA TRADING ESTATE, COBURG ROAD, WOOD GREEN,
LONDON N22 6TZ ENGLAND.

FIRST EDITION PUBLISHED BY AVON BOOKS: 1978
FIRST ALYSON EDITION: NOVEMBER 1998

02 01 00 99 98   10 9 8 7 6 5 4 3 2 1

ISBN 1-555583-294-6
(PREVIOUSLY PUBLISHED WITH ISBN 0-380-38992-4.)

LIBRARY OF CONGRESS CATALOGING-IN PUBLICATION DATA
MERRICK, GORDON.
THE QUIRK / GORDON MERRICK. — 1ST ALYSON EDITION.
ISBN 1-55583-294-6
I. TITLE.
PS3525.E6413Q57 1998
813'.52—DC21   98-20555 CIP

FOR CHARLIE,
WHO BULLIED ME INTO IT

"No. Please. I mean it. I want you to."

"It's too much, monsieur. I simply can't. We must be serious."

Rod laughed. Serious? He wanted to give the man a small painting. He didn't want to be serious. He had been learning recently that he didn't have to be serious about most of the things people insisted he should be serious about; he could turn life upside down and come out on top every time. He moved toward the door to indicate that the incident was closed.

"Truly," he said in French that was rapidly becoming idiomatic. "When people like my work I'd like to give them everything I've done. As you say, art should be a necessity, not a luxury." This plumber or electrician, whichever one took care of water heaters, had actually said it and had so delighted Rod that for the moment the idea of putting a price on pictures seemed beneath him. His enormous gamble hadn't been for money.

"If you refuse to let me pay, I will be here without charge whenever you're in difficulties," the stocky stranger said. "M. Valmer knows how to reach me."

"Perfect," Rod agreed, still laughing. A deal between specialists. His work had as much practical value as a functioning water heater.

The man picked up the tool bag at his feet and, holding the small canvas carefully by the stretcher, lumbered to the door. Rod followed. The man turned back to him and disengaged one finger and offered it in lieu of a handshake. Rod shook it and let him out amid expressions of mutual admiration and satisfaction.

He turned back into the big high-ceilinged room and looked around it with a proprietary grin. He stretched his arms out at his sides and flexed his finders. Space. His secret hideaway. Not even the girl he loved—who was thrillingly in love with him—knew where he lived. People might be sleeping in the Métro, but he, one of the Americans who were urged to "go home," had a place of his own in Paris. The price he was paying might drive him slightly schizo, but he wasn't even much worried about that anymore. He had the world by the tail.

He chuckled and dropped his arms to his sides and headed back to his easel. Everything was perfect. The enormous gamble, the gamble that had kept him in a paralysis of foreboding and indecision for almost a year, was paying off royally. Why had he ever doubted that it would? Why had he been so terrified of questioning the outmoded conventions that had ruled to first 25 years of his life? A month ago he would have been tongue-tied at the prospect of discussing art with a plumber—never dreamed that a workman would want one of his pictures. The fact that he had *given* it to the man was symbolic of his liberation from the prevailing obsession with money. Money. He was finally free of it; he knew what it felt like to be happy.

His biggest recent discovery was that torment was greatly overrated as a spur to creativity. He had never heard of the Greek who had said that no man could be counted as happy until he was dead, beyond the reach of life's hazards and vicissitudes. He hadn't learned that happiness is a volatile blessing frequently leading to folly. This had been the year of the big decisions. Next year they would bear fruit and make his name a household word. Let his future biographers make note of two crucial dates in the annals of contemporary painting: 1960 and 1961. Rod MacIntyre didn't have quite the ring of, say, Pablo Picasso, but it would do as well as Jackson Pollock.

He was right that the dates were crucial but in ways that were to come as a shocking surprise to him. Shrouded in secrecy, his name was soon to appear in a report given strictly limited distribution in an obscure office in the vicinity of Washington, D.C. It read in part:

REF YR 1274-27-C SIDECAR BADLY STALLED, SUSPECT NEW BIRD ABOUT TO FLY COOP. WILL FACILITATE DESPITE STICKY SITUATION WITH AUTHORITIES HERE. POSSIBLE MANSLAUGHTER CHARGE PLUS REALLY WEIRD SEX. YOU NAME IT, WE'VE GOT IT. SEE MY 746. IF SUSPICIONS COR-RECT, YOUR PEOPLE WILL TAKE OVER IN NY. NAME RODER-ICK MACINTYRE. FAMILY WITH BIG BANKING AND DIPLO-MATIC CONNECTIONS. KID GLOVE DEPARTMENT. SWORN ENEMIES OF OLD JOE AND THE BOY. SON A MAVERICK BUT CAN BE TAMED. WHY NOT? WE HAVE HIM BY THE BALLS. POSSIBLY USEFUL IN ONGOING INFILTRATION OF NIXON OPERATION. WORD IS OUT THE BOSS-ELECT ISN'T HAPPY WITH HIS NARROW WIN. BIG BREAK THERE FOR YOU, BOY. COMPLETE DOSSIER FOLLOWS AS Z-720-12. COTTON.

That lay in the future. But even if Rod had been granted a glimpse of things to come, he probably wouldn't have heeded the warning; he was more and more inclined to believe that the future would take care of itself. He had hit his lucky streak about a month ago and the gift of the picture was an offering to the gods who governed it. Luck had to be nourished whenever the opportunity arose.

In a sense it had all started with Lola. He remembered (only a month ago, but it seemed like another age) how close he had come to not seeing Lola again. He stood in the slight crouch he had adopted to compensate for the low ceiling of the cheap little hotel room and wondered if she was worth the bother of putting on a clean shirt and a tie. He glanced out the window, above which a small skylight has been added so that the management could rent the attic room as a "studio," and caught a glimpse of moldering gray masonry against a leaden gray sky. Depressing. Perhaps a brief wallow with the rich would be sufficiently grating to make him contented with his lot.

He backed away from his easel and his stacked canvases and the other litter of his work—the big portfolio of drawing paper, the newspaper-covered table strewn with tubes of paint, the jar containing a bouquet of brushes—and in a few paces crossed the room with his head down to another table and rooted about in a drift of letters and envelopes and gallery catalogues until he found Lola's card. He took another few steps and let himself collapse backward onto the lumpy bed and held the invitation up before his eyes. Beneath the coronet and the interminable name, a few words were written in a large, firm hand. "Come to tea on Wednesday the 12th at 5:30 (a drink of course). We must know each other."

A tie. He couldn't expect a woman like Lola to know a guy without a tie, although *why* they should know each other escaped him. Because "his grasp of the interrelationships of time, space, and matter have carried American painting a giant step away from the domination of the failing European tradition"? Because he had created "a world of astonishing architectonic solidity whose sharply defined patterns of vibrant color bring coherent order into the disparate elements of modern life"? Or because, according to one important fashion magazine, "people are talking about Roderick MacIntyre, whose soaring arabesques, whose fresh-from-the-paintbox colors have lit the Paulus Galleries with a blaze of young vigorous talent"? He laughed aloud. The memorized quotes from the art critics paraded gloriously through his head, but he doubted if they would make much more sense to Lola than they did to him. He had already met the lady, an imposing dowager who, through several of the more cosmopolitan members of his family, was a link with the life he had left behind. Out of affection for a favorite aunt, he had let Lola know of his presence in the city, he had been invited to a grand but boring party, and he had sent flowers. A social obligation had been discharged. Why have what was apparently intended to be an intimate meeting with her this afternoon? Perhaps he could use her as a test of his resolution to turn his back on all that she could offer him, on all that she represented. The hell with a shirt and tie.

He skimmed the card in the general direction of the table and looked at the ceiling. A long dark stain extended from one corner almost halfway across it. From the middle of the ceiling hung a wire; to the end of the wire was appended a light bulb covered by a misshapen but determinedly frilly shade. His eyes ran down over the wallpaper that crammed the tiny room with enormous, vaguely Cubist flowers interspersed with what appeared to be flashes of gray sky that was getting darker.

He pulled himself up into a sitting position, his long legs sprawling out in front of him so that his feet almost touched the opposite wall, and glanced at the trunk in the corner. It was not yet completely unpacked even though he had lived here for weeks. His glance took in with approval the tangle of clothes piled on a chair. The place was a mess, and it suited him. It was *his* mess, more his than anything had ever been his. Its impoverished impersonality soaked up his imprint as parched earth soaks up water. He burrowed into it and pulled it up around him–depending on it to cure him of the habit of money.

He looked at his watch. Almost time for Lola. He rose and hunched himself over to the window where he picked up the canvas he had been working on earlier and turned it to the last dead light of the dying day. His eyes probed into it, fixed and searching. It was dense, highly charged, and yet perfectly controlled. Architectonic. That was it. He could laugh at what the idiots had written about him, but he couldn't deny that they had played their part in his big decision. Without them he might still have his lucrative job with a successful firm of industrial designers. He might still be engaged to Carol–or even married to her. (He hadn't decided against Carol. It had been the other way around. She had treated him as if he had gone mad and turned a deaf ear to his suggestion that they let things ride until he saw how it all worked out. She had undoubtedly been right. She meant even less to him now than Jeannine, and that was saying something.)

He returned the picture to the easel and turned back into the room. He ran his hand over the dark stubble of the day's growth of beard. Unshaven, tieless, in a dirty shirt–this was probably the truthful way to go to Lola, the Left-Bank rebel invading the elegant sanctuary of the Right-Bank aristocracy, but there was no need to push it. The fact that he didn't have to shave every day was part of his new freedom, but he was still sensitive–oversensitive?–to the demands of propriety. He would shave for Lola. He would wear a clean shirt for her if he could find one in the depths of the unpacked trunk. He would revert once more to the Rod MacIntyre whose death sentence he had decreed several months ago after his successful New York show when he had sprung fresh from the paint box into the pages of the art journals.

He emerged from the dingy entrance hall of his cheap hotel into the lively streets of Paris. Paris. Why Paris? Some sort of concession to a dead tradition? Whatever it had once been, now it was just another crumbling bastion of Western materialism. Its most-notable features were De Gaulle's efficient storm troopers and the bombs that had been going off with increasing frequency since his arrival. He tried not to take them personally. There was something about the place that made you think that everything had been arranged for the individual. It *was* personal in a way he supposed most places used to be. Maybe not. He was still trying to figure it all out.

He buttoned up his raincoat against the cold and headed toward the Boulevard St.-Germain for the Métro, stopping to pick up an evening paper before forcing himself down into the stench and noise and crowd of the public transport system. He had almost never taken the subway in New York. He felt like a giant in the midst of this small, quick race.

He found a seat in an almost full carriage and ran his eyes over the headlines. Tension in the East. Tension in the West.

6

Tension in-between. The secretary for foreign affairs says that, with patience, war might be avoided. Patience. He turned the page. A body had been dragged out of the Seine. In Italy a woman had given birth to a fish. A bloody night at Orléans. An American GI, mad with rage, had availed himself of a gun at the dinner table and killed his French wife, his baby, his father-in-law, and himself. The mother-in-law, a bullet through one lung, was in precarious condition but–

Rod let the paper crumple against his knees and leaned back in the seat. He reconstructed the scene in his mind, the bodies slumped against the table. Possibilities for an interesting composition. Family Portrait.

Peace. It was wonderful. Almost everybody he knew had been shot at by someone somewhere. He had arranged his own entrance into the world rather cleverly. He had been too late for World War II–they weren't drafting children–and they hadn't given him quite enough time to be ready to be killed in Korea. If they managed to be patient for another four years, he would be too old for the next round of fun and games, although the French seemed to have left some loose ends in the Orient that Kennedy had been talking about quite a lot recently. Thailand? Vietnam? His geography was a bit vague when it came to the exotic East.

He got out of one train and moved in a surging wave of people to another. He climbed stairs and came out at the Etoile. The Eternal Light flickered softly in the misty night. The Unknown Soldier lay in eternal solitude under the crushing weight of the Arc de Triomphe. He wondered if there was really anybody in there. It seemed unfair to pile all that on top of one poor lonely bastard.

Crossing over to avenue Foch was like entering the gate of another city. Streetlights illuminated the immaculate and artfully landscaped garden strips, as artificial as something under glass, running down the sides of the broad avenue. Behind them, set back in their own garden plots and guarded by forbidding iron palisades, were the ornate 19th-century facades of apartment buildings that somehow had the effect of private dwellings, as a few of them had once been and still fewer still were. The automobiles that prowled silently before them were richly austere—Rolls-Royces and Bentleys and Daimlers. The occasional vulgarity of a Cadillac looked glaringly out of place. Nothing crumbled here. Just walking through gave him the old familiar sense of suffocation that he associated with money. He thought of the big house he'd grown up in—a country house, if you could count Greenwich, Connecticut, as country—but with the same air of overbearing privilege as this urban landscape. A big house set on a commanding rise of land and embedded in the pompom formality of hydrangeas. Cavernous white-columned verandas. A sweep of lawn falling away behind— with the pool at the foot of it set against a backdrop of woods. There were smells associated with it—the smell of fresh-cut grass predominate—but mostly he remembered colors, the cool green of the lawn, the sparkling blue of the pool, the scarlet and blue and yellow and white of the flower beds, the crisp white of awnings and housemaids' aprons. Clean, safe, and confining. Lawns and the rainbow spray of sprinklers demanded their price in taxes and conformity. It was no wonder the break for freedom and independence hadn't been easy, no wonder he still had moments of doubt about whether his decision would offer sufficient rewards.

He had been quite simply terrified of giving up his job, with a big raise in the offing and nothing but the few thousand dollars he had made from his show to weigh against it. He had had to stiffen his will to the breaking point to face his parents' disapproval and accept their unequivocal edict that no help would be forthcoming if he pursued his foolish course. In what he agreed was his slightly mad determination, he somehow convinced himself that he didn't need their help. He was madly determined to be a painter. Even the loss of Carol couldn't deter him. He was beginning to believe that nothing could deter him now that he had the Atlantic Ocean to hide behind. Of all the problems facing the world, that of a rich boy trying to earn the right to behave like a poor boy hardly came at the head of the list. But it was tougher than people realized, and he thought he was beginning to make some progress.

Halfway down Foch near avenue Malakoff, he turned in through a massive iron gate and walked back along the carriage drive that bisected the building to the elevator. A handsomely lettered sign hung on its door: "Temporarily Out of Order." It had been there when he was here before. He smiled with satisfaction. There were a few flies even in this rich ointment. He turned and mounted wide flights of carpeted marble stairs to the third floor.

He was received by a butler who took his coat and bowed him down an enormous corridor. The decor was such that detail was lost in the splendor of the whole. Even Rod's practiced eye had trouble coming to rest. It was flung from painted mirrors to delicately carved *boiseries* to looped and sculptured satins and brocades to ornate and crystal-bright chandeliers. He caught a glimpse of the great salons where the party had been held and was led to a door on which the butler rapped softly once before easing it open to reveal Lola seated on a sofa in front of a fire in a gorgeously furnished living room. Rod felt the suffocation gripping him again. God, to be trapped with all these possessions. He felt like going to the window and flinging it open. He wanted to stretch. He wanted to do something outrageous to prove that he didn't covet this array of riches and the power it represented.

"Good. I'm glad you came," Lola announced in a harsh and peremptory voice as he advanced toward her. She was well past 60, heavily built but wasted-looking, with an enormous nose and long uneven teeth. Her hair, which was thinning and wispy, was tinted a rich mauve, and her severely fashionable street dress looked as if it were holding together dismembered odds and ends of human anatomy—like a carelessly assembled package. She lifted a splotched and lumpy hand, palm downward and glittering with a tangle of rings. Only after he had taken it did Rod remember that he was expected to kiss it.

9

"Of course," Lola snorted as he fumbled with it. "I forgot. I'm supposed to give you a hearty grip like a ranch hand. You Americans. I imagine you'll call me Lola, too, even though we've scarcely met. There, sit down. René, the monsieur would undoubtedly like a drink. Whiskey? Good." She switched easily from French to English with only the trace of an accent in the latter. "Now let me look at you. I didn't have a chance to the other night. Fascinating eyes. Where do you Americans get your mouths? Absolutely ravishing. You're a very handsome young man, which makes up for a number of things." She uttered a startling bray, apparently meant to be taken for laughter, revealing the mouthful of long yellow teeth. Rod smiled, studying his hostess in his turn. A wonderful face, the ugliest face he had ever seen, very sketchable.

"Tell me about yourself," Lola continued in her authoritative way. "What sort of a place are you staying in? How long do you think you'll be here? I know you're only 20-something, so you're really still a child. You're a painter, aren't you? I don't know your parents, but I somehow never thought of your Aunt Irene as the sort who would have a painter in the family. All that money. You Americans are so marvelously rich. I adore it." She uttered the bray again, and Rod laughed with her. The old lady's down-to-earth coarseness appealed to him. No member of his family would talk about anybody being marvelously rich.

"You should see where I live," he said. "Irene would read me out of the family."

"Ha. I guessed as much from your address. Why must painters live like pigs?" She took an angry swallow from the glass the manservant had presented to her and went on accusingly. "I don't understand you young people anyway. How could I? In my day one wanted to make oneself as comfortable as possible. Nowadays, people seem content to live in one room with their feet up on the furniture. Ugh." She shuddered with magnificent disdain.

Rod drank his drink and waited to discover if there was any particular reason for his being here. The leaping fire cast a rosy glow

10

on the marble fireplace. The room with its soft rich old colors of fine fabrics and exquisitely carved woods was lovely; the museum piece in which he was seated was comfortable. He made a determined effort not to find it a blessed relief from his "studio."

"Whom did you talk to at the party the other night?" the old lady demanded abruptly.

"Oh, well, you know how it is in a crowd like that," Rod said, trying to remember. "Several people. There was a very attractive girl called Nicole something-or-other."

"Nicole de la Vendraye?"

"Yes, I think that was it."

"Ha. I knew it!" Lola cried triumphantly. "Wait until I tell Germaine."

Rod chuckled. "What are you going to tell her?"

"That we've found a presentable young man for Nicole at last. Handsome *and* rich. It's about time."

"Thanks for the handsome part, but I'm certainly not rich. Things don't work the same way in the States as they do here. Parents throw their children out into the cold hard world to fend for themselves."

"Ah, well, they can't live forever. I'm all for handsome young men. I knew you'd be perfect for each other."

"I wonder if Nicole knows how lucky she is."

"I'll take care of that, my young friend."

He was sure she would. He was about to tell her to lay off when a youngish woman whom he had also met the other evening made her entrance in a flurry of furs and jewels, trailed by a manservant. It was Germaine, Lola's stepdaughter.

"Ah, there you are, my dear," Lola said as Rod rose. "You two know each other. M. MacIntyre, but you must call him Roderick. We're being very American. No, that won't do. Rod or Roddy. How's that? Heaven knows what he'll call you. Germaine doesn't sound very American."

Germaine stood in front of an antique mirror beside the fireplace elaborately removing her hat. The manservant hovered nearby. As she smoothed her hair, she turned to Rod and gave him an insolently indifferent glance.

"Hullo," she said in a husky voice.

"That's a new hat," Lola snapped accusingly. "How sensible of you to have married so many rich husbands."

Germaine held the hat out for a brief inspection before turning it over to the manservant. Gloves and a mountain of mink followed. She made a number of small adjustments about her person with total self-absorption—like an actress about to make an entrance. When she was satisfied that everything was in order, she came alive and advanced to Lola with a flash of trim legs.

"I've got that thing from Cartier," she said. She held her hand out to her stepmother, focusing attention on a magnificent emerald bracelet.

"Aha," Lola exclaimed hungrily. She took Germaine's hand in both of hers and bent close to the glittering jewel. Her scrutiny was as rapacious as a pawnbroker's. "Splendid. Beautiful work. I told you the diamonds would have been a mistake. René, tell Minette to find my glasses. They're somewhere around my room. And the samples." She looked up nearsightedly, as if momentarily blinded by the bracelet. The manservant presented Germaine with a drink on a silver tray, bowed, and retired. Lola released the hand she had been clinging to and straightened.

"What do you think?" she exclaimed. "This charming young man has fallen for Nicole."

Germaine shot Rod a quick glance and then looked back at her stepmother with a curiously shuttered look. "I shouldn't think that would get him anywhere," she said. She ran her hand around her sleek head.

"We shall see. We shall see," Lola cackled. "Don't underestimate the Americans."

René returned with a pair of horn-rimmed spectacles and a couple of lengths of shimmering brocade that he presented to the old countess.

12

"That's the stuff I was telling you about," Lola explained, flinging the handsome fabric out on the sofa beside her. She scratched her heroic nose, settled the spectacles on the end of it, and made a preemptory gesture toward Germaine. The latter immediately unfastened the bracelet and handed it over. Lola hunched herself back in her seat and bent her head for a close study of the jewel. Germaine picked up one of the lengths of the brocade and let it ripple out at arm's length and cocked her head at it.

The atmosphere had turned as languidly and intimately feminine as a harem. Rod lifted his hand to loosen his tie but stopped himself in time. As a male he felt like an uncouth, superfluous presence. All this buying and possessing things, crowding rooms with *things* was essentially female. It had occurred to him that France, in its hysterical feminine way, had pushed capitalism to its logical extremes. He didn't think of himself as a big political thinker, or a big thinker of any kind, but he knew something was wrong with capitalism because it had produced his family. Even he could see that here the rich were richer, the poor were poorer, there was more violent rebellion and reaction, more gluttony, more rags, more gaiety than anywhere else he knew. It was a constant shock after the careful moderation of home, where everybody was pretending to be the same as everybody else. He had given up that game, so he supposed he didn't belong there anymore. He didn't need to belong anywhere. He intended to belong to himself.

"Roddy is a painter, you know. We should have him paint your portrait." Lola turned the suggestion into a raucous joke without taking her eyes off the bracelet.

"Roddy? Oh." Germaine dropped the cloth to her side and looked at him as if she were seeing him for the first time. It was a long appraising look, insolent still but with a glitter of interest that Rod felt in his groin. Their eyes locked, and he felt as if she had made his a proposition. "You're a painter?" she asked with a husky break in her voice.

13

"Not portraits and never on commission," he said, facing her down. It wasn't easy to display his new independent approach to life in this setting.

"Ha," Lola snorted. She removed her spectacles, straightened, and offered the bracelet to Germaine as if it were a trinket that had suddenly lost all interest for her. "I told you not to underestimate the Americans. It's time for another drink." She sucked up the last of hers and held out her glass. "Don't ring for that tiresome man. Roddy, will do it? Just a finger."

Rod took the old woman's glass and turned with polite inter-rogation to Germaine. She returned his look without any change in her expression and seated herself with studied non-chalance on the arm of a chair and made a display of her good points: sleek legs crossed, flat stomach, small firm breasts. All right, he thought. I've got the message. I'll keep it in mind if things get really tough. He knew of rich ladies who were very generous to their boys.

He congratulated himself for having such a cool, realistic thought as he carried the glasses, his and Lola's, to the table against the wall where decanters were set out.

"Scotch?" he said over his shoulder, and Lola croaked an assent. He began to pour the drinks, his back to the room, and heard movement behind him, a flurry of greetings, a new voice. He turned, holding decanter and glass, in time to see the girl he was supposed to have fallen for embracing Germaine woman-fashion, kissing the air first in the general vicinity of one cheek and then the other. They parted, and Nicole caught sight of Rod. For a second their eyes met with mutual pleasure and recognition. Then a cur-tain dropped in hers, and she moved on to Lola.

"How nice of you to ask me, darling." Her voice was as he remem-bered it, light and detached, with a ring of no-nonsense honesty.

Lola pawed at her vaguely as they embraced and then hitched herself around toward Rod. "You two know each other. Where's my drink, young man? Nicole will have Dubonnet."

Rod bowed briefly, trying to make eye contact again, but Nicole gave him only a friendly but impersonal smile before turning her back on him and seating herself. Rod resumed his bartending. Every detail of her was marked in his mind. She was dressed simply, as she had been the other night, not poorly but without the rich adornment of Germaine or old Lola. She wore her pale hair in an elaborate, rather old-fashioned way, drawn up behind and woven into an intricate knot. She wore lipstick on her delicate French mouth, but she needed no make-up on her large wide-set eyes or the well-shaped brows. She was built lightly, delicately, but suggested strength. He was more aware than he had been at the crowded party of how easy it would be to fall for her. An idea Lola had planted in his mind that he wouldn't allow to take root. He had neither the time nor the money to fall for anybody.

He handed around drinks and took a fresh one for himself and resumed his seat. He waited for them to get through their first rush of gossip while be observed Nicole covertly, absorbing brief sharp pictures of the tilt of her head, the long graceful line of her neck, the flutter of an exquisite hand as she made a point. He wondered if he would be the only man and suspected that he was. He was beginning to grasp the point of this slightly odd gathering of three generations of females. Lola, the old madam, was displaying her wares—Germaine for an uninhibited but casual roll in the hay, Nicole for more serious stuff. She was the sort a man would want to marry. He knew vaguely that the three were related, but he had the feeling that Nicole had opted out of their world. She didn't join in the gossip with their zest and flippancy, and at times her smile became withdrawn and faintly disapproving. It put her on his side.

As he listened to the lightning flow of their French, he was content to be left out of the conversation. His own French was serviceable enough, but he was sure it would sound barbaric here. Lola suddenly switched to English.

"Enough of this female gabble," she said readily. She addressed Nicole: "Are you aware that this superbly handsome young man is also a very important painter?"

"We're cousins too," Germaine contributed briskly. "His Aunt Irene–is that right?–yes, your Aunt Irene married the brother of one of my husbands."

"An American painter? Are there any? Nicole asked innocently.

He recoiled from it as if an ally had suddenly gone over to the enemy. Maybe her English wasn't very good; she had a pronounced and charming accent.

"Don't you know American painting?" he asked, giving her the benefit of the doubt.

"I don't suppose I do. Where would I see any?"

"God, you people are provincial about painting," he retorted with a bluntness he would never have dreamed possible a year ago. He had sworn never to be mealymouthed or apologetic about his vocation. He was glad he had settled on a tie and an expensive dark suit. It made his tone more socially acceptable. "Nothing good is being done here anymore, but you refuse to look anywhere else," he added impatiently.

"That's telling 'em," Lola crowed like a spectator at a sports event.

Nicole was really looking at him now, her eyes widening into his with a depth almost as palpable as tears. For a giddy instant she seemed to be completely open to him. Then she shrugged and resumed her studiedly distant manner.

"You're probably right," she said. "We have created so much and for so long that we no longer believe that is will save us. The Americans perhaps take it more seriously."

"If art is serious, I don't see how you can help taking it seriously," Rod said, defending everything he'd become since he had made his big decision. Whose side *was* she on? She was quicksilver. A mystery. "I'd gladly show you some of my things if you're interested," he said, exploring further.

"I'd like it very much," she said, sounding impersonal but genuinely interested.

"You must tell me how to reach you. I'll call and arrange something."

16

"I'll give you my card." She turned from him, apparently having gone as far in committing herself as she would in front of the others.

Talk became gossipy again. Rod followed it with more attention, anxious to learn all he could about the girl he was determined not to fall for. He picked up clues that indicated that she lived on her own, didn't work, was relatively poor. There were other clues that suggested there might be a man. So much the better. It would curb his impulse to pursue her, but it was at odds with Lola's roguishness and the brief candid welcome of Nicole's eyes. When the talk turned to general topics—the theater, a recently published novel—Rod joined in in careful French. He saw Nicole give him an approving if slightly astonished glance. The French never believed a foreigner was capable of putting together coherently three words of their language.

Eventually, there was a lull in the conversation, and Nicole stirred and looked at her watch. "I must go," she said. "I have to go home and change."

Rod took a final sip of his drink and stood up. "Me too," he said.

"I suppose I really ought to be going along," Germaine said.

"Not a bit of it," the old countess snapped. "I know what you're doing tonight. You don't have to go for an hour. I want to talk to you."

Rod guessed that this was part of her game as a matchmaker and smiled to himself as he went to her and managed to brush his lips over her hand more expertly than before.

"I can't thank you enough," he said.

"I told you, I have a weakness for handsome young men." She brayed happily. "Come see me."

While Nicole was making her farewells, he turned to Germaine. "It's been very pleasant seeing you again," he said.

She gave him a final appraising look. "I imagine we'll be seeing each other," she said in a way that managed to be both insinuating and insulting. He hovered near the door while Nicole exchanged a few last words with the other two and then followed her out. The butler appeared from somewhere and es-

17

corted them down the hall and helped them into their coats. Hers was cloth, he noted.

"Are they great friends of yours?" he asked as they started down the stairs. They could really meet now, liberated from Lola's cage.

"More like family really. Cousins. Like you. My parents are dead, you see. Without parents, cousins become more important." She spoke more directly and sweetly than she had before.

He looked down at her and considered offering to see her home. "What about that card?" he asked.

She stopped and leaned against the banister and lifted her bag to her breast and slipped a hand into it. He noticed that she wore pale polish on her nails. She didn't make a fuss rummaging through the bag but simply withdrew a card and offered it to him. He automatically passed a finger over it to find that it was engraved; he saw that she lived in a stylish neighborhood nearby. Warnings flashed in his mind. He was used to having girls and used to paying for the pleasure with dinners and shows and nightclubs. In Paris he hadn't yet discovered where you could take a girl like this without spending a fortune. Let her go. Dammit, I don't want to let her go, his old self balked.

"Would you really like to see my work?" he asked tentatively. He thought of the messy little attic room. She would probable expect a real studio.

"Very much." She leaned lightly against the banister and looked up at him with charming expectancy.

"It would have to be when the light's good. Could you have lunch with me tomorrow?"

"I'm afraid tomorrow is not possible," she said with a little laugh.

It grated on him. Polite society. Everything turned into such a bore. All he wanted was to tell her that she was a very intriguing girl and that he wanted to spend some time with her and maybe to go bed with her, but there always had to be complications. "Well, maybe I'd better call you," he said.

"Of course. Any time. Unless–"

He saw the expectant look fade and her eyes fix on his face assessingly. He knew very well what she saw, having spent hours studying himself in a mirror when he had no more interesting model to draw. He hadn't been paying much attention to his hair lately. It fell around his head in thick dark shaggy locks. Framed as it was, his face was like a work that had been intended to be rough-hewn but had been worked over too much and refined beyond the artist's intentions. It was his mouth that caused the trouble. It was delicately modeled, full but sensitive, so that the straight strong lines of nose and jaw were negated and the whole looked romantically rustic. He could start a drawing of himself looking like a hawk and end up with it looking like a pretty boy. Neither was the truth. People–girls–had told him that his eyes were fierce, but he suspected that that was because they found the idea of "fierce eyes" exciting. He knew that his eyes were simply penetrating and attentive.

"Unless what?" he asked before the silence between them became a problem.

"Oh, I thought that if you wouldn't mind leaving out lunch, I could come in the afternoon."

He smiled down at her, feeling that they were getting somewhere now. "No, that would be too much like business. Lunch is the part that interests me most. I'd like to talk to you. Can I walk you home now?"

"No, no," she said hastily. She returned his smile playfully, shadowed with guilt. "To tell you the truth, I will meet somebody around the corner. I don't tell those two everything. They are so wicked."

"I know what you mean. Lola had us married before you arrived."

"How dreadful of her. Were you terrified?"

"I could think of worse ideas." They were smiling into each other's eyes with open appreciation. Rod's thoughts became explicitly erotic. Perhaps he was making the complications. Perhaps she was ready and willing for an uncomplicated affair.

19

"I must go." She put a hand on his arm. "You *will* call? I look forward to it."

The hand made him jealous of whomever she was meeting. It also reminded him that he didn't want to make too much of it. He shifted his feet and used the hand on his arm to set her in motion once more. "Don't worry. I'll call," he said. Maybe he would. Maybe he wouldn't. Keep all the options open.

She withdrew her hand, and they descended the stairs side by side. The moment of parting on the sidewalk in front of the building became inexplicably awkward. They shook hands, and he held hers a moment too long. They simultaneously opened their mouths to speak and uttered brief laughter. Their eyes met and flew from each other. He made an effort to recover his social ease. He was behaving like an inexperienced kid.

"I'm glad we've seen each other again," he said. "I'd like us to get to know each other."

"Perhaps we will. You don't seem like an American in spite of your looks. Perhaps it's because you're a painter."

"You don't believe I'm a painter yet. You'll see."

They said good night and turned from each other and set off in opposite directions.

He turned his coat collar up against the night's damp chill and resisted an impulse to look back. He would call her, but not for a couple of days, after he had had time to find an undisturbing place for her in his mind. He wasn't going to fall for her. He didn't need her. He had his Bohemian pals on the Left Bank with their willing, undemanding girls. (Jeannine was such a good sport that taking her to bed had already become rather perfunctory.) He should probably start rationing his sex in any case, along with cigarettes and everything else, as part of his new aestheticism. Maybe he could learn to do without it except for holidays and special feast days like his birthday.

And no more Lola. It was too great a wrench from his customary life. He could still taste the expensive whiskey in his mouth. He could feel it too as he forced his feet to carry him back to the Etoile. He was launched on a very nice drunk. They didn't happen often, and this one was free. A bottle of wine with dinner would round it off beautifully. He plunged resolutely down into the noisome Métro.

Stale air rushed down a tunnel at him, and he found himself making his breathing shallow so as to inhale as little of it as possible. People pushed through a wicket, jostling each other, and he held back so that he wouldn't come into contact with them, as if they were diseased. His too easily seduced senses recoiled, left vulnerable by the scene he had just withdrawn from. The exquisite room, warm and faintly perfumed. A manservant moving silently through it. Jewels. A shimmering spill of brocade.

He pushed forward angrily, forcing himself to breathe deeply. He squeezed through the gate just as it was about to clang shut in his face, feeling its damp, gritty surface against him. It clattered metallically behind him, slamming on a world of luxury and ease, and he found himself on the long gloomy platform elbow to elbow with shabby man and women awaiting the headlong rush of the approaching train. This was what he had chosen. This was where his freedom lay.

He sat beside a murderous-looking Arab, breathing the stench of sweat-sour cloth. In the middle of the car, entwined around a pole, a boy and a girl clung to each other, their heads one against the other. Opposite him a massive heavily made-up woman wore an expression that proclaimed her unshakable conviction that she was the summit of civilization's achievement. Farther along, two schoolboys in cloaks and berets, both wearing enormous horn-rimmed spectacles, conversed sedately like little old men. Such wonderfully self-important people all clinging to their precious allotment of idiosyncrasies. A great deal of time and money had been wasted on trying to turn him into something he wasn't. Every day it was coming clearer what he was. He would make it yet.

He changed trains almost without thinking about it, proud of the expertise he had acquired so quickly. He was getting to be an old

21

Paris hand. He surfaced near St.-Germain-des-Prés and headed for the restaurant in the rue de Buci where his familiars usually ate. He didn't take a romantic view of this recently discovered Bohemia. He knew the same sort of thing existed in New York—Andy's crowd, Larry's crowd, others—except that here the food was a bit cheaper and much better. There was a more important, less tangible difference. With the emphasis on dope and kooky sex, Bohemia in New York seemed alienated, irrelevant. Catchwords, but they meant something. He didn't see how a painter could feel relevant in New York unless he was a commercial success. Here, people engaged in the arts were part of the city. They *were* the city. It made you feel important to be accepted by them regardless of whether you were making money.

He turned in at a low door and entered a narrow noisy room with an open kitchen at one end where men in tall white hats were milling about. Although it was early for dinner, the room was already beginning to fill up. He was on nodding terms with many of the people there, most of them his contemporaries, and he saw that a couple of members of his particular club were installed at the table they usually occupied. He hung his coat on a hook on the wall beside the blackboard on which the bill of fare was ornately chalked and went to join them. He was greeted, as he had expected, with ironic comments about his sartorial elegance. At the beginning the splendor of his wardrobe had caused him to be regarded as a harmless dilettante, but this attitude had been revised as word got around about his work. He had also stopped wearing his best clothes in order to make them last longer.

He asked Massiet if he had any news of the show he was hoping to have in a few months. Pichet described his plans for a wall he was going to decorate for a friend's new shop. Madeleine, Massiet's girl, filled his glass with wine while he was waiting for his own bottle. Lambert and Fargue joined them. They were all talented and tough and indifferent to fame or fortune. It was their toughness that Rod admired most. Hairy, bulky in shapeless woolen garments, they conveyed a total confidence in their indestructibility. By contrast, Lola and her lot, despite the surface toughness of acquisitiveness, seemed terribly fragile–like exquisite glass figures that could be smashed with a wave of the hand. With the exception of Nicole, maybe, but the less he thought about her the better.

He saw Jeannine enter and in a moment she had joined them, patting heads as she passed and stooping to kiss Rod's ear before dropping into the vacant chair beside him.

"*Salut tout le monde. Ca va?*" Her voice was rough and cheerful. She turned to Rod. "*Et toi. Tu es trop beau.* For whom have you made yourself so handsome?

"You of course." She was an ample girl bundled up in a thick gray suit. She wore an enormous knitted scarf looped around her neck and shoulders. Her hair was pushed about in an auburn tangle, and she had big green eyes, a long straight nose, and an inviting mouth. She managed to look both sexy and clever. "I hoped you were going to turn up." He touched her cheek. It carried the night's chill on it.

"I've walked all the way from the Louvre. If I'd known you were going to look like this I would have flown. I'm hungry. I'm hideously hungry."

She ordered a substantial meal, including lentils with great lumps of fat pork, which made her moan with gluttony and regret. She was a girl of big appetites, both at the table and in the bed. She had a faintly unwashed smell, masked by cologne–the smell of Paris–which Rod had forced himself to get used to. A poor boy's sort of girl, making no pretense of offering him exclusive rights or claiming any from him.

They ate and shouted good-naturedly at each other across the table. By the time he had his third glass of wine, Rod had decided to skip the evening sketching session at the Grande Chaumière. He'd almost forgotten how good it felt to get drunk. He hadn't had to pay for it–the wine didn't count–so he didn't have to feel guilty. All around him hunks of bread were being vigorously applied to empty plates and thrust into hungry mouths. Glasses were being drained. He had never known people to make eating such an unceremonial business of getting food into themselves. When there was nothing left, they began to drift off, leaving in their wake a litter of empty bottles and well-cleaned plates and stained glasses.

"Shall we go someplace for a while, beauty?" he asked Jeannine, slurring some of the words slightly and pausing to laugh at himself as he repeated them.

"You're in a very good humor tonight, *chéri*. We'll go to the Pagode and listen to your rocking roll. Why do you always laugh when I say that? Isn't that what it is?"

"Of course. Or rolling rock. Whichever you prefer."

They shared out their bill scrupulously, and Fargue and his girl went out into the cold night with them. They cut across to the Boulevard St.-Germain and down to their destination. It was a great warren of a bar, branching off onto various levels, balconies, discreet alcoves, erratically lit either by merciless fluorescent tubes or dim-shaded lamps. Near the door there was a rank of flashing pinball machines and farther along a many-hued jukebox of such agonizing design that it hurt Rod's eyes to look at it. They went to it and fed it money. It was the sort of place Rod wouldn't have gone near at home, but here he found it bizarre and rather jolly. It was swarming with young people; they appeared unexpectedly from around hidden corners. No dance floor was clearly indicated; couples moved to the blare of the music wherever they found themselves.

Prompted by Jeannine, he performed an energetic dance with her. They caught their breath with other couples. He wandered off to get beer. When he returned, Jeannine was engaged in a lively discussion with the group around her. He chatted. He flirted with a couple of girls. He fed the machine more money and danced some more, without paying much attention to the partners he picked, and went off for more beer. He was feeling slightly giddy, under control but getting pleasantly close to the silly stage. He danced with Jeannine again, feeling wonderfully uninhibited and sexy.

"Do you want to go home?" he asked.

"Oh, no, *chéri*. Not yet. This is much fun."

It was, although he wasn't sure how long it would continue to be. He was developing an unquenchable thirst that could lead to disaster. Other dancers moved in with them, so he was no longer required as a partner, and he broke away and headed for the bar and another beer. He had barely cleared the brightly lit area where he's been dancing when a youth barred his way. At first glance Rod took him for a schoolboy. He was short and wore a little beret on the back of his head from which escaped a mop of wavy dark hair. Rod saw that the cape he had taken for a schoolboy's was much more elegantly cut, with a dramatic collar adorned with big embossed silver buttons and a silver chain.

"You're a wonderful dancer," the youth said cheerfully with a French accent. "You Americans always are. You see?" He nodded toward the couples Rod had just left. "We turn it into some sort of ballet."

"You knew I was American?"

"Of course. I know many things about you. I'm a student of the occult." He said it with an ironic lilt in his voice.

Rod looked at him and was amused. He had a tilted Pinocchio nose like a drawing in a children's book. If caricatured, his wide mouth could belong to a ventriloquist's dummy. All the boy needed was a monocle to stand in for Charlie McCarthy. He looked up with merry, mischievous eyes. Rod laughed. "What else to you know about me?" he demanded.

"I will tell you." He took Rod's hand and lifted it in front of him and prodded the palm with a forefinger. "You're a painter."

"You're brilliant. Go on."

The boy bent the fingers back slightly to flatten the palm and ran his finger along its lines. "This is very important. You're going to meet–I'm not sure–perhaps you have already met a short dark stranger who will be very important in your life. You must do everything he says."

"Everything? That's a big order." Rod dismissed an impulse to withdraw his hand. It was being held with curiously tranquil intimacy. If a girl held it like this, he would have taken it as a sexual advance. As it was, it seemed simply warm and affectionate. He liked it.

"He will tell you only things that are good for you," the boy said with a gurgle of laughter. "He is your guardian angel."

"Really? How will I know him if you can't tell me if I've met him?"

"No. I see now." A finger prodded his palm with the agreeable intimacy. "You have met him but not for very long."

"Good," Rod said, keeping a straight face and prolonging the game. "Can you tell me his name?"

"I can tell you his earthling name. Patrice. I can't tell you the secrets of the spheres."

"Oh, no, I wouldn't want you to do that. OK, Patrice, I suppose you know mine name's Rod. My earthling name." They looked at each other and laughed. Patrice squeezed Rod's hand and then released it.

"You see?" You recognized me. You're very clever too."

"You're my guardian angel? Are you in the guardian angel business for many people?"

"No, no, no. We're given just one assignment at a time. You're mine for now."

"Good." Rod smiled down at the comic face. It *was* comic, but he could see that a drawing that didn't caricature the mischievous expression would bring out the elfin beauty that lurked in it. The mop of hair on his forehead was appealing. "I think I should have my guardian angel's undivided attention."

"Exactly," Patrice exclaimed delightedly, as if Rod had put his finger on a crucial point. "That's exactly how it works. That's why you must come have a drink with me."

"Fine. I was headed for the bar when you turned up. Come on."

"Not here. I want you to come have a drink with me at home."

"Is that one of the things I must do? It'll be good for me?"

"Definitely. We must discuss how I can best take charge of your case."

"I see. Do you live near here?"

"Quite near. Very near your hotel."

"You know where I live?"

"Of course."

Rod was taken aback. In his slightly befuddled state he was beginning to believe that this kid really *was* his guardian angel. He
glanced back and saw that Jeannine was still dancing. He looked at
the trim figure in front of him. He was immaculate in a very French
way, more pressed and starched under the dramatic cloak than
would be considered quite gentlemanly in some circles. He wasn't
a schoolboy, but he wasn't much older, just barely in his 20s, Rod
guessed. It was unusual for French kids to have places where they
could invite their friends. At least, he hadn't been invited to any. It
made him feel like an outsider still. Jeannine would keep him here
drinking beer for the next hour at least. The whole point of her was
that they could come and go as they pleased. He shrugged his
shoulders unconcernedly.

"OK, but it better be a quick drink. I've had a heavy evening."

"Yes, you've had much to drink, but that does no harm from time
to time."

"Right." He put a hand on the boy's shoulder and leaned toward
him but found that his balance wasn't all that it should be and
pulled back. "I think you're a very sensible guardian angel. Let's go."

"You had a coat."

"So I did. Where do you suppose I left it? Over there."

They went to a wall hung with coats. Patrice moved along them and
picked one out and handed it to him. "This must be yours," he said.

"Why?"

"Because it's the best."

Rod peered at it. "By golly, it *is* mine. You're amazing."

"You'll see. It's part of my job." Patrice guided him out the door
with a hand placed lightly on his arm, and they set off down the
boulevard. Rod saw that he was almost a head taller than his companion, but the latter swung along briskly at his side, the cloak bil-

27

lowing out around him. They crossed in front of the Flore and encountered a young man coming out as they passed. He spoke a word of greeting, and they both replied.

"You know him?" Patrice inquired with quick sharp interest.

"No, not really. He's just a guy I've seen around. Why? Who is he?"

"Oh, nobody in particular. Just, as you say, a guy one sees around. His name is François Leclerc. *Il est comme ca. Tu en connais d'autres?*"

Rod knew the expression and understood the question. "No. I didn't know anything about him." He felt that the stranger, François Leclerc, had somehow taken advantage of him by making him appear to be on friendly terms with queers.

"There's no reason why you should. He's no concern of ours. To the right." They passed through narrow side streets, turning frequent corners so that Rod lost track of where he was. He had been doing very nicely on the well-lit boulevard, but here on less-certain footing, he stumbled frequently and once or twice was almost carried away by wild lurches. Patrice was at his side offering tactful assistance. Rod was grateful for the way he did it. He was efficient without making a big thing of it, not making him feel a fool. They came out into a wider street that looked familiar to him. In another few moments they stopped in front of massive double doors, the kind of doors that, to Rod, gave the city an impenetrable and hermetic look. Patrice touched a button, and the door swung open an inch with a magical click. Patrice leaned against it and let them in. He pushed another button. Lights came on, and he leaned against the door again to close it. They were locked in a fortress. He called "Valmer" as they passed the concierge's loge and then crossed a courtyard and passed through a smaller ordinary doorway. Lights went out behind them, and they were briefly plunged into darkness. Rod swayed and reached out for support and immediately found his guardian angel's helpful arm. Lights came on in a decrepit stairwell. They mounted a flight of stairs. Patrice had just inserted a key in a lock when the lights went out again.

"*C'est toujours comme ca.*" Patrice's voice seemed to ripple with laughter in the dark. "Don't move. Do you need me? Here I am."

Rod found a shoulder to put an arm around, and for a moment he felt the boy's slight body against him as they advanced a few steps. He heard a door close behind them. Then a lamp came on, and they separated. Rod found himself in a large room, sparingly furnished with what looked like good old pieces. As Patrice moved about turning on lights, Rod's eye was drawn to a big skylight that took up almost all the upper part of one wall. Pipes writhed around handsome moldings. It was the sort of room, which in the innocence of his arrival, he had hoped to find for himself. Now that he had learned the facts of Paris housing, he knew that it was a treasure of inestimable value. He dropped his coat on a chair near the door and moved around the end of a sofa that was placed in front of an elegant marble fireplace with a real log fire laid in it. He became aware that the room was pleasantly warm without it.

"This is your place?" he asked with envious admiration as Patrice approached. His new friend had removed his cloak and beret and looked very dapper in a stylish suit.

"Yes. I was lucky. A friend helped me get it. Please sit down. I will get you a drink. I don't have the things you Americans drink. Scotch? Vodka? I will give you something special that you won't get anywhere else."

Rod sat on the sofa while his host went off to the end of the room. Patrice returned with a bottle and two small glasses. He filled them and handed one to Rod and looked down at him with a smile full of mischief. "You've been very obedient. I must arrange for the heavens to give you a special reward."

Rod laughed. "You're crazy. What am I doing here? I don't even know where I am."

"The rue de Verneuil. Your hotel is only a few blocks away."

"I guess it is. I'd better be thinking about getting back there soon. Why were you so anxious for me to come for a drink? I mean, I like it here, and you're a nice kid and all that, but nobody's ever asked me to his place since I've been here. I mean, none of the kids I know. I seem to have dumped my girl."

"You were bored with that place. So was I. We wanted to talk comfortably. Isn't that it? Cheers." He sat–perched–on a chair beside the fireplace and lifted his glass.

Rod took a swallow of his drink. The liquor was dry but fruity. It tasted strong but went down easily. "Wow," he said. "What is it?"

The boy laughed. "I don't know. My grandmother makes it. It's a great secret. If she tells nobody before she dies, we'll never know. Tell me about your painting. I don't mean the kind of pictures you paint. That would be stupid. About what it means to you."

"You're interested in painting?"

"Very much. Recently I've been learning about you Americans. You have some very good painters now. Isn't that so?"

"I think so." He thought of the dismissive references to American painting earlier in the evening and was delighted with his guardian angel. "Which ones do you like?" Patrice named names. Rod was impressed. In the soft light and with the mischievousness overlaid by lively interest, the beauty he had detected in the boy's face was more pronounced. He wasn't a comic oddity, although the ventriloquist's dummy made brief reappearances, but a guy with sense and taste and considerable knowledge. Rod finished his drink without being aware of it, and his glass was refilled while they moved into a wide-ranging discussion. Rod found himself talking more freely than he ever had about his own goals and the difficulties he had overcome in order to risk trying to attain them. He went on drinking, always finding more in his glass, but he felt he was speaking easily, even eloquently, with only occasional lapses when he tripped over a word or failed to find the one he was searching for. He eventually realized that his bladder was bursting with all he had drunk, and he interrupted a point he wanted to make to rid himself of this distraction.

"I better take a leak," he said. "Where do I go?"

"*Faire pi-pi?*" Patrice inquired. "I'll show you."

Rod rose and for a moment thought he was going to go right on over onto his face. Patrice was at his side offering support. He shook his head slightly and put his arm around the boy's shoulder. "Goodness. I wonder what's *in* that stuff."

Patrice laughed. "I think it is well that we don't know." He put an arm lightly around Rod's waist, and they moved together toward the end of the room while Rod pursued his thought.

"The point is, I'd love to be rich and famous and successful and all the rest, if it would just happen without my doing anything about it. Aside from my work, I mean. You know—without having to sell my soul. That's the problem in the States. It seems easier here. Maybe no. There's always Buffet. I guess it's up to the individual." His voice trailed off.

Patrice stopped in front of a door in a sort of corridor that seemed to be almost part of a kitchen and dropped his arm. "In there. You OK?"

"Sure. Fine." He have the boy's shoulder a little pat and entered a room the size of a closet where an antiquated toilet was installed, French fashion, in solitary grandeur. His thoughts drifted, and his eyes closed while he was relieving himself. He had to give himself a shake to wake himself up when he was finished. He made an effort to steer a straight course back to the sofa. Patrice had resumed his seat and looked up alertly as he approached. Rod dropped down and stretched out slightly with one leg up on the edge of the sofa and pulled off his tie and opened his collar. His eyelids felt very heavy. He had meant to leave when he was on his feet, but he was comfortable now, the bottle wasn't empty, and he was enjoying himself.

"Am I boring you?" he asked.

Patrice looked at him with lively eyes, bright with humor. "Far from it. You have no idea."

"I like talking to you. I wonder. I told you about losing the girl I was engaged to. I wonder if artists should expect to be alone." He saw that Patrice was speaking, but the words didn't seem to come through to him, and his eyes closed. "It's just that—" he began, wondering what was coming next. He'd intended to say something but didn't quite know what, and then he didn't know anything at all.

Patrice gazed with wonder at the big unconscious fish he had pulled out of the St.-Germain-des-Prés pond. Eventually he would have to throw him back, but he wanted to keep him as long as he could. At least for tonight, even if nothing happened. He heard Gérard's cynical laughter, but he didn't care. Sex was only part of it. He saw that Rod's wisdom and maturity were all in his eyes. Now that they were closed, he looked meltingly young and defenseless. Patrice asked nothing more than to take care of him. From the moment he had first seen him several days ago, he had practically been following him and finding out all he could about him. A real *coup de foudre.* Lightning had struck. The guardian-angel bit had been an inspiration of the moment, and he had been amazed at its success. He would remember it for the future, although the future didn't interest him much for the time being. He found the present too exciting and too unpredictable. What was he going to do with his prize now?

So far he had done everything right, and he wanted to keep it that way. He could leave him where he was, but the heat had already gone out in the building. In a little while it would be so cold that all the covers in the world wouldn't prevent him from waking up. The alternative was to get him into his bed, but lifting him also risked waking him.

Patrice rose and move lightly to the sofa and leaned over the sleeping figure, listening to his deep breathing. He longed to stroke the dark shaggy hair, kiss the deep-set eyes, run a finger over the strange male beauty of his lips, but he had no intention of losing everything for the sake of such secondary joys. The more untroubled his sleep, the better. He cautiously lifted Rod's other leg onto the sofa. Rod stirred and made muttering sounds and moved his hands down protectively over his crotch. You're quite safe, *chéri,* Patrice thought, with a smile that had no mischief in it. For tonight, I'm your little old maiden aunt.

32

Patrice straightened and decided to risk trying to get Rod to bed. Naked preferably, but that remained to be seen. He started for the door and stopped. He didn't want him to wake up and escape while he was gone. He went back to the sofa and looked at Rod's shoes. They were the sort Americans called "loafers," easy to remove. He removed them and carried them down the long corridor that led to the bedroom. He turned on a lamp at the head of the big bed on the side he expected to occupy. He pulled the covers back. The sheets were clean. He hoped his guest would find them irresistible. He undressed and hung everything neatly in the armoire above Rod's shoes. He pulled on a voluminous woolen dressing gown that turned his body into a shapeless bundle. Dozens, more likely hundreds, of boys had found pleasure with, it so he wasn't shy about it. But he had no idea what to expect of his sleeping prize. All the talk about girls. At first his knowing François had seemed significant, but apparently it wasn't.

Patrice hurried back along the corridor and adopted a more cautions pace as he entered the living room. He tiptoed the last few feet to the end of the sofa. Rod's breathing was so heavy, with a little gurgle of a snore in it, that he dared put a hand out and touch his hair. His heart accelerated uncomfortably, and he dropped his hand to his side and quickly stepped back. He went to the bathroom that was also the kitchen and without taking a real bath washed himself thoroughly in all the places that mattered. He scented himself with restraint and combed his hair into an artful arrangement of waves over his forehead and made a face at himself in the mirror. "Here we go," he told himself jauntily to give himself courage.

He returned to his sleeping American and, stomach churning with excitement, looked down at him for a moment to steady himself. Now. He leaned over and slowly lifted an arm. There was no reaction. He crouched down to the task and braced himself and put the arm over his shoulder and worked his own arm around Rod's back and lifted. He came up surprisingly easily. He slumped against him but hugged his shoulders as if he knew what he was doing. He seemed to be able to stay on his feet. Patrice took a careful step, and Rod moved with him. He got a firmer grip around Rod's slim waist and took another step. Rod was lighter than he had expected. He got him out of the living room and headed down the corridor without mishap. It was thrilling to feel the body in motion against him. As they entered the bedroom, Rod stumbled and muttered something. A name? Jeannine? When they reached the bed Rod straightened and pushed himself free and spoke clearly and distinctly.

"Bed," he said. His jacket fell from him onto the floor. He dropped forward and stretched himself out on his back and drew a deep sighing breath as all of his muscles seemed to go slack.

Patrice looked down at the peaceful figure with triumph. He had done it. He had landed his prize in his bed. It had been so easy that he didn't feel he had pushed his luck yet. He leaned over and with quick fingers unbuttoned Rod's shirt. The cuffs were fastened with gold cuff links, and it took him a moment to discover how they worked. He perched on the edge of the bed and carefully lifted Rod's shoulders. Rod's head fell forward and lolled against his own. Patrice slipped his hands inside Rod's shirt and up along his ribs and over his broad back and for a spine-tingling moment allowed himself to hold the naked torso close against him. The shirt slipped from Rod's shoulders, and Patrice disengaged the arms and laid him gently back on the pillow and gloated over him. It was the most beautiful body he had ever seen. All the muscles were long and sleek and lightly developed, an athlete's body—but an athlete who had engaged in sports that required speed and finesse. He thought of the swift symmetry of gazelles and antelopes and thoroughbred horses. The sparse hair on the chest was scattered along the lower edge of his pectoral muscles and gave them added definition. It wasn't curly but lay flat against the skin like delicate fur. There was a faint ripple of muscle above the deep hollow of abdomen that plunged down into his trousers. The ultimate goal. He hoped it wouldn't be too small. He couldn't deny that he liked big boys. He edged down the side of the bed and took a quick breath and began to unbutton the fly, commanding his hand to move briskly without a suggestion of a caress.

There were more buttons underneath, and he unfastened them and lay back the flaps of cloth and found a neat patch of hair that left the base of the sex visible. He paused to take in the whole breathtaking spectacle–from the shaggy hair to broad shoulders and chest down to narrow hips and the small furred triangle that pointed to the only secret that remained. He got a grip on the cloth and tugged gently while a cylinder of flesh was slowly revealed. To his inflamed imagination it seemed to go on forever. Perhaps the friction of the cloth was stretching it. At last the deep, elongated curve of the head was uncovered. He gave Rod's trousers a final pull, and they slipped down to his knees.

He stared. A big American. Bigger than he had dared hope. A friend of his said that all Americans were big there because that was where their brains were. It lay long and inert, its breadth almost concealing the testicles on which it was cradled. Patrice's hands clenched and unclenched on his thighs with the longing to touch it. He forced himself to rise and went to the foot of the bed and removed socks and pulled trousers down over long legs. The underpants came with them. He took another long look at the glory he had uncovered. A beautiful young athlete at rest.

He hitched up his dressing down to make sure he was properly covered. He had nothing particularly striking to hide, but it did stick out and was apt to find its way through the folds of his robe. He picked up the sheet and blankets from the bottom of the bed and drew them up but balked at covering his prize. He was proud of his self-control so far. He dropped the covers across Rod's hips and pretended to smooth and straighten them. When he picked them up again, his hands were carefully placed to make contact seem accidental. One hand brushed against pubic hair and the other came to rest on warm velvet skin. He ran them down along it to the convolutions of the head while he watched the peaceful young face. There was no change in the breathing, no flicker of eyelids or twitch of lips. He left his hands where they were, his fingers moving slightly to learn the feel of it. It was soft but thrillingly bulky and seemed to stir and throb with life. He drew his fingers back along its length and wished that he dared continue the caresses to see if he could arouse it.

He lifted the covers and looked. It had lengthened and filled out perceptibly. He could guess what it looked like erect. Magnificent. Some of Gérard's boys may have been bigger, but their immature bodies made them look grotesque. The muscular vigor of Rod's body demanded the complement of well-developed masculinity. Patrice had permitted himself the liberties he dared, and he resignedly pulled the covers up to Rod's chin.

Here he indulged in discreet caresses under the guise of tucking him in. He ran the back of his fingers along Rod's face. He touched his cheek when he straightened the pillow. He stroked the long hair on the back of his neck. He stood and stepped back from the bed and was filled with an almost suffocating contentment. The last few days of practically shadowing this stunning stranger, days of feverish fantasies, had culminated in this incredible reality. He was going to lie in bed naked with this beautiful naked boy. It was enough. He must be growing up. Nothing like it had ever happened to him because he had never known a boy whose presence made him happy without sex. He was in love even though Gérard had taught him that love was a fancy word for self-deception.

He moved silently around the bed gathering up Rod's expensive-looking clothes and took them to the armoire and arranged them lovingly among his own. He turned and looked back at the dark romantic head and the long body adorably snuggled down into his own covers. There was nothing more to keep him from getting in beside him. His heart was beating rapidly again but not unpleasantly. He wanted to laugh out loud with joy. He went around to his side of the bed and snapped off the light. Safe in the dark, he slipped off his robe and eased himself under the covers and lay with his back turned to his bedmate, a knee pulled up to conceal his sex. Rod immediately heaved about and flung an arm across him and muttered in his sleep. Patrice though he heard a name again. Janny? Could it be a boy's name? In the morning when Rod was awake and could tell him not to if he didn't want it, he would make his intentions clear. He tried to breathe evenly to quiet the pounding of his heart. The arm was heavy on him, but he wouldn't have dreamed of moving it. He could smell him—a fresh, clean, masculine smell, strongly flavored with his grandmother's liquor. He doubted if he would get any sleep.

Rod woke up with a naked girl in his arms. His erection was thrust up against some part of her, and he increased the pressure with a little contraction of his hips. He couldn't remember who she was, but he felt too awful to open his eyes and look. It couldn't be Jeannine; Jeannine was much more substantial. He began to suspect that there was something peculiar about the situation. For some reason this didn't feel like his own bed. Where was he? Hadn't there been a girl called Nicole? His erection made an additional lunge of excitement. He moved a hand over slight shoulders, and his curiosity was sufficiently aroused to open one eye.

He found a merry, unmistakably male face smiling into his. He uttered an exclamation and hastily drew back. He heard laughter. The boy wriggled down in the bed beside him, and Rod felt a mouth on his erection. He started to protest, but delicious sensations immediately stirred in his groin. He lay back to enjoy them. Fragmentary memories of the night before were beginning to fall into place. He had let himself get picked up by a cocksucker.

He thought of the other time this had happened to him under very similar circumstances. It had been almost ten years ago when he had been a freshman at Yale. There had been a big night of drinking, and he had awakened to find a senior performing this service for him. He had screamed the place down and threatened to report the aggressor to the dean. Now he couldn't see that it would do anybody any great harm. The mouth was marvelously knowledgeable. Hands were doing things that brought little grunts of pleasure from him. In a moment he knew it was going to happen quickly. He let out a little warning cry. The delicious ministrations of the mouth intensified, and he uttered another cry as he was shaken by his climax.

The mouth lingered on him briefly, and then he felt the boy scramble out of bed. He opened his eyes a slit to catch a glimpse of slim hips and a behind as prettily rounded as a girl's before a robe was dropped around it and the boy left the room. He closed his eyes, and his mind drifted around the small incident. He probably shouldn't have let it happen, but he was in no condition to put on a big injured-innocence act. He hoped it wouldn't cause difficulties between them. He remembered liking the kid. Patrice. His name was Patrice. He had always been wary of queers because he knew he attracted them, and he had never been tempted to go that way. He tried to remember if anything had happened that should have warned him. If so, he'd been too drunk to notice it. He must have passed out.

He stretched luxuriously in the big bed and became aware that his erection had only partially subsided. He felt as if very little would get it going again. His mind slipped back toward sleep. It was jogged into consciousness again by sounds of movement in the room. He opened his eyes and saw the short slight figure wrapped in the voluminous dressing gown approaching the bed holding a steaming cup. He remembered the fetching mop of hair on Patrice's forehead.

"There," Patrice said, standing over him. "That should make you feel better."

Rod lifted his arms out from under the covers and took the cup and grinned up at him. "You sure know how to take care of a guy."

Patrice's eyes twinkled. "Last night, you thought I was a girl. Jeannine? Lucky Jeannine."

"Lucky me. Thanks."

38

"You mean—you didn't mind?"

"Not if you liked it. I just think you ought to know I don't usually go in for that sort of thing."

"Oh. I wasn't sure. I shouldn't have done it. I'm sorry."

The boy looked crushed. Rod took a swallow of hot bitter coffee and tried to think of something to say to put the incident behind them. It wasn't his fault that he wasn't a cocksucker. "Oh, for God's sake," he burst out. "I don't want to make a big thing of it. If you like it, you like it. I mean, I'm sorry I couldn't do something nice for you."

"I wanted nothing more. It was wonderful for me but, of course, if you didn't want it—"

"I didn't say that. Oh, hell." He gulped more coffee. "Listen. This is ridiculous. We're getting all embarrassed over nothing. I don't have anything against queers. I just don't happen to be one, that's all. You wouldn't want me to pretend it didn't happen would you?"

"No." The sparkle returned to Patrice's eyes. "I think that wouldn't be very polite."

They both laughed. Rod finished the coffee and put the cup on the bedside table. "There. Don't let's worry about it anymore. What time is it?"

"A little after 9 o'clock. I will have to go to work soon."

"Yeah. I better get out of here." He pushed the covers aside and began the unwelcome labor of getting out of bed. As he did he felt his cock swing against his thigh. He didn't want to flaunt himself, but he didn't want to act self-conscious in front of the kid either. He managed to struggle to his feet and wondered if he would be able to stay on them. He put his hands over his eyes and groaned and stood swaying helplessly. In an instant Patrice's hand were on both sides of his ribs steadying him. Rod stood motionless for a moment and waited for his head to stop reeling. He felt a tremor in the hands, and then they began to steal, deft and light-fingered, over his chest. Rod intended to say a word of mild rebuke, but he felt the odd tingling sensation of a burgeoning erection, and he was too astonished to protest. Could a boy give him an erection? There was danger in permitting it. Somewhere in his mind a line was drawn, he wasn't sure quite where, beyond which Patrice would provoke his anger and disgust. The fact that he kept himself covered suggested that the boy instinctively knew this. He also instinctively knew where to put his hands to thrill and excite him. They moved slowly down over him, lingering, teasing, exquisitely caressing. They seemed to be achieving their purpose. He had never been handled like this without participating in any way, and it gave his cock an extraordinary independent importance. Without looking he couldn't be sure if it was fully operational, but in this case it hardly mattered. All the sensations were there. He opened his hands at the sides of his eyes like blinkers.

"Are you trying to corrupt me?" he asked of the averted face.

Patrice looked up and their eyes met and questioned each other. "Could I?"

"I always feel sexy when I have a hangover," Rod said. "You shouldn't pay any attention."

"Not pay attention when this happens?"

"What do you expect when you–" His breath was cut off by a new exploratory pressure, and he felt the independent appendage surge up and away from the support of hands.

"So big and hard," Patrice murmured, recapturing it. "*C'est magnifique.*"

"There's nothing magnificent about it. It's just a cock like everybody else's."

"It may be like everybody in the States, but here–*c'est extraordinaire.*"

"All right. Elizabeth Taylor couldn't make it any bigger or harder. Now what?

"You know what I want. May I do it again?"

"You didn't ask my permission before."

"No. That was wrong. Now I must know that you want it."

The kid hadn't crossed the line yet, but he was getting close. "It's obvious I want something," Rod said impatiently. He didn't want to

40

talk about it. "You haven't got much competition around here. Go ahead. Suck my cock if you like it so much. You're not apt to get another chance."

He saw Patrice drop down to the edge of the bed. He was pulled close, and the mouth was on him once more. With unexpected strength arms grappled with his knees, and he was toppled over and flung out on his back. He felt as if he had been struck by a tornado of passion. Nothing like this could happen with a girl. The hands and mouth were on him everywhere, from his neck (no higher) to the soles of his feet. He pitched and thrashed about on the bed. His arms and legs flailed. He cried out with stunned delight. He was carried to the edge of orgasm and held there in an agonized ecstasy of suspense.

"Oh, Christ. Do it," he shouted. "I want it, dammit. Do it. Please do it."

He heard exultant laughter, and he shouted with the approach of release and continued to shout as his whole body was lifted and flung about in the annihilation of his orgasm. He lay out with his legs spread and his arms thrown up over his head, his eyes closed, his chest heaving. The hands stroked his shoulders and chest soothingly while his breathing slowly returned to normal. He opened his eyes and found Patrice gazing at him with rapturous incredulity, still bundled up in his robe.

"You're really something," Rod muttered. "Where did you learn to do all that?"

"I went to a school for queers," Patrice replied, touching very nearly on the truth.

"I see. You must've graduated with top honors."

"You have the most beautiful body I've ever known. I wanted to make it good for you if it's the last time."

"It better be or you'll turn me queer for life. Come on. Show me where I can pull myself together."

Patrice rose and took his arm and helped him to his feet. They went along a corridor that Rod didn't remember to a living room

41

that he did. Patrice conducted him to the end of it, past the toilet he also remembered to a kitchen with a tub in it. All the fixtures looked old but clean. Patrice want to a cupboard and brought him fresh towels. "There. It's not the Ritz, but the water is usually quite hot. I'm sorry I don't have a spare dressing gown for you."

"I know who I want to be with."

"Thanks. I like you, you know, in spite of–well, the unmentionable." He chuckled and gave the shoulder a pat. "You're such a little monkey."

Patrice fled from his touch and, caught between idiotic tears and ecstatic laughter, returned to the bedroom and dressed quickly. He could do with some pulling together himself. He was close to insanity. To be in love with a boy who liked girls made it hopeless insanity but exciting. Rod might like girls, but he also liked sex, pure and simple. He might get used to a little monkey as a convenience when a girl wasn't available. Meanwhile, he would keep his body hidden except under the covers–if he was lucky enough to get him to bed again. No small physical contacts. Let him do the touching.

He went to the bed and pulled the covers back to air them. The dreams that filled his mind were the most virulent aspect of his insanity. He thought of himself as being armed with cynicism, but irrepressible optimism kept coming to the surface. He believed in old-fashioned things like human decency (a legacy from his father?) although he hadn't seen much of it. If love turned out to be a good thing, as some people believed it to be, then he could live for it and learn to do without sex. Insanity. How did he expect to fit Gérard into this romantic vision? Even if he broke all the rules and kept Rod a secret, he would be defying a destructive force that he had good reason to fear.

At the same moment he and Rod reentered the living room from opposite doors. Patrice was as jolted by his appearance as if he were seeing him for the first time. That he had shared the ecstasy of this superb young athlete, long hair combed, a towel hitched around his waist, lithe and virile, became a wild improbability. Despite an overnight growth of beard, Rod looked fresh and alert, his intent eyes giving him the look of maturity that he touchingly lost in his sleep. Patrice approached him but stayed out of reach.

"You wish to get dressed?" he asked in a businesslike way. "I hung everything up."

Rod smiled at him with a small residue of reticence that he regretted. This clever-looking youth in a stylish suit delighted him. Once he forgot the rest, he would be able to treat him with the friendliness he felt. "I must've been an awful nuisance last night. I'm sorry," he said. "I'll clear out and leave you in peace."

"And when will you show me your work?"

"I'm afraid I talked an awful lot too. Did I say I'd show you my work? OK. I apparently didn't let you get a word in edgewise. What do you do?"

"I manage a rather important antique shop. You might also call it a gallery."

"So young?"

"My training has been a bit—special."

Rod saw playful irony come dancing into his eyes. He felt his own smile broaden with uncomplicated pleasure. "I believe it. Your English is remarkable. This place . . ." He looked around at it, coveting it once more. The sky was gray, but the skylight pulled the day into the room. He had already decided where he would place his easel if it were his. "Marvelous space. The light makes me green with envy."

"It is better for work than your hotel?" Patrice asked, making a point of great importance to him.

"Oh, lord. Wait till you see. When do you want to come? It'll have to be during the day."

"Today at lunchtime? I could be there by one."

"Perfect. We'll have lunch together?"

"I would like that very much."

"It'll be on me to make up for last night." Patrice's eyes met his straightforwardly, but Rod was aware that they were being constantly tugged to other parts of himself. If they were going to be friends, they might as well get everything out in the open. "You like to look at me don't you?" he asked easily.

"Yes," Patrice blurted, rendered almost speechless by the unexpected question.

"I understand. I know my body's pretty good. It should be. A lot of money's been spent on it. I like to look at people too. It seems so silly to be shy about it. Hell, I don't *have* to wear this towel." He gave it a tug and let it drop to his side.

Patrice's eyes flew to accept the offer of a dispassionate inspection of the body he wanted insanely. He was being given a chance to demonstrate that he could look at it without flinging himself on it. The gentle swell of the sex was a startling contrast to the soaring power it had so recently possessed. He didn't know which way he preferred it. The whole body was so beautifully put together that that part of it, in repose, became an almost irrelevant adjunct to the graceful lines of the limbs and torso. He thought again of beautiful swift animals. He looked up and laughed. "Your guardian angel has a great deal to guard."

"OK, monkey? We don't have to be shy with each other. Your face fascinates me. I'm trying to discover why it makes me want to laugh. I'll sketch you later and find out. Now how about showing me where my clothes are?"

They returned to the bedroom, and Rod dressed haphazardly. Patrice watched the glory being obliterated by expensive cloth, perhaps forever as far as he was concerned. Rod folded his tie into a pocket and turned to him.

"Right. I'll expect you at one? You know where I am don't you? Yes, I remember. It's the top floor. Number 19.

They went along the corridor once more, and Patrice helped him on with his coat and opened the door. They shook hands French-fashion and smiled at each other with a lurking acknowledgment of what had taken place between them.

"See you shortly," Rod said and turned and clattered down rickety stairs. He remembered the courtyard and the big door. It was odd going out onto an unfamiliar street in broad daylight, his body still holding the imprint of passion on it. He hadn't been much of a partner, but he supposed it counted as a homosexual experience. Now that he was alone he was a bit ashamed of himself for having allowed it, but he thought he would recover. Hydrangeas and rolling lawns and precious Roderick carefully isolated from the big bad world. Guys had been known to have sex together. If it could happen to others, it could happen to him.

Within minutes he was hunched down again in his attic room. He shed his good clothes and put on his paint-stained jeans and an old sweater and was eager to get back to work to prove to himself that he hadn't been thrown off balance by his adventure. It went well, but there was a strange little twitch of special alertness kicking around in the back of his mind. He had rejected guilt, so it couldn't be that. It wasn't anticipation of further unorthodox pleasures. He felt no inclination to explore that terrain, and at the end Patrice has seemed content to drop it too. Perhaps it was simply an enlarged awareness of himself. He had felt in Patrice something he had never known or known that he wanted, an exclusive preoccupation with, almost an adoration of his person. It was very comforting after all the disapproval he had recently had to face.

It wasn't yet 1 o'clock when he felt that he had almost mastered his current canvas and was ready for a break. He began to clean up his work area and himself. He considered shaving but decided he didn't have to make himself presentable for Patrice. The less presentable the better. He flicked over the canvases that were lined up face to the wall and picked out half a dozen that he was ready to show. He remembered that he had invited Nicole for lunch today and tried to convince himself that he was lucky not to have to go through a big social effort. Aside from the sexual nonsense Patrice was awfully easy to be with.

He was checking his brushes for the afternoon's work when there was a knock on the door. In three strides he had opened it. Patrice entered, cape swinging, the little beret on the back of his head. He was brought to an abrupt halt by the dimensions of the room and looked up merrily. "You didn't tell me you lived in a closet."

Rod stood in front of him feeling that his welcoming smile was inadequate, wondering how you greeted a guy you'd been to bed with. It was almost far enough removed in time for him to be able to act as if it were part of a forgotten past—but not quite. Some small intimate gesture seemed called for. He settled for a pat on the convenient shoulder. Patrice ignored it and moved past him. That finished it. They needn't give it anymore thought. "Throw your things on the bed if you want," Rod said. He pulled the chair over to the window. "The only place you can see the pictures properly is here."

"You're amazing. You look as if your head is about to go through the roof. You're actually able to work here?"

"It's not easy. I'm soon going to have to decide what to do with the things that are finished." He had taken his work-in-progress from the easel that he moved back a few feet as Patrice seated himself. "You can say anything you like, you know. I don't expect everybody to be crazy about what I'm doing."

"They are yours. I will try not to like them too much." They exchanged a look of affectionate complicity.

"OK. Here we go. This won't take long." He picked up a canvas from the floor and put it on the easel and moved around beside Patrice to see if the light was right. He narrowed his eyes, verifying color and form, looking for the quality that he called tension but might be architectonic solidity for all he knew. He always saw a picture with a fresh eye when sharing someone else's first look at it. He glanced down at Patrice. He was leaning forward, his lips slightly parted, his eyes wide and active. He was no longer a bright, funny kid but a man with the single-minded attention of authority. Rod gave him a minute for a good look and then moved back to the easel and reached for the canvas.

Patrice lifted a restraining hand. "Not so fast," he said almost peremptorily without taking his eyes off the picture. He studied it for another few minutes and then nodded. Rod lifted it off and replaced it with another. The process was repeated, with Patrice taking longer for each picture. The atmosphere in the small room became dense with wordless communication. Rod felt as if his young friend were absorbing some essence of him from his work. By the time he had shown the six pieces, he was too keyed up to stop.

"Would you like to see a few of the things that aren't finished?" he asked in a muted tone so that he wouldn't break Patrice's concentration. He was amazed by himself. Not since his early art-class days had he allowed anybody to look at anything that was still in the formative stage.

"Please." Patrice was undergoing what seemed to him close to a religious experience. Years ago he had felt something similar, with adolescent confusion, for Gérard. But the older man had only used it to exploit his weaker nature. Seeing Rod in this tiny room so dedicated to creation, Patrice sensed a purity and goodness in him that reflected his own highest and most impossible aspirations. The pictures were thrilling—bold and virile yet evoking transcendent balance in a world Patrice had dreamed of but had never been allowed to believe existed. He watched Rod moving along the canvases stacked against the wall, bending, squatting, selecting, and all of his body and spirit seemed to converge in worship of agile strength and sensitive male beauty. A small flame of hope had been kindled in him far more precious than the roaring blaze of his passion.

Rod turned back to the easel holding a picture in front of him. "There's three or four that I think are far enough along for you to at least get an idea. Do you always look at pictures this way?"

"I see very much in the ones I like. It takes time."

"Of course. Still, you're amazing. I love to show them to you. I feel almost as if nobody's ever looked at then before."

"I don't think that could be true. You're very good. A friend of mine says that if a painter is good, there's no reason to say more."

"He sounds sensible."

"He knows a great deal about art. Of course, I want to say much more but only when you've shown me all that you want me to see."

47

They spent another half-hour looking at a few of the unfinished pieces and Patrice asking an occasional perceptive question about his intentions.

"I hope you have a long lunch break," Rod said finally. "We've been here for more than an hour already."

"I had almost forgotten lunch."

"I won't be able to do that sketch I want to do of you. We'll make it another day."

"Tomorrow?"

"Sure. Why not?" Rod said with a little laugh.

Patrice was on his feet. "Maybe by then I'll be able to tell you how much I love your pictures. I can come at the same time, but we will have lunch first so that I don't keep you starving to death. I will take you to a special place near here that is very good."

"Wonderful. You inspire me. Tonight I'll do penance. I'll go to the Grande Chaumière and sketch all evening. Come on. I hope you don't mind going to a place where they'll let me in looking like this."

"You look very interesting. For you to need a shave is intriguing because you look like a person who never needs a shave.

Patrice dropped the beret onto the back of his head and swung the cape around him. Rod opened the door and remembered in time not to put a hand on his shoulder as they went out.

He was ready for Patrice at one the next day. He had even got around to shaving. By 1:30 he was getting nervous and impatient. By 2 o'clock he was alarmed. It was inconceivable that the kid would simply not show up. It had been too important to him. Something must have happened. Was he sick? He would have called—the hotel was pretty good about passing on messages—unless he didn't have a telephone. Lots of people here didn't. Some sort of shortage. He abandoned the long wait and went down and left word where he was and went next door and had his usual lunch of beer and a sandwich (a yard or so of crisp French bread with a suspicion of ham concealed in it) at a workingman's bar. It was impossible for

48

him to imagine a situation that might cause Patrice to break their date. Of course, his being queer might make a difference. He had heard that queers were promiscuous and therefore fickle. Perhaps he was already caught up in a new infatuation. Rod couldn't believe it. The boy had as good as pledged himself to him. An accident or sudden sickness. . .

He went back to the hotel to check and then, knowing that the hotel added its own service charge for using the telephone, went on down the street to a *tabac* and paid for a token. He pulled Nicole's card out of his wallet and called her from the instrument next to the toilet. Of his recent new encounters, Nicole was the one who had really gotten a grip on his imagination–more so than he wanted to admit. When she answered he stifled his excitement by telling her that he had a couple of troublesome pictures he wanted to finish before he took any time off. She was cordial, and they agreed that they would try to arrange something the following week. He hung up satisfied that as long as he could put her off, she didn't represent a threat to his working routine. The mystery of Patrice still nagged him.

He went out and turned a few corners and was in the rue de Verneuil. He realized that he hadn't bothered to look at the number of Patrice's place, but he was sure that he could find it. He passed building after building with great impenetrable double doors. He was certain which side of the street it was on and knew it had to be right along here somewhere. It was only a few minutes from the hotel. He came to a wide cross street that he hadn't seen yesterday and turned back. Forget it. He didn't even know Patrice's last name. He had been picked up by a kid who had failed to turn up for a lunch date. So what? Was he afraid he was losing his sex appeal? His instinct to avoid queers made sense. They were odd and undependable, not capable of normal friendship.

He set off resolutely for the hotel and within minutes was back in his room. He went to work but remained fretful. When there was no longer enough daylight to gauge color accurately, he set out all the canvases around the room and studied them one by one for

49

flaws. Were they really as good as Patrice had said? His not showing up seemed a slap at his work. That was what bothered him. If
Patrice hadn't made such a fuss about the pictures, he could write
it off as faggot pique at Rod's not being fun in bed.

Eventually he joined his cronies for dinner in the rue de Buci.
He was evasive with Jeannine when she tried to pin him down
about his plans for the evening. After he had eaten—when the conversation around the table had reached a high pitch—he muttered
something about going to the john and slipped away. He headed for
the Pagode. There would be people he knew there, even if he didn't
find Patrice. He didn't care as much about finding him as making
sure that he was all right. His not showing up had spooked him.

He crossed the boulevard when he neared St.-Germain-des-Prés
but kept an eye on the busy sidewalk in front of the Deux Magots
and the Flore. He had almost reached his destination when he
caught sight of a trim cloaked figure swinging along toward him on
the other side of the boulevard. He plunged into traffic and heard
the squeal of brakes and saw headlights flash before he landed
safely in front of Patrice. He didn't know whether he was angry or
relieved. Patrice, his face radiant with mischievous delight, looked
as if they had been playing a game that had come to a satisfactory
conclusion. Rod decided he was angry.

"You're here," Patrice exclaimed.

"I'm here. I was at the hotel all day. Where were you?"

"You wanted me to come?"

"What a stupid question. We had a lunch date."

"And are you angry with me?" Patrice asked, still delighted.

"Angry? Why shouldn't I be angry? It's a fucking bore sitting
around waiting for somebody for an hour."

"Then I was wrong, and I'm sorry. Come with me, and I will try
to explain. It's good if you are angry. I know you'll forgive me." He
turned and started back toward the rue de Verneuil.

Rod followed automatically. "It doesn't matter whether I forgive
you or not. The fact remains, you loused up my day." He looked

50

down at the comic face and the appealing mop of hair and was glad to have found him despite being angry.

"I am truly sorry. I thought if you cared about lunch you might come by and look for me."

"I did. I tried to. I couldn't find your house. I didn't know the number."

Patrice stopped dead in his tracks. "You tried? You wanted to find me?

"Of course. I was worried about you. I thought you might be sick."

Patrice's smile faded. But in the uneven light of street lamps, Rod couldn't read what else was taking place in his face. He set off again. Rod followed. "Yes, I see," Patrice said almost to himself. He cleared his throat and spoke up. "Were you going to the Pagode to look for me?"

"I don't know. I thought you might be there."

"I hoped *you* would be." He laughed. "We timed it very well."

"Where are we going now?"

"But home, of course. You will have a drink with me, no?"

"More of Grandma's magic potion? I wish you'd tell me why you didn't show up." The prospect of basking once more in this kid's unstinting approval and adoration was unexpectedly pleasing. It could easily become a habit.

Patrice laughed again, this time with an apologetic note. "It's difficult, but I will try. You said not to be shy, but think how it is for me. All day yesterday and today I think about your work. You are a very good–probably a great painter. I think I shouldn't let you waste time on sketching me. And because I am queer–that word means other things, doesn't it?–because I am a homosexual I might imagine that we like each other more than it means to you. So I say to myself not to insist. Let him decide. If he wants to see you, he will find you. It was the most difficult thing I ever made myself do."

Rod detected a slight roughness in his voice as he finished, and he instinctively lifted a hand to his shoulder. "You haven't imagined anything. I don't go for the same kind of sex as you, but that doesn't

51

keep me from liking you. I was really impressed by you yesterday, the way you really looked at the pictures. Not many people know how. I wasn't even angry until I saw you looking so cheerful. I really worried about you this afternoon."

"And I–I was sick with worry that you wouldn't care if you saw me or not. You see, I think you're the most important person I've ever met in my life."

They glanced at each other across the considerable difference of their heights, and Patrice moved in closer so that Rod's hand slid across his shoulders, and he gave him a little hug. "OK. We're getting to know each other. Promise not to get me drunk again."

"Never. But truly it wasn't I who made you drunk. You already were."

Rod laughed, and Patrice joined in. They entered the maze of side streets that Patrice navigated with brisk confidence, turning corners as if there were no other way to go. They turned another corner, and Rod recognized the stretch of the rue de Verneuil that he had covered that afternoon.

"This is it, isn't it?" he asked as they approached a great double door. "Of course. I almost tried here, but I wasn't sure of your last name."

"It seems that we have gone very fast without stopping for a few important details."

He pointed up at an enameled plate over the door. "That is the number. My surname is Valmer. It's quite important for you to know because this is where you are going to live." He pushed the button and held the door open and called "Valmer" as they passed the concierge's loge. "I will tell her tomorrow. From now on when you come home after 9 o'clock, you must call 'Mac-an-teer,'" he said. Rod heard, but the suggestion was so outlandish that he could think of no rational reply and remained silent. They crossed the courtyard and mounted creaking stairs. And in another moment Rod was installed on the sofa in front of the fireplace. Patrice stood in front of him. "What would you like? Some wine or my grandmother's alcohol?" he asked as if he had never uttered his extraordinary proposition.

"I think wine would be safer."

Patrice went to the end of the room and returned with a bottle and two glasses. He filled them and lifted one ceremonially. "Cheers. Now you are home. I'm very glad."

Rod reached for his glass but was seized by a fit of incredulous laughter. The kid leaped so blithely to improbable conclusions. "You're as mad as a hatter," he said. "What're you talking about?"

"It's very simple, but we don't have to decide it now. I want you to stay here tonight. You have to. I must prove to you that you can stay without anything happening that you don't like. I will sleep out here if you wish. Tomorrow is Saturday. I don't have to go to work. We will have the weekend to get you settled here."

Rod's heart began to beat fast with astonishment, with gratitude, above all with excitement at the impossible possibility of having this room to work in. "You're mad," he said again, wanting to hug him for even suggesting it. "You're talking about my moving in here with you?"

"Of course. You can't go on working in that ridiculous room. If you don't want to move in with me, then I will go. This place must be for you."

Rod was stunned by the reckless generosity of the offer and immediately filled with dismay at having to refuse it. "Listen. This is crazy. It won't work."

"Why not? We don't have to talk about it tonight. Will you sleep here, please? It will prove that we're true friends."

"If you put it like that, of course." There was nothing physically displeasing about the clear-skinned, fresh-faced boy, nothing that gave him any qualms about sleeping in the same bed now that Patrice understood that passes would be unwelcome. "Just remember, if I stay here tonight that doesn't mean I'm going to move in."

"Of course not. Tomorrow you might decide that you really don't want to, but I think you would be foolish not to consider it at least. You would save the money of the hotel. You would have room to work. You say the light is good. I would try very hard to be what you want me to be. I love you. Is it all right to say that in English? In French I can say, *Je t'aime bien* or *beaucoup*. I must not say, *Je suis amoureux de toi*. That would mean I am *in* love with you. Do you understand the difference I make?"

"Sure. OK. I love you too. No, I guess that doesn't sound quite right in English. I like you, monkey, but we hardly know each other."

"That is only partly true, I think. I can't paint pictures that show you all of me. You are willing to discuss the idea?" Rod nodded and picked up his glass, and Patrice sat on the chair beside the fireplace. "Very well. You have showed–shown?–shown me very much of yourself and–"

"I sure have," Rod interrupted with a chuckle.

Patrice's eyes twinkled at him, and he burst into laughter. "You're very wonderful. I didn't want to talk about that. I'm talking about everything else. I will be very proud if I can make your work easier for you. That is the most important thing you should know about me. Please do what is reasonable for you."

"All right. Let's be reasonable. What would I do about girls? As far as that goes, how about you and boys?"

"There will be no boys. I can promise you. For you there is the room back there, very far and private. I can sleep here."

"No, monkey. It's too much. I'm not going to rearrange your whole life."

"Don't you know that you're a person whom people *should* rearrange their lives for if it would help you?"

"No, actually. That's never occurred to me." An unexpected lump in his throat made it difficult to speak. He was deeply touched. He tried to imagine what it would be like living here. Sharing the bed didn't bother him. Sharing his daily life was another matter. There was a fastidiousness about Patrice that suggested he would know how to avoid encroaching on his privacy, but he hadn't lived with anybody since his school days and hadn't intended to do so again until he got married. He liked the place. But as its owner had said, it wasn't the Ritz, so he could be reasonably sure that he wasn't being undermined by his habit of comfort. The thought of placing his easel where he had decided he would want it was the greatest temptation. He felt the boy's eyes on him and met them with an intense gaze as he went on. "Listen, I don't mean to sound as if I don't trust you–you're being so goddamn nice, but–you're not thinking I might turn out to be queer after all are you?"

Patrice met his eyes without flinching. "If I hadn't seen your pictures, I might still be thinking only of seducing you. Now I can truly say that it is much more than that."

"OK. No sex. Would there be any rules? Would you expect me to keep any regular hours, do things with you, that sort of thing?"

Patrice uttered his light merry laughter. "You mean, as if we were married? No, only things we might like to do together. We will lead our own lives as usual."

"You say there won't be any boys?" Rod asked. "I don't think I'm the first guy you've brought home with you." He watched Patrice's face turn very grave and his off beauty become striking.

"When you know me well you will perhaps understand," he said. "I've been with many boys. You make me very tired of them."

Their eyes held for another moment. Then Rod nodded and took a long swallow of wine. He wasn't about to believe that anybody would take a vow of celibacy for him, but maybe it was a problem that Patrice knew he could work out. His glass was refilled, and he lifted it and toasted him with it. "Well, it's all pretty crazy, but I'm thinking about it. Let's sleep on it. And I certainly wouldn't let you sleep out here. If anybody uses the sofa, I will. As a matter of fact, I rather like to wake up with my work beside me."

"I understand that. I would too. *Tu es amoureux de ton boulot.*"

"In love with my work? I suppose I am."

While they finished the bottle of wine, Rod asked Patrice questions about his life but seemed refreshingly indifferent to talking about himself. He learned that Patrice was an orphan (another one), that he had been brought up in the country by his grandmother until he was 15 and he had been sent to a family friend in

Paris. Rod got the impression that there was money in the background, although nothing specific was said. He was a little older than Rod had guessed, almost 22. He had apparently been actively homosexual since adolescence and referred to it with detachment as a fact of no particular significance.

When Rod had finished his last glass of wine, he lay back and smiled lazily. "I'm sleepy. I don't know about you, but I'm not much of a night owl. If you're not ready for bed, I'll go home."

"Please. This is home. You almost know that, don't you?"

"Maybe. Almost. It's funny. I wouldn't dream of it with anybody else. You're awfully easy to be with."

"The short dark stranger. I told you."

They looked at each other and laughed. They both stood. Patrice let the way down the corridor. He lit lamps and showed him where their clothes would be kept, and in a moment Rod was out of his. He didn't want to be a tease, but if two guys lived together, it was natural that they should see each other naked. It would be a bore to think about covering himself up all the time. Patrice straightened from turning back the covers and glanced at him as if he already took his nakedness for granted.

"I never wear pajamas," Rod explained. "Is that all right?"

"Yes. Very. I don't understand why people get dressed to go to bed. Do you expect me to wear them?"

"Don't be silly. I'll go do some washing up. OK?"

He turned away, and Patrice had his first chance to take a long look at his back as he left the room. It was as beautiful as the rest of him—broad shoulders tapering to a supple waist and small tight buttocks. The long legs gave the whole body a spring of power. He didn't know whether it was possible to live with happiness. He had never experienced anything like it, and his body felt uncomfortably stretched in the effort to contain it. He wanted to do all sorts of insane things that Rod would hate—cling to him, scream with laughter, fall to his knees in front of him. At least he had proved to himself that he retained some sanity by not appearing for their lunch

56

appointment. A test of willpower. What would become of his willpower if it turned out that he had found everything he had always longed for—father, brother, friend—everything except a lover? If he could do without that, he would have escaped Gérard.

"Please, God, let him stay," he prayed to nobody in particular as he undressed quickly and wrapped himself in his robe. In a few minutes Rod returned still casually, blindingly naked. He went to the foot of the bed.

"Which side is mine?"

"There. Where you were the other night. My turn for the bathroom." He hurried out, not trusting himself to watch Rod get into bed voluntarily.

Rod stretched out in the clean bed and pulled the covers up with a sigh. Everything was marvelously clean here after the squalid hotel. It was a nutty setup. Nothing like it could have happened at home, but this was Paris, thank God. He'd been taught not to leap into anything without carefully considering the pros and cons, but the hell with it. He's be crazy not to stay. The hotel was cheap, but the saving would quickly add up to another month of freedom. And another month. And another. He had put up the proper resistance to the offer. You mustn't be obligated to people. That sort of nonsense. Patrice was indifferent to such conventions. If he established his usual routine right from the start, it would be almost like having his own place. He might even put a daybed in the living room if sleeping together proved uncomfortable. Patrice thought he was important and wanted to do what he could for him. It was nutty but wonderful. An occasional girl. No difficulty about that. No need to tell anybody. Mail could still go to the hotel. Eat in. Less money on restaurants.

He was beginning to drift into sleep when he heard footsteps. He opened heavy eyelids and smiled up at Patrice as he came around the other side of the bed. He brought a sweet smell with him. He was still wearing his dressing gown when he turned out the light. He heard movement and the fall of cloth, and then the mattress assumed a new shape as his host worked his way down under the covers.

"Sleepy?" Patrice asked in the dark.

"Yeah. I haven't even thanked you. You're a sweetheart. Tomorrow I'll spend all day telling you how wonderful you are."

"Good. I will like that very much."

"Good night, monkey."

Patrice said nothing, incapable of being the one to close off communication for the night. He lay still, finding is less difficult that he had feared to keep his distance, lulled by the deep peaceful comfort of Rod's presence into a state of spiritual felicity more moving than any sexual experience he had known. He had always sensed that there must be more to life than physical license. Feeling as if all the world's happiness was contained in this room, he drifted off into peaceful sleep.

He was awakened by what registered in his subconscious as a big bang. Another explosion in the street. Quite close. Simultaneously, he realized that he was holding an erection. He moved his hand along its length with dreaming delight and found it so thrilling that it brought him fully awake. He remembered whose it was and snatched his hand away. He lay transfixed, listening to Rod's regular breathing until he dared edge himself over as far as he could go on his side without falling out of the wide bed. If he did anything when he was unconscious to drive Rod away, he would kill himself.

When he awoke again he knew it was day and felt Rod stirring beside him. His happiness was still stretching all of his body. "Are you awake?" he murmured without opening his eyes.

"Mmm. Here I am again. I have to go pee."

"I suppose that it's time to get up," Rod said. Patrice's eyes flew open as Rod threw the covers off and stood up, making no attempt to hide himself. Their eyes met, and Rod glanced down and laughed. "I wish it wouldn't keep doing this. I guess I need a girl much more than I want one."

He strode off, and Patrice scrambled for his robe and bundled himself up. If he had to face a sight like that every morning, it wouldn't be long before he began to question all his lofty resolutions. Gérard's training had left him with a feeling of obligation toward satisfying male lust.

When Rod vacated the kitchen Patrice prepared his usual café-au-lait for both of them. Rod joined him wearing shirt and slacks.

"Did you hear a big bang in the night?" Patrice asked, watching Rod's expression closely to see if he betrayed any awareness of the inadvertent caress.

"No. Another one?" Rod asked innocently. "I think they're trying to get me. You're not afraid to offer me asylum?"

"I'll risk it. It's all settled, isn't it? You will move here? You didn't change your mind during the night?"

"I guess I needed to sleep on it to make it seem real. Last night it sounded sort of crazy. I mean our not knowing each other very well and all that. This morning it seems more reasonable. I guess sleeping with a guy makes a difference. It's wonderful of you to have thought of it. It's going to make all the difference in the world to the work."

"That is the important part. Be sure to say you owe all your success to me when you're famous."

They had breakfast at the kitchen table and discussed details. To Rod's inquiries about contributing to household expenses, Patrice was firmly negative. Having a friend to stay would cost nothing extra. He agreed to let Rod pay his share of any food or wine they had together. They planned the move. They would need a taxi for the big suitcase-trunk, but Rod thought they could carry all the rest.

They set to work in a cold drizzle that slowed them down because of having to wrap the canvases carefully. They were further delayed when Patrice tried to take a shortcut and found the narrow street blocked off. Men were working around a shattered shop front. A twisted and crumpled car lay on its side.

"The big bang last night," Patrice said, "I knew it was close."

"They're getting closer all the tine," Rod commented dryly.

59

It took all morning to move the painting materials and equipment. Patrice picked up delicatessen food for lunch–pâtés and salads–but Rod was so excited at having the easel in place that he could hardly sit down long enough to eat it. He had his current canvas already mounted on it, and he kept jumping up and circling it to see the effect of the improved light.

"It's fantastic, monkey," he exclaimed. "I can see. I can move. I can stand up straight. I'll probably have to rework everything I've done here. I'm going into a whole new period. My Monkey Period."

Patrice's heart ached with pride and happiness. His dream was coming true. By evening Rod's things would be everywhere. He was here. He was his. The past would soon be a discarded and forgotten secret. At least he hoped he could manage that part of it.

They spent the afternoon packing and carrying and unpacking. The splendor and variety of Rod's wardrobe created a space problem, but Patrice rearranged his own things and crowded them together to give pride of place to Rod's. Soon they had everything sorted out and hung up or put away. For the first time since he had been in Paris, Rod was completely unpacked. He rather regretted his own mess, but he felt wonderfully settled down. Was he being seduced back into his old ways? Surely the necessity of brushing his teeth in the kitchen sink was sufficient guarantee that he was making no compromises for luxury's sake.

They had agreed to eat at home the first evening, and Patrice went to the kitchen to prepare the food he had bought earlier. Rod stripped and threw a dressing gown over his shoulders and followed him. He took a bath while Patrice prepared vegetables and meat. Rod's careless display of his body continued to raise tantalizing question in Patrice's mind about whether he was being overcautious. All the men and boys he had ever known expected nakedness to provoke sexual advances.

He set a small table at the end of the living room opposite the skylight while Rod lounged about in his dressing gown. "You must tell me if you want whiskey in the house," Patrice said. "I have *pastis* if you like that."

"Sure. I love it."

"Good. We'll have some." He served them the watered-down, milky-looking aperitif, and they sat in front of the fireplace drinking.

"This is the life," Rod said, his long legs stretched out in front of him. He had had a chance to look at the room in detail, and he liked it better than ever. The wooden floor sagged, the Oriental carpet was threadbare in patches, some of the upholstery was shabby, but everything in it was handsome. One of the pale gray walls was lined with books. There were four framed paintings on the other walls, semiabstract, interesting enough to confirm Patrice's good judgment.

"We have done a big day's work, I think," Patrice said. "I hope you like what I have cooked. I don't know what Americans eat."

"You can stop thinking of me as a special case. I'm sure I'll like everything you do. Nobody's ever taken such good care of me.

"That's what I'm here for. Let's have another drink."

He eventually served them artichokes with hollandaise sauce followed by veal cooked with mushrooms and cream. Rod found it better than any restaurant he knew. Patrice told him that his share of the day's shopping came to a little more than 1,000 francs. If he could eat like this for a couple of dollars, he could stay forever. They discussed the future. Rod explained his financial situation. He had hoped the money he had would last at least six months. Now he was beginning to think he might stretch it to ten. He had an understanding with his New York gallery that he would be given another big show in the spring. If it went as well as the first one, he would be able to stay as long as he liked.

Patrice felt as if they were entering into a contract for life. He hadn't been sure until now that he could think in terms of months rather than weeks. With a few economies of his own, he could surreptitiously shave a bit off Rod's bills to extend his stay. He would be eternally grateful to Gérard for the apartment that made everything possible.

They washed the dishes and tidied up the kitchen together and sipped wine and talked for another hour. They yawned simultaneously and laughed together.

"I don't know how I got so much junk in that little room," Rod said. "That was more exercise than I've had for months. You're such a pretty little guy, but you worked harder than I did."

"Would you like to go to bed? We have much to talk about, but we can talk there."

"Fine. I wouldn't mind stretching out."

They took turns in what now became the bathroom. Rod was already settled back against the pillows when his roommate joined him. With his back turned, but without turning out the light as he'd done before, Patrice slipped off his robe and ducked quickly under the covers. He lay out with singing contentment beside his friend.

"I am thinking of ways we can save you money," he said, resuming their conversation. "I can cook whenever you wish it. I will do your laundry when I do mine. I take my shirts out, but that's for my job. I can cut your hair but not right away. It looks wonderful long. I will think of other things." He paused and felt such deep peaceful understanding between them that he could no longer resist exploring its limits. "I wish I could make you happy in bed," he said simply.

"I don't see how you can, monkey," Rod said with a laugh. "Except that you're such a clever little devil I suppose I shouldn't be surprised if you managed to turn yourself into a girl."

Patrice rolled onto his side and propped himself on an elbow to face him. "I would be very glad to try."

Rod smiled at him with a little shake of his head. "I shouldn't have seemed too cooperative the other day. That was a fluke. You know that. I was half-asleep and drunk and hardly knew who you were. Now that we're friends, nothing would happen, if you know what I mean."

"You forget how good I am," Patrice declared with ironic innuendo. "And what if it has already happened, the way you were this morning? Couldn't I give you pleasure then?"

62

"No, monkey. I wake up with a hard-on every morning. That doesn't mean anything. Don't you understand? I wouldn't feel right lying back and letting a guy go to work on me."

"It is not what I call work, but I'm not thinking only of that. Don't some girls use something to make it easier?"

"Use something? How do you mean? You mean vaginal jelly, a lubricant, that sort of thing?"

"Yes, that's what it is. Have you used it?"

"Sure. I knew a girl once–" He broke off with a laugh. "It can sure make things very interesting."

"I don't want you to do anything you find strange, but if you've used it, it can't be strange. I have some. I can be your girl."

Their eyes met and held, and their gaze intensified. Only then did Rod fully grasp what Patrice was proposing. He'd heard guys say they'd rather have a clean boy than most whores. He had thought it was a joke but perhaps not. Perhaps it wasn't necessarily queer. Still, the idea chilled and shocked him. He found himself staring into eyes that had grown insistent with desire.

"I don't even want to kiss you," he blurted, "let alone–"

"Oh, kissing," Patrice said with a dismissive shrug in his voice. "Kissing is for being in love. I don't expect you to be in love with me."

Rod continued to stare at the boy wondering as the initial shock passed if it would be queer of him *not* to take what was offered him. His pampered background? Stripped of mockery and mischief, Patrice's droll beauty had a sort of sylvan innocence that made his proposal seem almost natural. He drew a hand out from under the covers and brushed it tentatively over the mop of hair on his forehead. He was struck again by the boy's fastidiousness. He couldn't imagine him doing anything messy or distasteful. "I thought it was agreed–no sex," he reminded him edgily. He was being made to feel that his reluctance was unreasonable.

"It is agreed, certainly. But this is something perhaps you haven't thought of. It wouldn't be like before–a guy working on you."

"You really want it like that," he asked slowly into his eyes, "as if you were a girl?"

"Very much. When I see your big erection, I feel a great need to be your girl."

"You go on about how big it is. Are all queers obsessed with big cocks?"

"Not necessarily big. Fortunately for me," Patrice said with a little giggle.

"If it's so big, I'd hurt you. I don't like hurting people."

"You won't hurt me. I have seen big boys before."

"You frighten me, monkey." He realized that much of his shock was rooted in fear. Fear of what? Fear of being exposed to the abnormal? He was training himself not to fear any experience.

"There is nothing frightening," Patrice assured him. "It is a pleasure we can give each other, more for me, perhaps, than for you, but we don't know that until we try."

"Oh, hell," Rod muttered. "I don't want to be coy with you and have you thinking I don't know what I want. I don't think my body is holy." He flung the covers off and lay without moving. "There. You'll soon see it won't work. If you think you can get any fun out of it, go ahead and try." He spoke and acted in a moment of bravado without reckoning on Patrice's skill. A fingertip strayed across his chest and was joined by others, followed by a mouth, playing amorous music on his body. Within seconds he knew the boy was winning. It wasn't desire; he was being undermined by a brilliant technical performance. He was filled with sudden unfocused anger. The boy was somehow taking advantage of him, paying exquisite homage to his body instead of making outright demands on it that it wouldn't be capable of satisfying. He flung his tormentor from him and sprang out of bed and snatched up his dressing gown and pulled it on. He had almost hit the boy. He could feel the violence in his hands and arms. He waited for a moment to calm down and then turned back to the bed. Patrice was lying with the covers pulled up to his chin. His eyes pleaded. He looked small and young and touching.

64

"Please. I am so very sorry," he said in a voice that sounded liquid with tears. "Please come back. You said I could try. I will never do it again."

"Oh, hell, monkey," Rod burst out with bewildered exasperation. "I just don't understand it. Maybe you can give me a hard-on. We both know it was beginning. You *are* good, but what then? I tell you it won't work."

"No. I was very wrong," Patrice agreed helplessly. He had made his first major blunder, been carried away by his American's gentle kindness, forgotten caution too soon. He was terrified by the hard, intent scrutiny of Rod's eyes. Faced with the abrupt end to all his dreams, he found courage to say more. "Please. I want only for you to be here and for everything to be as you wish it. I told you and you must believe me. It would be better for me to sleep on the sofa, at least until we're used to your being here and I will no longer make such mistakes."

"Dammit, you're not going to be put out of your bed. That's final. He continued to be annoyingly touched by the slight figure in the bed. He was a faggot who was trying to lure him into being his lover. If he hadn't just gone through the big move, the sensible thing would be to get dressed and go. He was trapped with a question he was forced to admit he hadn't quite answered to his own satisfaction. He took a step closer, his eyes fixed on the trouble young face. "Come on. Get up," he said, anger gone from his voice. "There's something I've got to find out." He turned and headed for the door.

Patrice scrambled for his robe, mystified but no longer frightened. He had heard the note of kindness that he knew now he must beware. He followed Rod down the hall back to the living room. Rod switched on all the lights at the end of the room that he had claimed as a working area. He collected a big drawing pad and some charcoal pencils and pulled up a chair. Patrice watched, beginning to dread what was coming. Rod turned to him. "OK. Stand over there by the easel. Take off that robe."

"But I can't. Please, *mon ami*. You don't like to look at boy's bodies."

"I'm used to male models. That's all you'll be while I'm working."

"But it will soon be cold."

"Then we'd better hurry." He sat and flipped open his pad and settled it on his knees.

Patrice moved with dragging feet into the light. "I wish you wouldn't. I have been most careful so that you won't see me without clothes. I understand that is what you want."

Rod laughed. "Do you think you can seduce me by staying all bundled up in that thing? Now listen. No boy has ever given me a hard-on before. I told you that the other day was a fluke, but you make me wonder. The only way I can learn anything is with my eyes. I'm not very bright otherwise. You say you want to be my girl. Let me see you, monkey."

The robe dropped slowly to the floor, and Patrice stepped away from it. Rod was glad to see that there was no sign of sexual excitement. A quick glance took in the modest accent of genitalia between slightly bony hips. It was a stripling's body, not coltish but slim and graceful and well-knit, the flat straight line from neck to thighs broken only by a faint swell of breast, charmingly fresh and virginal. He took a long hard look at it and watched the muscular tension in it smooth out and relax as Patrice adopted a casual pose. His hand began to move rapidly over paper. He looked at what he'd done and found that the problem was to make him look like an adult. He had drawn an adolescent. He smoothed out another sheet in front of him, and his hand moved rapidly again, refining the line, making sure to give the right weight to the shoulders. When he had finished he was satisfied that he had come as close as need be for a quick sketch. He studied the figure he had created, not looking at the model. Did he want this boy? He saw with the stirring of curiosity that the sensuality of the line was uncharacteristic of him, but physical response wasn't necessarily desire.

"Yeah," he muttered to himself. "OK. Turn around. Shift your weight slightly to the right. Good. No. Forget it. Walk around and

66

stand naturally with your back to me. Beautiful. This is going to be a bitch." He stared for a long time before putting pencil to paper. How to capture the long globes of the buttocks without making them look girlish? They were supported by slim legs and depended on their masculinity on the set of the proud shoulders. In quick succession he tore three sketches out of the pad and crumpled them and dropped them to the floor. He was drawing a girl. He closed his eyes and tapped his forehead with the pencil. *Look*, for chrissake, he told himself.

He opened his eyes and concentrated them on the torso before him. He bisected it, quartered it, subdivided it, searching for his error. He found the misleading girlishness in a half-inch, a centimeter of unusual length in the pelvic area. He took a firm grip on his pencil and moved it lightly, with an iron control that stopped his breath, over the paper. When he was finished the pencil slipped from his hand, and he took a long breath and looked at what he had done. Here was a slight male body that was waiting to be taken by him, and he knew he was going to take it.

The shock of it seemed to ricochet through his chest and settled in his groin. He had once had a girl in the way Patrice had suggested—not because he had wanted it but because she had—and remembered that there had been aspects of it he had decided to forget and that it had been exciting in a way he had supposed was perverse.

He lay the pad on the floor and rose silently and slipped off his dressing gown to be on an equal footing with his friend. Whatever happened he was determined to be honest with himself. He was aware that his sex was lengthening and growing heavy. He moved in behind Patrice and put his hands on his shoulders. Patrice gasped audibly and began to tremble but remained rooted in place. Rod ran his hands along the shoulders, finding the feel of his pencil strokes. He lowered his hands to shoulder blades and moved them out to the side so that his fingertips briefly entered armpits. Patrice's trembling grew more marked as hands moved down his sides. Rod held Patrice's waist for a moment while his erection lifted slowly between them. He placed his hands on the buttocks and parted them slightly as his fingers defined their elusive masculinity. Boy or girl, no matter how he might resist it, there was beauty in the body he held. He started to move his hands around to the front of it but remembered that they would encounter a flat chest instead of breasts, perhaps an erect cock—nothing was where he would expect to find it. He gripped the boy's waist and moved in closer to let him feel what had happened. "Where's that lubricant," he asked against his ear.

Patrice uttered a low cry and dived for his robe and trotted toward the door. "Come to bed," he called breathlessly.

Rod followed him, watching the almost girlish behind dancing down the corridor. When he entered the bedroom Patrice was stretched out on his belly with a towel spread out under him, his arms at his sides. Pausing at the bedside, Rod saw that one hand held a tube in a loose grip. He lifted himself over the supine body and straddled it and took the tube.

Patrice raised his head and looked over his shoulder. "Do you want me to—"

"No. Stay there." He squeezed some ointment into his hand and applied it liberally to himself. He tossed the tube onto his pillow and wiped his hand on Patrice's back. He got a grip on Patrice's hips, and they lifted to him. He overcame some brief initial obstacle and then drove slowly into the boy as easily as if he were a girl. He had barely completed his penetration when the body beneath him was seized by violent spasms. Patrice shouted and uttered a succession of hoarse cries, his hips writhed, his torso pitched about on the bed. He was finally still, sobbing quietly. Rod waited calmly for the storm of ecstasy to pass and then began the rhythmic thrust and withdrawal of possession. He was fucking a boy. It was a purely mechanical act—he had never made love without kisses and caresses—but it was a surprisingly satisfying facsimile of legitimate copulation. Since Patrice had had an orgasm and, unlike a girl,

68

wasn't likely to have another, he didn't pace himself but used the boy's body for his own pleasure and felt its passionate response. He was slowly filled with a sense of extraordinary power at exacting such total submission from a male. As he approached his climax, his movement accelerated, and his thrust became hard and deep. Patrice lifted himself on his arms and pressed his hips back to welcome the demands of the man he adored. His cries drowned Rod's long animal groan as they collapsed together in a deep stillness of shared repletion.

"Did you come again at the end?" Rod asked without moving.

"Yes."

"You liked it that much?"

"*Oh, mon amour.* I feel as if I had never been alive before." It had lacked passion, but it had been the way Rod had wanted it; Patrice couldn't imagine wanting it any different.

Rod lifted his head slightly and spoke with his lips against Patrice's ear. "*Tu es amoureux de moi, petit singe?*"

"*Follement.*"

"*Bon.* I can understand that, I guess."

"Thank you for letting me tell you. You understand everything now. Oh *chéri*, it's so big inside me. *Quand il s'agit de ta grande queue, il faut parler francais. Je ne veux pas dire des bêtises en anglais. Ta grosse bitte, énorme et tout-puissante. Quand elle est entrée dans mon corps, tout ce que j'étais cessait d'exister. Elle me possède, elle me joint à toi, elle me fait parti de toi. Sans toi, sans ta grosse bitte superbe qui me prend, je n'existerai plus.* I don't know if it is the same for girls. They grow up knowing they will have a man, so it must be different. For me it is forbidden, but the feeling is there. I didn't want it or ask for it. It is there, and it is forbidden, and so it grows and grows, with longing and without hope. Even with you there is no hope, but I don't need hope now. I am transformed, complete by being a part of you, even if this never happens again."

Rod was moved, if slightly daunted by the speech. The boy had offered him his life. To allow him to say such things would be an implicit acceptance of a commitment he couldn't dream of making. "You know it can't mean anything like that to me," he said carefully.

"Of course, *chéri*. That is what I cannot hope. All I wish is to be your girl sometimes and give you pleasure."

"Yeah. Well, that part of it seems to work all right. I'm sure it wouldn't with any other boy." He still couldn't place it as desire as he knew it because he felt no urge to fondle or caress the body he was lying on. Was it a growing acceptance of the bizarre and unfamiliar? Once you made an initial act of rebellion, were there no limits to which you might go? A sexual rebellion hadn't figured in his calculations, but if that was what this was, it was extraordinarily potent. Nobody had ever praised his cock so extravagantly. He knew that if he remained where he was, it would soon be ready to display its power again. He shifted slightly to withdraw.

"Keep it there for another minute," Patrice exclaimed rapturously. "When you are so much inside me, you make me—Oh, *chéri*, I am so much yours that I could almost paint your beautiful pictures."

"Maybe we better move the easel in here and see what happens." Their bodies locked together in a brief spurt of laughter. "You want to be mine, monkey?"

"All of me. All yours."

"You're giving yourself to me. What will you take? Girls always take something."

"I will take your big cock, and it will make me belong to you."

"I won't be yours."

"Have any of your girls made you hers?"

"Not really, but it'll happen someday, I suppose."

"We don't have to worry about that tonight. You fuck me sublimely. Better than the ones who like boys."

"Have you had guys before who didn't like boys?"

"Yes. A few. It happens sometimes if there's no girl. That's what I hoped with you."

Rod was reassured; he slipped slowly from the boy. His boy?

70

He did as he'd been told and lay on his back with his eyes closed while Patrice left him and returned demurely robed and carrying a warm washcloth and washed him thoroughly and dried him. Japanese girls were said to provide all sorts of special services. Was he going to have to think of Patrice as a Japanese girl? He laughed to himself. When Patrice turned the light out and got into bed, he put a hand out. The boy found it and held it and moved close enough so that their bodies touched lightly here and there.

Not too close, Patrice warned himself. He must give Rod time to get used to having taken a boy as a lover. There was a great deal they both would have to get used to. He would have to get used to love-making ending like this, in silence, without an exchange of kisses and endearments. It wouldn't be difficult. His body was filled with the feeling of the man he worshiped. It was far more than he had let himself expect. He had spoken openly of his passion. For tonight his spirit was at ease, and he was cradled in a cocoon of physical satis-faction. He pressed Rod's hand and murmured a good night.

"Good night, monkey." Rod closed his eyes and drifted toward sleep while his mind grappled with the impossible. He was shacked up with a fag in "gay Paree." If he had intended to do over his life completely, he couldn't have succeeded better.

It seemed like the moment for an appraisal of all that had gone before, but he found that when he tried to push his memory beyond the last five years, there wasn't much more there than a blur of miscellaneous images–school, girls, playing fields, ski slopes, country clubs, tennis courts, grand hotels, seashore, dances–dom-inated by the growing realization that he was different from his contemporaries. He could find nothing in them that corresponded to his passion for recording the world he saw around him with pencil and paintbrush. Unwilling to condemn himself to being an outsider, he had tried to minimize his passion. He had talked about becoming an industrial designer, which could mean anything from coffeepots to space ships, and was quite acceptable to the world he had been born into. He remembered the liberating revelation of his first complete sexual experience and the excitement of bedding other girls thereafter. He remembered that for his 18th birthday his father had opened accounts in his name with a New York tailor, a London bootmaker, and a Roman shirtmaker. This had presumably been intended to mark his coming-of-age, but it hadn't made him feel any different. It had amused him to send sketches of things he wanted to distant capitals.

He had been aware of being a member of an elite, but there had seemed to be such a great quantity of others who enjoyed the same privileges that it wasn't until he set up on his own in New York that he grasped that it was an elite of a tiny minority. His apartment was provided by his family and was large and comfortable. The generous allowance he had been given when he went to college was continued after he graduated so that the paltry salary he earned as an apprentice designer was quite irrelevant to the way he lived. He had enjoyed himself enormously until the passion for paint had gradually become a troubling obsession and he had begun to understand the price he was expected to pay for his privileges. He had finally come to the conclusion that there wasn't much point in being a rich boy unless he controlled the riches.

As a poor boy he was now apparently committed to living with a male lover. And why not? He began to see practical solutions to a number of problems in this unexpected situation. As far as money and comfort were concerned, it couldn't be better. That was obvious; there were more surprising considerations. He had known he must be prepared for a solitary life from the moment Carol had dropped him. An artist was a loner, more or less by definition. Patrice could save him from loneliness. The hunger for girls might let up a bit. He could afford to wait now until he found one who might be important to him. He had known from his first sober moments with him that Patrice offered something special—feminine solicitude without female demands, more than friendship but none of the burdens or thrills of a love affair, total dedication that would still leave him free. Patrice had ended by offering all of himself, knowing there were strict limits to what he could expect in return. Rod was glad of the quirk in himself that made it possible to accept him. Or perhaps it wasn't a quirk. He had discovered that he could accept sexual satisfaction where he found it. It made life much simpler.

He was suddenly aware, with a sudden rush of awareness, that he was grown up. He was an adult. He was a man. At 26 he no longer thought of himself as a boy. He tried to pin down and isolate the feeling, tried to define it, but there didn't seem to be anything in particular to define. There was only a sort of general easing of tensions as if he had slipped easily into clothes that hitherto hadn't set on him quite comfortably. For the last year he had been conscious of day-to-day shifts and changes in himself, but they hadn't added up to anything recognizably conclusive. Now everything in him felt jelled, focused. Only the other day he had been awkward and self-conscious with Nicole. He didn't think he would be now. He would make his play for her, and if it failed, try to forget her. Like a grown-up. He would see her and find out.

He wondered if the sense of power Patrice had aroused in him had brought about this real coming of age. Perhaps all men needed a homosexual experience in order to cast off the ambiguities of adolescence. He listened to Patrice's deep breathing. Asleep. He extricated his hand from his grip and reached for the beguiling mop of hair and stroked it. A boy could have nice hair. So much for the terrors of being queer. His whole life had become an act of defiance. He wasn't going to be stopped by conventional taboos. Patrice's hair was soft, and it soothed him to stroke it. He slept.

Rod attacked his work after breakfast the next morning, reveling in the new living conditions. Patrice told him there was enough food in the kitchen for lunch and went out early even though it was Sunday, a day for household chores. He intended to stay out all day. He wasn't going to let himself become an intrusive presence in the place. He felt more complete and confident of the future than he had believed possible. They would slowly find a home life together.

Rod returned that evening to his usual haunts. Jeannine was obviously beginning to feel neglected, but it had been time for them to drift apart. There would be others. He told nobody of his move. Yesterday, at a moment when Patrice had been otherwise occupied, he had arranged for the hotel to take care of his mail and telephone messages for a small fee.

When they had been sharing the place for a week, Patrice proposed an anniversary dinner. He spent a large part of the afternoon in the kitchen and lit a fire in the fireplace. They bathed and put on their dressing gowns, and Rod gorged himself, still marveling at Patrice's cooking. They moved back to the fireplace and talked while Rod grew drowsy in the friendly glow of the fire. There was a sharp knock on the door.

Rod was so startled that he leaped up and pulled his dressing gown closer around him as if he had been caught in a criminal act. Patrice was immediately on his feet in from of him, his finger on his lips, their eyes questioning each other.

"Do you expect anyone, *chéri?*" Patrice whispered.

"Certainly not," Rod replied, automatically adopting Patrice's whisper.

The knock was repeated more forcefully. Patrice stepped closer and turned his head aside and reached for Rod's arm, as if for support. Rod felt that Patrice was trembling and, shocked by it, yanked his arm away and gave him a push. Why should a knock on the door make anybody tremble? The knocking became more violent.

Rod charged across the room toward the door. Patrice flung himself in front of him, shaking his head, his eyes wild and pleading. The noise made whispers unnecessary. "Don't open it," he begged in an agony of terror.

Their slight scuffle pulled Rod's robe open down the front so that he was nearly naked. He gathered it together and decided he didn't want to confront a maniac in a flimsy dressing gown. He pushed Patrice aside again and made a dash for the corridor and ran back to the bedroom. He grabbed slacks and a sweater and pulled them on. What had he got himself into? Something to do with a sick queer world of demented perverts? He ran back along the corridor fastening up his slacks.

The knocking had become an insane tattoo that made the door rattle in its frame. There was no doubt in Rod's mind now; whoever was doing it was mad. Patrice was slumped against the wall near the shuddering door with his face buried in his hands. Rod seized him and half carried him back to the living room and set him on his feet. More self-confident in clothes and determined to put an end to the madness, he started back for the door. The hammering suddenly stopped. It was followed by a man's voice, cold and incisive and so accurately pitched that it reached them without sounding as if it had been raised.

"Very well. Enough of this," the disembodied voice said in French, making Rod's scalp crawl. "If you are there, and I'm quite sure you are, you'll regret this. This place isn't here for you to entertain your secret lovers. I think you'll have much to regret. You'd best start by looking for another job. Are you sure the lease here is absolutely foolproof? I doubt it. We shall see."

There were footsteps and the creak of stairs and silence.

The two remained motionless for a long moment while Rod slowly relaxed. He turned back to his shattered young friend who stood as if he were hanging from the ceiling by a thread, swaying slightly, his head bowed. "What is all this?" Rod demanded in a normal voice that sounded strident after the profound, welcome silence. "Some sort of faggot hysteria? I've heard about it, but I certainly don't want to be any part of it. Did you have somebody staying here before I moved in?"

Patrice pulled himself up and shook his head vaguely. "No," he said in a faraway voice. He had had a week of peace and happiness, more than he would have dared hope for if he'd allowed himself to count carefully the consequences of what he was doing. Almost two weeks, if he went back to when he'd started watching for Rod everywhere and had resolved never to resume the life Gérard had made for him, regardless of what happened with the unknown American. He had known he wouldn't be able to keep the secret for long if he embarked on what Gérard would assume was a silly little faggot affair. He had been prepared for questions, threats, reprisals; he had never dreamed of anything like this. Now that it had happened, now that he was recovering from it, he realized that he had nothing worse to fear, so that this was again a moment for hope. If he could gloss it over and put together the pieces, he might really be free. He had learned in a week that nothing Gérard could offer him, no extravagant pleasure he might dangle before him, could compare to the unpredictable joys he had found with the man he worshiped. He took a few steps toward the door in the corridor, listening, and turned back, determined to keep anguish out of his eyes, attempting a smile that he could feel was a disaster. "It's nothing, c*héri*. Please. Sit down. I will tell you everything," he said, intending to do nothing of the sort.

"I think you better." Rod sat on the sofa and prepared himself for lurid revelations. He knew very little about the boy, but he had seemed so open and easy and cheerful that it had never occurred to him that there was anything in particular to know. He hadn't seemed secretive so much as genuinely uninterested in talking about himself. Rod wasn't in the habit of grilling people. He glanced at his easel at the end of the room and wondered if this heavenly studio was going to be snatched away so soon. He didn't see how he could stay here with a maniac pounding down the door. He watched Patrice sit in the chair by the fire and saw that his hands were still shaking slightly. "OK, tell me," he ordered.

"I have told you almost all the facts," Patrice said, pleading for understanding with his eyes. "One is not very nice. You know I was sent to Paris when I was 15. I thought of the man I was sent to as my father. He immediately made me his lover. That is why I was there. I work for him now. That was he." Patrice dropped his eyes, and there was another silence.

"I see," Rod said stiffly, wondering what right he had to question him. He decided that bed gave him the rights. "Are you still his lover?"

Patrice's head shot up with protest, and he dropped his eyes again. "You shouldn't have to ask that. I haven't seen him since—how long? Since before we met. Almost two weeks. But not his lover for long before that."

"You work for him but you haven't seen him?"

"He has many business affairs. The gallery is only one of them. I don't have to see him often about work. I have avoided him."

"He apparently doesn't like that," Rod said, finding humor in the situation despite the menace of an unknown world. "Does this place belong to him?"

"No." His eyes met Rod's with the honesty of anger. "He helped me get it, but it's mine. He may try to take it away from me now. I don't know if he can, but he is very powerful, very cruel. He frightens me."

"What about the bit about secret lovers? Aren't lovers often secret? Private, certainly. Especially in your case, I should think."

"He expects me to tell him. He has taught us—me," he corrected himself hastily. "He has taught me to tell him everything about sex. He never wanted me to be faithful, only to tell about it. He likes to hear all the details. I will never tell him about you. That's the trouble. It makes him angry not to know. He likes to watch."

"Jesus." A little chill of revulsion ran down Rod's spine, the sound of the voice still in his ears. He gazed at Patrice. In the flicker of firelight he looked very young and innocent. His heart went out to him for having been subjected to such a training. At 15, for God's sake. "You've let him get away with this?" His indignation was directed at the older man, but the reproach included the boy.

"I have never known what it is to be in love. Little things long ago. Not truly, so none of it seemed to matter. I have been very wrong until now. I almost believed him when he taught me that love is nothing, only pleasure. I'm not good at hiding things from him. I thought of giving up my job. Now I have no choice."

"But this is crazy. Your talking about giving up your bed for me was bad enough. I'm not going to let you lose your job on my account."

"It *is* a very good job," Patrice admitted with a touch of pride.

"Then why don't you tell him the truth? Well, it *is* the truth. Can't you tell him I'm not queer and that you like me as a painter and want to help me by giving me a place to work? Hell, I'm willing to tell him myself if it would make things easier for you."

"No, I must be free to see him whenever he wishes, to entertain him with my lovers. He will give my job to somebody else whenever he learns I'm no longer what he wants me to be. I can get another, maybe not so good."

"Wait a minute," Rod said, studying the boy thoughtfully. "I'm not sure I've got this straight. Are you saying a man who's been more or less a father to you would throw you out if you won't let him watch what you do in bed?"

"You see why I cannot go on working for him?"

"Yes, but I don't like this happening on account of me." The boy was finally displaying the strength of character he had sensed in him all along and illustrating an unexpected kinship between them; they were both engaged in the discovery of their true selves. If his being here compensated for whatever the boy was losing, he damn well wouldn't leave the field free for "the Voice." "What about the other thing. This place. Do you really think you might lose it?"

"He frightened me. I feel better now. I will fight very hard if he tries to take it. It is for you, for us. If you weren't here, I would care little if he takes it."

"Is there anything else? Are you dependent on him in other ways?"

"Until I was 21, in every way of course. Then I wanted a place of my own, and he let me have it because he thought he had trained me to follow his ways. I thought so too, but I also knew I wanted something else. Now, very quickly, just in the last two weeks, I found out what it was. He will think me very foolish and perhaps I am, but I'm also happy for the first time in my life."

"I take it I won't solve your problems by getting the hell out of here." Their eyes met. The dismay and vulnerability in Patrice's made Rod regret having tried to make light of it. "How did he get hold of you in the first place? Is he a relative?"

"He was my father's comrade during the war–in the Resistance. They were blood brothers, heroes. My parents left me to him to be my guardian."

"They seem to have made a slight error in judgment."

"Something changed after the war, I think. I don't know what. He had made a cult of evil. Is that right? Do you say cult?"

"Sure. I know what you mean. He sounded as mad as a hatter."

"Perhaps. I don't want to be evil. I would rather be foolish with you."

At his most serious, something mischievous lurked in Patrice, and Rod smiled fondly at him. "Come here, monkey," he said.

Patrice sprang up. It was over. Rod's questions had made it easy for him to avoid lying. His one slip had given him a fright, but he had recovered himself in time. The dreadful moment had passed, and Rod was still here. This was the real beginning of a new life, and Rod would never have more than an inkling of the old. He sat beside his lover, confident of being able to bear his intent scrutiny. "I'm here, *chéri*," he said.

Rod ran a hand over Patrice's hair and toyed with the waves on his brow. The yearning in the boy was almost tangible, a yearning for his love to be met with equal love, a longing for passionate lips on his. He could give him only a fitful semblance of what he wanted, but he wouldn't betray the trust in his eyes. Patrice was counting on him to rescue him from whatever ugliness he had been living with. He leaned to him and planted an affectionate kiss on Patrice's forehead. He felt an ecstatic tremor in the boy as he did so. He sat back. "I didn't quite bargain for all this," he said musingly, "but it's obvious I haven't paid enough attention to you. I haven't even bothered to ask you what you've been doing the few times you've come home late. Tell me."

"I see friends. I go to the cinema."

"Are your friends all *comme ça*?"

"Most are."

"I'm not interested in details, but do you have sex with them? Having posed the question, although he hadn't given it any thought before, he wanted suddenly and unreasonably for the little he could give to be enough.

"At the cinema?" Patrice rolled his eyes comically. "No, *chéri*. It doesn't matter if you care or not. I can be only with you. I'm yours. I told you there would be no boys. Someday, I will go to bed only with boys who remind me of you. I don't think there will be many."

Rod ran an arm along Patrice's slight shoulders and gave them a squeeze. He was apparently going to be a good influence. He felt an odd paternal tenderness for the boy. An orphan. A kid who desperately needed a father. Judging from tonight's revelation, Patrice's emotional makeup probably led him to find passion in a father figure. If he were going to be a father figure, he hoped he'd be a better one than the madman at the door. "I guess after all this it would be pretty silly to say I'd go if it would help you. The main thing is, don't let my being here make you do anything you wouldn't do if you were on your own. Do you understand what I mean?"

"I understand, *chéri*. If I fall madly in love with a boy who is madly in love with me, we'll put you out here on the sofa." Patrice's sense of fun came bubbling to the surface and reminded them that the evening had been planned as a party. Flames leaping in the hearth and replenished glasses of wine revived their sense of well-being.

Their talk moved on to more familiar subjects, but Rod knew that the incident had marked their relationship and consecrated their living together. He was getting in deeper but not necessarily deeper than he was ready to go. When he picked up seriously with a girl, Patrice would find himself real lovers quickly enough.

Later, when they were in bed Rod made a conscious effort to extend the limits beyond which he couldn't go. He had been sparing in his caresses, but he found that with the growth of affection, his hands could find pleasure in fondling the body he possessed. He couldn't kiss him on the mouth or touch the part of him that made him a male, but he nuzzled his neck and bit his shoulders and heard his boy cry out exultantly. He felt rewarded for his effort. He had added something to their plan that wasn't strictly mechanical.

Patrice walked out of his job on Monday without seeing Gérard again. He checked with the management of his apartment building and found, as he had expected, that his lease was in order. Even if Gérard resorted to his most high-handed tactics, bribery and the threat of blackmail, he would have to go through the courts. Patrice had nothing to worry about for a year or two. He did worry about being unemployed, but he reported cheerfully to Rod that evening that he had another job lined up, counting on good friends, ex-lovers, and his well-known connection with Gérard to make it true. He wouldn't mind digging into his modest savings as long as they lasted to prevent Rod from noticing any change in their standard of living. His optimism was rewarded, and the following week he was back at work not far from Gérard's Left-Bank gallery.

For Rod, life had become rather like a dress rehearsal for a smoothly functioning, hardworking marriage. He no longer felt himself the beneficiary of Patrice's generosity but an integral part-ner in the household. He suggested, to Patrice's delight, that they have dinner at home together regularly. Spending so much time close to his work kept Rod marvelously free of distractions, but he assured himself that he wouldn't let it turn into too much of a rou-tine. An artist had to travel light, without too many attachments. He was already almost slavishly attached to Patrice's cooking. An en-graved invitation from Lola to what he guessed would be another grand party seemed like a signal to finally do something about Nicole. Life was so well-organized now that he could risk stirring things up a bit.

One morning after picking up his mail from the hotel, he went down the street to the *tabac* and called her. He half expected her to snub him for his two weeks' delay. But when he identified himself, she sounded pleased, and they quickly settled on a lunch date for a few days later. She remembered the name of his hotel, and Rod suggested meeting her there to save her the bother of writing down Patrice's address.

He was more elated by the date than he felt he had any reason to be. He was still smiling to himself when he turned into the rue de Verneuil and saw a familiar face approaching. He greeted the youth amiably before he remembered that it was the queer called François something-or-other that both he and Patrice had spoken to the night of the Pagode. Patrice had been interested in Rod's knowing him; he understood why now. He adopted a more guarded manner as the youth stopped in front of him.

"Hi there. I saw you the other night with that Valmer kid."

"That's right," Rod agreed, wondering why he had bothered to stop.

"He's quite a guy isn't he? Sensational in the sack."

Rod stiffened. Patrice had been frank about his past, but he didn't like being confronted with it. The youth spoke harsh, fluent, slightly inaccurate Americanese that grated on his nerves. "Is he?" he said coldly.

"If you don't know, Patrice must be losing his touch. He's got an in with some of the wildest action in town. Haven't you been to the club?"

"Not yet." Rod lingered in spite of himself in case there were to be further revelations about his bedmate. He congratulated himself for not having told anybody about his move; if it were known, he would probably be the prey of every queer in town. It gave him the creeps.

"He knows how to pick 'em. I'll say that. You're not only a looker, but I hear you're rich too and big buddies with your new president."

Thinking of the animosity that prevailed between his family and the Kennedys—something to do with business dealings he had never bothered to understand—Rod couldn't suppress brief laughter. "You've heard wrong. I'm sure as hell not rich, and I've seen Kennedy around at parties, but I don't think I've ever met him. Maybe when I was drunk. I'm not sure."

82

"That so? I heard you went to school with him."

"The same school for a while. Not at the same time. He's a lot older than I am." Rod was puzzled by himself. Why did he go on talking to this character? He refused to acknowledge him by actually looking at him; his gaze slid across him. He was aware that he was sharply dressed and that his face was curiously cold and expressionless. He was pleased by evidence that he was known and talked about, even erroneously, in his adopted village, but he didn't particularly want to be known by types like this. "I've got to be going," he said.

"Sure. You're not rich huh?

"Far from it. I guess you could say I'm the next best thing to being broke." Rod's puzzlement increased. Despite the youth's tough, low-key manner, there seemed to be something purposeful in his remarks. There had to be a point to this conversation or why were they having it? Rod's first suspicion that it was leading to a sexual pass was clearly mistaken. He waited impatiently for a clue.

"I have a feeling we may be seeing more of each other," the Frenchman said. "A lot of people have found François Leclerc a useful guy to know."

"I don't know what you're talking about."

"You never know till the moment comes. A guy gets in a jam, needs a little extra dough, I have ways of making a buck that might surprise you. Keep it in mind. I'll be seeing you around." He thrust out a hand. Rod gave it a shake and turned brusquely and continued on his way, pursued by a vague sense of menace. He tried to think why he had started nodding to Leclerc in the first place; somebody must have introduced them, but he couldn't remember who. He would ask Patrice about him. He shrugged him out of his mind as thoughts of Nicole brought the smile back to his lips.

He told Patrice that evening about the encounter. "Who is he anyway?" he asked.

"François Leclerc? He's a *pédéraste*. I believe he is engaged in many illegal activities. There are other rumors. Some even say he

83

is a secret agent, but nobody says for whom. *Ça c'est du cinéma.* I don't think he is somebody we need to bother about."

"He asked if you'd taken me to some club."

"A club?" Patrice picked it up with sharpened interest. "What club?"

"He didn't say. I didn't bother to ask."

"There are many gay bars," Patrice said dismissively. "His mind runs on one track. Do you say that? Can you imagine me wanting to take you to a gay bar?"

Rod wondered why he had let Leclerc bother him, and his mind reverted happily to what had grown into the major event of the day. He told Patrice that he'd called Nicole and made a lunch date.

"You want her, *chéri?*" Patrice asked with a teasing smile.

"Possibly. I'm not sure she's the sort of girl who'll let anything happen."

"With you? Then she must be made of stone. But I don't understand girls. I have heard the name. A very good family." Patrice was full of such bits of worldly knowledge, but Rod hadn't placed him socially. Serving rich clients would require him to know of the people in high society.

"She looks it," he said. "Anyway, I'm just going to show her the pictures."

"Of course, *chéri.* And anything else she wants to see." He laughed naughtily. The girls were beginning, and he found it exciting as well as disturbing. Rod was a man. He loved all of him and would love his having girls.

Two days passed while Rod's keen anticipation of the lunch date grew more intense. At the appointed hour he went around the corner and stood outside the entrance of the hotel. It was already hard to believe that he had once lived here, but he was glad that he had chosen it for the meeting; he didn't want Nicole of all people to know that he shared a place with a boy who was doubtless a notorious *pédéraste.* He hadn't been waiting for more than a few minutes when she alit from a cab. She saw him and smiled a greeting across the sidewalk, and he had a moment to observe her while she paid.

84

The quick dexterity of her graceful hands was one of the things he knew about her, as was the lovely line of her neck and the slim style of her legs. She was as quietly elegant as he expected and wore no hat on her intricately coifed hair. They met in the middle of the side-walk, and she held out her hand to him.

"How nice to see you again. I hope those pictures are no longer giving you trouble." She glanced over his shoulder. "This is where you live?"

"Yes. It's pretty grim. Don't worry. I'll spare you the squalor of my room. Since I saw you last, a friend had lent me a place to work. We'll go there after lunch." He remembered something withdrawn and mysterious about her but didn't feel it now. She seemed open and friendly and pleasantly pleased to see him. He took her to a nearby restaurant that Patrice had recommended. It turned out to be just the sort of place he would have wanted to take her, small and cozy with a fire in the grate, run by a motherly woman who made much of them when he mentioned Patrice's name. He felt a little glow of satisfaction at showing Nicole that he knew his way around. He mentally congratulated Patrice for his unerring good taste.

They had an excellent meal that featured fish soufflés, and they were soon talking freely about nothing in particular—just like old friends. Nicole's big wide-set eyes met his with intelligence and tranquillity. Her delicate mouth made Frenchified music of her English. He was stirred by her more acutely then before, although her physical appeal was muted and subtle. He could see sweet breasts under the smart dark green dress. He had never gone in much for brazenly sexy girls, with the brief exception of Jeannine, and he supposed (the thought depressed him) that he would always be drawn to "ladies." His whole body tingled at the thought of feeling her against him. He wanted to lie on top of her. He wanted to thrust himself into her and make her his.

"I wonder why every time I see you I always feel I'm about to fall in love with you," he said over coffee.

85

"Oh," she replied with a shrug and a friendly smile. "That is some foolishness Lola has put in your head."

"I'm not sure. What if I really do? That *would* be foolishness. Don't let me."

"I'm afraid I will have to leave that to you. You're a very handsome man. Girls always like handsome men to fall in love with them."

"But do they fall in love with the handsome men? I don't think so, as a rule."

"You're probably right. They like to look at them, but they usually end up with some ugly little old thing who is safer. However, it is always a possibility."

Their eyes met and held questioningly for a moment. Rod knew that his were telling her that he wanted her, but she must be used to men looking at her like that. Was she a girl he was ready to be serious about? Go slow. He wasn't sure of the message in her eyes. Hadn't there been some hint of a man in her life? He paid the smallest bill he had ever had in a Paris restaurant and again blessed Patrice.

"What a marvelous place," she said as they were leaving. "How do Americans find places like this? I must remember it."

He walked her to the rue de Verneuil and ushered her into the apartment and reminded himself not to refer to it as home. He took her coat and shed his own. She stood beside the sofa and looked around. "You really *are* clever. What a wonderful room to work. How do you find friends with such a place? I would give a great deal to have something like it."

"I've been damn lucky. The guy who owns it is out all day. I hardly ever see him. Come sit here." He pulled a chair over near his easel under the skylight. His interest was firmly fixed on her person, and he was anxious to get the showing over with. She was so elegantly aloof that he felt ready to devote months to plotting her surrender to him; having her now would save him from getting hooked by her and letting her disrupt his life.

86

He selected five canvases from those stacked against the wall and put one on the easel. In a moment it was clear that she didn't have Patrice's eye or concentration—or perhaps the pictures were of secondary importance to both of them. She commented on significant details but looked at him as much as the canvas. Nothing about her suggested that she would be an easy lay, but an exciting tension was growing between them that might soon exclude his work.

"I think I see something," she said while she was looking at the second. Her eyes strayed to him and dutifully returned to the canvas. She looked at the third. "Yes. If this is American painting, I understand why you were angry when I said I didn't know anything about it."

"I don't know if it's American or not. I'm an American, so I guess that comes into it, but there's so much American painting."

"Yes, but I think I see a difference. The French have become decorators. This isn't decoration. It's difficult for me in English but—it's so positive, like a statement. An affirmation. I'm afraid I can't say it right."

"Thanks for trying. You're not only beautiful, but you're also an art critic. I *will* fall in love with you."

"You mustn't make fun of me or I will be shy. You made me shy last time." She was no longer speaking to him as a painter. They were flirting.

"Is that what the trouble was?" he asked with a playfully insinuating smile. This was familiar territory, a move in the mating game, thrilling with expectation but without the sharp little edge of the unknown and the illicit that had marked his recent experiences. An ingredient he might find he missed? "I'm not making fun of you. What you said is all I'd want anybody to say. Anything else is literature." He brought the showing to a decisive end by removing the last picture from the easel and turning back to her.

Her eyes were on him. A current immediately leaped between them that tightened her expression with something like alarm. She rose slowly. He felt her desire like a shameless exposure of her body. He hadn't been so eager to get out of his clothes in months.

She touched her lips with her tongue, but when she spoke her voice was cooly self-possessed. "I'm grateful that you allowed me to see your work," she said, looking up at him warily as if she expected him to spring. "I think you're a true artist. I'm deeply impressed."

He held her eyes with his for a moment. "Enough to let me kiss you?"

A small smile twitched the corners of her mouth and was gone. She looked up at him gravely. "Yes. Enough for that."

The instant their lips met, he knew that she would offer no resistance. He was going to have her. Her responsive mouth opened to his. He was briefly astonished that it had happened so quickly and then totally absorbed in taking advantage of his good fortune. He put a hand on her hair and found pins and pulled them out. He fumbled with a zipper at the side of her dress and opened it and unfastened her bra. His hand on her naked breasts wrenched their mouths from each other with simultaneous gasps. He looked down at her and was stunned by the transformation he had accomplished. Years had dropped away from her. She was a child in distress, half out of her dress, her hair coming down but still partly caught up in the elaborate coiffure.

"You're not–not a virgin, are you?" he stammered.

She looked up at him with all guards discarded, her breath rapid. "How sweet of you to ask. Two others before."

"We have nothing to worry about? No problems about–?"

"No, no. You won't make me pregnant. It's all right here? Your friend–"

"Don't worry, we have plenty of time," he said hurriedly, spurred by shared desire. He couldn't figure out how her dress worked, but she helped him with it and stepped out of it and discarded the bra. She was a gorgeously provocative sight, naked to the waist and still in shoes and stockings. Her breasts were as exquisite as fine porcelain, the nipples hard and rosy. She lifted her arms to complete the release of her hair, and he bent to tender flesh. She began to tremble at the touch of his lips and dropped her hands to his head.

"I must sit down to take off my stockings," she said in an urgent whisper.

He straightened, and she stepped out of her shoes. He led her to the sofa. He was out of his clothes in seconds and found nothing lacking in the familiar experience of being vigorously aroused by a desirable naked girl. His erection looked too outrageously aggressive for such a delicate creature, and he wished he could hide it as he faced her. In another second they were tangled together on the sofa. She wanted him. She made no effort to disguise it. They moved up and around and over each other, their bodies performing extraordinary contortions in a passion to wring the ultimate ecstasy from each other. They slid across each other like snakes, their tongues provoking little cries and moans of anguished delight as they found and savored the most sensitive parts of each other's bodies. The sinuous ritual accelerated. Her hands gripped his sex and placed it against herself.

He glanced down to recover his bearings. "God, look at me going into you." He groaned with pleasure.

"I'm feeling it. It's heavenly."

She rode up his thighs, her legs gripping his hips to take all of him into her. She lay back in his arms, as wanton and shameless as a street girl and worked her hips on him. They rocked together and cried out to each other in a delirium of excitement.

"You like it, don't you?" he gasped with triumph.

"Yes, yes, I like it," she agreed breathlessly.

The sofa became a confinement, and they slid from it, still joined, and rolled about on the floor finding new joys in unexpected juxtapositions. When he could no longer bold back, he grappled her to him and used her without restraint. Her eyes were blind with ecstasy. A curtain of hair whipped about her face in the fierceness of his possession of her. She arched her body up to him, her legs in the air, and became an instrument for his satisfaction.

When he had spent himself in her, he pulled himself to his knees and gathered her into his arms and lifted her and lay her out on the sofa again. He dropped down and covered her with his body, belly to belly. They lay still in the lethargic aftermath of orgasm.

When he began to revive he lifted his head and looked down at her. Their eyes met with the peaceful knowledge of having experienced everything their bodies could give each other. He probed deep into hers and found them inscrutable except for the light of unextinguished desire. A girl's desire was the real thing, so rich in promise, stirring responses from the depths of him, particularly poignant in a girl who had seemed at moments all style and spirit. Was it the prelude to love? After this, what would they expect of each other?

"Say fuck," he ordered softly with is mouth close to hers.

"Fuck?"

"Yes, I want to hear you say it. Otherwise, I may ask you to marry me."

"If I say it, you won't?"

"It may seem less necessary if I keep reminding myself that what we've been doing is having a fantastic fuck."

"You won't want to give your wife a fantastic fuck?"

He saw humor spring up in her eyes. "I hope I do, but people don't necessarily get married for that."

"I don't know what they get married for. I love being fucked by you. More than anybody ever. I'm not sure why yet. You *feel* beautiful. This is very thrilling. Everything you do makes me feel you want me very much. You're a big man, much bigger than my other two. Lovely and slim but so much of you fucking me."

"Is that good?"

"I think it must be. If one likes to be fucked by a man, the more there is of him the better." They burst out laughing together. "Have I said it enough?"

"Yes, but it's not having the right effect. You make it sound so elegant."

"I'd like to have a husband who fucks me so beautifully."

Lethargy was passing. He felt none of the listless resentment he often experienced after the first time with a new girl, resentment at having surrendered something of himself for such fleeting pleasure. With this girl their bodies joined in a sort of witchcraft that promised an infinity of sensual rewards. That might turn into love if he let it. His voice hardened in an effort to be practical as he went on. "In another year or so, I might be able to think about getting married. In the meantime, I don't even know how I can see you very often. My work, no place to take you, having no money. All of it."

"I'm a French girl. We're very sensible about such matters. Do you want me to be your mistress? You can't live with me because that would cause a scandal, and scandals are usually more trouble than they're worth. Besides, you would be too far from your work. Do you want me to set aside an evening every week when you can come have dinner with me and fuck me? Some men arrange it like that with their mistresses."

He was briefly offended by her speaking of it so dispassionately. But second thoughts told him that she was offering him a great deal—a serious affair that wouldn't take up too much of his time. It sounded a bit like keeping a regular doctor's appointment—what if he didn't feel like playing on the prescribed night?—but he was sure she would keep it exciting. There was the mystery about her, something elusive, something that intrigued him. He felt it again, and his curiosity was agreeably stirred. There didn't seem to be another man, after all. Whatever it was, it had nothing to do with physical reticence.

He slipped off to one side of her to make their bodies accessible to their increasingly purposeful caresses and studied her delicate features. Her eyes were averted, her expression intent. The area in him that had been holding back, questioning, sending out warnings, seemed suddenly silenced. This exquisite creature was his. Her hands were exploring all the secrets of his body. She was his. It was as simple as that. Lola had known it was going to happen, so something must have been there all along. Why hold back?

91

She lifted her eyes to his, and whatever she saw brought an inviting smile to her lips. He made a little murmuring sound of acknowledgment. "If I see you only once a week, I'll worry all the time about somebody else fucking you," he complained.

"Do you want me to promise that nobody else will?"

"Is it a promise you can keep?"

"I haven't let anybody fuck me for almost a year. Before that, there was one man for about two years. He was married. And then, going backward, there was the first one. We were both very young, so it doesn't really count." She slurred over the last words in an odd way that caught his attention. Mystery?

"That seems to add up to only one man who did count. There *was* something sort of virginal about you when—well, until a little while ago."

"I am very bold and wicked with you, but you see that I haven't been promiscuous. And you—will you be fucking nobody else?"

He thought of Patrice, but that didn't count. "I haven't been much interested recently. Nor can I imagine wanting anybody but you. Besides, men are different."

"So they like women to believe. Never mind. If you are satisfied, I will be. At least until we see."

"See what? Do you think we really might get married?"

"You're an American but a fine artist. You're the only beautiful man I've ever seen. I'll think about it when you ask me. Not now. In a year if you're still interested. I must go soon."

He moved his mouth to hers. They kissed deeply and at length until they were devouring each other. Their mouths broke apart, and she buried her head against his chest and ran her mouth over it and kissed his nipples.

"Oh, darling, beautiful Nicole." He gently disentangled himself from her and sat upright. He drew her up and put an arm around her and held her close. She caressed the erection that lifted once more against his belly. "How marvelous. We're so good together," he murmured. "Thank you for saying fuck so

92

often. It makes me realize there's a lot more to it than that. Are we falling in love?"

"I think that means different things to different people. You're fascinating, not like anybody I know. That's why I want to be your mistress. I think you Americans are very sentimental. We say we're in love when we find the only person we think we can spend the rest of our lives with. To know that takes time.

"Did you know this was going to happen?"

"I thought about it. I believe men and women think about it a great deal, don't you? During lunch I knew you could have me if you wanted me."

"I wish you'd told me," he said with a chuckle. "I couldn't think about anything else while I was showing you the pictures. I've been afraid of you—afraid of falling in love with you and your not falling in love with me. I know that sounds ridiculous, but I've got to think like that. I just don't have time to run after a girl."

"Ah, when it comes to time you can't accuse me of wasting very much."

"No. That's what's so marvelous about you. So many girls pretend they're not interested in sex like men."

"How strange. You must mean American girls. French girls are interested in little else."

Their eyes met, and he saw tenderness mingled with the humor in hers, as well as desire. He marveled that in such a short time she could touch him on more levels than anybody he had ever known. Starting with the fire of passion that burned beneath her cool aristocratic surface, there was so much about her that satisfied him. Humor cut through her gravity. She was intelligent but with none of the superiority of the intellectual. She was beautiful, but unlike the beautiful girls he had known, she had yet to look at herself in a mirror. He tipped her over and lifted her legs onto his lap so that she was stretched out on her back, gloriously available.

"Isn't it marvelous being naked together? Some girls are always covering up. Half the fun is being able to look at a beautiful body."

"I'm beginning to find that out too."

He pulled himself up onto his knees and held her legs at his sides and advanced between them. She reached for him and guided him into her. They were joined once more.

"There. Just like that," he said with awe. "We become part of each other. Oh, God. Feel me inside you. Isn't it marvelous?"

"Heavenly. I don't think some ugly little old thing would feel quite the same."

Eventually he became aware of time and Patrice. They managed to call a halt and took turns in the bathroom. When he returned to the living room, she was dressed, looking cool and stylish and unattainable. He wondered how he'd ever dared make the first move as he headed for his clothes.

"I'm not covering up," she pointed out. "You said we must dress. That's different."

"I don't like being naked when you're not," he said over his shoulder. "Are clothes going to make us strangers to each other?"

"After this afternoon? I think not."

He tucked his shirt into his pants and turned to her. Their eyes met, and they burst out laughing. "Well, yes and no. Clothes make you look as if I ought to undress you. Can't we go to your place and spend the evening with nothing on? He went to her and held her lightly with his hands on her elbows.

She looked up at him with an unguarded smile that turned her young and virginal again. "We'll do that soon, my dearest. Tonight I have a dinner. A very dear friend just got married. Their first dinner. I would be unkind not to go."

"Yes, I guess that's the way it's going to be. You lead your life, and I'll lead mine. It's the way it has to be, of course. I hope it doesn't drive me crazy."

She lifted a hand and traced the shape of his mouth with a fingertip. Her eyes followed it with absorption and then lifted to his. "It's very confusing when there is so much desire. We mustn't let it make us foolish. I must remember, for instance, that a fantas-

94

tic fuck is not a reason for getting married. If we care for each other, it will do no harm to be apart a little. There is always the telephone."

"Yes, we've got to talk a lot. I'd like to know when you decided you want to spend the rest of your life with me."

"I doubt if it will be necessary to say it, but it might help us not to make unnecessary mistakes. There are always enough mistakes that are unavoidable."

"You sound very wise for a girl who's had only two men," he teased her.

"Women are born knowing more about love than men," she told him with mature serenity.

He had entered into his adult manhood in the nick of time. To deal with her shifts of personality, ranging from woman of the world to starry-eyed innocence, required adult confidence. He leaned down, and they exchanged a kiss that quickly became breathless. They broke apart, and he gathered up her coat.

He was prepared to escort her home, but she brushed aside the suggestion. He was delighted with her. Fifteen or 20 minutes in a taxi would contribute nothing to their intimacy; it was an irksome formality demanded by girls who were sticklers for the rules. He and Nicole had already reached a point beyond such petty rituals.

Getting her into her coat brought her into his arms again, and they clung to each other for another moment. Her hands on him were agreeable explicit. "I want to start all over again," he muttered. "We've got to get out of here."

"Yes, I must behave, but I love to feel it when it's like this. I'm not very ladylike."

"Thank heavens." They laughed unsteadily and let go of each other, and he headed her for the door. He stayed with her until they found a taxi. They exchanged a final kiss that brought smiles to the faces of passersby, and she was gone. The wrench of parting was so great that his first instinct was to grab another taxi and follow her. There wasn't one in sight. Standing irresolutely at the curb, he

95

had time to remind himself that if he would get into a state every time they parted, he has headed for trouble. He turned back with dragging feet toward home.

It was all very well to get carried away by a sensational girl, even to think he might he in love with her, but his life was organized for work; she had understood and accepted it. She was not only sensational but also sensible. He could at least try to be the latter. Perhaps planning on marriage in the indefinite future would help him keep everything in perspective and provide the cement for what could become a nerve-racking, unsettling once-a-week passion.

Patrice was there when he let himself into the apartment. Rod fell on him and gave him a great hug of greeting and immediately felt better able to cope with whatever he was getting into with Nicole. His monkey would save him from pangs of longing and help him keep everything under control.

Patrice looked up at him with mischief in his eyes. "You look as if you've been having a good time."

Rod chuckled. "I'll say. She just left."

"What did I tell you? She is not made of stone."

"God, no. She's amazing. I think this might be it, monkey." He still had an arm abound him and felt a slight stiffening in his friend's body. He gave him another hug and ruffled his hair. "Don't worry. Nothing's going to change, nothing important, not for months. I'm going to need you more than ever. Let's have a drink, and I'll tell you all about it."

He watched his boy move about the room, brisk and jaunty, and was suddenly overwhelmed by a sensation so intense and unfamiliar that for a moment he thought it must be physical, some wonderfully beneficent seizure. His legs felt weak and his arms and torso buoyant and bursting with an electric energy of their own. Images of Nicole flashed through his mind, and he guessed this was what it was like to be in love, his whole being suffused with love, as if she had uncovered a great untapped reservoir of love in him. It overflowed and brought the whole world and all of life's secrets flooding into him. He couldn't put it into words, but it was there, in his fingertips, in his eyes, and he was sure it couldn't have happened to him if he hadn't cut himself off from his stifling upbringing. Love wasn't struggle and torment. It was light and joy. It was— he could hardly believe it—happiness. That was the last thing he had expected. For a moment he almost didn't care whether he ever painted another picture. A profound transformation had taken place in him, and he wondered how it would affect his work once he had adjusted to it. It was bound to change the way he looked at things.

Patrice approached, bringing drinks, and Rod studied him, testing his sight, taking in the trim body, the seductive mop of hair, the contradictory beauty of his funny face. Love overflowed and encompassed the boy. There was plenty for everybody.

"I'll faint if you go on looking at me like that," Patrice said breezily, making fun of himself.

"Really? Like what?"

"With love, I think. You do sometimes, tonight more that usual."

"I love you, monkey. I really do. We've been together long enough for it to sound right now." He put a hand on his shoulder and leaned over and brushed his mouth with his lips.

Patrice turned rigid, as if he had fallen into a trance, eyes closed, not visibly breathing. He slowly came back to life and opened his eyes. He glanced down with a sigh that was almost a shudder. "I haven't spilled the drinks. How amazing."

Rod gave his neck a squeeze and took a glass. They settled into their usual places in front of the fireplace. Alight with euphoria, Rod talked exuberantly to his favorite audience, defining for himself what he thought the afternoon had meant for the future.

As soon as he had said enough to make it clear that their living arrangement wasn't threatened, Patrice was able to relax and enjoy it. He could face any eventuality except Rod's leaving. He wouldn't even mind if sex with him came to an end; he would prove to himself, to Gérard, that he was no longer a slave to his old appetites. He was ready to go back to the moment of their first meeting, when it had seemed unlikely that Rod could be had, and live for the platonic ideal of friendship. Virtue was the last quality he had expected to find in himself, but Rod would make him virtuous. He felt as dedicated as a monk, as pure as a priest, and he knew that a number of people would laugh like maniacs if they heard that *le petit* Valmer thought of himself in such a sanctified light.

"You say you're in love with me, baby," Rod said, fascinated by this vast and unknown subject. "What's it like? I guess that's what this is."

Patrice laughed a trifle ruefully. "There's too much to tell. Most of the time I feel like lying down at your feet and dying for you."

"Yes, I guess that's part of it, but please don't. I thought it would be more—I don't know. More exclusive maybe. I hated to let her go, and I'm dying to be with her again, but I love being with you. Everything's so wonderful. I can even imagine wanting another girl if the right one walked in. What if you found a beautiful boy with a cock twice as big as mine. Wouldn't you really be tempted?"

"No, never." A wicked gleam came into his eyes. "Twice as big? That would be a most extraordinary sight. I might be tempted for a moment, but I would hate it for tempting me, and that would be the end."

"I'm not sure that's the way it should be. I've seen too many people killing each other and calling it love. My sister and her husband for instance. I want to keep it all alive and exciting, the way I'm feeling now. I'm counting on you. As long as you're around, I don't think I'll lose my balance. The wonderful thing is that I don't think she's demanding in the possessive way some girls are. She understands that I've got to have some leeway."

"You're an important artist, *chéri.* You're in love with your work. Maybe you'll never fall in love the same way as most people."

"I'm not so sure. I'd say the main thing is not to let it turn into one of those big all-consuming passions you read about. That's what I'm apt to do. We mustn't let it happen."

Patrice was enchanted by Rod's rationalizations—his efforts to have it all his own way—and uttered adoring laughter. His sometime lover was such a man. Looking into his fiercely poetic face, the extraordinary eyes bright with joy and the wonder of revelation, Patrice was wrung by gratitude for being allowed to share the simple wholesome birth of love between boy and girl; it purged him of the residue of guilt remaining from his participation, under Gérard's guidance, in the sordid little intrigues of boy with boy. He prayed that he would never knowingly do anything to impinge on what was evidently a touchingly happy meeting and mating. Rod felt his selfless approbation; it confirmed all that he admired and valued in the boy. The evening was launched on a flood of mutual affection and good feeling.

Rod awoke the next morning with his usual erection, and habit turned him to the body at his side. Half-asleep, scarcely aware of what he was doing, and feeling himself prepared in the usual way, he took his boy automatically. As consciousness grew and he thought of Nicole, there seemed to be no conflict, and he didn't see why he shouldn't satisfy Patrice's need. The sense of power that this male submission provided was outside ordinary human experience, unlike anything he would want with a girl, related somehow to the superhuman power he felt when he was working. Patrice's happiness depended, not on sexual response, but on an act of creative imagination within himself and therefore deserved the best he could put into it.

When they were up and about, there was no need to make any reference to it. It fit into the complex of small automatic acts that made up daily life.

Alone, he set to work as usual but went out well before noon, finding that falling in love made it difficult to concentrate, and called his girl.

His heart leaped up at the sound of her voice. His words tumbled over each other in his rush to tell her how much he'd been thinking of her and that it was time to make their engagement official. "Definitely. With blares of trumpets and public proclamations. I've got to spend a whole day with you. When?

"But no, my dearest. Your time is too precious. You warned me how it must be. You must make a little money so that at least we'll have a place to live."

"Oh, God, darling. You're right, except that I've been thinking about you so much that I'm not working well. What do I do about that?"

"You must start to think of me very tranquilly—I wait for you and love you—oh, yes, my dear, so very much. I—yesterday was—"

He heard the catch in her voice and found it difficult to speak himself. "God, yes. Everything. Are you really—I mean, I'm nuts about you."

"Nuts?" She giggled. "Yes. Nuts. Is that right? We're nuts."

"Completely. When are we going to start having those evenings together?"

"Tomorrow?"

"Oh, fine. I was afraid you were going to say a week from next Tuesday." They laughed a bit hysterically and got themselves under control and continued to converse in broken phrases, sudden pauses, incoherent murmurings. Being in love apparently didn't make for eloquence; rapture could be contained in a monosyllable.

"It's all settled," he exclaimed, recovering the power of speech. "We're going to spend the rest of our lives together."

"That's supposed to take a very great deal of time to decide. I think we must wait at least till tomorrow."

They hung up, laughing, and he stood gazing at the telephone for some moments with a besotted smile. He would be able to work now—until the need to talk to her struck again.

Their first evening proved to be a confirmation of everything they thought they knew about each other, as sensationally satisfying as the first afternoon with an added peaceful sense of continuity. Her apartment, on the other hand, underlined the forces he would have to contend with. It was very small and very chic, every detail in exquisite taste, as he would have expected of her. There was no place for him to work even if his life had depended on it. She was definitely not a poor boy's girl. He would have to turn her into one. He was determined to remove her from the world she frequented as thoroughly as he had cut himself off from his own past. He brushed aside her reference to grand friends and relatives and was uncommunicative when she tried to draw him out about his family and childhood. Would she love him more if she knew that his great-grandfather had owned a railroad, that there were family banks and family foundations, even a family zoo? There was enough to find out about who they *really* were.

She didn't let him spend the night but insisted that he must go back to his hotel so that he would be ready for work first thing in the morning. He almost corrected her about the hotel but remembered his deception in time. Eventually he would tell her he had moved into the place where he'd been working. It was unimportant. Shortly after midnight he was back in bed with Patrice.

He and Nicole decided to make their first public appearance as a pair at the party to which Lola had invited him. Lola was at the head of his list of people to be eliminated, but under the circumstances he probably owed it to her to show up one more time. They made themselves conspicuous by their exclusive preoccupation with each other and provoked gleeful cackles from the old lady. Germaine treated them with brittle mockery; once, Rod caught a glitter of reproach in her eyes as she looked at him across the lighter he was holding to her cigarette. Had she marked him for her own?

The idea was more interesting than he would have expected because he'd discovered that she reminded him of his partner—a movie star, of all things—in his first full-fledged sexual experience. Marilyn Harvey had been a friend of his mother's and a rarity—a "lady" who had had an enormous success in the theater and films. One summer weekend when he was 17, after an afternoon spent with a large house party around the pool, she had somehow cut him off from the others as they were going in to dress and had quickly dropped her ladylike manners.

"Do you have a girl, Rod dear? Are you madly in love?" she asked as they were mounting the great central staircase to the upper floors.

"No, I can't be bothered with all that stuff," he replied dismissively, covering his shyness.

"Oh, dear. What a pity for the girls. Are you a virgin by any chance?"

"Well, I–"

"I suspected as much. That really won't do. You're just at an age when the boys might get you. We wouldn't want that, would we? You have the sort of looks that must drive them mad."

"How do you mean?" The incident with the senior at Yale had taken place only a few months before, and he found it uncomfortable to even think about.

"Never mind. If you don't know, so much the better. I suppose I seem frightfully old to you, but I dare say I could make you forget about that. Come along, darling."

His rooms were on the third and topmost floor, and he glanced longingly up the staircase as she led him along the wide corridor to where she was staying. He was frightened out of his wits but didn't see how he could run away from her. He couldn't believe that she would really go ahead with what she seemed to have in mind. Nice people didn't. He assumed that sex would happen in some undefined future, not here and now. Nevertheless, he was in her room behind a quickly locked door, his swimming trunks were gone, his cock was in her mouth with immediate and devastating results. He was so stunned that he hardly knew what was happening to him."

"With a boy built like you," she said complacently while he was still gasping for breath, "it takes a Marilyn Harvey to manage. I'm one of the best in the business, darling. We know now that I can make it hard for you, every splendid inch of it. That should eliminate any nervousness you might have felt."

He slowly came to his senses to find that a naked woman was taking extraordinary liberties with his body. It didn't take her long to prepare him once more, this time for orthodox copulation. He couldn't believe that his body was capable of offering him such exquisite ecstasies. He spent the rest of the weekend in a delirium of sexual release. He waylaid her at every opportunity—morning, noon, and night—and found that she was always ready to meet him more than halfway.

When she had gone he decided that he had found his vocation in life. He was going to have every girl in the world. He became a menace at all the parties that summer, drawing girls into dark corners and trying enthusiastically to get them out of their clothes. He discovered to his regret that there weren't many Marilyn Harvey's around; perhaps girls had to reach a certain age before they learned how to enjoy themselves.

Cheerful memories of Marilyn revived when he looked at Germaine. Although he stuck close to Nicole's side throughout Lola's party, there were a few moments when he was able to engage in a mildly titillating flirtation with her. It was a late party, and for the first time he woke up in the morning in Nicole's bed. He felt almost married to her until he had to put on his dinner jacket to go home.

When he got there he found a note from Patrice telling him that the water heater was out of order but that help was on its way. When the repairman admired his pictures, Rod was inspired to give him a small working sketch. He told Patrice about the incident but not Nicole. He had already discovered a practical streak in her that he was sure would be helpful in the future but that didn't suit his current euphoric mood.

Despite his work and evenings spent mostly at home, he didn't lose touch with his old Bohemian crowd from the rue de Buci. He frequently ran into Massiet or Pichet or Fargue in the streets around St.-Germain-des-Prés, and he always stopped for a beer and news of their latest projects. One day Massiet tried to interest him in an illustrating job for a deluxe edition of some classics that he'd been asked to parcel out to the best young painters he knew. Easy money. Rod immediately turned it down. It sounded too much like the old wage-slave days. If he ever again worked on order, he would be admitting defeat. He discussed it with Patrice that evening and received the approval he hoped for. His work was going too well for it to be interrupted. They mustn't think about money. He didn't tell Nicole. He didn't want her to think that he was turning down chances to speed the marriage they both took for granted now as the inevitable conclusion to their carefully paced but passionate love affair.

Christmas was coming, and plans were discussed in Rod's two households. To him, Christmas was so closely associated with family and big spending and trumped-up goodwill that he was willing to forget it. Patrice had always spent the holiday at his grandmother's house and wanted Rod to go with him.

"Does she know about—well, about you?" Rod asked.

"The unmentionable?" Patrice laughed. "Not really, but she may have an idea."

Rod couldn't see himself playing consort to an old lady's wayward grandson. Besides, there was Nicole. She had been invited to a stylish house party in a château not far from Paris and also wanted to include him. Rod declined. "Go ahead and have a final fling with your fancy friends," he said bluntly. "Even if I make a fortune, you won't drag me back to *la vie de château.*"

"But my darling, it's just a way for us to have a happy Christmas together. I will gladly stay here and have Christmas only for the two of us, but it would be quite expensive to make it gay."

"Exactly. It's just another day unless you do it up and spend money. I'd rather work. Go play with the rich folk."

"You sometimes sound as if you'd never known any rich people. Perhaps they're not nice in the States. Here, many people have been rich for so long that they don't realize they're quite poor now. The château will be freezing, but the food will be beautiful, which helps to keep you warm. Oh, darling. You're so adorable when you're trying to save me from my wicked friends."

He laughed, unable to scold her for long, and rose from the table where they'd had dinner. He moved around behind her and unfastened her hair and let it fall in a pale cascade down her back. "There. You look much too young to go anywhere on your own—just the right age to be seduced by an unscrupulous American painter. If we're going to spend the rest of our lives together, I don't guess one Christmas more or less makes any difference. You say Americans are sentimental. I'm learning to be as realistic as you are. Skipping Christmas is part of the cure. There's nothing sentimental about the way I want to go to bed with you."

She rose with light laughter and moved in close against his chest. "I'm glad we're both realistic about that."

It was all so new to him—the wonder of their unflagging desire and need for each other, her calm acceptance of their self-imposed conditions, the thrilling unclouded ripening of love even when they didn't see each other for days at a time. Whenever they came together they seemed to have attained a level of devotion higher than the one where they had left off. His only faintly comparable experience had been with Carol, and that had been so different that it could have happened to somebody else. They had begun with a powerful mutual attraction and had gone nowhere from there.

Carol had admitted to a conflict about premarital sex—she wanted it but felt guilty when she had it—so that he had never really felt sure that they were physically compatible. She expected constant daily attentions of the sort set by convention—dinner dates, flowers, down to never opening a door for herself. She wasn't interested in what he considered his real work. To her, work was real if it brought in money in comfortable quantities. Thinking of what life might have been like with her, he was stunned by the blessed fortune that had brought him Nicole. He held her and felt their bodies' unstinting recognition of their right to each other.

"When I'm with you, I never understand how I can possibly spend a night without you," he said.

105

"And when I'm with you, I know that when we're apart we will have to come back to each other, dear man."

So it was settled that his partner in each household would leave him to his own devices for a few days of the holiday season. He rather fancied the picture of himself working in austere solitude while the world performed the obligatory ritual of celebration around him. He had too much to celebrate to pretend that it had anything to do with a date in the calendar.

He and Patrice decided to have an evening out the night before Patrice was set to go to his grandmother for a stay that had been reduced from a week to two days. Nicole had left that morning. "It's time I let you out of the kitchen," Rod said.

"I know just the place I'd like us to have dinner. It will be almost as cheap as eating at home." For Patrice it was a major event. He knew Rod had been reluctant to be seen with him in public. An occasional film had been the extent of their outside social life. Perhaps having a girl was making him less shy of having people suspect that he might also have a boy, if it could be called that. He had been overjoyed to discover that sex with Rod wasn't to be cut off after Nicole's advent, but he kept his response subdued and unobtrusive and let Rod use him to give himself an orgasm. That was all, but when he thought he might have had nothing, it seemed a great deal.

For their evening out he was ready to settle for the restaurant where they weren't likely to see people they knew, but Rod suggested starting with drinks at the Flore. This was total exposure. Patrice was filled with inner glee.

They were both kept busy nodding and waving as they made their way through the crowded enclosed sidewalk terrace to a vacant table. Rod was so innocently unaware of the sensation they were causing among certain groups that Patrice could hardly keep a straight face. The protective arm was around his shoulders as Rod eased him toward a chair. That would set tongues wagging.

Before the dinner hour was over, the whole *quartier* would be agog over *le petit* Valmer's stunning American.

Their drinks had just been put on the table when François Leclerc pushed into the cramped space beside them and shook hands expressionlessly with both of them. Rod glanced at Patrice and eyed the youth cooly. He saw that the curiously immobile face had good regular features that seemed designed to conceal all signs of life. Rod pictured him stretched out in a casket. He probably would be quite handsome as a corpse. Patrice said something polite but dismissive.

François turned to Rod and spoke in his rapid-fire Americanese. "I haven't seen you around lately. This kid been keeping you to himself?"

"What's that supposed to mean?" Rod asked with a warning in his voice.

"Cool it, man. I see his point, but you're not my type."

"Lucky for all of us," Rod said with distaste. The young man struck him again as hard and self-assured and vaguely dangerous. An operator, sharply dressed for the part. He wished he would go away.

"So long as we have it clear I'm not making a pass at you. I don't want Patrice to get nervous. I've been looking out for you recently. I've got a hot deal going I thought might interest you. You've got dollars, haven't you?"

"That's my business. I'm not interest in deals."

"You might be in this one. I can guarantee to double your money. No risk. All I need is the capital. You give me 500 bucks, and I pay off 1,000 bucks in one week maximum. Ask your cute friend. François Leclerc is known around here. I'm not apt to do a flit."

Rod glanced again at Patrice who made a slight negative movement of his head. He looked up at Leclerc. "I'm keeping my dollars where I can get at them. Thanks anyway."

"I might work something special out for you. Think about it. I'm always in and out of here during the day. You can leave a message with the *caissière*." His face expressionless, he shook hands again

107

with both of them and began to thread his way skillfully through the crowded tables.

Rod turned to Patrice who looked cross. "What was that all about?"

"He shouldn't speak about his deals to you. He's probably honest with his partners, but what if he gets caught? He doesn't think of that."

"I wouldn't mind doubling my money. Have you told anybody I'm living with you?

"Certainly not. Nobody—except the concierge."

"OK." He gave his arm a squeeze. "The hell with François. Merry Christmas."

They had a second drink and were getting ready to go to dinner when Rod uttered an exclamation. He half rose and waved an arm and shouted across 100 heads. Patrice saw three youngish men hesitating near the door, turning to identify the source of the shout. They spotted Rod, and then they were all shouting. Rod charged through tables, and the four met in the open runway leading to the inside room. They shook each other and beat on their backs in exuberant greeting. Patrice picked up their drink stubs and trailed along in Rod's wake, feeling that he might be trampled to death if he got too close. Rod caught sight of him and reached out for him and hugged his shoulders while he introduced him. There were facetious references to mademoiselles and "gay Paree," and Rod suggested that they move into the main café lounge where there were some empty tables. They settled at one, and Rod called a waiter and ordered scotch for everybody.

Patrice could follow without much difficulty the loud slurred American accents, but there were too many obscure references for him to grasp what was being said. He wasn't even sure if Rod was glad to see these friends or was putting on an act. He had become someone Patrice had never seen before, a commonplace good-guy American whom he would never dream of picking up in a bar. When a second round of drinks were brought to the table, he realized with consternation that Rod was still giving the orders, still gathering the stubs. He was also getting drunk, as was Patrice. Whiskey didn't sit well on *pastis*.

Patrice waited until they were well into the third round before trying to catch Rod's eye. The group was growing more boisterous, backs were being slapped again. Rod was laughing a great deal at things that didn't strike Patrice as funny. There was something forced about his high spirits; it occurred to Patrice that he might want to be extricated from this mindless gathering. Patrice focused his eyes on him as insistently as his spinning head permitted. Rod apparently felt them because he glanced across at him. Patrice leaned forward.

"Shouldn't we be thinking about dinner?" he said, trying to drive his voice under the general hubbub for Rod alone.

"Hell, no," Rod shouted. "This is a reunion. Drink up. Everything's on me."

"Know something, Roddy?" one of the men asked. "I think your little friend here is a fairy. Looks like a fairy to me."

"Leave him alone," Rod said. "We're in love with each other. Nothing wrong with that." He joined in a great guffaw.

Patrice shrank from them. Big flushed faces seemed to loom over him, leering grotesquely in close-up like an old German film. A delayed shock hit him, followed by rare anger. He stood decisively, staggered slightly, and found his balance. "I must go now," he said to Rod.

"Sit down," Rod ordered. "Where the hell do you think you're going?" He made a grab at him, but Patrice stepped out of reach.

"Home," he said over his shoulder as he turned away. Once outside he began to curse under his breath. He hadn't known he could come so close to hating Rod. Anger kept tears at bay and sobered him. What had come over his thrilling lover? He had turned into a coarse and unattractive stranger. Worse, he was behaving like a fool. He must have already spent enough for several days' living. When it came to money Patrice had the right to be indignant. He was making less than he had with Gérard, and the few hundred francs he managed to knock off Rod's food bills every week represented a real sacrifice. He had had to dig into his savings on several occasions. He had given up buying anything for himself. They had explicitly pledged themselves to do everything they could to prolong Rod's stay. It was a betrayal of their understanding for either of them to throw money away in a bar. Anger seethed in him and kept his pace brisk until he got home.

Alone in the apartment so filled with Rod's presence, he was gripped with anxiety. How long would Rod go on? Should he have stayed with him and tried to limit his folly? His heart began to beat rapidly. He almost feared Rod's return. He had discovered that he wasn't so besotted with love that he couldn't make a stand about an important issue. He withdrew nervously to the bedroom and set about making as much as possible of packing in order to kill time. He was bitterly disappointed about their evening, but if he let himself think about that, anger would dissolve into self-pity. He yanked a pair of slacks out of the armoire but decided they weren't suitable for the country and carefully hung them up again.

He was still trying to turn the selection of two shirts into a major enterprise when heard the front door slam. His heart gave a leap, and peace descended on him. Rod called his name. He answered and dropped the shirts and headed cautiously down the corridor. Rod was standing in front of the fireplace, swaying slightly, looking disheveled but familiar. Everything in Patrice dissolved into happy relief at his lover's return.

"What do you think you were up to?" Rod demanded belligerently. "I thought we were supposed to have dinner together."

"I wasn't sure we could afford dinner."

"Would you like to tell me what's on your mind?" Rod's tongue tripped over the words.

"I know we can't afford to buy whiskey at the Flore."

"We? I didn't notice you paying for anything. You owe me for two *pastis*."

"We can afford that."

"What's all this 'we' business? It's my money, isn't it? He was in a rage with himself and didn't need Patrice to tell him what an ass he'd been. "Jesus. I'm sick of counting every penny like a miserly shopkeeper. I'd rather spend it all and forget it. It'd probably do me good to starve to death."

Patrice had to fight back laughter. He was so sweet and silly. "You know you wouldn't," he said firmly. "You know I wouldn't let you. That's why I say 'we.' Are those friends of yours so important that you would to without eating for three days so that they can drink?"

"They're no worse than that queer black-market friend of yours."

"We didn't buy him a drink."

"Goddammit. I'll buy drinks for whomever I goddamn please," Rod roared. "I, not you or we. Jesus, you'd suppose I was going to marry *you*. I'm getting a bit fed up with it."

Patrice felt all the muscles of his face stiffening. He didn't know whether he wanted to hit him or burst into tears. "Very well," he said with a display of calm that surprised him. "I'm going away tomorrow. When I come back I can go somewhere else. I've told you that if you don't want me around, this place is yours. Let Nicole come live with you. I probably should have insisted on it at the beginning."

All the fight drained out of Rod. His shoulders sagged. He ran his hand through his hair and shook his head to clear it. "Come here, goddammit," he growled.

Calling on all his reserves of will, Patrice stood his ground. "No, I want you to admit that I have the right to say 'we.'"

"I don't know what you're talking about," Rod growled.

"I'm talking about important things. If it will help you to bring Nicole here, I will go and there will be no 'we.'"

"You're nuts. You'll leave your own place to go live in a cheap room somewhere? Maybe you could get my old room at the hotel. Wouldn't you love that? Jesus. All this sweetness and light. I'm getting sick of it."

"There's no sweetness and light when you do stupid things with our money. *Our* money. There. I've said it again. Anything that has to do with your work is ours as long as you're living here."

"That sounds like an ultimatum."

"You know it's not. I have a responsibility to you as a painter. If I didn't know you were very good, I wouldn't care. We can forget everything else. Just you as a painter. Painters are usually imbeciles about money. I see you're no exception."

"Thanks." Irony seemed an easy way of putting Patrice in his place. He had the impression that they were talking in circles; this conversation might conceivably make sense with Nicole but with nobody else. He had known he was getting in deep with his boy, but there must be limits. Nobody had the right to claim a responsibility for his work. His work was his own. His mind drifted for an aimless moment and came up with a question. Hadn't Patrice made it possible for him to work in a way he never could have at the hotel? He knew that he'd been in the wrong all evening; this added to the dull resentment that had replaced rage. "All right," he said abruptly. "Let me tell you something. I accept 'ours' and 'we' only here, within your own walls. What I do outside is my own business. Is that understood?"

"I understand the words, but I don't believe they mean anything." He was amazed by himself. He was being downright foolhardy, but he was drawing on love. If he planned on living for love, it had to be tough enough to stand up to tests. "Inside and outside is all the same. What if I start serving champagne and caviar every night and ask you to pay your share? It would be my right, but you wouldn't like it. When I go to my grandmother I always travel second class and she pays. Tomorrow I will go third and keep the difference. It will be very uncomfortable and will also be cheating her, but it gives us a little extra. It makes no sense if you throw away what I save. It is ours."

"What're you talking about? You sound as if you're keeping me. How does what you save affect me?"

"It doesn't. Not at all," Patrice said hastily. "I get mixed up when I'm always speaking English. I mean only if I save, you too should save. In case you need it."

"I see. I hope that's what you mean. You swore my being here wouldn't cost anything. I don't want your money."

"Of course not. I'm talking about *your* money."

"So it's mine again," Rod said with a small smile, his resentment fading. He loved the kid. There was no getting around that. "You're a sneaky little devil. I hope you haven't been cooking the books."

"Cooking?" Patrice understood and seized on the first thought that came to mind to get away from the sensitive subject. "Who were those men?"

"Classmates at college. We were friends. God knows why. They've heard I've had a big success as a painter. To them success means money. How can I tell them I can't afford a couple of whiskeys?"

"*Mon pauvre chéri.* Do you still think in that way?"

"Yes, when I'm drunk, I guess. I turn into an American drunk. Being poor is socially unacceptable. I've gotten over it, but when I'm drunk it catches up with me."

"Now you help me to understand. Thank you." He took a few paces toward Rod and felt the softening in him. Now that hostilities were ending, he wasn't sorry for the angry words that had been exchanged. He had found a strength that Rod must have given him. For once he hadn't behaved like a lovesick maiden. "Are you hungry?" he asked, scaling his voice down to normal. "Hadn't I better make us an omelet?"

"It'll save us a restaurant bill, but you were supposed to have a night off from the kitchen. I've fucked that up. I'm sorry."

"I don't need a night off. I make quite good omelets, and I love cooking for you. At least we can be comfortable. Why don't you put on your dressing gown? Patrice turned away.

"In case it makes you feel any better," Rod said to his back, acting on his suggestion by kicking off his shoes and tossing his jacket onto the chair, "I was furious with myself. Why should I show off for those assholes? They don't know a painting from a comic strip. They'd be more impressed if I did illustrations for *Esquire*. You're the first person who's made me feel important. Really important. As important as a bank manager or an insurance salesman. Maybe eventually I'll be able to tell all my classmates to fuck off. I'm working on it."

Patrice stopped on his way to the kitchen and turned back with a sudden sunny smile. "That's good. They will all want to buy *you* drinks. I'm sorry I was angry, but it was for your sake. Also I don't like being called a fairy when it's meant to insult me."

"The stupid bastard. I felt like socking him. You're right to be angry. Are you drunk too?"

Patrice laughed. "I was. Walking home made me more sober."

"I don't think it had the same effect on me." He had peeled off his socks and unbuttoned his shirt. "Come back here for a minute."

Patrice obeyed. When he was standing in front of him, Rod looked carefully into the familiar devoted face. He put his hands out and placed them on Patrice's shoulders, his chest, his hips, and dropped them to his sides. "It's funny about people, why you get all tied up with one instead of another. You mean so damn much to me and–well, it's unique. I mean, if you lose somebody you're in love with, it's likely you'll fall in love again. But this is different. I'd never find another monkey. I wonder how it happened. Our peculiar little sex life?" He put his hands on Patrice's waist and drew him closer and kissed his eyes and cheeks. He had so little beard that Rod felt only a slight abrasion of whiskers under the fresh skin. His body was inert against him. It took so little to make him happy. Life was too wonderful for silly little quarrels.

Daring an additional offer of tenderness, Rod kissed Patrice on the mouth and pulled back as if he had been burned. "My God," he exclaimed. "Maybe I'm drunk, but your mouth is sexier than a girl's. How amazing. I've never known that." He leaned down to him again and parted his lips with his tongue. For an instant Patrice was galvanized into tense immobility. Then a cry was torn from him, and his mouth opened voraciously. He responded to the kiss with uninhibited longing. Rod's love for the boy sent a sexual shock racing through his body. He was startled by it, startled by the

114

thrill of the unerringly provocative hands that were stripping him, taking possession of him. A pattern was wrenched out of shape; Patrice hadn't taken the initiative since the first morning.

The kiss was broken off with a stifled cry, and a mouth joined the hands in whipping up all his body's erotic sensibilities. Rod stood naked before the boy, his feet parted, his head thrown back, his shoulders bunched, his hips thrust forward to offer his rigid flesh for adoration. At moments with Nicole, he was still slightly embarrassed by the gross blatant virility of his erection, but he knew it couldn't be too big for Patrice. Looking down he felt he should curb an unfamiliar pride in it, shake off the heightened awareness of it that had begun with Patrice's rapturous praise of it; everything in him seemed dwarfed by the bold male organ that demanded adoration.

"Jesus, baby," he gasped as hungry lips drove him to the limits of his control. Some sixth sense seemed to link them so that he felt himself becoming what Patrice was in him—a god-hero in an almost innocently childlike vision of triumphant masculinity. All remnants of self-consciousness passed. He was a naked god accepting obeisance. Hands and tongue and lips worshiped the vision until Rod felt as if his body would crack in the blaze of passion it had aroused. His orgasm almost toppled him off his feet.

When the spasms had subsided Patrice rose and looked at him from eyes that were glazed with incredulous gratitude. "I'm sorry. I've wanted it so much," he murmured.

Rod stood close to him and ran a hand through his hair. Having received a gift of unbridled selfless dedication, he was filled with tenderness and solicitude for his boy. "Don't be sorry, baby. *I'm* sorry. You know that. I wish so much it could be the same for me."

"You kissed me. That's more than anything." A sparkle came into his eyes. "I had to think of a way to thank you." Patrice tore himself away and headed once more for the kitchen. It required a superhuman effort to lightly dismiss something that had so profoundly moved him, even though it had been edged with shame. For a moment he had almost allowed himself to believe that he could take him away from his girl. He knew that he couldn't, and he knew that even if he could, he mustn't. But he had felt Rod's near-participation and been tempted to tear off his own clothes and achieve a total act of love. The quarrel had given him an exaggerated sense of his importance. He was glad he was going away; it would give him time to readjust to accepting passively whatever Rod was ready to offer him.

Rod missed his boy more than he had believed possible. Instead of enjoying having the place all to himself, as he had expected, he felt out of sorts and alien. He had gotten used to being taken care of. He missed Nicole too, but he was accustomed to that after the last month of once-a-week meetings. It was an entirely different feeling, not unlike having money in the bank; it felt good to have it there even if you weren't spending it. His need for Patrice was immediate, and his absence was an upsetting as having a hand incapacitated. Rod welcomed him home with affectionate exuberance and made him very happy.

A few days later he called Nicole the day after her scheduled return.

"Oh, it's you at last," she exclaimed when she heard his voice. "You gave me such a fright, my darling. Did you get my message?"

"Message? No. What message? Is anything wrong?"

"No, of course not, dearest. Not now. I came home a day early. To tell the truth, I was quite bored by my rich friends and wanted to see my poor one. When I called your hotel they said you weren't living there anymore. I knew it was some silly mistake, but it made me feel so horribly cut off from you. If you hadn't called, I was going to do something quite drastic like sit on your doorstep until you came home."

"I'm sorry. There's an idiot there who always gets everything wrong." His first impulse had been to blurt out some semblance of the truth, updating his move to the last few days, but she had given him time to decide that it would sound too pat and contrived. He would tell her when he could leap up to it of his own accord rather than making it sound as if it had been forced out of him. "The main thing is you're back. You came day before yesterday?"

"Yes. It seems ages. I'm quite desperate to see you, my darling."

"Same here. Tonight?"

"Yes, please."

"I'll raise hell with the hotel. Damn them. We could've been together last night."

"That's what I had been longing for."

"Were you, sweetheart? I'll spend the night to make up for it. I have the right to get to work a little late tomorrow. I'm the only person in the world who worked all day Christmas."

They exchanged additional endearments and grew repetitive without being aware of it, entranced by the sound of each other's voices, and hung up reluctantly. Rod returned to work wondering why he clung to his small deception. If Nicole knew he had a friend he shared an apartment with, she might expect to be introduced to him, but he could think of ways of avoiding that. He couldn't quite face the thought of getting through a social occasion with the two of them. It was a harmless secret that could become dangerous only if someone found out, but there was an element of danger in all that was unorthodox, and he had given up playing safe. Nothing he had observed or had been taught about human behavior had convinced him that there were infallible rules. He would invent his own. Nicole. Patrice. They were both necessary to him in very different ways.

With the coming of a new year (he had ushered it in quietly with Nicole), he and Patrice decided that 11 of the pictures were ready for their transatlantic voyage. A complicated procedure was required to clear them out of the country; a special branch of Customs had to be convinced that there wasn't a Rembrandt secreted among them. Crating and shipping was expensive. Rod had the impression that his funds were suddenly melting away. It really didn't matter. The spring show was no longer a distant goal but an immediate reality.

Ten thousand dollars had been mentioned as a sum he might reasonably expect this time. The things he could do with $10,000! The shipment was practically a guarantee that payment would soon be made. A letter from the gallery arrived little more than a week after the pictures had gone, too soon for it to be an acknowledgment of their arrival. He read it with puzzled disbelief. It said nothing definite but hinted at a postponement of his show. Heavy commitments to more established painters. Hitting the market for abstract art while it was still hot. A possibility of showing a few of his new things in an important group show in order to boost his prices. Blah, blah, blah. He crumpled the letter in the grip of sudden panic and had to smooth it out carefully so that he could show it to Patrice. He was probably reading more into it than was intended. It simply raised some questions without answering them.

He spent the rest of the day in a state that was familiar to him from the last weeks in New York, torn between defiance and dread. As evening approached he became restlessly impatient for Patrice's return. His boy was the only person in the world he would willingly discuss the letter with, knowing anything he said would be shrewd and to the point. Nicole might see it as a defeat, a possibility Patrice would never consider.

As soon as he heard a key in the lock, his nerves unwound, and he was able to put on a welcoming smile. Patrice made a cheerful entrance, carrying a string bag distended with groceries.

"Go put your things away," Rod said. "I've got something to show you."

Patrice gave him a curious look. "Good or bad?"

"That's what you're supposed to tell me." He stood in front of the fireplace holding the letter while Patrice went to the kitchen. When Patrice returned, Rod held it out to him and moved around beside him so that he could read it once more.

"Is this the way Americans talk about art? Patrice asked without lifting his eyes from the sheet of paper. "They sound as if they're in the sausage business."

Rod uttered a brief laugh. "They're very dedicated to money. Do you think it means they're going to postpone my show?"

"It seems possible. Of course, they haven't seen the new things yet. I think that you don't have to pay too much attention to this until they do see the works we sent."

It was just what Rod had hoped he would say. "Thank God you're here. I've had a bad day. It gave me a shock."

Patrice looked up with a reassuring smile and rubbed his shoulder against him and handed back the letter. "We better have a drink." He fixed them strong ones, and they settled down opposite each other. "You don't have a contract with these people," he said.

"Not really. Just an agreement. It was firmly understood that they're giving me a show in the spring."

"Yes, but if they delay, you can take your things to somebody else?"

"I could, but you don't know how things work in New York. I'd have to go back and make contacts, and even then I probably couldn't get anything set up before fall. I don't have the money to wait."

"We must think. Is it a good idea what they say about having a group show."

"It could be, depending on the group, and if they promise to follow it up with a show of my own."

"I think you must write them. If they sell only a few things, it would be enough for us to get through the summer. When they see the new things they will pay attention to what you want. They should be there by now. Don't worry. It will be all right."

"You really think it's the best work I've done, don't you?"

"Without any doubt. Everybody will think so. Your gallery's idea to show just a few first is probably very smart. A few to put the price up and then a whole show to make you rich. You must write and tell them that's the way to do it and ask for $1,000 so that we don't have to worry about the summer. I sell things better if I have an investment in them."

"You're a smart monkey." Rod looked at him with gratitude. His unwavering faith was wholly masculine. Girls always suspected

119

men of being dreamers and trying to shirk their practical responsibilities. A man was supposed to be first and foremost a good provider. Nicole was bound to see that Patrice's suggestions would further delay any serious plans for marriage. Anyway, everything was too much up in the air to bother her with it.

He drained his drink and felt all the worries of his troubled day dissolving and melting away. "I'm so damn lucky you found me. I guess I've said it before, but I go on being amazed by you."

"I may amaze you more," Patrice said with a sly smile. "A girl came into the shop yesterday. She was so pretty and looked at me as if she liked me so very much that for a second I thought I might get hard for her. Do you think I might stop being queer? I admit she was very boyish."

They laughed, but Rod wasn't as pleased as he thought he should be. Patrice was his. He needed him more than ever now; he needed all his love and attention.

Letters began to spread past each other over the Atlantic. Rod wrote, the gallery wrote, and Rod wrote again. But none of the letters answered any other. Gradually some order emerged from the correspondence. The difficulty turned out to be that the three partners in the gallery were at loggerheads over Rod's new work. One didn't like it, one did but didn't want the partnership to break up and agreed that it might not be commercial. The third, whose name was Herbert Kappenstein, was Rod's determined champion. Mr. Kappenstein was so determined that if Rod would go along with him and he could pick up a few other young painters to form a viable "stable," he would consider setting up on his own. In the midst of the controversy, nobody bothered to answer Rod's question about money.

Patrice read the letters with glee. "You see, *chéri*? Only the really good ones make violent feelings. If it were here, there would be fistfights in the streets, and you would be a celebrity overnight. If those people had any sense, they would show your work even if they hate it."

Only the fact that there was still hope made it possible for Rod to forget from time to time that almost another month had passed, his money had further dwindled, and he didn't know where more was coming from. The threat of being back where he had started, with money once more the dominating factor of life, drove him to great distraction.

He admitted to Nicole that he was having trouble getting a firm date for his show, but he did his best to make light of it. If they were going to have a lifetime together worrying about the rent, he didn't see any point in starting before it was necessary. It turned out that she had a problem too.

"I have an announcement," she said when they were seated at the table in the dining area she had cleverly created in a corner of her entrance hall. Big-leafed plants turned the place into a tropical bower. The table bore a handsome display of silver and china and glass. He paused between spoonfuls of soup and looked at her for a clue to what was coming. She looked her most serene, exquisite in candlelight. "I thought of dropping it gaily into the conversation with drinks, but it might have seemed frivolous. I think now, before you've eaten enough to spoil your digestion. I'm pregnant."

"You're *what*?" He let out a whoop of joy before she could repeat the word and was on his feet and crouched down beside her, his arms around her, his head pressed to the fine wool that covered her breasts. "Oh, darling. How fabulous," he crooned.

She stroked his hair. "But do you understand?" *Enceinte.* Pregnant. Is that the right word?"

He looked up with misted eyes. "It's the perfect word."

She laughed gently. "Dearest friend. How adorable of you to take it like this. I hope you will be equally happy in a year or two if it happens again."

"Don't worry. We can make it an annual event. I want to take you to bed and find out about you all over again, little mother." She filled the universe; there was no room for anybody else. Nobody had so completely possessed all his senses and thoughts and emotions.

She touched his face with her fingertips. "You are so very sweet. Perhaps I chose the wrong time for my announcement after all. Do you want to miss quite a good dinner?"

"No, but only because you took the trouble to cook it. I'm afraid I won't notice whether it's good or bad." He drew her to him, and they kissed tenderly. He straightened and resumed his seat. Their eyes met. He sprang up again and leaned over her, and they kissed more ardently. He sat and gazed at his soup with a bemused smile. "My goodness. I'm a father."

"Yes. It's lovely knowing it and feeling it there, but we mustn't let it stay very long."

"What do you mean?"

"I must have been careless. It's hard to remember everything when we're making love. This will be—what do you call it—a preview performance."

"I see. You mean an abortion?" He was still riding a wave of such dizzying delight that the word made no dent on his consciousness.

"Of course. There's no worry about that."

"Wait a minute," he said as he reached for her hand across the table. "Don't start being sensible too soon. How long is it safe to wait?"

"Oh, of course, the sooner the better, but there's no big hurry. If I arrange it in the next few weeks, it will be all right."

"Have you thought of not getting rid of it, not having an abortion?"

"Oh, my darling, if we're going to talk about that, I'd better change the plates." She gathered them up and left him.

His sense of the world turning around two people who had become one was so vivid and extraordinary that he was incapable of forcing his mind into practical channels. He drifted in a daze of ecstatic completion—as if he were taking part in his own birth—until Nicole returned and served more food that he didn't bother to identify. "I think we should talk about having the baby," he said.

"Oh, dearest, I would love to, but how can we?"

"Well, I guess it wouldn't be fair to have a bastard, so maybe we'll have to get married."

"But we can't afford to get married. We know that. We certainly can't afford to have a baby."

"How much does having a baby cost? I've told you, if the show comes off in a month or two, there should be plenty of money for the time being. A couple of months of uncertainty doesn't seem much to pay for the kid's life. You have some money, don't you?

"So little. I've had some family things that I sell, but they're almost all gone. The rest is a tiny income that nobody could live on. In the States I would have gone to work long ago, but here a girl earns so little that it's been easy to put it off. You see why Lola was so anxious for me to catch you."

"Some catch." The tide of elation that had carried him beyond the financial facts of life was beginning to recede under the pressure of the all-powerful words: cost, afford, money, income. The only thing to do about them was to pretend not to hear them. His adoption of more enduring values would have to be sustained by an act of faith. He made a quick mental list of his potential assets.

If his parents knew that the life of their grandchild was at stake, they might be willing to part with a bit of their precious capital. He thought of François Leclerc. If he put up $1,000, very nearly all he had left, in a week it would be $2,000, and the profit could pull in another $1,000 and so forth until the baby and marriage and even an apartment were paid for. He thought of Mr. Kappenstein but knew that the best he could hope for from him was a minimum to get by a little longer, certainly not enough for a wife and baby. Life's marketplace—bargaining, jockeying for advantages, calculating every move, buying and selling things that shouldn't have a price. A slave market.

"Listen," he said. "All I ask is that you wait as long as possible before you do anything drastic. So long as there's no risk for you, naturally."

"You're very surprising. Usually it's the man who feels trapped when this happens. I don't want to trap you."

He reached for her hand again. "How could I feel trapped? I mean, if I'm trapped, it's because I want to be trapped. By you. I

123

sometimes think you let me feel almost too free. Is there any reason why we can't get married and just go on the way we are until we see what happens?"

"Please, my darling. That is one thing I don't want. When I get married, I want to feel truly married." There was an uncharacteristic sharpness in her voice.

He looked at her, puzzled. "How much more married *can* we feel? I didn't realize you thought a little ceremony would make that much difference?"

She looked briefly flustered, but when she spoke she had recovered her habitual sweet tranquility. "I don't mean the ceremony. I mean the way we would live, in our own house, together. Until then I would rather be your mistress. Mistresses are supposed to take care of their carelessness."

Rod groaned. "Damn money. Isn't an abortion expensive?"

"I'm afraid so. I've been thinking whom I can borrow from."

"Don't, for God's sake. I'll take care of it if that's the way it turns out. Please, sweetheart, let's think about having the baby as long as we can. It makes me so damn happy. We've got to stop this once-a-week routine. I want to be with you as much as possible."

He insisted on spending the night with her and got home as Patrice was preparing his café-au-lait. He broke the news happily and hugged his boy and kissed him on the mouth. "I'm a *father*," he exclaimed. "Isn't it incredible?" I don't see how we can keep it, but for right now I'm a father."

Patrice treasured the kiss, knowing that this could drastically alter their lives. "You're beautiful when you're so happy and excited. Nicole must be mad about you as a father."

"She's all ready for an abortion, but we have a couple of weeks to decide. I want to spend more time with her until it's settled. When I do come home at night, I'll have to start using the sofa. I told you I like to wake up with my work. You understand, don't you monkey? It may be superstition, but I'd be afraid that God would strike me dead if I did anything that a son of mine might not be proud of."

124

"Of course, *chéri.* I wish you would let me have the sofa, but I understand about your work." He also understood that Rod's pride of parenthood and a matter-of-fact attitude about abortion were on a collision course that threatened disaster. It alarmed him, but there was nothing he could do except pledge himself once more to self-sacrifice and selfless love. He was ready to be tested. "That girl I mentioned came in again yesterday. She pretends to be interested in a very expensive vase, but I think not. Shall I invite her into my empty bed? You make me want to have a baby too."

Rod was grateful for the lighthearted note, but he couldn't sustain it. "One at a time for God's sake," he protested with inappropriate intensity. "I've got to find some money, monkey. "What're we going to do?"

"Wait until we get a final answer from New York."

"What about that François character? Don't you think I should talk to him just to find out what he has to offer?"

"No, *chéri,*" Patrice said decisively. "He frightens me. It would be nice to have double your money but not so nice to have none at all. It's a big gamble. And dangerous, I think."

"I'm sure you're right, but the way things are now, having none at all wouldn't make much difference." One possibility stricken from his list. When he thought seriously of writing to his parents, everything in him balked. The list was canceled.

"Don't worry," Patrice reassured him. "I'm your guardian angel, remember. There are still many pictures. People buy pictures here. We will wait."

Rod ended by sending an ultimatum to Mr. Kappenstein pointing out that if he didn't receive an immediate advance on his work, he would have to make other arrangements. A question of survival.

Seeing Nicole almost daily, he felt her beginning to occupy areas of himself that had been reserved for Patrice. That was as it should be, as it must be ultimately, but he hoped it wouldn't mean losing his boy quite yet. Patrice remained a buffer against unleashed, unmanageable passion. If he surrendered to Nicole—body and soul—as everything in him was straining to do, the tranquility they had carefully nurtured would be lost, all his defenses against a misbegotten world would crumble. He glimpsed havoc and prayed for Patrice's patience and understanding.

Before there had been time for a reply from Mr. Kappenstein, Rod received final word from the gallery. The partners had decided that they all needed time to cool off. If they were to undertake the expense of a show for such controversial work, they must feel sure that they had given it every advantage of preparation and exploitation. It was in Rod's interest not to rush it. When the second shipment arrived, they would go into the matter again with some expert outside opinion. It was still possible that the one firmly negative vote would be turned in Rod's favor. Whatever the outcome, they all agreed that the fall was a more favorable time for a show of this nature. Meanwhile, he was free to go elsewhere if he wished.

Rod stood in the entrance of the hotel and read through the letter several times trying to give it the optimistic interpretation that Patrice always managed. This wasn't failure. They still wanted to see the second lot. The negative partner was apparently wavering. Great. He was still as solidly architectonic as ever. He might be less so after five or six months of starvation. He shoved the letter into his pocket and went to the *tabac* and called Nicole to share the news that had hitherto been reserved for Patrice. Before he had finished his report on the letter, he could hear the anger mounting in his voice. Would she think he was angry at her? Patrice understood his anger. "I'm fed up with all of them acting as if I could wait indefinitely," he explained, trying to keep calm. "At least we know the show's off or not. Jesus."

"My poor darling. It's terrible for you to have all these worries at the same time. I wish you would let me have my share of the responsibility."

"Short of arranging a show for me, I don't see what you can do about it. Just tell me I'm the painter you love most in the world and help me to stay sane. I'm beginning to wonder if I shouldn't hold back some of the things and try selling them here. I'm going to talk to Patrice ab–" He bit off the word, and his mind whirled while he tried to force himself to say something, anything, so that she wouldn't notice the abrupt silence. "What was I saying? Oh, yes, you know–the guy who's letting me use his place. He knows quite a lot about the art market. As a matter of fact, he' been suggesting that I move in with him and save on the hotel expenses. Every little bit helps. I may decide to take him up on it."

"Yes, well–" It was Nicole's turn to fall silent.

"Are you there?"

"Yes, darling. I was thinking that perhaps we make things needlessly difficult for ourselves, but we haven't invented the housing shortage. If only we could find a place where you could work, I could be your housekeeper. Will I see you this evening?"

"Of course, if you're not getting sick of my nerves."

"You have the right to your nerves. I don't want to be the one to make them worse."

"Silly darling. Actually, I don't really mind the damn letter. One less thing to wonder about. When I hear from my friend Kappenstein, we'll know exactly where we stand." He hung up and breathed a sign of relief. Patrice had finally been brought into the picture. In a few days he could tell her he'd moved. No more secrets.

He found her thoughtful that evening. Several times he caught her giving herself a little shake to bring her attention back to him, as if her mind were miles away. It happened for the third or fourth time when he was wondering ironically if they should lay the baby on Lola's doorstep as a tribute to her skill as a matchmaker. With an obvious effort to play along with him, she asked if he wanted to go to the old lady's next party.

"That's right. There's another one coming up any day now, isn't there? I forgot to answer the invitation. How dreadful. I'll probably be dropped from her list. Think of the savings in flowers."

"Be careful. If we ever get married, she can be counted on for a handsome present."

"I'll run right home and send her my regrets. That should keep me in good standing."

He stayed the night, but when they parted it was understood that they wouldn't see each other for a day or two. Nicole had some sort of family gathering that evening, other engagements the following day.

Mr. Kappenstein's letter arrived promptly two days after the gallery's. A chill ran through Rod as he read it, and there was an odd numbness in his hands so that he couldn't feel the paper he was holding. It was brief and straightforward. As there was every reason to believe that his partners were moving closer to his viewpoint, it would be to Rod's benefit to wait until they could all get together and give him a real push. There was no doubt that the new work would put him way out in front of the field. If things didn't turn out as Mr. Kappenstein expected, he would be eager to reopen the discussion of alternatives. He didn't think it would be ethical to act independently at this time.

A heavy weight fell on Rod's chest. There was a hollow ache in the pit of his stomach. Not a word about money, not even an offer of a loan. His arms and legs felt stiff. He could no longer focus on the blurred paper. He managed to get to the café next door and ordered a beer without hearing his voice. He swallowed half of it in one gulp and closed his eyes and felt things loosening up a bit. He had said glibly that it was better to know exactly where he stood. He stood exactly nowhere. He would have to agree to the abortion now, but killing the baby wouldn't put money in his pocket. Time was up. The good provider was a flop. He finished the beer in a second gulp and ordered another. It had an effect. His mind began to slide around the hopeless aspects of his predicament. Things had a way of looking up when they were at their blackest. He could get through another couple of months of hard work before giving up. He'd have a serious talk with Patrice about selling here. He might yet pull off a miracle of some sort.

When he finished his third beer, his mind seemed to have suspended operation and he thought he could talk to Nicole without shouting with rage and frustration. He went to the *tabac* and dialed her number and listened to it ring. After a moment he realized that it wasn't going to be answered. He hung up and recovered the token and dialed again, a reasonable precaution with the French telephone, again without result.

Probably just as well. By evening the first impact of this final blow would have worn off and he might even be able to make light of it for her sake. It was the least he could do considering the decision that was being forced on them.

He went through the day with a knot of fear tightening around his heart. He had more or less known the baby would have to go, but now even his being able to stay in Paris was threatened. What was going to become of them? There was no getting around it—in another couple of months he would have to go.

The thought made his hands tremble so violently that he couldn't apply paint to canvas. He stood with his head resting against the ledge of the skylight while the future solidified into an unbearable burden in his mind. Alone in New York—or sitting out the summer in Connecticut. Nicole and Patrice living their lives without him. He saw it so vividly that tears sprang to his eyes and a sob broke from his chest.

He couldn't stand it. What had become of the splendid grip he had thought he had on life? He was helpless. His only hope was to take Nicole to New York and get a job and marry her. How long would they survive with all the joy and happiness ground out of them by the drudgery he had so recently escaped? He had been edgy enough here; she would quickly find him unbearable. He dashed tears from his eyes and pressed his head between his hands, trying to relieve the pressure that threatened to split it.

Patrice wouldn't let him go. That thought and the fact that it was barely conceivable to him that he might find himself completely penniless helped to steady him. Work. He had to use the little time that remained for work.

Later he went out to try Nicole again. When the line had buzzed twice, he was struck with a certain knowledge that she wasn't there. He held the instrument to his ear while a premonition took possession of his mind. She was doing it. She had taken the responsibility upon herself. She would no longer be pregnant when he saw her next. He fumbled the instrument back onto the hook and stood in front of it and kneaded his forehead with tense fingers. She couldn't. She wouldn't. She knew these were crucial days when a word from New York could change all their prospects. It would have to be done, but deciding on it together would be, in some strange reversal of nature, a manifestation of parenthood, a function of their union. She knew this. Action on her own would reduce him to no more than a lover. Impossible. Premonitions were simply a reflection of one's worst fears, and he had been a prey to fear all day.

When Rod got home Patrice was there. Patrice had been keeping irregular hours recently, and Rod never knew when to expect him. Rod gave him a distracted smile. "I hoped you'd turn up. I've got something to show you."

"Don't tell me. I know even without reading your palm." They had shared so much bad news that they could joke about it. "Mr. Kappenstein isn't going to give you any money."

Rod bowed in tribute. "Spoken like a true clairvoyant. His letter's sort of interesting." He handed it over.

Patrice burst into laughter as he read it. "You sound like a horse, *chéri*. Isn't that what being out in front of the field means? No matter. He knows a good horse when he sees one. It's obvious what we must do. We will pick out four of the pictures, and I will sell them. You will be very angry when I tell you how much, but nobody here will admit that an American can paint. They might have more value if I say a horse did them."

130

As usual Patrice made everything a bit brighter. "Can you get enough so that I don't have to worry about leaving? That's what's been driving me crazy all afternoon."

"You must never worry about that," Patrice said, immediately serious and authoritative. "I know a few collectors. I think I can get maybe $500 for four."

"But that's crazy. I can make $1,000 with that François character."

"Perhaps, but this is not a gamble. When you've finished the 25 you must have for the show, then you can do a few more to sell here. Anyway, when all the pictures are there and a date is set, they will surely give you a little advance."

"But don't you realize that sending the next lot will cost almost all I have left."

Patrice remained unperturbed. "I make what married men with children are supposed to be able to live on. I don't see how they can live on it, but perhaps we must find out."

"Now you're talking about keeping me," Rod protested distractedly.

"You're supposed not to think like that anymore. A few months maybe. We can do anything, but you mustn't consider leaving."

He was a rock on which Rod could rest. He wished he was sure Nicole wasn't going to be home this evening so that he could ask Patrice to stay with him. "Shall we have a drink? Are you going out?"

"I will meet friends. You aren't going to Nicole?"

"I can't reach her. She was sort of absentminded yesterday. I remember she said she had things she had to do today. She'll probably be there later.

"This is rather important news."

"Yeah. We're going to have to go ahead with the abortion now. There's nothing more to wait for."

Patrice's expression became grave. He took a step closer to Rod. "I'm sorry. I would do anything I could. I joke about you funny Americans, but I don't joke about this."

"I know. There's nothing anybody can do about it. The baby would be arriving just about the time I *might* be having a show.

131

The timing's all wrong. It's infuriating for a few months to make a difference. I guess we should try not to take it too seriously. It was an accident. There'll be plenty of babies when the time comes."

"Yes, that's the way you must think. I know it isn't easy for you."

"Nothing's easy at the moment. For a while there everything was too good to be true. How about you, monkey? Everything OK? I haven't been bad to you have I?"

"No. Never," he asserted with calm conviction.

"I'm glad. I couldn't see any reason not to break some of the rules. The rules cut too much out of life. Do you realize how beautiful you are these days? You've changed somehow."

"It's the light of purity shining from my soul."

"Really? No temptations? No beauties looming on the horizon?"

"Oh, the beauties are always there," he said with a shrug and a merry gleam in his eyes. "It's so restful not feeling that I must chase them."

Rod moved to him and draped his arms around Patrice's shoulders and leaned down so that their foreheads touched. "I miss not being in bed with you, monkey. You understand about all that, don't you?

"Of course." Patrice had accepted, had even tried to believe that he welcomed the end of their nightly physical intimacy. He didn't need sex to sustain his love. This was unequivocal evidence that the good he had found in life was real, that nothing in his past could undermine the strength and purity he had found in his devotion to Rod. He wanted to fix his conviction in words. He drew his head back and looked up. "You've given me more than if you were queer and in love with me. You don't divide everything into categories. The way you hold me now is better than making love with anybody else. You allow me to be in love with you because you know how much I need it and are not embarrassed by it. That is truly extraordinary."

Rod ran his hands over the familiar body and drew him closer and moved his mouth to his. They exchanged a long kiss. He drew back and looked down at him. "What a mouth. I'm glad I got as far as learning to kiss you. You're very sweet, monkey darling. Run along and have a good time."

"You don't want me to stay with you?"

"I do, but you better not. I'm all bottled up inside. I don't trust myself. I've got to talk to Nicole and get started on a whole new phase. I don't know what I'd do without you. We'd better leave it at that."

When Rod was alone he quickly drank a whole bottle of wine to keep his mind blurred and harmless. Too much trouble to go out and try to call Nicole again. He was asleep on the sofa long before Patrice returned. When he called Nicole in the morning, she was in.

"Oh, my darling. I've been waiting for you to call." There was a little flurry of urgency in her voice.

"Here I am. What happened to you yesterday?"

"Yesterday? I was in and out. You called?"

"Of course. Morning and evening. I had things to tell you."

"Yes, I understand. I too–I was–When are we going to see each other? Her voice was beginning to sound less normal, the urgency thinning out into an undercurrent of apprehension.

"Is anything the matter?"

"Of course not, my dearest. Just that I miss you. I've been spoiled by seeing you so often. The telephone is no good. When will you come?

"This evening?"

"Of course. There's nothing in particular. We'll talk this evening. You never take time off for lunch."

"I have for you." She was definitely peculiar. He had rejected his premonition. Another possibility leaped to his mind. Had she seen a doctor who had given her a fright? "Listen. I'll come out right now. You sound very strange."

"I'm sorry. There's nothing, just that I'm looking forward to seeing you."

"Fine. You'll see me in about half an hour."

"No. Please, darling. I don't want you to–"

"Don't be silly. I want to see you too. *A tout à l'heure*." He hung up, suddenly in a rush to get to her. She had to be all right. There was nothing that could make an abortion dangerous for a healthy woman as long as it was performed right. They had gone into all that. She had a reputable doctor who was willing to risk an illegal operation.

Twenty minutes in the Métro gave him ample opportunity to meditate on death and the corruption of the flesh. He was tense with anxiety when he reached her door. The minute he saw her, he knew that she had done it. He gathered her into his arms , and they clung to each other in motionless silence. He had seen her pale face. He held a damaged body. Relief passed. Something vital and precious seemed to shrivel within him. A cry of protest choked his throat.

"Why?" he asked.

"I couldn't bear what it was doing to you. You've had too many worries, my dearest. This one I could spare you."

He drew back and rubbed his eyes with the back of his hands. "Have I been as bad as that?"

"Not bad, dearest. Too good and loving and kind. It's been agony for you."

He dropped his hands and looked at her dully. They were no longer the glorious pair enthroned at the center of the universe but only a man and a woman who liked to fuck and who had created a tiresome problem for themselves in the process. A saner view, perhaps, but sadly commonplace. "You knew I've been waiting for money. It might have made all the difference."

"But it hasn't? You've heard?

"Yes. Nothing." He supposed he ought to tell her that he would probably be gone before the summer was started but saying it might make it true.

"Then we had no choice. That worry is over."

"But don't you understand, darling? It was something I wanted us to do together–to decide together. It would have helped to make it less awful somehow."

134

"There is nothing awful, dearest friend. Just tiresome and a little painful. I told you I must share the responsibilities." She turned from him and started slowly, painfully toward the living room.

He followed her. She was wearing a severe housecoat that aged her. The way she moved was a reproach. He didn't feel the unique all-encompassing claim on him that she had somehow established while she was pregnant. He was in love with her, of course, but even that had momentarily dimmed. Only momentarily. It was too tremendous to pass quickly. Tears started up behind his eyes.

"You're all right, aren't you?" he asked as they slowly crossed the room and seated themselves.

"Of course. These things are never quite as simple as they say. I was at the clinic almost all day yesterday. I got home quite late. They don't like such cases to stay overnight. If you die, they prefer for you to do it at home."

"Jesus, darling. Thanks for telling me now. How could you have done it all alone?"

"It would have been the same if you'd known. It's very hush-hush. You do understand? You're not angry?"

"Angry? No, just horribly disappointed." He slumped down in his chair with his long legs stretched out and dropped his head onto the backrest and looked at the ceiling. "I don't blame you. I know I've been difficult lately. You must think I'm such a sensitive soul that I can't face facts. I'm going to pay for it you know. How have you handled that part of it?"

"Don't worry about it, dearest. The doctor is an old family friend. He doesn't care when he's paid."

"Fine. Now my girl's a charity case. I really am a prize catch." Gloom enveloped him. He couldn't afford a baby. He couldn't afford a girl. Quite simply, he couldn't afford to live. What idiocy made him think that he could plan a normal married life without money? No plans–the choice he had made but had been bewitched by impending parenthood into forgetting.

135

He gathered himself together and sprang up and took a turn around the small stylish room. Still acting out his life in luxurious surroundings. They should be in a slum. Exposure to raw poverty might make him tough enough to take an abortion in stride. He had no business being here. He stopped beside her and touched her shoulder. "I guess everything will work out. I know we couldn't wait any longer to do it. I feel like hell about what you've been through, but it's easy for a man to say that. You've been very good about it. Thanks." The effort it required to say the conciliatory words made him realize how much had been lost, how diminished was the current that ran between them. The magic people created together was probably bound to be ephemeral. Still, they had had it. He had the impression that most people never did.

She put her hand on his and pressed it. "I was sure it was right. Don't feel you have to sit around here, darling. It's been a strain for both of us, much worse for you than for me. It's been wearing you out for weeks. Was your latest news very bad?"

"No. Aside from money it was pretty good. They seem to be getting organized for a show in the fall. If I live that long."

"Why don't you go on back to your work? It was sweet of you to come so promptly. I felt I had to see you, but that's all right now. I must be quiet for a few days, and then I'll be as good as new. You should have a complete change, a little holiday. Forget your worries and your useless girl. Isn't Lola's party tonight? You should go and devour all her expensive food and wine and look beautiful in your dinner jacket and let all the girls fall in love with you."

"With you here barely able to walk? What a swell idea. At least I can take care of you."

"No, my dearest. This is nothing we want to share. Natalie is coming in this afternoon. Suzanne will cook something for me tonight. She has had it done too. We will talk woman's talk. Tomorrow the pain will be gone. Let's wait until we can be lovers again, and then we'll forget all about it."

"Well then, I'll fix you some lunch. I can do that much."

136

"If you want to eat too, that will be pleasant."

He doubted if it would be. Duties seldom were. She was probably right–this was a good time to have a holiday from each other.

Thinking of not seeing her for a few days made him begin to miss her, so lunch turned out more pleasant than he had expected. At moments he could feel the strands of their disrupted love being mended and reknit, and he resisted the process. They would start afresh when they could make love again. A holiday. Time to assess what was there without the magic.

He got back to work feeling less bruised and defeated. A small ember of defiance was rekindled in him. With Patrice's help he'd show the gallery guys that he didn't need them. He was looking forward to a couple of evenings with his boy again. Simple, undemanding friendship. It might release the flood of love in him that seemed to have been dammed up by his battle against impossible odds. Marriage and children were out. Make the most of the possible. Start all over again.

When he had cleaned his brushes for the day, he poured himself a drink and wandered about the room and waited. He couldn't assume that his friend would show up. On the contrary, he would more likely stay out; as far as Patrice knew they might be busy arranging for the abortion. All the same . . . his guardian angel . . . what was he a student of the occult for?

He wandered over to the skylight and looked up into the murky Paris night. He was in no mood to stay alone here all evening. If he went out, he'd spend money–even a little would be too much. What else? Go to Lola's after all? His Left Bank pals envied his connections and thought he was crazy not to use them. The rich existed to be conned. Only Patrice understood that his work was too important to play games with. If Lola and her lot liked it, he would begin to wonder what was wrong with it. Even going to eat her incredible food would be an admission that she had something he wanted. And why not? Take what you want and spit in their eyes. He hadn't answered her invitation. He didn't have to send flowers. He could be as ill-bred as he liked. Actually, he was rather fond of the old lady; it was the others who drove him wild.

He pulled off his clothes and took a leisurely bath. There was no hurry. Patrice might still come in. If he did, he'd forget Lola. He had another drink to postpone dressing. Once he was in his dinner jacket, there was nothing more to wait for. He mustn't let himself be too dependent on anybody.

As he cut across the windswept circle of the Etoile toward avenue Foch, he noticed that there were a great many policemen about, standing in groups like flocks of some strange fowl, their capes flapping like wings in the bitter night. The wooden barricades that were always produced for parades or demonstrations were piled up in stacks here and there. An odd time for a parade. Somebody was threatening to march on Paris and put de Gaulle to the sword. As least they hadn't been trying to blow him up recently. Count your blessings.

Once enclosed by the artfully simulated rural landscape of the avenue Foch, it was impossible to imagine danger of any sort. Rebellion had no more chance than originality in this artificial world.

When he had passed through the handsome ironwork portal of Lola's building, he found that even the elevator was working for once. He rode up in it, and Lola's door was opened by the butler in full dress who greeted him by name and took his coat and directed him unnecessarily to the grandest of the grand salons. The room looked as if it had been moved from Versailles—gilded, mirrored, glittering with crystal chandeliers, the furniture pushed back against the walls.

As he entered it he saw that he was early. Should he have waited longer for Patrice? The hell with that. He was on holiday. Where were the girls who were going to fall in love with him? People were seated in stiff groups. Waiters moved about with trays of drinks. Rod took a whiskey. The hum of conversation was so discreet that a woman's laughter was a sudden discordant note. Lola advanced to greet him. She was wearing a purple dress of complicated design that seemed to catch her around the knees and threaten to throw her to the floor. She lifted a hand to be kissed, and he pulled it down and briefly clasped it. Enough of fancy foreign ways.

"Did I know you were coming?" she demanded in harsh peremptory tones. "I'm losing my memory. Nicole called to say she couldn't."

"She's not feeling well. Some sort of bug."

"No wonder. This weather. I don't know why I'm not in Cannes. I've got a very expensive villa, but I never go near it. Come over by the fire and get warm. Did you have a frightful time getting a taxi? I hope you've got a woolen undershirt under there." Lola was wearing a sable stole that she hitched closer around her. She put a hand on his arm and tottered toward a great fireplace on the opposite wall. Rod admitted that he'd never owned a woolen undershirt.

"You're a fool." She uttered her harsh bray of laughter. "All these people are bores. Maybe it'll get better later on. The bores always come early. They have nowhere else to go." Rod laughed, and she added impatiently, "I don't mean you, of course. You're part of the family."

Rod glanced about him as they moved across the room, finding it odd to feel so at home in this gathering. A few famous faces had already arrived. Lots of money was the price of admission. They knew who he was. Probably quite a few of them would buy his pictures. All he had to do was kiss a few asses.

There was a literary group—an editor and a newspaper publisher centered around the slight, misshapen figure of Frédéric de Bellecourt, the famous critic and essayist. He recognized a strikingly handsome French film star who was holding a small white dog on his lap. The women were all beautifully dressed and looked as if it would take all night to dismantle them.

As he entered the orbit of heat thrown off by the fire, he saw Germaine disengage herself from a nearby couple and come toward him without looking at him, obeying a law she had apparently laid down for herself of never acknowledging an interest in anybody. When she was almost upon him, she turned her head and faced him directly. Among all the stylish ladies she dazzled.

"Hello, cousin," she said. The husky voice, trained to innuendo, filled the two words with a wealth of possibilities.

Rod smiled down at her, checking her necklace, her earrings, the brooch close to her breast. He wasn't an expert on pearls and emeralds but guessed that she was wearing no less than $100,000.

"Hello," he said to the largest emerald.

"This is your night, my dear," Lola snapped. "Your boyfriend's left his girl at home. If you don't get him tonight, you never will. And for heaven's sake, buy him some woolen underwear. He hasn't any."

"Buy him some yourself," Germaine said rudely.

"I haven't had as many rich husbands as you. Ha." Lola displayed her teeth once more to utter her alarming laugh and struggled off, clutched around the knees by the purple dress.

"She's wonderful," Germaine said with crisp admiration. She looked him in the eye. "So we've disposed of Nicole for tonight?"

"She's a bit under the weather."

"I suppose I should pretend to be sorry. You must feel so married to her by now that you'll soon be looking around for a mistress."

"Are you applying for the job?" He felt a new hostility in his inclination to flirt with her, hostility that he supposed was directed at the moneyed philistinism that she represented and that threatened to push him under. If she made a pass at him, it would be a pleasure to turn her down. Would it be a worthwhile evening's occupation to make her suffer in some small way for forced abortions, marriages blocked by poverty, ill-treated artists? There must be some reason for being here.

"You could do worse," she said with the little vocal trick that loaded everything she said with ambiguity. "You're old enough not to be shocked by a few wrinkles and creases. I haven't many, but I can see them as well as anyone. I'm rich. That should interest any young man who's making his way in the world. If you're any good, I could do wonders for your career. It makes such sense that I wonder why I haven't done anything about it. You *are* extraordinarily attractive. I suppose you think you can have any woman you want."

"Quite the contrary," he said. "I've always wished women would make it less difficult to figure out what they're after."

"You Americans! You're such children about sex. If you'd be honest with yourselves, you might learn something about life."

"If you want honesty, let's start with you. Do you want to go to bed with me?"

"That's not being honest," she snapped. "That's just boorish and tiresome. What I mean by honest is doing something about what you want."

"I'm sure there's a subtle distinction in there somewhere. OK. If you won't answer a simple question, let's get drunk. That's really what I came for." He was being an ass. What if she'd said yes to his question? He wished Patrice had come home. It had been dangerously wrong to expose himself to so much that he detested in the world.

She put a hand on his arm and steered him toward great double doors that opened into the smaller salon. He glanced down at her for another quick appraisal. A good figure. Pretty breasts were half exposed by her low-cut dress. Her face had no striking features, but the whole was clever and chic. She looked no particular age, around 30, although he knew she was closer to 40. She was such a gorgeously expensive package that it was natural to want to see what was in it. Nothing would come of it, so there was no harm in playing along for whatever fun he could get. Nicole had given him a holiday. He hoped his poor darling was feeling better.

Germaine lifted her eyes to his. "Are you trying to decide whether you want to go to bed with me?"

"Something of the sort."

"Men usually decide that they do, thank heavens. I'm very choosy, despite those four husbands."

"And you haven't chosen me? I admit I sort of thought you had, even when we're being rude to each other."

141

"I dare say it could happen, sooner or later. At first I thought you were much too young. Perhaps you've grown up in the last few months. I'm beginning to think you're tough enough for me."

"And what about Nicole?"

"Heavens. Adore her. Marry her. That doesn't mean you're going to be faithful to her. I've never known a man who had the faintest idea what fidelity means."

"No one can accuse you of being starry-eyed, cousin," She reduced life to its lowest dog-eat-dog level. He felt her as a challenge to the high hopes and dedication that had helped him through the winter. He wanted to prove to her that he was beyond her reach, but the only way he knew he could score on her was through sex.

An elaborate buffet was set up in the other salon. A hired pianist was banging out American jazz. Several servants were fussing over champagne bottles in ice buckets.

"Are you going to get civilized drunk or American drunk," she asked.

"Does champagne made it civilized? You're all such conventional snobs. Drunk is drunk. As it happens, I like champagne." He abandoned his whiskey, and they both took wine. They nodded at each other over the rims of their glasses and drank.

"Do you want any of this rubbish?" She waved a disdainful hand at the array of hors d' oeuvres on the long table. "There'll be some real food in a little while. Oh, I forgot. I suppose you people over on the Left Bank never get anything to eat. Here. The caviar's not bad. Stuff yourself. You won't have to buy any food for days."

Rod sipped champagne and munched toast thickly spread with caviar and wondered how much of the lavish outlay would be thrown away. Jolly party thoughts. The caviar alone represented enough to keep him for several months. A child had been destroyed, two lives may have been permanently scarred, but the rich had to have enough to waste. It was time for another revolution. He would gladly strike the first blow by slapping Germaine silly. He drained off his glass and held it out to the waiter to be refilled. "Tell me about the wonders you can do for my career," he said after he had taken another swallow of wine.

"Oh, that's easy." Her clever face took on a shrewd business-man's look. "I'd see that you meet the people who really count. You have to know Paris awfully well to know who they are. No outsider, no matter how rich she might be, could manage it. They always end up with the *pédérastes*."

"You'd have to charm them, of course, and accept their invita-tions. I'd hang one, two at the most, of your pictures in my salon and give a few dinners for the people who should see them. There would be gossip about Germaine's new American. Within a month you'd be a celebrity of sorts in a small circle. Then it would be time for an exhibition. That's where the money comes in. The good gal-leries are expensive, none of your Left Bank holes-in-the-wall. I'd have to pay the critics and journalists to get the kind of publicity we'd want. You'd be famous overnight. New York would automati-cally follow."

"New York doesn't follow so automatically these days. You make it sound as if it could all be bought and paid for, regardless of the pictures."

"That's about what it amounts to. Of course, you'd have to have *some* talent. It wouldn't work with a complete dud."

"And it won't happen unless you're my mistress?"

"It could, but why shouldn't it? It would take time and money. Naturally, I wouldn't be bothered unless I was enjoying myself."

"I see. I'd really be more a whore than a painter." He held out his glass, and it was filled again.

"It always takes a bit of whoring to get ahead. I wouldn't be rich if I hadn't put up with a few inconveniences along the way."

"I'll think about it," Rod said, deciding that he'd rather get an honest job digging ditches than play her game. His Left Bank friends talked naively about conning the rich. The rich were way ahead of them. If he weren't getting a bit light-headed and silly on champagne, he might burst into tears of frustration at having to turn his back on such an easy solution to all his problems. All he had to do was go to bed with an attractive woman.

"Don't think about it too much. You might be disappointed," she warned. "I haven't said I wanted to be your mistress, only that it would make great sense."

The room was filling up around them while they talked. The hum of voices became a roar. They leaned their heads closer to hear each other. Rod kept holding out his glass to be refilled. People surrounded them to greet Germaine, dissolved in bursts of laughter, were replaced by new faces. More food appeared—ham and chicken and lobster—was picked at and left amid crushed cigarette butts. The pianist continued to bang out ill-tempered American tunes.

"Are we drunk yet?" Germaine demanded. Her eyes were bright, and she looked younger than usual, her manner softer, no longer the shrewd businessman.

"I think I must be. Let's dance and find out." They took a few turns around the middle of the room. He was steady on his feet but had reached the point where drink was acting as an aphrodisiac. Holding her, brushing against her, aroused him. He made no attempt to conceal it. She didn't withdraw from the contact but encouraged him by moving in against him.

"Dreaming of Nicole? she asked in her forthright way.

"What a bitch."

"Are you planning to do anything about it?"

"It feels as if I'll have to. I've seen some lovely ladies tonight. I'm thinking of ditching you and finding somebody who appreciates me."

"Who gave you a lovely hard-on?"

"It's not a hard-on. It's simply a preliminary display of manly prowess." He giggled, delighted with being so rude.

She laughed lightly. "We *are* getting to know each other better."

"I'll say. How much more friendly can a guy get than showing a girl his cock?"

Time flowed and began to exist only in isolated moments. He was still with her when a vision of beauty swam into his sight. For a few seconds he didn't think of it as male or female, only beauty incarnate. Then he saw a tall young man with golden hair and a lovely rosy complexion bend over Germaine's hand and straighten with limpid blue eyes then melting into his.

"Beauty," Germaine exclaimed. "Are you here? I didn't see you."

"You've been much too busy with this devastating man." Rod felt bathed in blue, and then the eyes flowed back to Germaine. "Yes, I'm here. Haven't you seen a film star with a sweet little doggie on his lap? I thought everybody knew that I sometimes take the doggie's place."

"Cousin, darling, this is the Prince de Lussigny-Forbain. Rod Mac-Intyre, an American. Beauty is called Beauty for obvious reasons. You've got to excuse me for a moment. I see one of my husbands. Don't tell me I've never done you a favor, Beauty. I don't think you're Rod's type, but I'm sure you'll find out for yourself."

Rod didn't see her go. He was staring at the prince. A short straight nose, exquisitely curving lips, a lean line of jaw terminating in a subtly dimpled chin, all too perfect to believe, radiant with youth but firmly chiseled so that there was no weakness. Rod's sight was slightly blurred around the edges, enclosing the vision in an appropriately golden aura. He shook his head slightly and saw that the prince was regarding him with a still, effortless smile.

"You've got to forgive me for staring." Rod blurted. "I've never seen anything like it. You're the most beautiful human being in the world."

"I'd gladly have you stare at me all night, preferably with nothing on, but my hands are full for this evening. Can we make a date for tomorrow?"

"No, you don't understand. Nothing on you—that is—would be fine but just because I'd love to see what kind of body goes with that head. It's a problem of aesthetics."

"Dear me. I don't like to be a problem of any kind. You're not interested in sampling my considerable charms in bed?"

"No, I'm afraid not."

"It's quite all right. Unlike Germaine, I don't expect every man I meet to fall at my feet. I know a few are left who actually prefer women. They're usually the ones I want. Like you?"

"What? Preferring women? Yes."

"Are you by any chance Nicole de la Vendraye's American?"

"Yes."

"How divine for her. Darling Nicole. Tell her I invited you to my bed. She'll laugh like a drain. We've always had the same taste in men."

The thought of Nicole laughing like a drain about anything, let alone about men making passes at each other, struck him as so odd that he wondered if they were talking about the same girl. He missed something the prince was saying."

"–appalling. I'd like to go to the States."

"Would you? What for?"

"A change. Do Americans find homosexuality shocking?"

"In general, yes. I don't." He wished Patrice were here. He'd be fascinated by the prince. He started to mention his name to find out if they knew each other, but his habit of keeping his life compartmentalized was so ingrained by now that he thought better of it.

"I'd adore living where people knew nothing about me," the prince explained. "If nobody knew I was queer, I wouldn't go around acting so queer. There's much to be said for guilty secrets. Everybody's so *tolerant* here. That's why we all behave so outrageously. There's nothing to feel guilty about. Who do you suppose let Henri come tonight?"

"Henri? Who's Henri?" Rod's eyes were having such a feast of beauty, studying how the face was made, that he wasn't keeping a very firm grip on the conversation.

"Henri Poncennet. One of her husbands. The chap she's just gone off to speak to." The effortless smile returned to the prince's lips, sweetly modest and winning. "Your eyes are fascinating. You

146

must let me take you and Nicole to dinner soon. Seeing you together might save me from falling in love with you."

"Dinner would be great." Rod supposed he ought to be cultivating the people who really counted, but the prince counted a great deal to him. "Henri Poncennet. Isn't he one of the big guns who was put in jail after the war? Collaborating with the Nazis or something? I remember my family talking about it."

"Exactly. Careful. Here comes the vampire."

Germaine was with them once more. "Beauty hasn't carried you off yet, cousin? You must be quite fanatically heterosexual. How reassuring. I gave you your chance, Beauty."

"You may be sure I made the most of it. I like him so much that passion is slowly subsiding into undying devotion."

"You have the most peculiar effect on people, cousin. What are we both doing with empty glasses? Shouldn't we–?"

Germaine was interrupted by Lola who stood before them, her eyes blazing, her habitually belligerent expression monstrous with rage.

"De Bellecourt's an ass," she roared. "Never will I allow him in my house again. Never, do you understand? If you take my advice, Germaine, neither will you."

"What's he done, darling?" Germaine demanded, laughing at her stepmother's heroic outburst.

"What's he done? Nothing to laugh about, you silly little fool. He's walked out because of Henri. The pompous dwarf. He said, 'Good night, my dear countess. I'm afraid I can't approve of your choice of guests.' Approve of my choice! How dare he–"Be quiet, darling, be quiet," Germaine cut in in an undertone. A look of alarm crossed her face that she replaced with a fixed smile as she glanced about her. "Do you want everybody in the place to know about it? There'll be the most–"

"Know about it? Everybody knows about it already." Lola continued to bellow. "If they don't, they will in five minutes. There were a dozen people around me when that gruesome little monster–'I cannot remain under the same roof with Henri Poncennet? As if I care whose roof he remains under!"

"Intolerance at last," the prince's indolent, very British voice said in Rod's ear. "De Bellecourt is my hero."

"It's too ridiculous." Germaine sounded as querulous as a child. "What do people expect me to do? I was married to him. I can hardly pretend I don't know him. I must say, I don't think it was very nice of Frédéric."

"Very nice! It's an outrage. If anybody else wants to go, let him. And good riddance! I'll invite whomever I like to my house. What's the matter with people? They shouldn't go on thinking about the last war. They should be getting ready for the next one. Even you Americans know that much."

The last was directed at Rod. He could think of nothing to say. He felt as if he had been rudely awakened from a peaceful dream. The carefully preserved fabric of ease and security was about to disintegrate like a mummy exposed to the air. He heard the piano banging away relentlessly, the tinkle of decorative laughter, the pop of a champagne cork. It was febrile and without gaiety. He was practically sober again.

"It's the Russians," Lola proclaimed disjointedly. "We should have fought them instead of the Germans."

"You do talk the most ridiculous nonsense, Lola," somebody said in an even voice. Lola's face sagged, and then she brayed with unexpected laughter. Rod turned and found a stranger at his side, of medium height, compact, with an unhumorous face that was hard and lean and with close-cropped graying hair that fit his head like a cap.

"Now Gérard, don't *you* get started," Germaine broke in.

"Oh, let him rave." Lola squared her shoulders aggressively. "Everybody knows he's a Communist."

"Do they? How very odd of them," the man called Gérard said. His voice was curiously cold and penetrating, and it reminded Rod of something he had heard before.

"A Communist or a crackpot. It's all the same. Why don't *you* leave? There must be somebody here you don't approve of."

Gérard shrugged and smiled cooly. "My dear Lola, I haven't worried about being compromised by association for years."

"My film star is looking lost. I'd better go," the prince said. Rod turned to him and took the card that was offered him. "Keep that in case I can solve any problems of aesthetics. I'll call Nicole." They shook hands. To Rod's sobered eyes the prince was still a phenomenon, but he hoped he hadn't made a fool of himself by carrying on about his beauty. He wondered what Nicole would have to say about him.

Germaine took advantage of the moment to ease Lola back into the party. "There, darling. Do go along. You don't want to stand here all night carrying on about politics. Go talk to people. Treat the whole think as a joke. That's much the best way." She gave the old woman an affectionate little push and turned back to Rod and the stranger. They eyed each other with the uncertainty of people in formal circumstances who haven't been formally introduced.

"Gérard, I don't think you've met Rod MacIntyre. This is Gérard Thillier, cousin. One of the people I was telling you about. Rod is a very fine painter."

The two men shook hands. Rod's was held for what seemed to him a beat longer than necessary. "You're a friend of the prince?" Thillier asked.

"Hardly. We just met."

"I see. You looked very striking together. A study in contrasts as it were. You're a painter, eh. And an American? American painters interest me." Thillier's self-confidence was so pronounced that he made it sound as if interesting him was the basic foundation of art.

"In what way?" Rod had been jolted into a premature hangover and was feeling edgy and out of touch with his surroundings. How many days had he been here?

"Oh, the obvious. The greatest industrial nation in the world with no traditional ties to the past or any particular culture. Will

149

you be a liberating force or will you simply industrialize creativity? There appears to be an alarming trend toward the latter."

"You're right. It's something to fight. That's why I'm here. I mean, it might look as if I'm running away, but I'm just giving myself some time. I'll be going back soon enough."

"Yes. Paris is rather passé as a cradle of the arts."

Rod looked at him with sharpened interest. He was the first Frenchman he'd encountered who seemed ready to admit that Paris wasn't the unique source from which all culture flowed. It was a strange face, closed and hard, yet hints around the eyes and mouth suggested that some things might make him laugh–like watching a baby being drawn and quartered. His body looked dangerous, crouched, ready to spring, but the intelligence in his face warned of more cerebral power. Tentacles. He made Rod uneasy and defensive. "Paris isn't really the point. There were too many distractions in New York. I wanted to be some place where I could just work."

"This is an odd place to find you if that was what you wanted."

"Well–"

"I'm thinking of taking him under my wing," Germaine cut in with the air of an acknowledged patroness. "He's shown in New York. Don't you think we should arrange an exhibition for him here?" She included Rod. "Gérard controls three very important galleries," she explained.

"Only one is wholly mine," Thillier corrected her. "Perhaps I should see his work."

"Naturally." She swept on imperiously. "Why not tomorrow? I could go with you. Let's make a date."

"Some of my best things are in New York," Rod objected, trying to retain some possession of his work. Germaine had caught him off guard. What had become of the sexual string?

"That doesn't make any difference," she said flatly. "Anybody can tell you've got something."

"An unknown American? To do it right would cost a great deal of money," Thillier pointed out.

"I told you I'm considering taking him under my wing. Go see his pictures, and then we'll talk business."

"I'm always happy to find new painters at no cost to me." Thillier withdrew a slim notebook and a gold pen from an inside pocket. "Rod MacIntyre," he said writing. "And the address?" Without thinking, Rod gave him Patrice's. The pen was arrested. Thillier stood motionless for a moment, looking down at what he'd written. Then he flipped pages and pulled out a card. "On second thought I'd prefer for you to come to me. The atmosphere of a painter's studio is often wrong. Bring one picture. If a man can paint one good picture, he can paint dozens. You seem to be collecting cards this evening."

There was a hard glint in Thillier's eyes that seemed to probe secrets. Rod blushed as he took the card. "Thanks. I'm working very hard these days. I won't call you until I feel like a break." It was the least he could to to establish his role in the deal. Germaine made him almost irrelevant. She knew he "had something" without a glance at his work. Quick and simple. You knew somebody with a gallery. You told him to arrange an exhibition. You paid. In a month he'd be famous. So much for struggle and heartbreak. He waited for some exhilaration to kindle in him but felt nothing. Germaine and Thillier were getting ready to pull strings, manipulate an event. It had nothing to do with art. Maybe when he told Patrice about it ...

"Choose your own time," Thillier was saying. "And I don't think we'll invite your female admirer. We'll be able to talk freely."

"Don't forget where the money's coming from," Germaine snapped unnecessarily."

"I'm sure you won't let me." Thillier gave her a little bow. "Now, if my departure won't be interpreted as a political gesture, I must go." He raised Germaine's hand to within a few inches of his face, nodded to Rod, and left. Rod was almost sorry to see him go. He was a troubling personality, but he wasn't intimidated by Germaine. The thumping of the piano was nerve-racking. The cacophony of voices was beginning to deafen him. He was depressingly aware of his own dull sobriety.

Germaine sighed and ran the back of her hand across her forehead and smoothed her hair at the side and attempted a note of brisk satisfaction. "There you are, cousin. I told you it was all a question of knowing the right people."

"I thought nothing would happen until you were my mistress."

"I'm told disinterested acts are good for the soul. Anyway, I had to carry on so people would forget about Henri. What a bore. I'm quite sober."

"Me too. I suppose we could start all over again," Rod suggested halfheartedly. "Thanks for plugging me. Maybe you should see what I do before you go any further."

"Heavens, darling, what good would that do? I haven't liked a painter since Fragonard."

"Jesus Christ," he exploded. How insulting can you get? You want to prove you can make me or break me regardless of what I have to offer? Quite a few people think I'm important. Damned important. That means more to me than being put on show for some creepy gallery owner." He was eager again to slap her, to humiliate her in whatever way would hurt her most, but she looked up at him with a shy and undeniably beguiling smile.

"Poor cousin darling. I've upset you. I'm sorry, but why pretend to be something I'm not? I know my world. I know how to use people. You have no idea what an introduction to Thillier, backed by money, would mean to a young French painter."

Backed by money. Sex offered the only battlefield where he might defeat her. "I'm getting out of here," he muttered. "You can tell Thillier not to be surprised if he doesn't hear from me."

"Now, cousin." She tucked a hand under his arm and moved with him toward the hall. "Don't throw away a marvelous opportunity just because you're cross with me. We'll talk about it when you've calmed down. I'm ready to go too. You can drop me off, and the car will take you home."

Was it going to happen at last? A grope in the car. A brutal rejection. He would have evened the score. He pressed her hand against him with his arm and looked down at her with a smile that he hoped was warmer than he felt. "I'm not really cross. I guess I'm still a bit drunk."

Outside, cars were lined up at the curb. They walked along them until Germaine found hers, a stately Bentley. The chauffeur was inside, slumped over the wheel. She rapped on the window. The chauffeur straightened with a start and leaped out, fumblingly obsequious with sleep.

"I've told you not to sleep in the car. I don't expect to have to tell you things twice," Germaine said peevishly.

"But madam-" The man was holding open the door.

"Don't argue." Her voice became as cutting as a knife. "I won't have you sleeping in the car. Sleep at home." She got in and settled into deep cushions. He sat close enough for their knees to touch. He wanted to go home to Patrice. He wanted to go to bed with Patrice not for sex but for the comfort of his presence. Patrice knew how to minister to his easily bruised ego.

They rode in silence up the avenue and around the Etoile and down the Champs-Elysées. He didn't know where she lived, so he had no idea how much time they had. If she let him go without making a pass, she would have won all the way down the line. They turned into the avenue Montaigne and drew up next door to Christian Dior. Germaine stirred and sat up.

"Here I am. Pierre will take you wherever you want to go." She snapped open a little gold mesh bag and bundles of crisp 10,000-franc notes spilled out of it. Several notes fluttered to the floor. They lay at her feet, pale in the light of a street lamp. "Get those for me, will you, darling? I've got to give him some money for the morning."

He saw, as if it were being run on a film, what he was going to do. He reached down and obediently retrieved the bills. She took them and crumpled a couple into her palm and stuffed the rest back into the little bag. He watched her with much interest. She probably didn't even know how much she had.

"Aren't you going to ask me in?" he said. Making the first move was another point for her but the only one he intended to concede.

She snapped the bag shut and looked at him. "I generally let the man take the initiative. I must say I find it difficult to keep up with your moods."

"That's because I'm a very talented genius. You know, artistic temperament."

"I'm very much inclined to send you home. Still, you *were* rather fun earlier. Have you decided to be nice again?"

"Like when I was showing you my cock?"

"Really. You're impossible, but I'm beginning to think you might be rather interesting in bed. Different at least."

"I doubt that. How can a guy be different when he's fucking?"

"Perhaps I'll let you show me. Come in if you want."

"That's what I like–being begged. We're a very passionate pair."

"I hope you can get it up at least."

"It's the other way around, isn't it? I hope *you* can get it up."

"I've rarely failed." The chauffeur was standing holding the door open. Germaine slid out in a ripple of fur, and Rod followed her. He found it exciting to treat her as she deserved to be treated. He wondered how far he could push her before she would fight back.

They entered an ornate portal, crossed a court, and mounted a short flight of carpeted stairs. She let them into a dimly lit entry and took his hand and led the way down a wide corridor to an open door. Lights flashed on in a bedroom, and she closed the door behind them.

The white and gold room was wide and high-ceilinged with enormous sprays of flowers everywhere, on the mantle, beside the big bed, on the bureau. She flung her coat and bag onto a chaise lounge. "I'll slip into something more comfortable, as the saying goes. There's some champagne there." She indicated the silver ice bucket on a table against one wall and continued across the room to a bathroom and closed herself in.

Rod could hear water splashing as he opened the bottle and filled a glass. He finished the champagne in a few quick swallows and filled the glass again.

"Are you getting undressed?" she called. "There's a man's dressing gown in the closet if you're modest."

He went to the chaise lounge and dropped his clothes onto it. His eyes were on the small gold bag. For some reason he wanted to do it when he was naked. He glanced up at the bathroom door and then leaned over and snatched up the bag and opened it. His tense fingers extricated the first bundle of bills they touched. He saw the bank's pin still in the corner. A bundle of ten. A couple of hundred bucks. He snapped the bag shut and dropped it. Stealing was sexy. His cock swung out and lifted vigorously as he picked up his jacket and shoved the bills into a pocket. She might not miss them immediately, but when she did she'd guess where they'd gone. He let the jacket fall over the bag and ran a hand out along his cock with self-congratulation. His $200 cock.

He retrieved his glass and took up a position in front of the bathroom door, still toying with himself to keep everything in shape for her. He was more befuddled than he had realized. The glass of champagne seemed to have reactivated everything he had drunk all evening. He couldn't figure out why he thought he'd scored such a great victory over her. He'd taken her money, but she might never know it was gone. Instead of keeping himself all worked up for her, wouldn't it be more to his purpose to relax and force her to really work for it? An impotent man could drive a hungry lady wild. He dropped his hand to his side, but being naked in this feminine room with a woman nearby getting ready to be taken was enough to keep him operational. He might find a way to take her that would make it an act of revenge. He thought of Patrice and wondered how she'd like a little queer stuff.

He was draining his glass when the door opened and she appeared, wearing a slim negligee, her face pale but gentler without makeup.

She stopped in the doorway. Her expression became fixed as she gave him a thorough inspection. "You Americans," she said lightly. "You're all such strapping lads. With a body like that you hardly need talent."

"Thanks." He stood his ground and let her approach him. She did so slowly, still inspecting him. When she reached him she put a hand on his erection. It gave a little leap at her touch.

"Heavens. Does it get bigger?"

"That's about it."

"And quite sufficient too. You can't deny you have a hard-on now."

"No. It's the genuine article, but you'd be amazed at what did it."

"Dreaming of Nicole again?"

"Let's leave her out of this."

"Gladly, but fancy that delicate little thing having such a stallion. How does–"

He slapped her face, not hard but hard enough to bring tears to her eyes. Better. Hitting her was even sexier than stealing from her. "I told you to leave her out of it. We make love together. I'm not going to make love to you. I'm going to screw you."

She brushed her cheek with the back of her hand. "I didn't mean to be offensive," she said. "I'm sorry. By all means, screw me. That's what I like, and for as long as possible. This feels as if you could do it beautifully." She dropped her hand onto him again. The other joined it. "Such a lovely long thing. Come to bed and screw me, darling."

He started to open her negligee but checked himself. Her urgency was a guide. He looked down at the hands moving over him eagerly, assessingly. "You're much too well-dressed to go to bed. Go ahead. I've never had a girl jerk me off. Let's see how quickly you can make me come."

She snatched her hand away. "But, darling, I want you to take me. I want us to be together."

"You know what a cock feels like inside you. This is different. We'll watch together." She started to duck down before him, but he caught her and held her close against his side. "I've had plenty of

156

blow jobs. I'm sure you'd enjoy doing it. This is going to be strictly for me." A hand once more caressed him. "Go on. Like that. All the way to the end. Lovely." He felt a warm tingle of approaching orgasm and had to keep himself firmly in check in order not to pull her robe off and take her the way she wanted to be taken.

"But it's such a waste." Her voice was a moan of frustration. "All this lovely equipment for nothing."

"Nothing? You're making me come. Faster. Out there more. Masturbation is like everything else. You've got to learn how to do it right. Here. I'll show you." He placed his hand on hers and manipulated himself provocatively until he didn't dare touch himself an instant longer. He was bursting with a sort of gleeful rage. "Take over," he ordered. "Have you ever felt a harder cock? Imagine what it would be like ripping into you."

She broke from his restraining arm and tried to get in against him. He held her at arm's length and released his tensions with a peal of laughter. "God, look at it. I didn't know it could be so big." He seized her hands and held them on it and drove it back and forth between them. "That's great."

He planted himself with his feet apart and put his hands on his outthrust hips. "Do it. Make it good. Now. Oh, Christ. Look out or I'll come all over you." He let out a cry. She stepped aside still stroking him, and he saw the ejaculation leaping from him, being flung across the room. When it was finished he pulled away from her grip. "Not bad," he said indifferently. "Have you ever watched a guy come before?"

"Certainly not. The men I've known have had better things to do than stand around and make a mess on the floor."

He laughed and moved in closer and put his mouth on hers. She welcomed it voraciously. While his erection subsided he engaged in what would ordinarily have been preliminaries. It was an exercise in technique, and he set out to make it as tantalizing as he knew how. He put his hands under her robe and caressed her everywhere. She was damp between the thighs. She writhed in close against him. He went on until he could feel that she had com-

157

pletely abandoned herself. Then he pulled back and looked down into a face suffused with craving. "If you'd told me how much you wanted me, maybe I wouldn't have made you do that."

"It still feels hard. Quickly. If we–"

He swayed himself against her and made her breath catch. "It may feel hard, but it isn't. It has to go down before it comes up again. Maybe I'll let you work on it when I've had a drink. Why don't you tell me you're wild for me? That might help."

"Oh, darling. I am. You're the most thrilling man I've known for years. I'm glad we did that. I'll know what it looks like when you're coming inside me. Ravishing."

"If you said things like that more often, I might get to like you." He broke from her and headed for the ice bucket. He was still holding a glass. He filled it and another for her, which he held out to her. He could see her habit of domination struggling with the desire to be near him. Desire won. She sauntered toward him. She had rearranged her negligee so that it covered her elegantly again. She took the glass and managed to look like the leading lady in a drawing-room comedy as she lifted it to her lips.

"Why do you wear that thing?" he asked.

"Mystery, darling. Any woman past 25 wants to guard a little mystery except under the most favorable circumstances."

"If you feel that way, you shouldn't fool around with younger guys. Take it off."

"No, darling. Not until we–"

"Take it off, I say." He reached for her and gave the negligee a tug. Something ripped her. Her glass made a small thud on the carpet as she dropped it. He tugged again, and the flimsy garment fell around her feet. She moved in close to him, hiding herself against him. "It's getting bigger, darling, much bigger," she reported breathlessly.

"This is ridiculous–waiting around for an erection as if it were a streetcar. It's late. We've both had a lot to drink. I better go."

"Oh, no, darling. Please. It's happening. You've got to spend the night." He hadn't dreamed he could subjugate her so completely. She was as tame and docile as a lamb. His revenge was almost complete.

"Pick up your glass, and we'll have a nightcap together." She did as she was told. He refilled her glass and saw why she wanted to keep herself covered. Her breasts were still youthful, and her legs were shapely, but in-between there were strip marks and bulges and a few small folds of crepey skin at the midriff. In spite of her being taller than average, she looked somehow dumpy. But she was a woman, and she wanted him. She would probably get him eventually, but she still hadn't paid the price she had goaded him into demanding. He put down his glass and held her breasts in the palm of his hands. "Pretty good, considering. There's nothing wrong with these. Still, you can hardly expect a guy to be consumed with passion unless you know how to get him started."

"It's getting hard, darling. I can feel it. It was beautifully hard at the beginning."

"Sure. I probably would've screwed you by now if you hadn't been such a smart-ass. You can suck it now. That should perk it up."

"Can't we go to bed?"

"I'm fine here." He backed against the edge of the table and watched her obey. Her mouth wasn't as exciting as Patrice's, but she knew what she was doing. He didn't care whether she succeeded, which made it more likely that she would. Wishing for an erection was the best way to kill it. He took a sip of champagne and glanced around the wide white room. He might yet end up in a garret, but it was taking a long time to get there. His eyes lingered on the chaise lounge. Should he relieve her of another neatly pinned bundle. His $400 cock? He looked down at it and the naked woman crouched in front of it and chuckled. "You look so funny doing that. The elegant Germaine Powers, working for a fuck. I think the streetcar's coming. Yeah, it is. You do that very nicely. I'll have it that way this time."

159

She released him and looked up at him with stricken eyes. "Oh, darling, it's all ready to take me. You said you would if I made it hard again."

"No, I didn't. I want you to suck my cock. If you argue about it, you'll undo all your good work. It's not ready yet anyway. Look at it. Do you call that hard?"

"Almost."

"You were getting there. Go on." He lifted his burgeoning erection in one hand and pulled her head back to it. She drew it into her mouth again and began to redouble her efforts. Watching her obediently perform this service was as exciting as the physical sensations she was producing, and together they restored his virility.

After another moment she drew her head back and spread her hands out flat on his belly and looked at what she had accomplished. "You can't say it isn't ready now, darling. Magnificent." She darted her tongue around it and made it leap in response. "It's no hardship for me, sucking a gorgeous cock. Shall I go on? It's entirely up to you, darling."

"That's more like it. I may yet teach you how to treat a man." He settled back on the edge of the table and spread his legs and leaned over and lifted her by the arms. He dropped his hands to her very womanly buttocks and pulled her in hard against him and looked into her eyes. He saw a middle-aged woman in the grip of anxiety and desire and was touched by her. He was so firmly in charge now that he could let her have what she wanted without compromising anything of himself. "Jesus, all this fuss about fucking. We're naked together. What is there to do *except* fuck now that you've proved you really want it?"

"Do you always expect so much proof?"

"I've never behaved like this in my life. You're such a spoiled bitch you asked for it. I'm in no mood these days to be pushed around by anybody. Mmmm. Nice tits. Go lie down and we'll pretend we're just getting started."

He gave her behind a pat as she turned from him. He stood and drained off his glass and followed her. She stretched out on her back to receive him. He dropped down on her and drove into her, feeling no need for any additional buildup. She gasped, and he felt a great shudder pass through her, and then she went limp beneath him.

He had planted himself as deep in her as he could and held himself there, stirring slightly to let her feel it. "Satisfied?" he asked.

"Yes, darling. Utterly. Your cock is sublime. It's going to make me come very quickly. You're really quite a prize all over, cousin, one of the most perfect physical specimens I've ever seen. Who would have guessed? I really did almost let you go. And now all this. Your heavenly body taking possession of me."

"People are weird. Just because a little part of me is inside you, we're supposed to think something important is happening."

"Far from little, darling, and it *is* a rather intimate thing to do," she drawled, her voice playing its complicated tricks. "For you, of course, I'm just another woman you can take or leave, but I've never wanted a man unless there was that little extra something that happens when people want to know each other. It's something you can't pay for."

"If you get what you want, what's wrong with paying?" His cheeks were burning. He had no intentions of returning the money, but his sense of fair play operated even for her and demanded that he do his best. He withdrew from her and then drove slowly into her again while she uttered little cries of delight and lifted her hips to take him. "Wouldn't you pay for that?"

"Heavens, it goes on for miles. Oh, yes, darling, but only if I felt it would happen even without paying. I know I can't pay you."

"How amazing. You get a reward for that. I was sure you thought you could buy anything." He lifted himself to his knees, pulling her up with him and put his open mouth on hers. She devoured it and gripped his hips with her thighs and flung herself about on the hard flesh within her.

"Are you going to make me a famous painter?" he asked coolly while her body was swept by a frenzy of lust.

"Yes. Anything. I haven't felt anything like this for ages. More and more. Oh, God, do it, darling. Do it."

Rod climbed out of a taxi in front of the big doors in the rue de Verneuil wearing his dinner jacket in broad, unexpectedly sunny daylight. Whores could afford taxis. All his thoughts were focused on Patrice, the only person he could tell about his night, the only person who could help him over the feeling of self-disgust it had left in him. Waking up in bed with Germaine, riding home in his stale evening clothes, he had tried to convince himself that it was all part of the toughening process that was helping him to shed his background. He had to adapt. He had to be ready to exploit every situation that arose.

Stealing from the rich might be justified for an important cause. Hitting and humiliating women, being unfaithful—everything could be justified—but it left him in a confusion of guilt and self-doubt. He had tried to give value for money; that was the only redeeming feature of the squalid episode. Seeing it through Patrice's eyes might reveal others.

He let himself into the apartment and stood listening by the door for a moment. He heard an indistinct noise from the kitchen and called. He met Patrice in the living room as he came bustling out, wearing his robe and looking fresh and saucy. Rod immediately felt better. The hangover that had been making his head pound seemed to subside.

"There you are, *chéri*. I hoped you'd come in before I had to go."

"You're up early."

"So are you." They smiled at each other. "You have been with Nicole?"

"No." He remembered that Patrice didn't know about the abortion and told him.

The boy's face fell. "I'm very sorry, *chéri*. You knew it had to happen but—it's good you didn't have to worry until it was over."

162

"I guess so. It's as good an excuse as any for the way I behaved last night."

"You were very wicked? You have the hangover?"

"I'll say. At least I did. It's better now."

"Come. Coffee is just ready."

Rod unfastened his tie and collar as he followed his friend. They sat at the kitchen table with steaming cups in front of them.

"I went to Lola's party after all," he explained. "I was so upset about Nicole that I couldn't stay here alone, not that you'd have known it from what happened. I hoped for an evening with you."

Patrice reached across the table and touched his hand. *"Merde.* I assumed you'd be with Nicole. Was it a glamorous party?"

"Lots of people." He reached into a pocket and found a card and pulled it out. "This is one of them. Jean-Marie Andre' Phillipe et cetera et cetera Lussigny-Forbain. A prince."

"Beauty Lussigny? He was there?"

"Yes, and a beauty he is. You know him?"

"I did. I haven't seen him for a long time."

"You've been to bed with him?"

"Yes, that is one I don't regret. He was in love with me for a week or two."

"He invited me to his bed, as he put it."

"I'm sure he did. You weren't tempted?"

"Don't be silly. Of course not."

"You will tell me if you ever feel like that for a boy?"

"I never could, but suppose I did. You'd want me to tell you about it?"

"Of course. Not the details but that it happened. I would be glad. It would mean I'm not entirely a–what do you call it?–a quirk of your nature and that you're not always thinking of girls. Except Nicole, but that is love."

"The prince gave me the idea that she might understand about a lot of things." He stroked the hand that lay beside his. He turned it palm up and placed his over it and experienced a moment of profound relief. He was home and safe after a particularly stormy voy-

163

age. He help Patrice's hand in both of his, gently, not wanting to stir an amorous response. His own looked brutal by comparison. "You're a sweetheart, monkey mine. As soon as Nicole's better, I want you to meet her. I thought a lot about you all night. We can start sharing the bed again if you want. The sofa's a bore."

Patrice's fingers tightened around his. "You mean it?"

"Why not? I always feel as if things might turn out all right when I'm with you. It's something we have—it's ours—nothing to do with boys the way you mean it. You're being very discreet about last night. No questions. You don't still suspect I worked in a fling with the prince, do you?"

"No. Only for a second when you pulled out this card."

"I have a more important one here somewhere. I admit I'm curious about his body. Is it as beautiful as that head?"

"I thought so at the time. I'm sure not as beautiful as yours. He was an adorable lover. I remember that."

"I do believe I'm jealous. How strange. Do you think I'm a bit in love with you without knowing it?"

"Don't even say it. It's too much at 8 o'clock in the morning."

Rod laughed and relinquished his hand and gave his hair a tug. "Maybe I'm still drunk or maybe it's the company I've been keeping. As a matter of fact, I've been with a lady—the one I've told you about, Lola's stepdaughter with the American name."

"Really? Why?"

"Why indeed. For various reasons I'm ashamed of. It was a lousy thing to do to Nicole."

"I don't think you should worry about that. It is something the French don't understand about American girls—that they expect men to be faithful. French girls don't. She would mind only if you had a serious affair."

"At times I get the feeling that that's what we're having."

"Yes, but with a boy she wouldn't think it serious."

"No. I suppose not. Still, I'd like her to understand a bit how much you mean to me. I've been brought up to believe that I ought to be faithful to the girl I love. Maybe you Catholics have something. Confession. Am I absolved for fucking Madame Powers?"

"If you did nothing to hurt Nicole. If Madame Powers won't tell."

"I'd kill her if she did. Maybe I should warn her. That's not all of it." He felt for the money and pulled it out and put it on the table. A card slipped from it, and he picked it up. "Here's the one I was looking for."

Patrice was gazing at the money.

"Why are you carrying all that, *chéri?*"

"I stole it."

Patrice looked up and his eyes widened. "You mean it?"

"Absolutely. She was–Germaine–she was carrying on about all the wonderful things she could do for me if I–well, if I fucked her was what it amounted to. I decided that if I was going to be a whore, I wanted to be paid in cash. Piles of the stuff were falling out of her bag. I could've taken more. I'm not much good as a thief."

Patrice studied him for a moment, and then his eyes began to dance with mischief. "You're a very expensive whore. I can't afford you. How much is it?"

"I haven't counted it. It's still pinned. A hundred thousand, I guess."

"You must have been very angry with her."

"Yes, only you would understand that," Rod said gratefully. With Patrice, life always seemed to make some sort of cockeyed sense. "She'd been treating me like a gigolo, like a new toy. I had to get back at her. Stupid."

"For you to fuck somebody is a funny way of getting back at them. I'm sure many people would like you to get back at them in that way."

"Yeah, she got what she wanted finally, but I made her work for it."

"And what are the wonderful things she's going to do for you?"

"That's where this comes in." He flicked the card with a finger. "She introduced me to a guy who owns a gallery, or galleries. They didn't say which ones. Well, hell, you probably know him. A guy called Thillier." He held out the card. Instead of taking it Patrice did something clumsy with his hands, and his empty cup overturned with a clatter. His expression was suddenly closed and defiant, shadowed with fear. Rod put down the card. "What's the matter, baby?"

"Nothing," he said in a strained voice. His hands flew about wildly. They briefly clutched at his hair and came to rest on his chest, gripping his robe. He choked and made an odd sound like a croak. His eyes stared. "You just–Gérard."

"Thillier? What about him?"

"He is the one–the man I told you about."

"Told me about what?"

"The one who came here."

"You mean 'the Voice?'" It was Rod's turn to stare as it all clicked into place. "Your so-called guardian?"

"Yes."

"Oh, for God's sake." Rod picked up the card and put it down again. "I don't believe it. I should've known. There *was* something familiar about his voice."

Patrice made a visible effort to get control of himself. He dropped his hands and leaned forward. "You must tell me everything, everything that was said," he demanded sharply.

"There wasn't much. Germaine told him he should give me a show. He said it would be expensive, and Germaine said she'd discuss it with him. That's about all."

"Did he know who you were?"

"Who am I? An unknown American painter. Germaine told him that much. He wrote down my name."

"No. I mean, did he make no connection with me?" he asked with startling force.

"How could he? Wait a minute. I remember. I was pretty drunk. We were arranging for him to come see my things and he asked for my address. I gave him this one and he changed his mind. He said something about not liking artists' studios and asked me to bring a picture to his place. Of course. He must've known."

"Did he act peculiar after that?"

166

"He acted peculiar the whole time. I didn't like him. He must've seen the prince give me his card. At the end when he gave me his, he made some crack about my collecting them. I'll be damned. So that's Gérard Thillier."

Patrice was staring at space, looking so hunted and haunted and lost that Rod's heart was wrenched. He rose and went around the table to him and put his hands on his shoulders and kissed the top of his head. "Come on, baby. Take it easy. What difference does it make?"

"You don't know. He's been biding his time, probably because he thinks I've lost my head over some silly little faggot and will come to my senses. Now that he has seen you, he will know it's not that. He will do everything he can to destroy everything good between us. He has very important connections. He could have you put out of the country."

"Don't be silly. Why would he bother? All he's suggested is that I come see him and show him a picture."

"Yes. Why? He will never give you a show. He will try only to hurt us both in any way he can."

"How? I don't even have to go see him, for God's sakes."

"No, you mustn't. Not until I've had a chance to talk to him."

"Now listen." Rod squatted beside Patrice and put his hand under his chin and turned his head to face him. Their eyes met. Rod took a deep breath as all his protective possessive instincts seemed to gather in a knot in his chest. He hadn't realized that his boy was still so under the influence of his discarded father figure. "You're mine. Right? That's the way we're going to keep it. I'm not going to let Thillier give you a rough time so forget him. We don't need him."

"But you don't understand, *chéri*. He is very dangerous, but he could also help. If this woman is ready to pay for a show, it would be very good for you. He knows Nicole. I could perhaps convince him of what you said before–that we're just friends and that you will soon be married. He could also tell her that you're living with a notorious pervert."

"Are you notorious, baby?"

"Yes, but I swear to you that I–" Something in Rod's eyes made his voice trail off.

"No, don't say it," Rod said gently. "You don't have to. I thought you might be, but I know it's all finished, whatever it was." Their eyes searched and probed and assented to everything they found in each other. "Forget what I said about being in love. That's silly. But I really do love you, baby, more than I can show you. If it had more to do with sex, it would be easier." Rod ran light fingertips over the troubled face. "I've missed you for the last few weeks, but you understand why I had to sort of pull back. That's over now. I can't imagine being without you, so don't worry about anybody spoiling things for us."

"I'm scared, *chéri*." He moved in closer and buried his face in Rod's chest. "*Mon grand beau.* I can give you so little, yet you are ready to take care of me."

"Naturally. We take care of each other. I couldn't have gotten through the last few months without you." He searched for the word or act that would eliminate Thillier once and for all. He added, "I need you."

"Please do. I try not let myself think about how much I need you. What I need is unimportant. Only when you–you say you love me do I feel very important."

"I've been so selfish with you." Rod slipped his hands under the robe and moved them over the slim body. The night's guilt urged him to make up to Patrice for all his shortcomings. "I don't know anything about being queer but the hell with it. It doesn't matter what people do with loving. I guess I better show you what I mean. I'm all fucked out, so I'm not being carried away by some crazy impulse I might regret. This is a good time to do it. He hoped he could go through with it. He ran his hands along Patrice's shoulders and pushed the robe down over them, exposing the tender stripling's chest. Patrice held the robe firmly closed at his waist. Rod chuckled. "There's no use putting up a fight. I'm bigger than you are."

"Please, *chéri*." There was a note of panic in Patrice's voice. "Please don't. You know what happens when you touch me. You don't like to see me like that. I'm your girl."

"I've got a girl. I want you to be my boy. We've been together long enough for me to find out if you've got a cock. Let go." The robe fell open. Patrice's legs were crossed, locked together. "You're such a pretty guy, you must be fed up with my not paying any attention to this." Without looking, he unlocked Patrice's legs and found his boy's erection and held it for the first time. It felt bigger than he had expected. He was inexplicably proud of it, and he smiled slyly into Patrice's eyes as he caressed it.

"Please, *chéri*," Patrice begged. "You don't like it. You mustn't force yourself."

"Sure I must. Anyway, I'm not forcing anything. It feels nice and sexy. If you decide to take on that girl you keep talking about, I'm sure she'll be delighted with it." He stood and pulled Patrice to his feet. His boy tried to cover himself again with the robe. Rod pulled his hands out of the sleeves and took it away from him. Patrice tried to duck away around the table but Rod held him firmly in front of him. His head was bowed. "I keep telling you how much you mean to me, but I never do anything about it. Words. It's time for action." The boy struggled against his grip. "Why not? If I can do something that pleases you, it doesn't matter if I like it or not as long as it doesn't kill me." He dropped to the edge of the chair and pulled Patrice to him, feeling every muscle in the boy's body coiled to tear himself away. He looked up at him. "Please, monkey. Relax. I probably won't be very good at it. Don't make it more difficult for me."

He lowered his eyes and finally took a close look at a man with an erection. It strained up to him, looking so taut that he wondered how he could get it into a drawing. There being no visible source of tension added mystery. It would be like drawing a man on the rack without showing the rack. He regretted not having studied it before, so fascinated that he almost forgot

169

what he set out to do. He fought a final battle with ingrained repugnance and conquered it. He leaned forward and opened his mouth and drew the rigid flesh into it.

Patrice cried out and tried to pull away again, but Rod had a firm grip on his hips. He tugged at Rod's hair. "Stop. You mustn't. I don't want it. You'll hate me for letting you."

Rod tried to overcome his resistance by reproducing the things he had learned from him, but it was such a mouthful that he was unable to experiment freely. He wondered how Patrice managed with such apparent ease. It struck him as a grotesque act, yet it had been performed often for him, apparently with pleasure. He remembered the shock of letting Patrice make love to his body the first morning and wondered how he had come so far along this unknown road. He had a cock in his mouth. At least he was doing it for someone he loved, which made it more honorable than anything that had happened during the night.

Patrice continued to protest, his voice hoarse with tension. "You're making me come. I can't help it. Oh, please. Please, *chéri*. No. Oh, God. No." His body lurched. his knees buckled. Rod's mouth was filled with a musky fluid that was thick and warm.

He tried to swallow it and gagged. He wanted to take all of it, but it overflowed his mouth. He sprang up and made a dash for the toilet and spat it out. His stomach heaved. Sweat broke out on his forehead. He thought he was going to be sick. He swayed over the toilet and continued to spit. There was so much of it.

His hands were shaking violently, but when he looked at them they stopped. He felt totally cut off from himself, at a loss as to who he was or where he was going. He thought that this was what it might be like to go mad. He had to find a recognizable face to present to Patrice and act as if he was sure of himself. Any trace of embarrassment or uncertainty would be misinterpreted. He wiped his damp forehead with the back of his hand and straightened his clothes and went out to demonstrate that he had taken the incident in stride.

Patrice was seated at the kitchen table, wrapped in his robe. He didn't look up at Rod's approach. Rod touched his shoulder.

"It happened," he said, sounding as unconcerned as he could have wished. "I don't guess it was very good for you, and there's no use pretending it's something I'd ordinarily be absolutely crazy about, but it's the thought that counts."

Patrice lifted his eyes. They still looked haunted. "You're not disgusted with me?"

"Oh, baby, how could I be? You tried to stop me. I guess the first time is bound to be a bit–unexpected."

"It certainly was for me." They studied each other for a moment, and Patrice's eyes cleared. They carried Rod beyond the act to the meaning he had tried to put into it. Perhaps it was as simple as he had wanted it to be, leaving him intact and unaltered. The only way to find out was to get on with the day's business and pretend it was behind them. He touched Patrice's hair and pulled a chair around and sat close to him, facing him.

"I'll be having lunch with Germaine," he said with a switch of conversational gears. "She wants to talk about Thillier and the show. What should I say?"

"It doesn't matter as long as you do nothing until I talk to him."

"You don't know Germaine. She'll probably be having the posters printed up by this evening. I don't want you mixed up in something that upsets you so much. Germaine surely must know of other galleries besides Gérard's."

For you, Gérard is the best. He's known for discovering important new painters. I must find out what game he plays. Not just about the show. It could be almost anything."

"Like having me thrown out of the country?"

"He has done it before. I will try to find out today."

"You're planning to see him?"

"I think I'll have to."

"Well, take it easy, baby. Don't worry about me. I have some pretty important connections myself."

"I better dress. I want to get to work promptly. The day may be difficult later." He rose and hesitated. He suspected that Rod wanted to obliterate with talk the sexual act, and he still feared its consequences. There had been no desire in it. The feel of his beloved's mouth on him was a promise of bliss he wouldn't let himself believe in. He couldn't undo it, but he could help Rod see it as a matter of no importance. "I think now I will let you see me naked sometimes. After all, there is nothing very terrible to hide."

"I wish you'd burn that damn robe."

"Not yet. But slowly I may learn not to grab it so quickly." He shot Rod a merry glance. "I owe it a great deal. All this time I have been disguised as a little lump of wool. Now I think you're ready to know the truth."

"Just keep smiling for me, monkey."

Patrice did so, and Rod rose and followed him back to the bedroom. He hung up his clothes while Patrice dressed and climbed into the unmade bed and was asleep before Patrice had left. He awoke with a start an hour later. Had he dreamed it all—Germaine, Thillier and Patrice, what he had done with his boy? He put it all together slowly and found that it was real. He had been unfaithful to Nicole. Thillier was the villain in Patrice's life. He had sucked a cock. His mind reeled again and settled on Patrice's theory that it would have to happen with another boy before it could be considered anything but a quirk. Sucking a cock didn't make him a cocksucker; he didn't know what it had made him. He drowsed and dawdled and dressed and went out into a day of balmy sun. It was suddenly spring. Everywhere he looked, the grim gray city had been transformed into vistas of unknown delight. He went around the corner and called Nicole, glad for another day or two to pull himself into some recognizable shape. He couldn't believe that the things he had done hadn't marked him in some way. He told her he'd gone to Lola's party.

"I know, my dearest. I've heard already. I've also heard that Germaine was doing her best to console you for my absence."

172

"She was very attractive. She even sent me home in her car. She's suddenly decided to become a patron of the arts. I'm supposed to have lunch with her in a little while to discuss my future."

"Lunch? I *am* jealous. I thought I was the only person you had lunch with."

"The only person I want to have lunch with. Shall I ditch her and come see you? The party threw me all off as far as work's concerned."

"No, darling. Give me a day or two, and we'll be together again. It's too frustrating to see you when I'm like this. You were a great success last night. Beauty Lussigny just called and asked us to have dinner with him. I told him to call again at the beginning of the week. He's mad about you, of course."

"He told me you were pals. I was amazed. I didn't know you knew such racy people."

"Men who don't want to flirt with me often turn out to be good friends. Beauty is adorable. My first man—only a boy really—actually went to bed with him. He told me all about it. It sounded so sweet and absurd that I didn't mind it in the least."

"Well, aren't we sophisticated. You must tell me more when we see each other." He liked the new Nicole; he had been doing her an injustice in thinking he had to hide Patrice from her.

"What do you say, my darling? Shall I accept?"

"The prince? Sure. I love to look at him."

"It's mutual I'm sure. I think I'm going to be somewhat *de trop* at this dinner. I hope he doesn't make a habit of borrowing my men."

Very civilized and adult. He wondered if she had been hiding a lot too. If they weren't to be figures in a great romantic passion, it was nice to discover that she was more relaxed and easygoing than he'd realized. They exchanged lingering farewells, and he hung up and called Germaine. He was passed through servants, one male, one female, before the lady was on the line.

"Good morning, darling," she said briskly. "I've been waiting for your call. Is it as heavenly as it looks?"

"Wonderful."

"I've thought of the most perfect place for lunch. Nobody I know would dream of going. We'll be the soul of discretion."

"It doesn't matter. I've told Nicole we're having lunch together."

"Never mind. It's always a lark to be clandestine. Meet me at the restaurant in the Eiffel Tower. The food is excruciating, but it has a nice view. I'll book a table in your name. About half an hour?"

"Fine." He hung up feeling as if he'd been talking to a casual acquaintance with no sense of her being a woman he had been to bed with. So much for infidelity. Patrice was right as usual. He went out again into the balm of sun and was once more overwhelmed by beauty that had been hidden from him for months. His eyes were busy with the light effects that had caused this transformation and the color in what had been a misty monochrome landscape. He walked wishing someone he loved was with him, Nicole or Patrice or both of them, to share it.

Young lovers and Paris in the spring. Banal but potent magic. And he was off to lunch with a bitch whom he was going to try to con into salvaging his life. He doubted if last night's lessons would mark her for long. Her invitation to lunch had sounded dangerously like a command. He had no intention of taking her to bed again unless she had something very good to offer in return. Unless. A whore's thought.

Some of the bloom seemed to fade from the day. He crossed the vast open spaces of the Invalides, guaranteed to make even a megalomaniac feel uneasy, and followed the river, with the Eiffel Tower looming ahead of him. He wanted to turn back, run away from his meeting.

He experienced a strange massive slippage within himself, so physical that he stumbled and slowed down to recover an even stride. It scared him. He had known something was wrong. Everything in him was falling into a new precarious balance. Infidelity, his boy, money, his work, even love—looked at from a certain perspective–everything became trivial. He was filled with a sense of the futility of life. Little desires. Little fears. Little hops and ambitions. How could an artist transcend the general triviality of humanity?

He glanced up at the street sign. Quai Branly. The address on the prince's card. The prince who was mad about him. Additional triviality. He came out into the Camps de Mars. The Eiffel Tower sat astride it, a contradiction in filigree power. Rod shrank from it; it was terrifying. In the distance he could see unusual activity in front of the Ecole Militaire. A number of police vans were drawn up, and a crowd was milling about. He wished they'd have their revolution and get it over with.

The unseasonable day had brought many people out as if they had been standing in the wings, fully mobilized, awaiting this call. The little ice-cream wagons were out, the balloon men, the children, and the mothers. It was a cheerful scene. He forced himself to see the gaiety in it.

The monstrous skeleton of the tower seemed to float just off the ground, lifted on a shimmer of pale sunlight. It straddled space like a huge mechanical beast. There was the beauty of impossible equilibrium in it, and he determinedly closed his mind to the menace he irrationally sensed in it. He wanted to suspend all the sensitive irrationalities of his senses. It was time to add a layer to the protective toughness that had barely begun to insulate him from the tough life around him. It was important to keep an upper hand with Germaine and beware of whatever danger Thillier represented.

Rod approached the foot of the tower reluctantly and took his place in the tilted elevator, alone with the operator. Gates clattered, the elevator trembled, and they ascended sideways across the sky.

The wide platform on which he was deposited was spliced into the sky. He hadn't been in the elevator long enough to have risen so high. He was drawn irresistibly toward the edge. Paris lay far below him along the Seine. He caught his breath as giddiness plunged down through his stomach, and he was afflicted with a sense of the fragility of his human package. What did it all matter?

175

One false move and it would all be gone—worries about money, worries about love, ambition, pride, determination. The void exerted a terrible pull. It was foolish to go on struggling when it would be so easy to stop. Giddiness rocked his stomach again, and he felt it unhinging his legs. With an effort he stepped back and turned away from the unsettling panorama. He stood for a moment to compose himself, feeling life take charge once more. He was getting really nutty, mooning over a low railing a mile up in the air. His heart was beating rapidly as he walked over to the entrance to the restaurant.

It was more elegant than he had expected from Germaine's reference to it. His hand went immediately to his jacket pocket, forgetting that he was Germaine's guest. He had brought only a few hundred francs. He supposed Patrice had taken charge of the stolen fortune for him. He was greeted by a mâitre d'hôtel in morning dress.

"You are looking perhaps for Madame Powers?" he asked in English.

Rod nodded. His attention was directed to a far corner of the big room where he saw Germaine silhouetted against a window, looking quite dazzling. In spite of himself he felt a little thrill of pride at having possessed her. She was dressed with stunning chic, but clothes couldn't obliterate the memory of her as she had been last night. That she had been able to put herself together again so successfully was a small miracle. He approached her with a little swagger left over from his triumph over her.

"Well, there you are, cousin," she said briskly as he stopped before her. Her eyes ran over him in quick appraisal. "Quite nicely dressed for a struggling artist. I won't have to waste money on your clothes. If you leave me any." She stirred about in the expensive litter she had created around herself—bag, gloves, jeweled cigarette box. "Here. Sit beside me. We'll be tourists and gawk at the funny Frenchmen. My pocketbook will be within easy reach."

The two references were fairly obvious. He was glad he didn't have her money on him. He was still enough of a proper gentleman to give it back to her. "What's that mean?" he asked as he edged in beside her.

"Oh, come, darling. You don't really think I don't know when I'm robbed do you?" she said. "It doesn't matter. I'd have given it to you if you'd asked. I told you how I feel about paying once I know it isn't a condition. I don't mind at all. I'm really quite generous. There." Her hand sought his under the table. He felt something being pressed into his palm. He started to pull away, but she was too quick for him. He had no choice but to accept the crisp paper left in his hand. He brought it up and put it on the table. Another 10,000-franc note.

"What's this for?"

"Please, darling. Be a little discreet." She looked quite flustered as her eyes darted around the half-empty restaurant. "It's just to pay for lunch. Put it away for heaven's sake."

"Why can't you ask for the bill and pay for it like anybody else?"

"Darling, you can't expect a woman of my age to be seen paying for a young man's lunch. Think of the way it would look."

"I guess it would look as if you have more money than I have. Why didn't you suggest going somewhere I could afford?"

"I would have thought you could afford almost anywhere today. But then it wouldn't do for you to buy my lunch with money you stole from me. Now be a lamb and put that away."

He did so, scoring the first round as a draw but pleased to have opened hostilities. He wasn't going to make it easy for her to become a patron of the arts.

A waiter appeared before them, brandishing large cards. Germaine ordered authoritatively in a French way he didn't like, adding sharp commands as to how the food was to be prepared and presented. It was knowledgeable in the way one might be knowledgeable about a machine. And for him it took all the pleasure out of eating. "Don't you want to order the wine, cousin?" she inquired.

"No. You're doing fine. Just make it two of everything."

She finished her business with cards and waiters and took a cigarette from her box and handed him a small gold lighter that he dutifully operated for her. She blew smoke at him and smiled with a hint of the complicity of the night before. "It will all be quite dreadful," she said, dismissing her efforts over the meal, "but we must keep them on their toes for the tourists' sake. Wasn't last night the first time you'd met Gérard Thillier?"

Rod's attention quickened. "Sure."

"That's what I thought. How odd. He called a little while ago. He spoke of you–not exactly as if he knew you–I can't quite put my finger on it–as if he knew a lot about you, I suppose."

"He can't possibly." He felt that he must modify the force with which he had said it. "How so?"

"Well, he said what a coincidence it was meeting you, for one thing. He wanted me to make a particular point that it was very important for him to see you in the next day or two. I didn't get the impression that it was necessarily about your work. Do you suppose he's after you?"

"How do you mean?"

"Just that, darling. His reputation is quite lurid. I've heard things that have even shocked me. Have you ever heard of the *Cercle Vert*?"

"No," he said, thinking of all the odd hints Patrice had dropped from the beginning.

"Well, you won't hear about it from me. Ask Nicole. Green, I imagine, for Oscar's carnation. A green club. She'll tell you. She's gone in more for the funny boys than I have. Come to think of it, why didn't he call her if he's so anxious to reach you? He knows her quite well. He must know she's engaged to you."

"I don't know anything about it. Didn't you talk about the big show?"

"Good heavens, darling. Did you think I wouldn't after last night? I told him I'd definitely decided to back it whatever it cost. You see? You don't have to rob me." She dropped a hand to his thigh and moved it toward his crotch.

"If you're wondering if my cock is still there, it's all bunched up on the other side." He shifted and opened his legs to make it more accessible. Doing so he stirred it to life; when she found it, it was no longer bunched up. "If you want a real grope, help yourself." He unzipped his fly. He wondered how far she would play along with this shameless game. He felt her hand on his naked flesh. By the time she had freed it and lifted it out, it had begun to function on its own. "Carry on. A guy gets nervous if he's left sort of twixt and between. He wants to make sure it's going to go all the way." He glanced at her as she caressed him. Her face was beginning to dissolve into the expression of blind hunger he had seen last night. He felt himself surge up in her hand. "That's it. You're holding a nice hard cock, and there's nothing we can do about it. This is hardly the time or place to jerk me off."

"How frightfully wicked of me. I'd love to see it."

"I don't know of any law that says a lady can't look at her escort's cock in a stylish restaurant. There it is." He lifted the tablecloth and sat back, surveying the room to make sure they were unobserved. The hand on him did some interesting things, provoking a rigorous reaction.

"Gorgeous, darling. We'll take care of it after lunch."

"That remains to be seen." He dropped the tablecloth. "Unhand me, madam. It can't stay like that indefinitely, and I don't want you to feel it getting limp." She did as she was told. "Now then. We'd better talk about Thillier. I have a friend–I'll tell you later."

Waiters had arrived bearing dishes. They were held out for Germaine's inspection. She nodded to them as if they were distant acquaintances. Plates were removed and replaced. There was a great whisking of napkins and brandishing of cutlery. Rod took advantage of the commotion to get himself back into his trousers. The sommelier brought up the rear. His bottle, too, had to be inspected, the cork removed, sniffed, and held out for Germaine's approval. Food was put on her plate, a thimbleful of wine poured into her glass. They all stood back, side by side, in exquisite suspense. Germaine nibbled and sipped with regal indifference. Assured apparently that she wasn't going to throw anything at them, the servants sprang into action once more around Rod. He expected them to start putting food in his mouth.

"Will you for chrissake tell them to go away?" he growled.

"*Ca va ca va*," she said with a wave of her hand. They were immediately alone. "What were you saying about Thillier, cousin?"

"I've been thinking. I talked to a friend of mine this morning who knows him. He agrees with you that he's pretty kooky. He told me he'd probably be after me, as you put it. I want you to hint that I'm interested. Push the show and tell him that I seem very anxious to get to know him personally. I can play games too."

"Be careful cousin. From what I hear, Gérard is not a man to play with."

"You let me handle this," he said, thinking of Patrice's warnings. "I want him to think that I've been mixed up with a boy, but I'm trying to get out of it." This was for Nicole's benefit, something he must remember to tell her. If Thillier carried any tales to her, she would think she knew the source. "I can play him along for a month or two, long enough to get a show on."

"All this talk about boys," Germaine objected. "How do you think it'll make me look? People will think you've made a complete fool of me."

"Who the hell cares? Can't you take an interest in a faggot? There must be plenty of faggot painters. Let's have the bottle put on the table."

"Are we going to get drunk for the next month? How do you think all this is going to work as far as Nicole is concerned?"

"After last night I'm not worried about that. Not just last night, darling. Just now. You're rather pleased with that cock of yours. Justifiably so, I must admit. As long as ladies share your enthusiasm for it, I'm sure you'll find opportunities to indulge their weakness." She put her hand on it again and laughed complacently as it responded.

Rod experienced again the odd massive slippage in himself, this time in reverse, like the old Charlie Chaplin sequence of a house teetering on the edge of a cliff with everything careening from one side to the other as the balance shifted. Values resumed their meaning. A sense of his own dignity and worth returned. What had

180

possessed him to open his pants? Why was he bartering his decency, if only by hearsay, for the favor of a vicious corrupter of youth? Poor Germaine was a saint by comparison.

He didn't want to get drunk, but wine offered some relief from his anger with himself, and he finished one bottle and signaled for another while they progressed through a meal that was ornate without being distinguished. They were waiting for the bill when Germaine was greeted by a tall middle-aged man who was elaborately tailored. He stood in front of their table, bowing over her hand with a mannered grace that immediately made Rod want to do something boorish.

"*Tiens*, Gilles. What in the world are you doing here?" Germaine asked.

"I wondered the same of you. Perhaps we're starting a trend."

"I hope not. I've never had such a ghastly lunch. This is Rod MacIntyre. An important American painter."

Rod lifted himself a few inches from his seat and shook hands. The newcomer scarcely glanced at him.

"I'm planning to launch him in Paris," Germaine went on. "Wait until you see his work. You'll want to do a piece about him for your paper. I'll let you know when the time is right."

"Splendid. He's a very lucky young man. I'm sure he'll be an enormous success. Wasn't the last one a prizefighter? The catholicity of your tastes is admirable."

"You dreadful man." They laughed as the man took his leave. She turned to Rod full of brisk decision. "That's Gilles Delannoy. He has *Les Arts Francais*. Very influential. We must plan our campaign. I'm not sure I understand your plot with Gérard. I can count on Gilles. There are others you must meet. It's important not to spread ourselves too thin. With a handful of the right allies, the rest fall into line or attack you, which is good too."

Rod listened without feeling that it had anything to do with him. His St-Germain-des-Pres friends jeered at *Les Arts Francais* as the mouthpiece of academic reaction, but they'd quickly stop jeering if it meant solving their financial problems. Were his really over? "You seem to have everything well in hand," he said with only a faint shading of irony. If she was aware of it, she ignored it.

"I'd have done it sooner if you'd given me the slightest encouragement. It's too stupid for you to go on grubbing in some wretched attic."

They had brandy and coffee, which threatened to shift the balance in him once more. His response to Germaine became warmer, jocular, and slightly drunken. He made her laugh and laughed himself. He paid the bill and pocketed the change. They left in a gale of laughter somehow inspired by him, clinging to each other to support their merriment.

"We do have fun, don't we cousin?" she said with a comfortable sigh when they were in the elevator. "I'm so glad they haven't pulled the tower down yet."

Rod felt as if he were being returned to the scene of some catastrophe. He resisted the pull of the earth. Nothing awaited him there but insoluble problems. More disloyalties? More whoring? Honorable starvation?

They left the elevator and, following Germaine's lead, strolled toward the river. "The car's waiting in the Quai Branly," she explained. "We can give that handsome cock the attention it demands, and then we can decide what to do about Gérard."

"I've decided," he said quietly, knowing finally that he had. "Here's your change." He handed her a few bills.

She drew away. "Don't be silly. I must give you more. You'll have expenses. I'm going to introduce you to Lucie Dessailley. You'll have to flirt with her a bit, send her flowers. It would be obvious to a blind man that people make a fuss over her because of her connections, but she goes on believing that her charms are irresistible. Silly goose."

"Look, Germaine–"

"Now, darling, don't be tiresome. I'm determined to do this thing right. You must act like a success in order to be a success. You Americans understand that. We have a lot to talk about. We must make plans."

"I've had enough of your plans. I don't want your money, goddammit." He halted abruptly. Germaine turned and looked at him coolly.

"You seemed to want it rather badly last night, darling," she said.

"Goddamn you," he gasped in a voice choked with welcome rage. Here was something simple and straightforward to deal with at last. He threw the bills he was holding into the air and leaped at her and seized her pocketbook and wrenched it from her hands. He sprang back and held it up before her.

"There. Now I've got it," he cried. "Why don't you call the police? I'm a real thief. A purse snatcher. You can have me arrested."

He saw her poise draining from her as it had at the party. She glanced around with panic-stricken eyes.

"How dare you—in public—" Germaine stammered. "You must be insane."

"You'll see how mad I am. How much have you got in here this time? A couple of hundred thousand? Half a million? How much do you think it will take to launch my career?" He tore open the pocketbook and clawed through it and brought up a bundle of bills. "What do we care about money? Let's throw some around. Flowers for Lucie Dessailley. Flowers for *Les Arts Francais*. Flowers for Gérard Thillier. Flowers for all the whores and perverts who really count in artistic circles." He shook the bundle loose. Bills spilled and fluttered around him. He brought out more and flung them into the air. "That's for anybody we've forgotten. Now I'm a success. A genius has been born. I can throw as much money around as you can. And if you try hinting around to Nicole about any of this, I can get a lot madder. Just remember that." He hurled the pocketbook at her. He saw her hands go up in self-defense as he turned and strode away.

He walked fast, expecting at any moment to hear sounds of pursuit, whistles, angry shouts, running feet. Nothing happened. As he calmed down he realized that it was part of his insanity to suppose that anything would. She was a coward.

So much for Germaine. He had no more lessons to teach her. So much for Thillier. So much for the whole fucking art world. He was out of the market.

He had no commodity to sell. He had stripped everything down to a simple question of survival. You had to be tough for that, and he could see that it might easily turn you into a real shit.

He slowed down and became aware of the painful pounding of his heart. Easy, he told himself. There was nothing to get worked up about. He'd never had any intention of having an affair with Germaine. He didn't want anything she could do to launch him. If he hadn't been more or less drunk for almost 24 hours, he wouldn't have let her go so far. Survival had nothing to do with his work. Survival was money. For most people there was a connection, but for him they were two separate things. Hang onto that fact.

He passed elegant doorways, one of which must be the prince's. Should he pay a call and indulge in the luxury of contemplating beauty as an antidote to the ugliness that had ruled his life since yesterday? The prince would quite understandably assume the obvious. He didn't need that. He needed Patrice, but Patrice was either at work or trying to straighten things out with Thillier. Survival was money, not work. Money might come from almost anywhere if you kept your eyes open. He hadn't succeeded in putting that weirdo François entirely out of his mind. For once he didn't agree with Patrice; his boy was being overcautious. There was no harm in at least finding out about the deal. Double your money. If he doubled his money only twice, he'd be set until fall. François had said he could always be reached through the Flore. He turned into an avenue that led up to the Ecole Militaire and headed for the nearest Métro. He'd like to have some good news for Patrice for a change.

Patrice was filled with dread as he approached the handsome old house on the Ile-St-Louis. The day was piercingly sweet and made him feel as if he were defiling it just by coming here. He had

184

first seen this street, with its trees leaning romantically over the river, seven years ago, and he still remembered the innocence and the boyish sense of adventure he had brought with him. The innocence hadn't survived long, but the sense of adventure had been intensified when Gérard had taken him to bed and introduced him to the pleasures that seemed to have been stored in his imagination, waiting to be realized from the moment he had become aware of his sexuality. It had not been a reluctant capitulation. He had been Gérard's lover, sequestered and shielded from the household's realities barely a week when he learned that his status was no different from that of the two older boys whose residence predated his.

The number of boarders (he soon thought of the place as a sort of school) fluctuated. There were never fewer than two and sometimes as many as six. Gérard's standards were high. He demanded some degree of physical beauty in face and body, and any boy who was particularly well-endowed between the legs was granted almost automatic admission. It took Patrice the first year to adapt to the basic house rule–total obedience in sexual matters. They were permitted, even encouraged to go to bed with each other, but any display of preferences, of emotional involvement, of love, was strictly forbidden. He had found it difficult at first to respond sexually to boys he disliked, but they were all taught tricks calculated to overcome the most deep-rooted resistance. After his body had been used in every possible way by men that he found actively repulsive, he had become an adept in simulating desire. Neither he nor any of them, while in residence, had been whores in the sense that money was paid for their services. Whatever value others placed on them accrued to Gérard's benefit.

They were recruited from all over France and across the borders in Germany and Italy and even North Africa. They shared one characteristic–they were all orphans or sons of widowed mothers. Patrice learned eventually that Gérard protected himself from the

185

law by insisting on being their legal guardian. The establishment was known throughout Paris as the *Cercle Vert*, green for youth and perversity, although only the habitués knew exactly what it was. It was primarily a social center for exclusive homosexual gatherings. The boys were there for Gérard's pleasure and to strengthen his hold on his influential friends. The boys met leaders of the arts and industry and politics. They were sent to good schools, and Gérard encouraged whatever talents, outside of bed, he might detect in them. The turnover was high because he lost interest in them as they approached manhood. He let them go to qualified suitors or arranged for them to complete their educations outside the home.

Patrice had been there two years when he sensed that the end was approaching for him, but a literary man of such worldwide celebrity that even Gérard deferred to him fell passionately in love with him, and he was kept on to satisfy his weekly demands. The literary man was followed by an elderly politician who had served several times as prime minister. By the time the politician's ardor had cooled, Patrice had become a fixture. He was good with the younger boys, helping them get through the traumas and confusions that he had experienced at the beginning. He had developed a diplomatic finesse that was useful on one occasion when scandal threatened. Despite Gérard's disdain for conventional affections, Patrice knew that he had established some obscure power over him. Even for the last year, living on his own, he had continued to act as a kind of house mother and sexual coach to newcomers who attracted him, under Gérard's active surveillance. He looked at his watch. Gérard had told him to come after lunch, sounding cordial enough and not surprised to hear from him. "After lunch" in Gérard's rigidly regulated life meant a quarter to three. He was on time.

He was admitted to the austerely magnificent first-floor apartment by a coarsely handsome manservant with whom he had shared many boys long ago and who was one of Gérard's few dis-

186

coveries who had sunk rather than risen in the world. When Gérard had discovered that the man was in love with a girl, he had promptly married him off and obliged him to take the first job he could get. They exchanged friendly greetings, and Patrice was informed that he was expected in the salon where coffee had just been served.

The big room with long windows giving onto the river was sparsely furnished with formal groupings of Louis XVI pieces and a few striking Renaissance treasures. The paintings and sculptures, half a dozen of the latter, were severely contemporary. Gérard was sitting on a sofa alongside a youth dressed like a schoolboy–slacks, pullover, white shirt with an open collar–and didn't rise for his visitor. Patrice went to him and took his outstretched hand and leaned over for the ritual kiss on the forehead that Gérard customarily bestowed on him. The youth had leaped to his feet while Gérard spoke a few words of introduction, and Patrice turned to him and received a kiss on the lips, a greeting that all Gérard's boys were taught to offer their male elders. He felt in the mouth that was pressed to his a tendency to linger, and he hastily pulled back. The boy was a bit taller than Patrice and slightly chubby, with dark curly hair and pert features and lingering traces of baby fat that made him look very young. Gérard's type. He had an cheerful grin that reminded Patrice of himself at that age. He was as friendly as a puppy. Patrice seated himself in a high-backed armchair, and the boy stayed with him, leaning against the chair above him and grinning down at him, giving the impression that he wanted to wag his tail and lick Patrice's face.

"It's so thrilling to meet Patrice at last," he said in a breathless rush. "We hear so much about you. Everything we do has to be just like Patrice or we never hear the end of it."

"That must get rather boring. Your name's Georges? Thanks for not hating me, Georges."

"I know you're the greatest lover in the world. Everybody says so. Now that I've seen you, I'm going to dream of finding out for myself."

Patrice glanced at Gérard. He was watching impassively, a faint trace of amusement in his face, as fascinating to Patrice as ever. Had he turned Georges loose to seduce him? He acknowledged the boy's efforts by taking his hand and exerting slight pressure. "We should've met sooner. You wouldn't have had to dream."

The boy took Patrice's hand in both of his and held it lightly on the front of his gray flannel slacks and moved almost imperceptibly against it. "You have an American lover. Have you sworn vows of fidelity?"

Patrice felt flesh hardening under the expensive fabric. He was sinking involuntarily into the sex-ridden atmosphere of his old school days. He started to remove his hand but didn't want to start out by making too much of a point of having rejected Gérard's training. He left his hand where it was and shifted in his seat to ease the slight stir of excitement in himself. "What makes you think he's my lover?" He looked back at Gérard. "He's a good friend. As a matter of fact, he's in love with a girl."

"How strange. Gérard says he's your lover. Wait till you see Christian. He's fantastic. He's older than I am, but I'm quite grown up in ways that matter."

"You are indeed." He looked up at the boy and winked. His hand was being held against imposing manhood. Perhaps not one of Gérard's major discoveries, but something he would ordinarily want to have a look at. He rejected the temptation but allowed his hand to be moved along it slowly and felt it lifting against confinement. He dropped his eyes to it. Its outlines were visible and its size obviously exaggerated by the bulk of cloth. He looked determinedly back at Gérard. "I haven't a great deal of time," he said, hearing a plea in his voice despite his resolution to take control of the situation. "I have to talk with you in private."

"Of course. Later. Christian will be here in a moment. He's going to show us his new dressing gown. I have allowed the boys to skip school this afternoon in your honor. They're so anxious to please the famous Patrice. I hope that you're not going to disappoint them."

Patrice's heart sank. Conditions were being imposed. He was to be the quid pro quo for Gérard's declaring a truce concerning Rod. His hand closed on stiffened flannel. "Georges knows he pleases me very much." The realization of how completely Gérard retained control made his voice falter. He looked up at the boy without seeing him. "Don't you, Georges?"

"I hope so." He darted his head down close to Patrice's and whispered. "It's going to happen if we don't watch out."

"I'm glad to see that you can at least still enjoy a quiet grope," Gérard said. "Let's abandon ourselves to pleasure for an hour or two, and then we can have a private talk if we must."

The way Gérard spoke of abandoning himself made it sound like work. "There's really no need for privacy," Patrice said, determined to force Gérard to make an explicit offer in return for what was expected of him. "You've met Rod now."

"Yes, that was quite a coincidence. Who would have guessed that little Nicole de la Vendraye's fiancée was your lover? He's a very handsome young man. Very intriguing. Does Nicole know about him?"

"Know what? Why should somebody who's in love with her be my lover? He's an extraordinary painter. I persuaded him to move in with me to save him money. He didn't tell her because–well, I warned him that a lot of people know about me. But now that you know the whole setup, he's going to. If you think you can make trouble by telling her, go ahead. He doesn't care."

"I see. There seems to have been a rather peculiar misunderstanding. If he's nothing but a friend, why have you exiled yourself from the scene of your erstwhile passions? We've missed you."

"I knew you wouldn't believe me. He means a great deal to me. I don't deny that. I've wanted to be free to do everything I could for him." His heart was beating rapidly, but all trace of his fear was gone. He had been bullied and fascinated over the years into thinking of Gérard as an omnipotent spirit of evil. Now with all his thoughts fixed on Rod, he saw him only as a rather commonplace, rather despicable, and entirely contemptible man. His final liberation had been accomplished in an instant. All that mattered was to remove any lingering suspicions he might have of Rod. "Are you going to give him an exhibition?"

"We shall see. I was afraid you were going to make a speech about the sanctity of love. Still, I don't find you quite convincing. If you have no lover, what's become of your sex life?

"That too," Patrice said. "I promised him when he moved in that there wouldn't be any boys." His heart was beating more and more rapidly with the effort of being untruthful about something more precious to him than life. He assured himself that nothing that happened here could touch him. He'd said he would do anything for Rod. Now, if necessary, he would prove it. "If you give him a show so that he can get married, that'll be the end of that," he said, praying that it wouldn't be.

"Then do I take it you're ready to return to the fold?" Gérard asked.

Patrice kept his eyes on his adversary while he lifted a reluctant hand and deftly unbuttoned the flannel slacks at his side. The boy made little yelping sounds, and his body jerked in an odd little dance of participation. Patrice pushed shirttails aside and an eager organ leaped out and filled his hand. He held it an instant while his eyes struck a bargain with Gérard, and then he turned and looked at it. As he expected it wasn't as big as it had appeared under wraps, but it was gratifyingly substantial. He leaned forward and offered it his expert attentions. He heard the boy gasp. In another few seconds his mouth was filled with the ejaculation. He swallowed and felt flesh begin to go slack and released it. He looked up at the boy and winked again. Georges sank down on the arm of the chair beside him looking dazed.

"Oh, Patrice," he whispered.

Patrice turned back to Gérard. He was sitting with a tight little smile of satisfaction on his lips. "Have I passed the test?"

"I'm delighted to see that you haven't changed after all. You always do that with such panache. I'm more than ever anxious for you to meet Christian. It should prove quite fascinating."

"I told you, I can't stay now. I have a job, remember." The aftertaste in his mouth made him want to cry with wounded pride, but the act was nothing; whatever fleeting excitement it had given him was only a sort of reflex action, a hangover from his old obsession with any big male part. The only body that could thrill him was Rod's, no matter how incomplete his experience of it was.

"The afternoon has begun so promisingly," Gérard said. "I'm sure you're valuable enough to your new employers to allow yourself a little time off. Perhaps you should have your old job back. In any case we still haven't really fully discussed your friend's exhibition."

"Then let's. When you see his work, you'll want to do it. You know now you can't have any personal objections to it."

"You remember how easily you always managed to have your way with me. If Germaine Powers is ready to put up the money and—ah, here's our laggard beauty."

Patrice's first impression was of a blaze of color lighting up the austere room as he turned and saw a young man entering. He was wearing a rich robe of heavy brocade that swept the ground, turquoise and jade and azure, shot with gold. He had a mane of thick blond hair artfully coifed in waves that swirled over his brow and ears and around the back of his neck. His enormous eyes were blue, his ornately sculptured mouth was crimson. He moved with a lordly tread.

"Christian! Angel!" Georges exclaimed. "Look. Here's Patrice."

The spectacular youth ignored the yelps of his puppy friend; he had eyes only for Gérard. He preened and paraded in front of his patron while the latter made appropriate comments about the robe. It was shaped and tailored to enhance the contours of what appeared to be a splendid body, and yet there was something fragile and feminine about the model despite his considerable height, his big bejeweled hands, and his big feet encased in burgundy needlepoint slippers. His nose and chin were strong and nicely formed, but his face gave the impression of being all eyes and mouth, a corrupt face despite its youth. Patrice guessed he must be at the outer limit of Gérard's age range, 18, even 19.

Gérard's spate of praise was more fulsome than Patrice had ever heard from him, but he checked it abruptly like a light being switched off. "We're being rude, my child. I haven't introduced you to our guest of honor. This is Patrice."

"Isn't it thrilling, angel?" Georges exclaimed from somewhere behind the chair. "We're finally meeting Patrice. You won't believe what just happened. He's thrilling."

Patrice saw huge mindless eyes turned on him, and then the startling youth drifted in his lordly fashion toward him. He rose to meet him. As long as he was here, he might as well live up to Gérard's expectations. Georges could be taught subtlety to offer himself less exuberantly, but he wondered if anything could jolt Christian out of his lethargic self-absorption. The youth stopped in front of him in a cloud of heady scent and leaned down to him. Patrice was ready for a perfunctory brush of lips against his. He gripped robed arms and opened his mouth and treated the boy to the fruits of his considerable experience. The effect was satisfactory. The body came alive against him. Soft lips worked with increasing abandon. When Patrice pulled back, the great empty eyes were wide, not with intelligence but with a startled lust.

"You're *exciting*," Christian breathed, the first words Patrice had heard him utter.

The embrace had somehow made the gorgeous robe look disreputable. It was open down to the waist, exposing a smooth chest. Glancing down, Patrice saw that the rich brocade was lifted slightly in the middle, suggesting that the body beneath it was entirely naked. As Christian started to move away, Patrice saw what looked like the heavy swing of a club giving the robe a more pronounced lift. He still knew what to do with a willing boy; the embrace had left him coldly detached.

192

"He's extraordinary, don't you think?" Gérard asked, immovable on the sofa.

"Yes, but I'm already quite fond of this baby," Patrice said, turning to Georges. The boy rushed forward from behind the chair and stood expectantly beside him. Patrice resumed his seat. Georges mirrored his move, dropping onto the arm of the chair and cuddling close with an arm around his new champion's shoulder. Patrice put a hand on his thigh and patted him.

Christian was arranging himself elaborately beside Gérard in a semi-lotus position with one leg crooked up under him, foot tucked against knee. He had shed his slippers. Under the triangle of draped brocade formed by his spread thighs, the swing of the club was still discernible as he settled himself. He put his hands on it and lingeringly arranged the draperies to display it to its best conspicuous advantage. This was surely one of Gérard's major acquisitions. Patrice determined not to let himself be mesmerized by it. He could feel enormous eyes fixed on him.

"I'm very pleased with both of them," Gérard said. "I suppose they arrived just after we last saw you. I'm expecting two more charmers in a week or two. We'll need your invaluable guidance. Or should I say—inspiration? I can't tell you how delighted I am to see you here again."

"Thanks. It was silly to get out of touch. I'll make sure Rod calls you tomorrow at the latest."

"You're not going to say you have to go again. I must admit, I'll feel much less favorably disposed toward a friend of yours if you treat us in such an unfriendly fashion."

Delivered in Gérard's oddly cold and penetrating tones, it was the crack of the whip. It had always struck terror into his depths. He wasn't frightened for himself any longer, but he still feared for Rod. "I honestly *have* to go. You can't think I want to leave these two without getting to know them better." He tried to cover an attack of nerves by filling his voice with all the regret he could muster.

"You hear, my children? I'm counting on your attractions to keep him. Really, my dear old companion. You don't want to hurt all our feelings, do you? You always bring out the best in our young friends. I'm looking forward to seeing you with these two."

Out of the corner of his eye, he was aware of Christian stirring again, rearranging his draperies. "I'm looking forward to it too. We'll try to–" Georges ran his hand possessively over his shoulder and ducked down and kissed his hair.

"Don't go," he begged.

Patrice looked up at him distractedly and patted his leg again. When he turned back his eyes flew uncontrollably to the other youth. He had flung open the robe and let it drop back over his shoulders so that he was as naked as he could get without removing it altogether. Only a flap remained as precarious covering for the club that stood up now against one thigh, a gaudily wrapped package. The body was a figure in alabaster, fragile and extraordinarily smooth, with no strong muscular definition, a body created out of erotic fantasies. Patrice wanted to make a dash for the door.

"Magnificent, isn't he?" Gérard asked softly.

"Yes. I–" His eyes were trying to bore through the remaining covering, and he couldn't think of anything to say.

"Doesn't he remind you of Alain?"

"A bit, I suppose." Long ago he and a boy named Alain had attempted to conduct a secret love affair. When Gérard had found them out, he had debauched them both so thoroughly in each other's presence that they had quickly despised each other. The memory helped him to collect himself.

"As you can easily see, there's one quite spectacular difference– one of the most spectacular that even you and I have come across. Are you still in a great hurry?"

"I don't–" he tried helplessly to direct his attention away from the gaudy wrapping. He wanted to shout obscenities at the room in general and get away. "About the exhibition–I'd like to know you're planning to go through with it," he managed to say calmly.

"As I told you, when you wish to have your way with me, you usually succeed. I think we can say that you can count on it, now that I see we have your full attention." Gérard reached for the robe and gave it a little jerk, and the club was finally unveiled. It slowly lifted from the thigh where it had been resting and stood upright, no longer a club but a majestic scepter. Patrice felt all his face going numb, and he ran the tip of his tongue along his lips while his eyes adjusted to its magnitude. It was an enormous phallic assertion.

The youth rose with a breathtaking unfolding of his body and let the robe slide down his arms. The phenomenal phallus seemed to lift free of the body, growing in stature and majesty. Patrice remembered a few others like it, but he had never seen a body so suited to carrying this glory. He watched the phallus advance toward him, not swinging now but solidly immobile in imperious extension.

"Isn't it fantastic?" Georges said excitedly. "Every time I see it, I almost faint."

"Didn't you hear him, my little one?" Christian asked. "He wants us to persuade him to stay. Take your clothes off."

Patrice's eyes were fixed within reach while he determinedly obliterated everything outside it, everything that was precious to him, everything in him that was dedicated to Rod. A shudder of dread and desire passed through him as he prepared to resume his duties as master of the revels.

Patrice hurried through darkening streets. Winter had returned with the setting sun, and he was pursued by demons. Laughter and cries of ecstasy, accompanied by Gérard's sinister voice, rang in his ears. The feel of young bodies tumbling about with his was still in him. After the months of cautiously giving only what was wanted of him, of holding back, of disciplining his natural responses so as not to offend, all of him had been used again for pleasure and passion and young lust. He had enjoyed it.

It was a fact he couldn't get around, and it plunged him into a howling prison of despair. Everything good and clean and decent

195

that he thought he had discovered in himself was a sham. He had plunged headlong back into the vicious world that Gérard had taught him was the only real one.

He had done it for Rod. He had thought he could stand outside it and engage in acts that no longer meant anything to him, but the corruption that had been planted in him had proved a sturdy growth and had lost him his love. He could never belong to Rod again. He had enjoyed it.

He would go on serving Rod in every way he knew how, but even if his friend did not notice a change, the corruption in himself would eventually destroy it all. That was the lesson the afternoon had taught him. He had attempted an act of dedication that was beyond his powers. He tried to drive away the afternoon's memories and felt as if he were beating his head against prison walls. He was trapped in his old obsessions. He longed for Rod to perform some miracle that would make him his again. He was flooded with unshed tears for his loss.

He became aware that his rapid pace was carrying him toward home. He veered off into another street. It was too soon. He couldn't face his lost love yet. He would waste an hour at work and try to recover some outer semblance of peace of mind. He had to make sure he had his story straight. There would be no secret about his having seen Gérard. He had gone to convince him that Rod's version of their life together was the truth and had succeeded. Gérard was prepared to go ahead with whatever arrangements could be worked out with Germaine as soon as he saw one of Rod's pictures. To make it all up, he would have to drop in a word about seeing Gérard again from time to time as evidence of their reconciliation. Rod wouldn't like it, but he could hardly object to cordial relations with the man who was going to give him a show. A show. Rod was going to have a full-scale show in Paris. It was almost too good to believe. If he concentrated on what he had accomplished for Rod, his guilt might seem somewhat mitigated.

Rod paced his working area impatiently. It was time for Patrice to get home. He had wasted the day, but at least he had come to an important decision, and he had things to discuss that he could discuss only with Patrice. He hoped he was planning to have dinner at home.

The minute he heard the key in the lock, he ran to meet Patrice and threw his arms around him and gave him an affectionate kiss. He was surprised to feel his boy resisting it, and he let him go with slightly hurt reluctance. He was pleased to see bundles in his string shopping bag. "I've been waiting for you. Are we going to have dinner together?"

"Of course, if you wish it." Patrice wondered if he had only imagined that Rod's greeting was more loving than it had ever been. It was a greater punishment than if he had turned from him with disgust. How could he have *enjoyed* the things he had done? It required an agonized effort to face the undeserved love in his loved one's eyes without shrinking from him with shame. "I bought some things."

"Good. I've got a thousand things to tell you." He removed Patrice's cape and beret and gave a few touches to his hair to arrange it the way Patrice liked it to look, then took the string bag. He put an arm around him and started for the living room. He still felt what he interpreted as resistance in his boy. He gave him a hug and a little shake. "What's the matter, baby? I somehow have the feeling you're not all that glad to see me. Did that girl finally get you?"

"It was written in the stars. We spent an afternoon of mad passion. I never wish to touch a boy again." It helped to talk nonsense that had some trace of truth in it. He was going to have to employ all the ruses at his command to keep everything going in a routine cheerful way. Rod's eyes were sharp.

Rod laughed. "I should've known it. Just when I'm turning into a great lover. We'd better have a drink."

Patrice filled their glasses while Rod dropped the bag in the kitchen. Rod put his arm around his boy again as they went to their accustomed places. "Now listen. I've made some decisions. First, I'm not

197

going to fuck around with Thillier and Germaine and all that. What I need is money, and my work shouldn't have anything–" A small sound escaped Patrice. Rod stopped and looked at him questioningly. Patrice shook his head and lifted his glass to his lips. Rod went on. "Anyway, I went by the Flore and left word for your friend François to meet me there at noon tomorrow. I'm going to find out what it's all about. If I've got to get some money, I'm going to get it in ways that don't affect my work. Last night. Today. I can't take anymore of it."

Patrice somehow managed to swallow a sip of his drink. He didn't think he could speak. "It's all arranged," he choked out in a dead voice. "Your show. He's going to do it. He realizes it was crazy to think I'm your lover when you have a girl. All you have to do is show him a picture and tell Madame Powers to arrange everything with him."

Rod reacted with hilarity. "Oh, baby. Wait until I tell you. I've screwed that up but good." He told Patrice about his lunch and ended with more, rather shamefaced laughter.

"But you can apologize," Patrice persisted, still forcing his words out. "She sounds as if she would put up with anything from you."

"Maybe, but I don't want any more of it. That's final. I've tried whoring and I'm no good at it. It might be difficult if my work didn't get mixed up in it. We'll have to find me a rich lady who's never heard of painting. What's the matter, baby?"

Patrice hadn't known that misery could cut so deep. He had done it for nothing. He no longer had even the small recompense of thinking that he'd accomplished something for Rod. He struggled to keep from looking as if he felt like dying. "Nothing's the matter. It's just that–well, I didn't like seeing Gérard very much. I wish I'd known. I need not have bothered. At least after this afternoon, I don't think he'll worry about you anymore."

"I'm sorry, baby. Everything just sort of happened at once, and I couldn't take anymore of it. You'll come see François with me tomorrow, won't you? I arranged it for your lunch hour especially."

"Very well," he agreed listlessly, not really taking in what they were talking about, "but I don't like to see him very much either."

"At least there won't be anything personal about it. He can do something with my money or the hell with it. Don't you understand? I don't like whoring, not just for Nicole's sake but for you. I guess what's happening *is* pretty crazy, but at least we know it means something to all of us in various ways. With Germaine it was just sex and wanting something in return. I hated it."

Patrice took another swallow of his drink. A knife was being turned in the wound. If he could tell himself truthfully that he had hated it, perhaps he could confess and get back to Rod somehow, across Christian, across Georges. He had hated it, but it had also satisfied a need. "Just sex. Isn't what you do with me just sex? I mean for you." He realized he was trying to exonerate himself with some vague accusation against Rod and hated himself even more.

"It isn't sex at all. You know that, baby. It's you and me. I've tried for sex because I know how much it means to you. You love me, and that's the way it works for you. When people love each other, all sorts of things can happen that wouldn't ordinarily. I love you more every day. There's a line somewhere that I feel I'm getting awfully close to crossing. God knows what'll happen if I do."

Patrice sprang up and took a few steps toward him. Then he turned abruptly and drifted toward the kitchen.

"Hey, wait a minute. There *is* something wrong. What is it, baby?"

Patrice stopped but didn't turn. "Nothing. Honestly. Seeing Gérard upset me. You know what he does to me."

"I told you not to bother with him. We can manage very well without him."

"Of course. I'd better do something about dinner." He continued on his way.

Rod rose and followed him. Only something seriously wrong could dim his monkey's high spirits. He stayed with him while he prepared the simple meal he had brought home. The recent changes in the pattern of their lives had caused a falling off of the cuisine, and Rod was ready to get back to the old routine now that he would be again on a once-a-week basis with Nicole. He wooed and cajoled his favorite cook and had the impression that he was making him forget whatever was bothering him.

Patrice served them in the living room, and they discussed their day's encounters in greater detail. Patrice filled out the dialogue he was supposed to have had with Gérard, eliminating the two witnesses to it.

"He more or less expects to start seeing me again, for me to be part of the household as I used to be. He even talked about giving me my job back."

"Well, that's out. I mean, you said it had a lot to do with taking boys to him. Forget him."

"Yes, but it's difficult. Once I'd convinced him that he was wrong about us, there seemed no reason for things not to be as they were. I agreed so that there wouldn't be any difficulties about your show."

"All the more reason not to have anything to do with Thillier and his lousy gallery. I'm really sorry I let you get sucked into it again, even for an afternoon."

"There are things I suppose you shouldn't do even for the person you love most in the world. It was a mistake." Rod's sweet loving solicitude was beginning to break through Patrice's misery. Was there still something to hope for? He could think of only one thing that might save him, an impossibility, but everything that they had shared had seemed impossible until it had happened.

They changed the subject, but Rod felt that contact between them remained slightly out of focus. At moments when their eyes met, he sensed something calculating in Patrice's, something almost flirtatious, which puzzled him. There had never been anything overtly sexual in his boy's manner toward him. If there had been, he would've probably taken to his heels right at the start. It was another wrench to the familiar shape of their relationship, and he wondered if his boy was about to spring one of his surprises.

They had a few glasses of wine after dinner in front of the empty fireplace. It was still early when Patrice stood and stretched. "I'm going to have a bath and wash the day away. I must be new and fresh to welcome you back to your bed."

Again Rod caught a flirtatious look as he turned away. Something to do with this morning's incident? He expected repercussions, but he hoped to avoid more emotional strain. After the day's strange disturbances in his mind, the weird shifts of perspectives, he was looking forward to his return to the comfortable bed and to a good night's sleep. He finished his wine and rose and puttered about in his studio area getting things ready for the next day's work. He'd be interrupted at noon, but that shouldn't take long. It would be wonderful to work again without a thought of shows and galleries.

After he had studied the unfinished canvas on the easel and lined up colors and brushes, he went to the kitchen door and called to Patrice. "Can I brush my teeth? I've bathed enough for today."

"Of course, *chéri*. Come in." He gave a final touch to his hair, and his heart sprang up. If he could lead Rod to uninhibited sexual union, his dream of ideal platonic love might be replaced by the satisfaction of his body's passion. All the monumental cocks in the world would be no danger then. He would be trespassing on territory he had conceded to Nicole, but he could no longer pretend that he was capable of monkish self-sacrifice. He had been trained as a whore; it was all he had to fall back on. He felt Rod approaching, and it affected him in the way it always did, in the way he wanted it to.

Rod stopped halfway across the kitchen. Patrice was standing in front of the mirror over the sink. His hair was loosely combed in soft androgynous waves. His charming boy-girl back glowed with cleanliness. Clean smells filled the room. As Rod watched, Patrice turned with a sensual shifting of his balance and displayed himself without reluctance or reticence.

Rod wondered why Patrice looked so different before he realized that the robe was gone. He gazed, for the first time in its entirety, at an aroused naked male body. His eyes widened. Was it possible

201

that a boy, all exquisite balance and clean spare line, was more aesthetically satisfying than a girl? Sex had blinded him to the question. Patrice was an entrancing priapic youth from a pagan vase painting. For a moment Rod wanted to be naked too and have him on the kitchen floor. He wanted to make love to him. The realization came so easily that he was scarcely aware that all his feelings had altered. Having grown to love Patrice, he found it quite natural to want his glowing young body.

Their eyes met, and they exchanged secret little smiles as they moved to each other. Neither spoke. The silence became taut with unspoken questions. Rod reached for the slim erection and let his fingers stray over infinitely smooth skin. He felt it swell, and Patrice swayed his hips to encourage the caress. Rod's eyes registered one of the strange shifts in his mind's perspective. He was confronted with a shamelessly inviting stranger, a Patrice he could place now in the fragmentary scenes he had sometimes conjured up when his boy referred to his past, lurid sketches whose details he had never wanted to fill in, perverse, obscene, secret. He was the central figure in the unimaginable—wanton and unnervingly desirable but beyond the known range of Rod's desires. His scalp prickled, and he turned quickly away and bent over the sink. He felt as totally at odds with himself as he had this morning when he had fled from Patrice to the toilet.

What was expected of him now? Events had crowded him, imposing loss after loss, until even his boy seemed to be slipping from him. He had been odd all evening, first withdrawn, then provoking him sexually in a way he never had. Was it possible to make love to a boy in the way he made love to a girl? Patrice seemed to be inviting him, daring him to abandon restraint. Had he gone so far that he could suspend distinctions between male and female? If so, he was only a step away from falling in love with his boy. A shiver ran down his spine. He was torn between flight and surrender. He had pledged himself to discovery. He had drawn no line there. He rinsed his mouth and spat into the sink.

Patrice waited, worshiping the power in the shoulders and hips that were turned to him. His heart was beating rapidly as the conviction grew that he had depressed more of himself than necessary. Rod had reached a "line," and he had failed to lead himself across it. With nothing left to lose, he was determined to do so now.

Rod dried his hands, and they exchanged a look in the mirror that neither quite dared to interpret. Patrice silently led the way to the bedroom. Rod pulled off clothes as they went. Patrice almost dreaded seeing him without them for fear the afternoon had robbed the worshiped body of the special glory his eyes had always seen in it.

He opened out the sheets and made sure that everything was ready for them. He glanced across at Rod as he moved away from the armoire, and his breath caught as always at his nakedness. His manly beauty could have no equal; nothing could diminish the impact of his virility. They came together in a few quick strides and put their arms around each other and exchanged a kiss that swept many questions away, although they each had different ones. When they drew apart Rod's eyes held Patrice's intently.

"It feels like a long time, baby. This morning–something's changed. I think–maybe I really want you." Rod seized Patrice and lifted him. They tumbled into bed.

Patrice wriggled away and scrambled to his knees and faced him. "Are we going to make love? I mean really?"

"We'll soon see." Rod gathered himself together and butted his head into Patrice's stomach and toppled him over and took possession of him with a mouth that was no longer fastidiously awkward. He was suddenly discovering passion that he hadn't known existed in him. Within moments, Patrice escaped with a joyful cry and slid in against him and faced him.

"Something's changed, all right," he said against Rod's mouth. They rolled and pitched about on the bed, vying with each other in sexual audacity. Patrice was a shameless leader, but Rod quickly

203

learned that he could follow. A battle raged within him. His body was learning how to keep Patrice his. In fleeting moments of disengagement, his mind recoiled from what he was doing. How long could it contain his warring spirit? He felt as fragmented as if one of those bombs had finally gotten him.

He drove the boy to a pitch of excitement so intense that he found himself contending with a hard, demanding male. Without breaking the flow of their bodies' ecstasies, Patrice prepared them for coupling, and Rod entered him in easy domination of the masculinity he had himself uncovered, claiming it, absorbing it into himself, becoming—master? protector? confirmed lover, satisfied and satisfying? Fragments.

They reached a climax together and lay in silence while each tried to define the new balance that had been established between them. Rod had made him his boy again, removed him from wanton scenes of the unimaginable, but he had gone a long way toward accepting the unimaginable for himself. His mind seemed to teeter toward chaos in the face of his body's adaptability.

Patrice was fighting back tears.

"I can do anything with you now," Rod admitted at last.

"Let me up, darling," Patrice said abruptly. He left, recognizing despairingly all that they had missed. There wasn't a particle of him that Rod hadn't known and loved and used, and his body's needs were finally fulfilled. It was there for the future because they were true lovers now, but he couldn't unlearn the afternoon's lesson. He would never belong to Rod as he had dreamed of belonging to him—with a complete, unquestioning surrender of himself. He was closer to total happiness than he had known was possible and knew that it was too late for it to mean what he had thought it would mean. They were lovers—nothing more. He had dreamed of much, much more.

He returned and washed his lover proudly and climbed into bed beside him. Rod put an arm around him and held him close. "I guess I better marry you, monkey," he said.

"I accept."

"I'm not kidding, really. You've become so much a part of my life. I don't see how it can change. If I ever go back to New York, we'll fix it so that you can go too. Nicole will have to know about us–not necessarily the gory details but enough so that she can guess there might be something going on if she wants to. As you say, she probably wouldn't take it seriously." He thought he might be able to talk it into the shape of a life he could imagine living. Rod lifted himself on an elbow and leaned over him and stroked Patrice's hair. "I am sort of in love with you, I suppose. It doesn't sound so peculiar. You know, don't you?"

"Yes, I know. We're just finding out. I'm still amazed. I didn't expect it to go this far." He felt the magnificent erection beginning to fill out and gather strength against him. He hoped it would subside. He had led Rod far enough.

"Can anybody be in love with two people at once?"

"Why not? If one is a girl and one a boy, it must be very different."

"It is." He kissed Patrice on the lips and inched closer to him. "No matter how queer you're making me, I still want Nicole. I don't expect that to change. Do you?"

"No." He could probably dispose of Nicole now but only because he had brought Rod down to his level. He didn't want to keep him there. "You want children for one thing," he added firmly. "You need a wife. Even when we get married, which I'm planning to do tomorrow, I'm afraid you'll want a lady wife too. And other boys, I think."

"Other boys? Why should I want that? You don't count. You're a monkey. Other girls, maybe."

"No. You've always wanted to be free of girls, free of anybody you might need too much. Much of you is only for your work. Boys are nice for loving and leaving. Nicole must be very good and very clever to know how to make it right for you. Oh, *mon amour.* I've wanted so many foolish things with you. And now we have everything. For tonight."

"That's just it. Why tonight? Did it have something to do with what I did this morning?" He was still trying to come to grips with what it meant for him, trying to assemble a more stable self that could encompass it. "Now that it's happened, it's hard to understand why it didn't long ago."

"It's odd. If you had been queer–I've heard people say gay. Is that better?–if you had been gay and I had–if my life had been different–would we have fallen madly in love and lived happily after? I have doubts. If you had been gay, I wouldn't have fallen in love with you and that would have been that. You've been my god. I've worshiped you. You know that."

"Yes, but I'm not sure it's good for me to be worshiped. It's better like this. I'd started to wave my cock around as if it were the only one in the world. Only queers do that."

"Perhaps you are more queer than you know." The thrust of flesh against him diminished, and he drew a quick breath of relief. He wasn't ready for his own body to be put to the test again. "You don't hate the idea, do you?"

"After tonight? Oh, my baby." He gave Patrice a little hug. "But how do we explain Nicole? Either I'm both ways and have to get used to the idea, or you have to get used to being my quirk. You can't say I'm not turning into a willing lover, whichever way it is."

"You're a divine lover, *mon amour*. Better than–better than any boy I've ever known." He was close to a confession but knew it would only be self-indulgence, a relief for him but for Rod an unpleasant discovery that he had allowed himself to be seduced by a skilled whore's tricks. He realized that his greatest responsibility now was to keep up the pretense of being worth loving. "We're both tired. It has been 24 hours to be forgotten, except for the way it's ended." He reached for the light ands turned it off.

"You're the nicest quirk I know," Rod said, stretching out with a sigh in the comfortable bed. Perhaps everything would make sense in the morning.

It was a little after noon and another magical day. Rod's eyes lit up, and the little tightening of anxiety in his chest eased as he saw Patrice emerge from the crowd and come swinging into the Flore. They shook hands in the French way, their hands lingering together until Patrice had seated himself. Their knees touched under the table, and they looked at each other and smiled.

"This is OK," Rod said with an optimistic renewal of his recent high spirits. "If this weather goes on, I'll want to come out and meet you every day. You want a beer? We have time." He handed Patrice the note François had left with the *caissière*. "I've forgotten where rue Monsieur is."

"Not far." Patrice glanced at the note and nodded and handed it back. "Ten minutes. It's a good address."

"That's reassuring. Come on. Don't look so disapproving, " Rod said.

"Not disapproving—yet. Worried. You didn't bring much money with you, did you?"

"It's too soon for that. I hope it doesn't turn out to be a total fraud. It's so wonderful not thinking about Mr. Kappenstein."

"I understand, *chéri*. Artists shouldn't have to think about their work for paying the rent or for babies or for anything. In time I'm sure we'll find you a patron, not like Germaine or Gérard, but a true patron who cares about your painting and nothing else. That's what we should be looking for, not playing crooked games with François."

"But just think. If I let him do whatever he does with $1,000 just twice, I'll have $3,000 and no more worries until fall."

"Have you told Nicole about François?"

"No. I'm sure she won't like it any more than you do. Why have I asked you two to marry me? Actually, I have a feeling she doesn't want to marry nearly as much as you do." He saw the mischief spring up in Patrice's eyes, and they burst out laughing. Another beer was put in front of them, and they drank lazily in the sun. "The next time I talk to her, I'll tell her I've moved," Rod said, having reached that point in his thoughts. "I'll tell her you're queer in case she's heard of you or finds out and thinks I'm trying to keep it a secret, OK? I'll make a slight point about sleeping on the sofa, not much of a one. She can draw her own conclusions as we go along. Would you mind cooking for us, monkey? I'd like to ask her for dinner."

"It would be very exciting."

It wasn't the word Rod would have chosen. The light of his happiness was fading already, as it seemed to do easily these days. He felt a terrible hollowness in what he'd been saying. The battle he had provoked in himself last night had left him still feeling deeply fragmented. Every effort he made to regain a grip on some inner reality increased the sense of fragmentation. Had he gone too far? Was there a rule about bringing his girl and his boy together that even he couldn't break? Had something happened within him that he still didn't know about but which demanded that he make a choice between them? Perhaps money still stood in the way of understanding. If he could stop worrying about money, he'd be able to think straight about things that mattered.

"It's time," Patrice said. "The note says 12:30. We'll be only a few minutes late."

They paid and set off at a brisk pace. Patrice guided them across a maze of intersecting angled streets and along the straight line of the rue Babylon, and in just less than the ten minutes he had predicted, they were standing in front of a golden oak door. Rod pushed the bell, and François appeared before them.

"Hi there. Come on in," he said, brisk and expressionless. "You've brought your cute friend. I get it—the buddy system." He shook hands with both of them, and the cold contact reminded Rod of how much he disliked him. He couldn't imagine François's doing anything decent or straightforward or without calculation. He was made for petty cruelty and shady deals. He led them across an entry and through double-glass doors into a vastly overfurnished room, all dark upholstery, dark pictures, and bric-a-brac. A tall old man rose at their entrance. A round little old woman was embedded like a raisin in a great cake of a chair. "My grandparents," François said and performed careless introductions. They all shook hands with each other. "Go ahead and start lunch," he said in French to the old people. "I have some business with my friends. I'll join you in a moment."

The old man bowed in a courtly fashion in front of the little old woman, and the couple marched through another pair of glass doors into what Rod saw was a darkly furnished dining room. François waved his visitors into chairs that engulfed them in upholstery.

"Been thinking my deal over, have you?" François asked Rod. "You're a smart cookie. You can't beat it. Did you bring some money with you?"

"Of course not. I don't know anything about it. You'd better explain a few things." Rod was observing the old couple seated at table within the frame of the glass doors, performing like actors in a silent film. He noticed the ceremony with which they treated each other to exchange remarks. Absurd and old-fashioned but charming compared to their grandson's brusque manner.

"The less you know, the better for you, mister," François said in his fake Americanese. "You've got the picture. You invest your capital at 100% interest. What more do you want?"

"How do you do it?"

"I take a little trip and do some people a favor. How much have you got?"

"I was thinking about maybe $1,000. It depends."

"A grand, huh?" François appeared to ponder it but was obviously impressed. "None of these bums around here have any dough. That's why they stay bums. It's nice to talk to somebody with some class. When can I have it?"

"I haven't said that you can. I'm still waiting to hear what you do with the money."

"Listen. You don't want to know, see. You're still worrying about letting your money out of your sight? I could maybe fix that."

"How do you mean? If I don't let the money out of my sight, how come I won't know what you're doing with it?" He saw the old man lift his glass to his tiny wife and suddenly wondered if his rebellion would look to an impartial observer as unwarranted as this youth's rejection of the old couple's charming ways. Could he too be considered an affront to decency and simple morality? He glanced at Patrice and wondered if they should leave.

"It's not quite that simple," François commented with a thin smile. "A real team. All right. The kid's pretty, but he's a lot tougher than he looks."

"Do you want to do it?" Rod asked his boy.

"I don't see why you should go with him. He's obviously not going to tell us what it's about, but I think you can trust him."

"Why should I?" he turned back to François. "You have a car?"

"Of course. We'll drive down."

"OK. If you let me keep the keys when we're separated, it's a deal."

"Cagey, aren't you." François seemed to hesitate. "Taking taxis. I don't like to change my routine. It might be unlucky."

Rod saw the old woman rise from the table and gather up dishes. The grandfather dabbed at his mouth with a napkin and looked at the group in his living room. Rod felt like an intruder, a spoiler.

"What did you do with the message I left you?" François demanded.

"Nothing." Rod felt for it in a pocket and pulled it out. François reached for it and tore it into several pieces and made a ball of it and dropped it onto the table beside him. "We don't want to leave things around that could prove a connection between us."

"That's pretty dumb. What about the *caissière?*"

"You don't have to worry about her. I tip her plenty. She wouldn't want to lose a good customer."

"Do you ever get into trouble with this business of yours?" Patrice asked.

Rod saw the old man rise and come to the glass doors and open them. "Your grandmother is about to serve the roast," he said.

"I'll be there when I'm finished," the grandson replied curtly. The old man caught Rod's eye and seemed to like what he saw there and continued into the room toward him. Rod rose politely. The old man was

210

dressed in a dark business suit and an old-fashioned hard collar and wore a gold stickpin in his necktie. His mouth looked surprisingly sweet and youthful under a neatly clipped white moustache. He reached into an inner jacket pocket and withdrew a wallet.

"You're an American?" he asked. "Fine people. I'm always pleased when François makes friends with Americans." He opened what turned out to be a leather folder containing two photographs and handed it to Rod. The latter looked at young intense faces, a man and a girl. "My son. François's parents," the grandfather explained. "Perhaps he hasn't told you. As far as we can learn, they were killed by the Germans the day before you Americans liberated Paris. Having their child to care for gave us a reason for going on living. Life is hard and cruel, but we've found our consolation in him, in giving him the chance in life that his father didn't have. That's why I'm delighted he's making American friends. You are, after all, the leader of the world today."

"I'm not much of a leader," Rod mumbled uncomfortably, returning the folder. Why didn't he clear out? He was ashamed of being here under such false pretenses.

"You must forgive me if I've embarrassed you with private matters. The old can never fully understand the young. If François has certain shortcomings, we must always remember that he has had the great handicap of being brought up by people so much older than he is. Are your parents living, sir?"

"Yes."

"You're very fortunate."

"I'm sure I am," Rod agreed in deference to this grave exposure of the old gentleman's tragic preoccupations. He hadn't felt particularly grateful for his parents' survival for some time, but in this land of orphans, he was beginning to be aware of something lacking, a break in the chain of tradition that left everybody terribly exposed and dependent on their individual capacities for improvisation. He was, in a sense, an orphan too. This awareness had the effect, perhaps intended by the old gentleman, of softening his feelings toward his partner in whatever crime they were planning.

211

"I don't want to interrupt you young men." The old man returned the folder to his inner pocket and shook hands with Rod. He turned to Patrice, who rose, and shook hands with him. He stopped briefly in front of his grandson. "Try not to let your food get cold." He returned slowly to the dining room and closed the doors behind him as the old woman placed a platter in front of his place at table.

Rod faced François. "Is that it? We leave in the morning? You'll have $2,000 for me at noon on Monday?"

"Check. If we leave by 9 A.M., we can be in Marseille by Sunday afternoon without getting arrested for speeding. You'll have the dough, won't you?"

"Of course. That's the whole point, isn't it?"

Rod asked a few more needless questions as he tried to convince himself that this simple transaction was going to solve his financial problems. He tried to get Patrice to take part in the discussion, but there seemed nothing to say. They agreed to meet in front of Patrice's building, and François let them out.

As soon as they were in the street, Rod threw an arm around his boy and gave him a big hug in a burst of relief at being back in the familiar world. "Is everything all right, baby?"

"It seems so. If the weather stays like this, it will be very pleasant driving to Marseille with you. I wish François didn't have to come with us."

"Yeah. For a minute there I almost wanted to back out of it. The old boy was so nice and sad that it seemed shitty to use his place for that kind of deal. But hell, it's not my fault François is the way he is. *I* didn't launch him on a life of crime."

"No, it's not your fault, *chéri*." Day before yesterday it would have hurt Patrice to hear his god resort to such a banal justification, but he was still suffering too deeply from his own imperfections to judge another's.

"Don't you think it was a good idea to suggest going with him?" Rod asked, anxious to feel that Patrice was in this with him.

"Perhaps, but I don't worry about that part of it. He's been around very long, and I've never heard that he cheats or lies about money. Of course, if he says nothing, it's easy not to lie."

Rod chuckled, welcoming the mischievous note. "He's got saying nothing down to a fine art. Do you have any idea what it's about?"

"No. It's difficult to imagine what could make such a good profit. He surely makes as much for himself as will make for you. A few years ago it might have been something to do with the black market but there's little of that anymore. I suppose it must be drugs, but I thought drugs were organized on a very big scale."

"Me too. The Mafia and all that. A thousand dollars is peanuts to them. I guess having dollars is the main thing. Think of it, monkey. In a month we might have $5,000 and no more worries until money comes in from the show. That's what counts."

"It does. I'm thinking of it."

"We better grab a bite to eat. I'll take care of the money when you go back to work."

When he was alone Rod called Nicole. She said that she was feeling much better than she had been before.

"The doctor says that tomorrow I can go back to all my wicked ways. Shall we have a Saturday night celebration, my beloved?"

"God, sweetheart, I'm ready for one but here's the thing. I'm going away for the weekend with some guys I know. It's too complicated to explain, but it may be a way of making some money."

Going away for the weekend to make some money? How very mysterious."

"Making money is the most mysterious thing I know. At least it has nothing to do with my work. How about tonight?"

"I think we mustn't, my darling. I feel so nearly right that I wouldn't trust myself, and the doctor says not before tomorrow. How are all of Germaine's glorious plans for you?"

"She was beginning to get tiresome. She was acting yesterday as if she were planning to take over my whole life. I told her not to bother."

"I'm rather relieved, my darling. If she'd turned you into a success overnight, I would have felt left out of it."

"Oh, listen, speaking of money. I've decided to move my stuff into the studio later today. It's silly to go on paying for the hotel. I've just found my new roommate is a friend of Gérard Thillier. I gather you know what that means."

"I have an idea. Is he a beautiful blond child?"

"No. Small and dark. Very nice. You'll like him. Germaine was planning to get me hooked up with Thillier. That was another thing I didn't want. I feel as if everything is getting organized again after some sort of total catastrophe. I guess your trouble threw me for more of a loop than I realized. I'm sorry about the weekend, honey. We'll make it Monday, won't we? I'll call you as soon as I get back. You can go on using the hotel if you want to leave a message."

"Shall I make a date for dinner later if Beauty calls again?"

"Sure. Anytime. Get lots of rest and be ready for a big night. I love you, sweetheart."

He went to the bank and left with all the money he had in the world folded into a small wad of cash provided, in defiance of currency controls, by a family friend on Rod's assurance that it would be returned at the beginning of the week. Germaine's money was his only cushion against something going wrong in Marseille.

He and Patrice were out in front of the building the next morning a bit before 9 o'clock and had been waiting only a few minutes when an inconspicuous four-door sedan drew up and François signaled to them. Rod sat in front with him. Patrice dropped a small bag containing their few necessities into the back seat and sat beside it.

Now that they were embarked on the venture, Rod wanted to see the best in their leader, and he immediately approved of his driving. François maneuvered expertly through the morning traffic, getting ahead of the pack without taking risks. They were soon passing Fontainebleau and heading south. The passengers settled down for the long trip, having offered to take turns at the wheel and been turned down. The day was less dazzling than the last two, but the weather was good for driving. Rod and Patrice found plenty to comment on in a winter landscape of great charm and frequent beauty. François joined in from time to time. Rod began to feel that the omens were auspicious—he was going to make some money without having to work for it, with a pleasant drive through France thrown in.

They stopped in a small town for a simple lunch. François abstemiously limited himself to a single glass of wine, and the other two shared the rest of the bottle and were feeling relaxed and mildly festive when they returned to the car. They got into the backseat together, and the afternoon became a chauffeur-driven tour of spectacular Burgundy country. It was getting dark when they came out of the hills into Lyon.

"I know a good cheap hotel about 15 miles south of here," François said. "We can stop there and be all set for an easy run into Marseille tomorrow."

Something he had read made Rod wonder if it was wise to let François decide where they would stay, but after the cheerful afternoon it was only a fleeting thought, and he made no objections. They had another good meal and more wine, and when they had finished he was in the mood for a convivial evening. But he found that he couldn't play off Patrice as usual. Was his boy still disapproving, still worried?

François pushed his chair back from the table. "You two have a good time. I like plenty of sleep."

Rod withdrew his attention from Patrice long enough to remember his stipulation. "You better let me have the keys," he said. Because the distrust that inspired the arrangement had been in abeyance all day, he felt obliged to add an apologetic note. "Don't get me wrong. I trust you, but that's the way we said we'd do it, and we might as well stick to it."

"Help yourself." The keys were tossed onto the table. They all shook hands and wished each other goodnight.

"One thing about him," Rod said when François was gone, "it's awfully easy to forget he's around."

"I could say that about everybody when I'm with you."

Rod looked at his boy lovingly. "We're all right, monkey. I guess we'll have an early night too. This isn't the liveliest village in France." He looked around at the empty provincial dining room. "The deserted inn. A perfect place for skullduggery."

When they'd locked themselves into their small room, Rod put the money and the keys in a sock and tucked the little bundle under the head of the mattress. He looked at Patrice and laughed. "I feel pretty silly, but I have to put the money somewhere. It's a lot to leave lying around." They undressed and got into the double bed and lay quietly together. "I don't know what I'd do without you, baby. Have I said that before? It's true. If I were starving to death, I still wouldn't be able to do this if you weren't with me. It's not the sort of thing you'd do with a lady wife." He hugged his boy and gave him a tender kiss.

Patrice couldn't shake off his sense of unworthiness; it seemed to affect his muscles, impeding free movement. If he were as heroic as he had dreamed of being, ready to sacrifice all for his love, he would find a way to simply vanish. His misery was aggravated by the fact that he had won Rod's sexual surrender with the artificial and practiced wiles of his debauched boyhood. Self-condemnation was hardening into sexual disgust. He was sick of his body and made no response to Rod's kiss; it hadn't even given him an erection.

He had had an intimation the night before that something of the sort was in store for him when Rod had pleaded a delayed hangover and had gone to bed very early. He had stayed up alone, glad for an excuse to avoid physical intimacy, trying to find some solid ground between Gérard's doctrine of absolute evil and his own lost vision of absolute purity. If it existed, he suspected he would find it sterile and cold.

Now he felt himself being lulled to sleep by the motion of the road that remained in him and for the first time in his life felt no

216

compulsion to offer satisfaction to a willing male. He wondered what would happen if Rod wanted him and was asleep before any further move was made.

The next day they drove down into a new gold and silver landscape of vineyards and olive groves framed by the dark exclamation points of cypresses. The air had a bite in it despite the bright sun, and it was full of sharp, pungent smells. Rod was intoxicated by it and by the new shapes and forms unfolding before his eyes.

"It's terrific," he exclaimed. "I've been down here before–but when I was a kid–with my mother and sister. We've got to come back, monkey. It's got such guts, much better than Italy. We'll let François here make us some money, and we'll come back for a couple of weeks later on. There's so much to look at. Is it a date?"

"Of course, *mon ami*. It's a date."

They smiled at each other. Rod saw Patrice's eyes suddenly glistening as if they had filmed over with tears, and the boy turned quickly to the window and exclaimed over an old farmhouse they were passing. Rod gave Patrice's shoulders a hug. He supposed it had something to do with their big night. They hadn't had time to follow it up and learn where it was leading them. He felt as if he had left bits of himself scattered all over Paris. It seemed reasonable to make plans that didn't include Nicole, but that didn't mean that he would exclude her in serious ways. She was teaching him that they could be independent within their relationship. That was what he wanted. At least he thought he did. He gave Patrice another hug.

They stopped for lunch in the tree-crowded square of Aix. By midafternoon they were driving through the center of Marseille toward the Vieux Port. Rod had never been there and was disappointed. He had expected something exotic and vaguely Eastern, but this was just another hustling heavy northern city. A few palm trees here and there looked like bad jokes. François turned into a side street within sight of water and boats and parked the car. With a quick movement he withdrew a small gun from the glove compartment and slipped it somewhere inside his clothes. It happened so quickly that it took a second for Rod to convince himself that he'd really seen it.

"Hey," he exclaimed. "What's that for?"

"I'm not going to shoot you. Don't worry. The people here are a bunch of nuts. You never know. I don't come down here for my health."

"I'm sorry to hear it. I've been enjoying myself until now. So what's the program?"

"I have things to do. You have time to take in a movie if you want. We can meet at 8 o'clock. There's a restaurant called Le Pecheur du Port right around the corner down there. Turn left at the end of the Cannabiere and go along a little way until you come to it. You can't miss it."

"I thought you said we'd be together except for half an hour."

"That was before I knew you were going to cover yourself. You get the keys. What more do you want? I can use the time for business. You might as well give me the dough now."

A sudden thought struck Rod. "How do I know you don't have another set of keys?"

François made a little mirthless sound of laughter. "I wondered if you were going to think of that. You're not dumb. I haven't."

"Thanks for telling me that piece of information. However, I still like the original idea of half an hour better."

François hitched himself around in his seat and looked at Patrice. "Listen, old lover of mine. Will you explain to your boyfriend that people know me? Why would I want to fuck up for 1,000 lousy bucks?"

"I have said that. He can decide for himself how he wants to handle it. You made an agreement. Why not follow it?"

François stared impassively out the window, drumming his fingers on the back of the seat. "OK, if that's what you want. What I don't see is how you're going to manage to part with your money even for half an hour."

"I can stand being nervous for half an hour. Three hours might throw me into a breakdown."

"Funny. Well, we don't have to sit in the car. We can *all* go to a movie. Or maybe we should go take a room and have a daisy chain if we're going to spend the rest of our lives together. Jesus."

François got out. Rod winked at Patrice, and he winked back as they followed. It was colder than it had been in Paris. Rod closed his raincoat over his chest, and Patrice buckled his cape while François locked the car. He came around the end of the car and dropped the keys into Rod's hand.

"You might as well have them in case I get kidnapped," he said.

Rod had had time to decide that their leader was reacting convincingly and satisfactorily. He pulled the money out and handed it to him in a closed fist. François glanced at it and quickly pocketed it.

"I must've done something right. Thanks. Eight o'clock at the restaurant. You better eat something while you're waiting. I don't like to hang around when the job's done. We'll be driving all night."

They shook hands, and François was swallowed up in the flow of pedestrians surging around them. Rod turned to Patrice. "OK, baby?"

"About giving the money? I think so. I'm glad you're not carrying it anymore. What did he say about shooting you? Does he have a gun?"

"Didn't you see it? He pulled it out of the glove compartment."

"Your eyes are very good for this adventure. Tell me if anybody starts to shoot me."

"Don't worry. My money's gone, but nobody's going to get you. At the moment I must be the poorest friend you've ever had. Do you love me despite it all?"

"Yes, *chéri*. I almost wish your money was really gone so that I could do something astonishing for you like murder my grandmother and give you my inheritance. *Tiens*. Why haven't I thought of that before?"

They found a film Patrice wanted to see. Rod tried to concentrate on it while forebodings of destitution fluttered around his heart. Patrice, and to some extent François, had convinced him that the deal was on the level as far as he was concerned. Still, it was strange to be watching a movie at a jumping-off place on the Mediterranean without enough in his pocket to live for a week. His thoughts turned automatically to his parents and cables for help, but he sternly suppressed them. He and Patrice would somehow make it. He kept his arm around his boy's shoulders, seeking protection as well as offering it. Nobody at home would believe any of this. The thought made him briefly pleased with himself.

It was dark when they came out. A bitter wind was blowing, but they made a detour to make sure the car was still there.

"I knew it would be, but still–" Rod said, noting that the splash of paint on the curb lined up with the mudguard as it had before.

It was almost 7:30 when they reached the restaurant. It looked unpretentious, but a glance at the bill of fare revealed that it was expensive. At Patrice's suggestion they ordered a single portion of bouillabaisse, which he maintained would be enough for two, enough to get them through the night's drive. It turned out that liberal additions of bread to the soup made it a meal, of sorts. The clock on the wall was approaching 8 P.M., and they were halfway through their bottle of white wine when a blast of wintry air announced François's appearance in the doorway. He glanced around the room and crossed quickly to them and, without taking off his coat, dropped into a chair they had kept for him. Rod saw immediately that, to the extent his neat expressionless features would permit, he looked worried.

"Everything OK?" Rod asked, trying to sound casual despite the sudden agitation of his heart.

"Sure. That is, not exactly. Something's funny. People aren't where they're supposed to be. Getting around in taxis doesn't make it easy. If–"

"Where's the money, for chrissake?"

"Don't worry. I've still got it. That's what's funny. I haven't been able to turn it over."

"Oh, for God's sake." Rod found that he had been leaning forward tensely, and he sat back with a sigh of relief. "Let's just forget it. If it didn't work, it didn't work. Give me back my money and we'll maybe try it some other time."

220

"That might suit you, buster, but it's not good enough for me. Do you have any idea how much this trip costs? I didn't come down here for nothing. There's a lot of red tape in this business. You have to go through channels. If I had the car, I could take some short-cuts, check things out. Let's make a deal. I want the car. If I haven't got things squared away in half an hour, I'll call it quits. Three quarters at the most."

"No. The hell with it. It's my money. I want it back. I don't want you taking any risks with it."

"Who said anything about risks? If I don't make the right con-tacts, nothing happens. Right? If I do, we're in business the same as before. So we've lost an hour. So what?"

"What can you do in your car that you can't do in a taxi?"

"Don't be dumb. There're certain places I can't have a taxi dri-ver take me. Have you forgotten where you are? One more body on the sidewalk isn't going to bother anybody very much. The taxi drivers are all part of some mob. I've had to do a lot of walking. When I find a taxi to take me someplace else, the lead's cold. The minute I saw there'd been a slipup, I should've dropped it and come here. I've been wasting my time."

As they talked, Rod's disappointment at losing the opportunity for easy money weighed more and more heavily against caution. He'd been counting on it. Whatever the difficulty was, it apparently was a technical one, not something inherently wrong with the project. François's being here proved that he wasn't trying to pull any funny business. "If you take the car, you really think everything will be OK?"

"I've never had any trouble before. I told you it was unlucky to change the way I operate."

"If you go on having trouble, you swear you'll drop it and bring my money back?"

"Listen. You can meet me outside at 9 o'clock. I wouldn't keep a dog waiting around on a night like this."

Rod hesitated another instant, looking into eyes that were cold but not shifty. He nodded and pulled out the keys and handed them over.

François accepted them with a faint smile. "You're not the easiest guy I've ever dealt with, but at least you'll listen to reason. Good. Go on back to the Cannebière a little before 9 o'clock. There's a big cafe right on the corner with a glassed-in terrace like the Flore. You can watch for me in there, but come right out the minute I show. Don't get cozy over a cup of coffee. I like to keep moving. Right?"

Rod was prepared to shake hands, but François was up and gone without further ado. He turned to Patrice. "The plot thickens. Amazingly enough, I'm beginning to trust the guy. You were right. I hope it works this time."

"I think it will. I'm impressed by him. It seems quite complicated, but he acts as if he knows what he's doing."

They had finished their wine by 8:30 and decided to go to the corner cafe and coffee right away in case François turned up earlier than expected. They found the place an excellent observation post. Big glass windows offered a clear view of all the activity around the old port. They ordered coffee and paid for it as soon as it was served so that they'd be ready to take off at a moment's notice. Rod observed the flow of traffic. It moved in waves as it was released by the lights up and down the broad avenue. François might approach from any one of various directions, but Rod assumed he'd pull up just across the sidewalk in front of them, pointing toward Paris. He picked out the door they'd use to get to him. They finished their coffee and kept glancing at their watches. For once, they had nothing to say to each other. The clock behind the bar inside was a few minutes slow by their time. When it said 8:55, Rod shifted in his chair to ease his nerves.

"I deserve something out of this," he said in a hushed tone. "If we decide to do it again, I certainly won't come with him. Let him sweat it out on his own."

"He'll be here any–"

"There." They were on their feet and moving toward the door. They crossed the sidewalk and, without thinking, Rod jumped into the front seat and Patrice into the back. They slammed the doors, and the car pulled away.

"Well, what about it?" Rod asked. "Did it work?"

"Of course. I told you it would."

"You mean you'll have the $2,000 for me in Paris?"

"That's the agreement."

Rod swung around to Patrice. Their eyes gleamed at each other in the light of the traffic. They reached for each other's hands and squeezed. "OK, monkey?" Rod asked with quiet triumph.

"*Tres* OK, *mon ami.* Don't you want to be back here?"

Rod gave his hand another squeeze and released it. "It's better for you to have it all to yourself. You can stretch out and get some sleep. You have to work tomorrow. We can trade when we get close to Paris maybe." Facing front, he saw that they had turned off the Cannebière and weren't going in the direction they had come from that afternoon which he had assumed was the main route from Aix to Paris. "What're we doing now?"

"Just checking to see if we're being followed. It happened once before. I'll drive around the center of town for a few minutes."

"Who would want to follow you?"

"I don't know. I'll see in a minute. I know how to shake them." He turned onto another street and accelerated.

"Why go through all this? Why not just clear out?"

"And take the chance that somebody'll pick a nice secluded spot along the way to have a little chat? No thanks."

"Did you collect what you said—your package?" Patrice asked from the backseat.

"That's what I came for."

"Where is it?"

"Here. Where you couldn't find it without pulling a few things apart."

"I think I'm beginning to know what this is about." Patrice spoke with unexpected authority.

"How do you mean?" Rod demanded, swinging back to him.

François turned another corner. "This is no time to go into that. It looks as if some people might be asking you questions if I don't play this right. You don't know anything. Keep it that way. Here we go."

"There's somebody after us?" Rod looked out the rear window and saw a confusion of dimmed headlights.

"Don't either of you look back, especially the kid back there. Just act as if we're out for a Sunday drive." He made a right turn and let the car coast slowly toward a red light that Rod saw controlled traffic crossing the Cannebière. The light changed as they reached the avenue, and François crossed slowly and made an immediate left turn. After a few moments he muttered, "All right, buster. Let's see how smart you are." He accelerated and took another fast left turn. Rod's heart began to beat rapidly. He glanced back at Patrice who was staring straight ahead. François swung out to pass a loitering driver and got back into line within inches of hitting an oncoming car. Lights flashed at them. They were across the Cannebière again and racing. Tires squealed as he took two right turns in quick succession and got the rocking car under control and sped toward a green light. It turned red as they passed it, and the arrested traffic to the right and left surged forward. François clapped a hand on the horn and shot across the avenue for the third time, pursued by a cacophony of horns challenging his. Cars jolted to a halt and leaped forward again. They were safely on the other side. Rod saw François ease himself back in his seat and realized that his own fists were clenched in a spasm of fear and that his nails were digging into his palms. He unfolded his fingers with a great effort, as if they were locked into position, and he took a deep breath.

"That should take care of that," François said with cool satisfaction.

"I must say, you know how to drive this thing," Rod said, his voice sounding unsteady. "That was pretty hair-raising."

They drove in silence for a few minutes—fast but not fast enough to attract attention—through a part of town that combined new blocks and old crooked rows of houses. Traffic was light. They passed cars. A few cars passed them.

"I'll hit the road that runs along the main port in a minute," François said as if instructing himself. "I'll circle around and pick up the road to Aix, and we'll be on our way."

They drove on a few more blocks. François kept lifting his head slightly to check the rearview mirror. He slowed down. He sped up. He made a quick turn and turned again and followed a straight downhill street. "Oh, shit," he said.

"What's the matter?"

"The fuckers. They're on us again. Maybe there're two of them. They must've guessed where I was heading."

"Are you sure?"

"No, it's all a big dream. I don't like being out here where it's so deserted. I'm going to make a run for it." He pulled the gun out from somewhere in his clothes and placed it between his legs and accelerated. The car lunged forward and careened out onto a wide road. Pure luck ordained that there nothing in their way. "Sorry. I didn't see that." The motor roared as François opened it up to its limits.

Rod felt his feet pushing down through the floorboards, his body stiffening, bracing itself. Hands dropped onto his shoulders from behind and held him firmly. He couldn't tear his eyes off the road. They were racing through a sort of no-man's land of open storage yards and warehouses. A wire fence ran along the far side, and beyond the warehouses he saw cranes and masts silhouetted against the sky.

"This is dumb," François said above the roar of the motor.

"They still there?" Rod asked through clenched teeth.

"Gaining a bit. I can't go faster."

"I hope not."

A big truck came around a curve ahead of them, approaching rapidly. They were about to pass each other when François swung the wheel and braked violently. The truck loomed hugely at Rod's side as he was thrown about in his seat. The air was filled with sounds of disaster, the squeal of tires, the crash of hardware, and they skidded sickeningly across the road. For an instant Rod thought the car had been wrecked, but then it shuddered through gates and picked up speed again.

"Sorry if I scared you," François said. "That might create a diversion back there."

Patrice's hands were no longer on Rod's shoulders. "You all right, baby?" he asked as soon as he could speak.

"Very well, thank you. I've always wanted to be killed in a car crash." The voice was jaunty. Rod still couldn't force himself to turn and look at him. They were going fast again across a wasteland toward a group of sheds and warehouses.

"Shit. I didn't think they'd dare come in here," François said. "Maybe they're police." He accelerated up to full speed again. As they approached the buildings, Rod saw that the area looked like some sort of military installation. Army vehicles were parked near one of the neatly painted buildings. When they reached the first building, François braked violently once more and swung in behind it and pulled the car around in a wrenching U-turn. A man in uniform came running toward them shouting.

"So long, mister," François said. "We can't wait."

They shot out from behind the building and headed back toward the gate and the main road they had so startlingly left. Headlights flashed on in front of them. François flicked his on full and hunched down in his seat and set the car on a collision course. He dropped a hand from the wheel and picked his gun. Headlights rushed at each other, devouring the road between them. All of Rod's muscles were gathering into an enormous bone-crushing knot. A shout was rising in his throat. His whole body became a scream of protest. It had never been subjected to such torture. He hoped he'd be able to move when it came time to grab the wheel. There were only seconds left. He made a lunge for it just as the other car gave way, and they hurtled past each other with a blast of air that rattled the windows. He heard a small crack somewhere like metal snapping.

"Don't fool around while I'm driving." François tapped his hands away with his gun. "You're apt to get hurt. That was a lousy shot."

"Shot?"

"Yeah. They nicked the car somewhere."

226

"If there's shooting," Patrice interjected briskly, "I think we must have a plan. How big is your parcel?"

"About the size of two books."

"I see. Because it *is* two books? I think we should be back in the center of town. There are plenty of people still out."

"That's where I'm going if I can get there. The sons of bitches have turned around already."

"They're not interested in you. They're interested in the package. That's true, isn't it?"

"As far as I know. Hold on." He sped through the gates and roared out onto the main road just in front of another truck. Brakes screeched, headlights flashed, but they were off in the direction of town.

"You can't go on driving like this forever," Patrice pointed out calmly. "You've been lucky, but soon you'll kill us all."

"I'll try to shake them once more. If it doesn't work, we'll see."

"Not if we're dead. They're very good at this. Even in the center of town, people will be going home soon. We can stop somewhere safe where there are lights and people—a gas station for instance—but they wouldn't let us leave. Is that right? You want to keep moving. Pretend to shake them, but drive more carefully."

"And then what?"

"Then we'll give them what they want," Patrice said with decision. He couldn't permit this to go on any longer. When the truck had loomed over them, he had seen Rod dead in his mind's eye and had wanted to die with him. He had never felt his responsibility to Rod so intensely and had to get him out of this. "It's very simple," Patrice went on. "I'd like to be near the train station. Lead them there. When you're sure they're watching, I'll jump out with a package and they will follow me."

This severed Rod's hypnotic preoccupation with the road, and he swung around to the backseat. "Are you out of your mind? Those people were shooting at us. What if they start shooting at you?"

"At the station? I don't think they will."

"Anyway, it's out of the question. Forget it."

"Don't worry, *mon ami*. I'm very quick and–"

"Why don't you call me *chéri*? You always do."

"But he–I thought–" His smile was radiant even in the dark. "Thank you, *chéri*. That's very wonderful. Now you must let me do what I say. I think there's a late-night train to Paris. I know there's one early in the morning. I'll be there as soon as you are."

"OK, then I'll come with you."

"No, *chéri*. You must stay with François to see that all goes well in Paris. Besides, alone I will think only for myself and will be very clever. If we're together, we'll think more for each other than of the others. That might be dangerous."

"I don't care what you say. If you get out of the car, so will I."

"And you, François. What do you think? Will you do what I say?"

"It's not a dumb idea. What'll you have in your package?"

"It will be some clothes carefully folded so that they will look all right at a distance. It's important for everything to look convincing so that they think they know what we're doing." He didn't think there was any great risk in what he was proposing but wouldn't have cared if there were. If he could perform one unequivocally unselfish act for Rod, his life would be complete. "If they're still with us at the station, I'll jump out. Not right in front of the station. So many people stopping and getting out might confuse them. You know that street that leads up to it with the cheap shops? It's always crowded. That's a good place."

"Check. But I'd still rather shake them," François said. "Here we go again." They came to a traffic light, and he made a fast turn into built-up streets. He began his maneuvers again, turning right and left haphazardly, working his way into the busy part of the city, driving as fast as the increasing traffic permitted but no longer bringing Rod's heart into his mouth. "They're staying much closer to us," François reported. "Why not? We all know what we're doing now. It's not going to make it easy to pull off any tricks."

228

"You know how to do it. Wait until you're far enough ahead when you turn a corner so that you can stop for a second and start off again when they come around after you. It will look as if you thought you were doing it when they weren't watching. Of course, they must see it or they'll chase you all night."

Rod heard the fastenings of their bag clicking in back of him. He turned again. "You really want to go ahead with this crazy idea?"

"It's better, *chéri*. I think François's driving is more dangerous than those people back there."

"Fine. I'm ready when you are," Rod said.

"I wish you wouldn't, *chéri*. It will be very distracting if I'm worrying about you. If you think for a minute, you will know I'm right."

Rod faced front. He heard the fastenings click shut. He didn't see Patrice reach forward and squeeze François's arm. François grunted.

"Anything wrong?" Rod asked.

"No. We're getting close to the station."

"My package is ready," Patrice announced. His lips were suddenly against Rod's ear. "You're my life, *chéri*," he whispered. "Whatever you do, be careful."

Rod put his hand on the door, ready to get out. He had no idea what would be expected of him. If Patrice ran, he would run after him. If he stood and confronted their pursuers, he would confront them too. He couldn't believe any great harm could come to them in a crowded street. He was as ready as Patrice to put an end to this chase. He was amazed by his boy's apparent knowledge of what they were doing.

François turned another corner. He gunned the motor in a sudden spurt of speed and slammed on the brakes. Rod was pitched forward and hit his head on the windshield. He heard a door slam, and he fumbled for the handle beside him and felt another blow on the head. He was thrown back in his seat and spiraled down into a black pit of unconsciousness.

Rod came to slowly, aware that his head was aching. He burst into full consciousness with a start and knew that it was still night and the car was moving. He whirled around. The backseat was

229

empty except for the hump of their small bag. He swung back and made a lunge for the ignition keys. François struck him in the head with his gun.

"I'm not going to kill you, but I'll sure as hell hurt you if you make any trouble. Sit back and relax."

Rod saw they were on the outskirts of the city again, speeding along a wide highway. "Where is he?" he asked.

"He got out a block from the station. It worked perfectly. I timed it damn well, if I say so myself. The last I saw, he was trotting along the sidewalk, and our tail was pulling to the curb behind him. We're in the clear. Don't worry about him. He'll probably get back before we do."

Anxiety was already beginning to gnaw at Rod. He felt all at odds with himself being separated from his boy. If he insisted on going back, he might not be able to find him, which would make it worse. He became aware of his aching head. "What in hell was the idea of knocking me out?" he demanded.

"He didn't want you with him. He was right. If he wants to make himself scarce, you'd have been in the way. I just gave you a little tap. You've been out only a few minutes."

"This is the Paris road?"

"That's right. Finally. We won't get there until noon or later. Put this thing away, will you?" He handed Rod the gun. The gesture was a token of trust, and Rod was glad to get it back into the glove compartment.

"Why did he sound as if he knew all about what you're doing?"

"Not all about. Something, maybe. He's had an interesting life. He's been laid by a lot of big shots. I guess you know that. Somebody may have talked out of turn."

"He's not in on it in any way, is he? I mean, those guys who were after us wouldn't connect him with anything?"

"Oh, hell no. Unless they happen to be pals from the *Cercle Vert*, and he'd certainly know how to handle anything like that." François made his mirthless sounds of laughter.

"OK. Cut that."

"I'm not knocking him. He's an amazing kid. I guess you're nuts about each other."

"We're friends," Rod said coldly. Without Patrice being here it sounded almost like betrayal. His mind was full of prayers for him to be waiting at home. He'd go wild with worry if he were delayed. "OK. I guess we're nuts about each other in a way," he said grudgingly to propitiate fate. "There's no point talking about it. I doubt if you'd understand."

"Probably not. I'm strictly for one-night stands. You're not really my type, but I get a special feeling about a guy when I've been through some excitement with him. If you feel like some fun along the way, let me know."

"Jesus. Thanks," Rod said, drawing away with anger and distaste. Slowly his mind cut free from the wrench of being parted from Patrice, and his thoughts were redirected toward their reunion. He'd want to get to his shop as soon as possible, but he'd leave a message at home first. They would celebrate the money tomorrow evening. It would soon be this evening. He remembered Nicole. He'd be worn out after this all-night drive. Maybe he'd put her off until the next night. Patrice was probably already at the station looking up trains. He imagined the street scene that would have just taken place, the men moving in beside him, Patrice showing his little bundle of clothes. They might ask questions, but Patrice would know how to answer them. Nothing to worry about, nothing more than what could happen in any busy street. *I wanted to be with you, but the shit hit me over the head.* His mind conveyed the message to his boy, willing him to receive it.

He was tired. After the tensions of the last hour or two, the steady movement of the car on the open road was soothing. He supposed François must be tired too. "We could take turns at the wheel, you know," he said. "It seems as if you've been driving this thing without stopping for the last ten years."

"I like it. I hate being driven. Sleep if you want. I'm OK."

After the verbal pass, Rod didn't want to get any more friendly with him. He sank back into his corner and soon was dozing. He awoke with a start, anxiety congesting his chest, and turned quickly to the backseat. Patrice wasn't there. Of course, he wasn't there. He was safely on a train going to Paris, probably sleeping peacefully. He dozed again but experienced similar moments all through the night—the sudden awakening, the agitation at sensing Patrice's absence, the reassuring thoughts to lull himself to sleep again.

At dawn they stopped at a truckers' place for coffee and croissants. Like most of the other clients, Rod had a glass of wine. They drove on in thickening traffic and arrived in Paris under gray skies just before 1 o'clock. Rod felt as if he'd been gone for a month. François drove him to the rue de Verneuil.

"What now?" Rod asked when he stopped in front of the door.

"I go and finish the job. I'll bring the dough back here if you want. I'll be about an hour."

"Fine. I'll wait for you. I wonder if Patrice is back."

"If not, he will be soon. See ya." They shook hands, and Rod pulled the bag out of the back seat and went in. He called Patrice's name the minute he had the door open, but there was no answer. They usually left messages on the floor just inside the door so that they couldn't miss them, but there was nothing there. He went through the silent apartment—checking in the kitchen, his work area, back in the bedroom—to make sure Patrice hadn't chosen a new place, and then he returned to the kitchen and poured himself a glass of wine. There was no point in waiting and wondering. He would find out what trains there were so that he'd know when he could expect him.

He drank off the wine and went out again and walked around to the hotel. He picked up some mail that he was glad not to be interested in and went on to the *tabac* and called the Gare de Lyon. He found that there were a number of trains, of various classes and categories. Patrice obviously hadn't taken the night train or he'd al-

232

ready be here. Assuming that he'd want to economize as usual, Rod chose a day train getting in after 5 o'clock as the most likely. He could always check at the shop later just in case. He went home and found some cheese and absentmindedly finished off the bottle of wine. Now that he had had time to think it over, he knew that François was out as a source of income. The extra $1,000 would do. Perhaps by the end of summer he would again be desperate enough to do anything for more. For the time being, he could thank his lucky stars that he had experienced the nastiest couple of hours of his life, had had a taste of crime, and had survived. Another layer of insulation to protect him from the world he had chosen to live in.

There was a knock on the door. He leaped up with a happy smile of welcome until he remembered that Patrice would let himself in. He went out to the hall and admitted François. He had shaved and looked as fresh as he had the day they left. He stopped in the hall and turned to Rod holding out a wad of bills.

Rod took it and looked at it, noting with satisfaction how much it had grown. "Thanks," he said.

"You don't have to be polite. Count it. I would if I were you."

Rod riffled through it. "That's all right. I'm sure you haven't shortchanged me."

"I've done what I said I'd do, right? That's the end of my obligation. If anyone asks, you can say François Leclerc keeps his word. I don't have to say any more, but the kid was a big help last night, so I owe you both a favor. Something fishy's going on. I haven't figured out exactly what yet but last night was part of it. Have you heard from your pal?"

"No. I checked the trains. I don't expect him until later."

"Fine. Until you know he's here, why don't you go out? I don't think it's a good idea to hang around here. Don't ask me why. It's just a hunch. When he gets here he'll maybe know more than I do. I'd clear out until you know he's all right."

"Of course he's all right. What're you talking about? I was just going to get some sleep."

"A guy like you shouldn't have any trouble finding a bed to sleep in. The concierge knows your name. I asked for you rather than Valmer. I'd slip her a little something to forget it for the next few days. I'm just trying to do you a favor. Pay no attention if that's the way you want it. I may have it all wrong." He made a nervous move toward the door. "Don't try to get in touch with me. I'll let you know if I find out anything you should know. I've got to clear out of here."

Rod opened the door, and they shook hands briefly. François slipped out looking wary and oddly furtive. Rod was left in a state of irrational, undirected alarm. What was he supposed to be worried about? Reprisals from the underworld? Trouble with the police? He wished Patrice would hurry up and get back so that they could talk about it. He caught sight of the small bag he'd dropped at the door to the living room. If it had something to do with the police, maybe François had been trying to tell him that it would be better if they weren't so obviously living together. Should he take a room again at the hotel so that he'd have an official independent residence? Maybe that was what Patrice would want him to do. He was lost in this situation without him. He went to his work area and drew with charcoal on a piece of paper: "Welcome home. I'll be back at 6 o'clock. For the evening. Love." The train got in just before 5:30. Patrice would take the Métro and walk from the nearest stop. Half an hour at the most. They'd be together by 6 o'clock. Allow some time for the train to be late and other delays. No point getting worked up over nothing. Patrice would be back by 6:30 at the latest.

He dropped the note in front of the door and picked up the bag and left again. In a way it made sense to go to the hotel since that was where Patrice would leave a telephone message if he were trying to reach him. If he understood François correctly, it would be a mistake to go by the shop. They wouldn't know anything anyway. His boy would get in touch with him before anybody else. He decided not to call Nicole. He would be in no state to talk to her until

Patrice was back, and by then it would be too late to plan an evening. She'd probably assumed already that he'd been kept out of town an extra day.

As he entered the hotel he was unmistakably cruised by a youth who passed on his way out. He instinctively turned to look after him. The youth did the same so that their eyes met briefly. Rod cursed to himself as he went on to the desk. That had never happened when he was living here. Had being with Patrice marked him physically?

He found that there was a room available but on a lower floor than his old one, so there would be no skylight. He smiled to himself at the fuss they made over their silly little skylight. He had a whole wall of light with which to work. He walked up two flights of stairs. As he reached the second floor, he heard footsteps behind him and glanced back. It was the youth hurrying after him. The boy looked up at him and smiled invitingly and said, "Hi."

Rod sighed with exasperation and went on down the corridor looking for his room number.

"Are you just moving in?" The youth had caught up with him and was at his side.

"No. I've lived here for months."

"I haven't seen you before. My room's right down there. Can I look at yours? I'd like to see if they're all the same."

Rod stopped in front of his door and put the key in the lock. "Listen. Why don't you bugger off? I'm busy."

"Well. You don't have to be rude about it."

Rod shut the door in his face. He didn't look at the room. He didn't want to stay in it but could think of nowhere else to go. The wine had added weight to his exhaustion. He dropped the bag and fell onto the bed. He didn't think he could sleep even though it would help him get through the afternoon. He closed his eyes. Within seconds he was drifting off into unconsciousness.

He awoke in darkness and didn't know where he was. He felt as if he were facing a disaster so appalling that everything in him cringed from it. It took a moment to find his way around in his mind, and he realized that he felt like this simply because he hadn't yet heard from Patrice. He was being idiotic. The night before seemed like a dream. Poor Patrice had had the rotten luck to have to spend a miserable night in a station and get through a long train trip alone. That was all there was to it. He sat up and found a light by the bed and switched it on and looked at his watch. It was nearly 5 o'clock. The hell with François. He'd go and wait for Patrice at home. Only an hour or so more.

He found soap and a comb in the bag and tidied himself up at the washbasin. He needed a shave, but that would help pass some time when he got home where the water was really hot. He put on his coat and put his razor in a pocket and left. He must have been slightly drunk to have taken the room, but because he had to pay for tonight, he'd leave the bag for appearance's sake until tomorrow.

He was keyed up with anticipation at the end of the short walk. He could have guessed wrong. Patrice might be there. He took the stairs two at a time and fumbled with the key in his haste to get the door open. He flung it wide and saw his message lying on the floor. His spirits sagged, but he hastily reminded himself that he hadn't really expected him until 6 o'clock or 6:30. He shed his coat and turned on all the lights and began to feel happy at being home. He realized how grubby he felt after God knows how long in the same clothes and went to the bathroom and stripped.

He shaved while he ran a bath and emerged after half an hour in the kitchen feeling like a new man. He put on fresh slacks and a clean shirt and an old jacket. They would spend the evening at home. Patrice would probably stop along the way to pick up something for dinner. That was something he hadn't thought of that might delay him. He poured himself a stiff *pastis* and drank it slowly while he fiddled about in his work area. The canvas on the easel began to absorb him, and he studied it in detail. His hands itched for tubes of paint and brushes. Before he knew it, it was after 6:30. Nothing to worry about. He poured himself another stiff drink and returned to the fascinating canvas.

It was almost 7:30 when he forced himself to face the possibility that Patrice might not return that evening. His heart was fluttering uncomfortably, and he poured himself another drink with hands that had developed a slight tremor. He thought of the unhappy afternoon he had spent back at the beginning when his boy hadn't kept their lunch date. Was he pulling some trick like that now, testing him in some way? Impossible. He hadn't been his boy then. There was nothing to test now. What else? He thought of the scene on the street last night as François had described it. The car pulling to the curb. If he'd been forced to go somewhere to be questioned, he would have quickly convinced his questioners that he didn't know anything. To imagine even that much stretched credulity. Movie stuff. Pure fantasy. If anybody tried to force him to do anything, he would shout the skies down. If he had a gun stuck in his ribs? See it as a movie scenario. What then? A gun in the ribs. A ride in the car. Questions. He knew nothing. He had nothing on him anybody would want. End of scenario.

He poured himself another drink—his fourth? fifth?—and saw that his hands were steady. Nothing like a drink to calm things down. A doubt he didn't even know was in him began to move into the forefront of his mind. You could never be sure with queers. It was so easy to give in to temptation. Patrice might have picked up with somebody he found attractive. If he discovered he had a long wait for his train, it would be almost difficult to blame him if he agreed to go to a hotel. If the somebody had a big cock, one thing could lead to another—time forgotten, postponed partings, missed trains. He felt his muscles beginning to tighten with anger. He'd beat the shit out of Patrice if it turned out to be something like that. It was the only reasonable explanation.

He drained his glass and filled it again. This one would fix him up so that he wouldn't care if Patrice never came home. Let him have his big cock. Cheap. Sordid. Patrice wasn't like that, but even the best of them couldn't seem to get enough of it. The thought of Patrice in some lousy hotel made Rod sick. The drink settled his stomach. He went a bit unsteadily to the bottle for a refill. He wasn't going to hang around all night. Go out and have some fun. He could let himself spend a little money for once. Maybe find a girl. No, he had a girl. Go find the old crowd in the rue de Buci. He was hungry.

He put his fortune in the brown jar on the kitchen shelf where Patrice kept their spare cash. He took a couple of thousand francs of Germaine's money out of it. There were signs everywhere of his having been here, so there was no need to leave a note. He didn't know when he'd be back. To make sure he was insulated against shock, he had one more drink and wrapped a scarf around his neck and put on his coat and went out.

He found Massiet, Pichet, and Lambert at the restaurant without their various female attachments. The first two had just finished dinner and were going on somewhere together. Lambert, the gentlest, dreamiest member of the group, had just sat down, and Rod ate with him. He drank a bottle of wine by himself and ordered a second to share with Lambert. He was drunk but pleasantly so.

"You doing anything this evening?" he asked his friend in French as they were getting to the bottom of the second bottle.

"I've been invited to a party. I think I'll go."

"Oh. I don't know what I'm going to do," he said pointedly, in the mood to tag along with anybody who offered companionship.

"I'd suggest you come too, but I don't think you'd like it. There'll be only boys."

"Oh. No, I don't think much of that idea. I mean, if that's what you like—I just didn't realize you were—"

Lambert smiled vaguely. "No, I'm not like that, although I've often thought it would be much more convenient if I were. I have friends who are. I used to go their parties because the poor dears were very careless with their valuables. I used to pick up odds and ends that helped pay for food. Now that I work quite a lot, I go for the free drinks. They know I don't wish to be molested."

Rod liked his easygoing attitude. He liked his admitting that he was a thief. "Well, if it's like that, maybe I'll go with you. I mean, if it's all right for you to take me."

"It will be very much all right with the other guests, although bitterly disappointing for them if the word spreads that you too don't want to be molested. They always manage to keep quite calm with me, but you'll be the big star of the evening. You've never been to this kind of party?"

"No, never."

"Then you may find it very strange. It took me many times before I got used to it. Of course, you can leave if it upsets you."

"That's what I was thinking." With Lambert to run interference for him, Rod doubted if he'd have much trouble rejecting advances. His friend wore a rag-bag assortment of sweaters and scarves, baggy tweeds and shiny flannels that appeared to cover a minimal body. He had a neat little beard that followed the line of his jaw, and his hair stuck out all over his head with no discernible attempt at design. Rod had been to plenty of stag parties; one roomful of men couldn't be much different from another. It might be something funny to tell Patrice if the little bastard ever turned up. He might even be able to make Patrice jealous. He certainly deserved to be.

"We can walk," Lambert said when they were out in the street. "It's not that far from here."

They weaved their way through many narrow intersecting streets, heading in the general direction of the river as far as Rod could tell, though he quickly lost track of where they were. He had to make an effort to avoid lurching, but he managed to navigate well enough. Eventually they entered an old building and climbed bare wooden stairs. Lambert led the way to a door and pushed a bell. The door opened to a gust of male voices. He found himself in a small entrance hall, his coat was taken from him, and he was introduced to a well-tailored middle-aged man who greeted Lambert with friendly carelessness and reserved a speculative scrutiny for Rod.

"I haven't brought you a recruit," Lambert explained. "He's another impostor like myself."

"What a great pity. He's the handsomest man here."

"I thought that would be the case. You'll all have to be content to just look at him. You somehow manage to be satisfied simply by my picturesque presence."

They moved on into a large handsomely appointed room that was not overly crowded with males of all ages—some very young, a few old, most somewhere in between, the assemblage giving the impression of having taken great care with appearances. He and Lambert were sloppy enough to warn everybody off. He was aware of lulls in the conversations around the room as groups here and there registered his arrival. Eyes were turned to him. Although they all stayed where they were, he felt in the room an almost physical movement toward him.

Before he had time to be disconcerted by it, the beautiful prince appeared before him. They shared an instant of mute astonishment, and then Rod could feel the delight in his smile responding to the sweet modesty of the prince's.

"It's really you. I couldn't believe my eyes," the prince exclaimed.

"I can't believe mine. How marvelous. I've been hearing so much about you. I was looking forward to seeing you again."

They shook hands, and Rod touched the other's shoulder. Their eyes met from equal heights, and a surge of exhilaration lifted his spirits. This dubious occasion was going to be fun after all. For some reason, perhaps because he knew Nicole, the prince seemed like an old friend.

"Speaking of eyes, yours are extraordinary. Just as I remembered," the prince said in his lightly mocking manner. "Shivers run up and down my spine. I've dreamed of you without a moment's letup for almost a week. Quite exhausting. Don't let's say another word until I get you a drink. What do you want?"

"Anything that's going. Whatever it is, be a pal and make it a strong one, will you? I've started a drunk."

"A whiskey should do it. Don't move. Above all, don't talk to any strange men."

The prince moved off through the crowd. Rod saw that his pale gray suit was beautifully molded to a powerful body. His memory was of a willowy youth. His eye had slipped up there. A boy approached and tried to start a conversation. Rod answered briefly, paying no attention. When the prince came back, he wouldn't be bothered by the others.

His beautiful friend emerged from the crowd holding two glasses. Rod looked at the arch of brow, the wide gentle blue eyes, the exquisite modeling of nose and cheeks and jaw, the full but delicate curve of lips, and he gave his head an incredulous little shake. The clear rosy skin and golden hair were bonuses no one deserved.

"You're unbelievable," he said, taking the drink that was offered him without looking at it, turning his back on the unknown boy. "I've never seen such perfection."

"You don't flatter by halves, do you? You're outrageously sexy with your clothes sort of thrown on you like that. It didn't show so much in your impeccable dinner jacket. I hoped knowing about Nicole would cool my passion, but I'm afraid it's a lost cause. I talked to her today. She said you were away for the weekend. You're both supposed to have dinner with me on Thursday, subject to your approval."

"Wonderful. Listen, about the weekend. You haven't seen me tonight. I got back late, and what with one thing and another, I decided to wait until tomorrow to call her and tell her I stayed away an extra day. That's why I'm here. I was at loose ends. A friend brought me." Their eyes met, and the prince smiled with understanding.

"I wasn't absolutely speechless with astonishment at finding you here," the prince said. "Little birds have been twittering."

"Pay no attention to birds. People have been twittering about you. Everybody says you're adorable. I wanted to find out for myself."

"If I can be adorable for anybody, I can certainly be adorable for you. Come over here where I can concentrate on it." He held Rod's

241

arm and led him toward an armchair against some bookshelves in a deserted corner. Rod saw they would be conspicuously isolated from the party and went willingly. He could relax.

"Does anybody call you Marie?" he asked as they moved to the chair.

The prince uttered youthful laughter. "Some have tried but haven't been encouraged. You've been reading my card. That's promising."

"I'm not going to call you Beauty. That's as silly as Marie. I might as well call you Phil. I can't think of a name that suits you less. See? I know your card by heart. I even know your address. I almost dropped in the other day when I was in the neighborhood."

"You get more fascinating by the minute. Why didn't you?"

"Do you really want to know?"

"I can guess. Are you sure you wouldn't have liked it?"

Rod laughed. "Maybe I was afraid I might. Actually, I was sort of upset and didn't think I'd be at my best. It's as simple as that." The prince squeezed his arm, and Rod hoped he wasn't being a tease. The prince's interest was so explicitly sexual that he couldn't ignore it. He wanted him to make his pass and get it over with so that he could simply enjoy his company. They stopped in front of the chair, and the prince put him into it and balanced elegantly on the arm, one long leg stretched out for support, the other hitched up beside him. Rod looked up at him, and their eyes met and held.

"What about your aesthetic problem?" the prince asked. "Do you still want to see me with nothing on?"

"I think I'll have to sooner or later, but we'd better put it off until I'm used to you," Rod said. "You've got to excuse me. I have this passion to look at you. I even told Nicole. I can understand your thinking it's something else."

"And it isn't? Oh, dear, what am I going to do with you? So near and yet so far. Now that I've found you, aren't you at least going to come home with me?"

"No." Rod broke eye contact and took a swallow of his drink. He wished the prince had made it a convincing invitation for a drink, but his new friend wasn't even trying. He was talking about bed. Rod couldn't imagine making love with a wholly masculine man like the prince. There was nothing ambiguous about his beauty; it was unequivocally male. He wouldn't even dare muss his hair. If it turned out that he was going to swing both ways, it would be because he was fascinated by the androgynous quality of boys like Patrice. He simply had an urge to strip the prince and look at all of him.

He lowered his glass and looked at the hand resting on the thigh beside him. A shiver of delight ran through him. "Oh, damn," he said. "Look at that hand." He reached out and, holding the prince's wrist, lifted the hand and turned it slightly. It was big but superbly made, with long graceful fingers. "The most beautiful hand I've ever seen. You must drive sculptors mad." He turned it over and was suddenly reminded of the night he'd met Patrice and was stabbed by a pang of longing for him. He took another quick swallow of his drink and felt it loosen his mind and set it adrift. Better. The prince took his hand in both of his and drew it toward him and pressed it between his legs. Rod felt what he was intended to feel and extricated his hand and ran it along to his knee. He glanced hastily around the room and saw a number of eyes on them. "You're supposed to be adorable. Don't embarrass me. My being here is giving you the wrong idea."

"It's very difficult to get the right idea with you. I can't remember anybody who seemed to like me so much. It makes me quite giddy. Your extravagant praise of my person is quite unsettling too. I don't want to make too much of the twitterings, but any little secrets you have from Nicole are safe with me, I can promise you that. Don't you think you really ought to come home with me and help me straighten it all out? Preferably with nothing on, but I'll leave that up to you."

Rod looked up at him again, and their eyes met and probed each other. "I don't know. Maybe. We'll see." His hand closed on the knee he was holding. He seemed to be prolonging this flirtation, which hadn't been his intention at all. He was a thief like Lambert, an outlaw. He was stealing pleasure. The fact that he was beginning to feel more at ease in this gathering was a step in the right direction, a new experience. He was all in favor of experience.

The prince moved his hand down close to Rod's so that they were almost touching. "There *is* something, isn't there? I don't want to be a bore about it, but I can't help asking one question. In a broad general sense, regardless of me, do you or don't you?"

"Fair enough. To be as truthful as I can be, the answer is more or less no."

"More or less. You're not letting me off easily. If I'm the most beautiful person in the world, shouldn't it be, for me, a little less no?"

"I don't think so. That's the trouble with beauty. There's nothing you can do with it. It's all complete in itself. You can't make love to it because love is exchanging things, and there's nothing to add to it. All I can do is look at it. Say I go for me. It wouldn't make any difference. If you're as perfect all over as the parts of you I can see, all I could do is sit and stare with wonder. You can't desire perfection."

"I might have something to say about that. I have fairly conspicuous procreative machinery and a big ass. I doubt if there's anything perfect enough about me to induce total paralysis."

Their eyes danced to each other, and they burst out laughing. Rod tilted his glass back and drained it. "I better get another drink before I talk any more crap."

"I'll get it. I'll make it really strong this time." He took the glass out of Rod's hand. "I'm here to serve you."

"Good. I like being served by princes." He watched the prince's big ass as he moved across the room. It was narrow, but its rich curves had a massive thrust, something else he wanted to look at. He would strip him as soon as he had made himself quite clear on the sex question. He was pleased with his speech about beauty. That was telling it straight.

Two men appeared in front of him, one young, the other middle-aged, both pleasant looking, and began to ply him with questions about what he was doing in Paris and how he liked it and where he was from. He answered politely. He supposed he ought to get up for them, but he didn't trust his legs. He hadn't felt drunk with the prince, but now he wasn't so sure. The prince returned with full glasses.

"I say, I hope you chaps will excuse us, but we're having a rather private chat." He resumed his seat on the arm of the chair and handed a glass to Rod. "I hope you don't mind my dismissing your suitors. I want you all to myself." He dropped an arm around Rod's shoulders and pulled him closer.

"That's the way it should be." Rod took a grateful sip of his drink and felt his eyes closing heavily. He dropped his head against fabric and looked up. "Nice. Schoolboy necking. That's what you are, isn't it–all you guys who like other guys–aren't you all just retarded schoolboys?"

"Rather depraved schoolboys, I'm afraid. I think Narcissus comes into it somewhere too."

"Yeah, that's it. That's probably why I'm not queer, not so you'd notice it. I've never really fallen for myself."

"Perhaps you would if you'd allow me to worship you in the way I'm quite prepared to."

"I thought it was the other way around. I thought I worshiped you–from a safe distance."

"That's because I haven't dared tell all yet. I'm absolutely mad about you. I'm beautiful, if you insist, but you're the handsomest man I've ever seen. Everything about you thrills me. There's a marvelous menace in you–I don't know quite why I feel that, but it's breathtaking. Those eyes. That irresistible mouth. The chills keep running up and down my spine. Those great hands that look as if they could twist anything into any marvelous shape you want. I can see you've got a glorious body. Tonight it looks as if it ought to be naked always. We're clearly made for each other in all sorts of obvious ways. The light and the dark. The effete princeling and the noble savage. I won't belabor the point but I'm trying awfully hard to seduce you."

"It's probably impossible. You forgot to mention oil and water. What if you succeeded but one of us didn't like it? Wouldn't that sort of spoil a beautiful friendship? I like things the way they are."

He reached up and found the hand on his shoulder and held it. His eyes closed, and he pried them open. When had he last had some sleep? He pulled his head up and drank some more. He hoped the prince wouldn't decide to go after somebody else once he was convinced he had nothing to hope for from him.

"You're so bloody sweet, aside from everything else. I'm beginning to slobber over you, which isn't my style at all. Don't let me."

"I *like* having you slobber over me. It's the least you can do after I've told you you're the most beautiful human being in the world." They looked at each other and smiled and pressed each other's hands. "Am I very drunk?"

"I'm not sure I've seen you absolutely sober, darling. It's hard to tell."

"Maybe I better pee and get rid of some of it." He lifted his glass to his lips and discovered there was nothing but ice left. "I'll be damned. Need another drink. Where did you say I could pee?"

"Right out there and across the hall and the first door on the right. Do you want me to go with you? I hope not. I might be tempted to make a pass at you in the toilet and that would be worthy of me."

"I'm fine. First on the right."

"You won't let anyone make off with you, will you?"

"Why would I do that? You're taking me home with you, aren't you?"

"Yes, darling. I certainly am."

"Good. I thought that's what we agreed. Don't want to go home by myself."

He pulled himself up with an effort and stood unsteadily for a moment to get the feel of the floor under him. Then he squared his shoulders and turned to the prince and moved in close to him and ran a hand over the golden head. There were no equivocal stirrings in him. They were friends now. "See? Sober as a judge. You *are* adorable. I agree with everything everybody says."

"Don't be too nice to me. Go pee, and then I'll take you home."

Rod put his hands on the prince's shoulders and left them there for a moment while he looked thoughtfully into his upturned face.

He wondered how such beauty managed to escape the least trace of effeminacy. If he looked like a girl, he'd probably take him on the spot. He smiled down at him and gave him a little shake and turned to start his careful progress across the room. The floor had a tendency to tilt, but he managed to make allowances for it. Men spoke to him. Hands reached for him, and he brushed them away. He caught a glimpse of Lambert's back and remembered how he had got there. He followed instructions and found himself in a closet with a toilet. He had the hiccups. A bad sign. He never had the hiccups except when he was very drunk. He held his breath while he relieved himself. It was difficult doing two things at once. It made the hiccups worse. He couldn't talk to the prince with the hiccups. Lie down for a minute. That always fixed them. He fastened himself up and left the closet and stumbled along a corridor. He saw a big bed through an open door and went in and fell on it and was asleep.

He awoke with something pressing against his side. It gave him a claustrophobic sense of being hemmed in. He stirred with annoyance to free himself. He tried to push it away but couldn't get a purchase on it. He opened his eyes slowly and gazed up into a vision of beauty. Annoyance subsided into the peace of being held, cradled, watched over. His mouth dropped open as the vision swam toward him. Soft lips brushed his, and he thrust his tongue into a cavern of delight. He drifted back toward sleep while his tongue continued its indolent explorations. He felt arms tightening around him, a body moving against him, something hard thrust up against his hip. He lifted his hands and found bare shoulders and cool skin. The mouth withdrew, and he opened his eyes again and looked up into a soft blue gaze.

"Did that wake you up, darling?" the prince asked.

"You're naked?"

"Stark. You would be too if I hadn't been afraid I'd never get you back into your clothes."

His hands moved down over a bare back and found the heavy swell of buttocks and strayed between them. Flesh leaped in response. The prince was taking a lot for granted, but he was a plea-sure to touch. Rod decided to make allowances for a friend.

"Is that what you want, my wicked darling? I don't usually, but in your case I'll surrender to superior forces. Later, darling. We don't want to go into all that fuss here."

"Where are we?"

"At the party. A divine party as it's turned out."

The prince slid down along his side and kissed Rod's chest. Rod realized that his clothes were open all down the front and that he had an erection. He had an impulse to cover it, but the prince's mouth was moving over him toward it. He'd have to stop passing out on strange beds if he expected to keep his pants on. He put his hands on the bobbing head and ran his fingers through thick gold-en hair and let himself sink into a haze of sensual bliss.

In a moment the prince lifted his head. "You *are* well armed," he said. "I'll finish that in a minute. First I should show you what you've wanted to see." He lifted himself to his knees and straddled Rod and sat lightly on his abdomen. "Here's all of me," he said with an angelic smile.

Rod tried to focus his blurred vision. The light beside his head fell on rounded expanses of rose-gold skin. Stripped at last. Not the exquisite sculpture he had expected but the most ripely voluptuous body he had ever seen–big bones covered with smooth lush flesh, bisected at the groin by what he was ready to acknowledge as a princely erection lifting from a froth of golden curls. His eyes fixed on it despite the other attractions displayed before him.

For a moment longer he held the buttocks that were resting on him, but his hands were drawn elsewhere. He moved them around and lay them flat on the straddling thighs, framing the extravagant display of masculinity. He saw the mysterious tension he had noticed with Patrice, magnified to such a degree that it had a physical im-pact, and his heart began to beat more rapidly. Unlike the modest one he was growing familiar with, this filled the eye and demanded attention. It was a curiosity that anybody might find mesmerizing.

The prince ran a finger out along the under side of it, lifting it and showing it off. "I'm afraid I can't match you here," he said.

"You can't?" Rod asked, startled.

"You can see for yourself, darling. We're quite a pair, but you win. I don't mind. I adore having a big one—it's so marvelously vulgar, the only mark of the beast that hasn't been bred out of me—but I also adore finding bigger ones. It happens more rarely than you'd expect." He rose on his knees and tilted his torso back and eased his hips forward so that it seemed to soar above Rod's dazed eyes. The prince held it with both hands and looked down at himself. "Narcissus, darling." He lifted his eyes and looked at Rod. "Do you want me to bring it up there to you?" Rod rolled his head back and forth on the pillow in negation, unable to admit to any interest in the offer.

"I thought not. There are some things that boys who like girls don't want to do. Do you mind holding it?" He reached for Rod's hand and placed it on himself. Rod's other hand crept up to join it. He experimented with a gingerly caress.

He'd known he would eventually see the prince naked, but his imagination hadn't included a compelling erection. His hands became more freely caressing. Patrice was egging him on, claiming that he was no longer a quirk. It was strangely agreeable to fondle a big hard cock. He felt a twinge of envy but remembered that he was the winner. His hands delighted in the silken surface, testing its core of rigidity. It swelled hugely when he touched a place near the head. His eyes were spellbound. He moved a hand back and forth there, fascinated by the effect it had. He was performing this ultimate intimacy with someone he had only just met; faggots made sex dangerously easy. He wanted to satisfy his curiosity without appearing to enjoy it, but he knew his hands were betraying him.

"I guess you've seduced me after all," he said, grudging and self-conscious.

The prince reached behind him and lifted Rod's erection and exerted pressure against it to make him feel how fully aroused it

249

was. "At least I haven't paralyzed you." His smile was full of open uncomplicated pleasure untainted with triumph at his apparent success.

"How did I get a hard-on?" Rod demanded.

The prince's smile broadened. "We're all human, darling. With something like that to play with, any schoolboy would be inspired."

"I didn't even know it was happening."

"No. That doubtless gave me an advantage. I was afraid that when you came to, all my lovely work would be undone."

"Yeah. That's the thing. Why does it stay hard? You couldn't seduce me while I was asleep, so I guess you're seducing me right now."

He used the word while he resisted it. He still couldn't imagine making real love with this superb male.

"I've sucked your cock, darling. I'm going to make you come in a minute. When we get home I'll let you fuck me to your heart's content. I don't know who's seduced whom. It doesn't matter as long as it hasn't spoiled our beautiful friendship. I mean that." He put his hands on Rod's and held them still and bowed his head. He took a deep breath. "Careful, darling. Waiting for you was a bit of a strain. If you want to make me come, you can in about five seconds." He dropped his hands and straightened. "I love to see you hold it. I love what you're doing to it. You feel as if you're learning to like it."

Rod had to admit that he liked it very much. He wasn't stroking it just to be polite. The prince wanted him. He was apparently stroking it to make the prince want him even more. If he intended to stop at that, he was definitely being a tease. In another moment he felt it get so hard and inflexible that he knew the climax was near, and he reluctantly released it. He wanted the prince to want him, not come all over him.

The prince dropped back on his heels, and his hand took over. "Shall I? It's awfully close. I'm longing to suck you off, darling. Then we should get out of here."

To forestall orgasm, Rod gathered himself together and pulled himself up and grappled with the lush body and forced it down beside him. He tried to lift himself onto it but was tethered by his tangled clothes.

The prince looked up at him with happy encouragement. "You *are* waking up, darling. Are you going to be a sublime lover?"

"I don't really know. Am I? How can I be anything all dressed up like this?"

"I told you, darling. I wanted to be able to make a quick getaway."

Rod leaned down to him and opened his mouth again with his tongue. Boys' mouths were extraordinary. The prince's body writhed in under him. Their cocks pressed up hard against each other as if locked in combat. Their bodies strained to each other while the prince pushed clothes aside to expose more of Rod's. The naked golden body against Rod's nakedness was a searing delight. He responded blindly, feverishly, from flesh to flesh without conscious thought of queer or normal, with little sense of his partner's identity, knowing only that he no longer wanted to resist whatever it was he had felt he should resist. He heard animal sounds caught in a strangled throat. He wrenched his mouth free.

"All right," he cried. "If it's going to happen, I want it now, while it feels as if it has to happen, not planning it and getting up and going somewhere for it." He looked down into a beautiful face alight with passion.

"Please wait, darling. We need something and–and afterward. You know. Washing and all that. I hate using other people's towels."

"You want me now. You want me to take you. You want my cock up your ass." If he had been seduced, his seducer might as well face facts.

"Nobody ever put it to me in just those terms, but yes, darling. I do. Madly. We know it has to happen. It'll be the same later.

"No. It won't be natural anymore. Right now I want to fuck you as much as I've ever wanted to fuck anybody. Maybe it's because

251

I'm drunk. I thought you were so elegant, but you're all crazy up-side-down sex. All you guys seem to be overflowing with it. I'm going to fuck you silly."

"Darling, if you go on talking about it, I won't be able to wait."

"We're not going to. Get those damn clothes off me."

"We're both mad." The prince struggled up and helped Rod into a sitting position with his legs dropped over the edge of the bed. He unfastened his cuffs, and Rod pulled his arms out of sleeves, and his shirt and jacket were tossed aside. The prince pressed his golden head to his chest and slid down against him onto the floor.

Rod leaned back and propped himself on his arms while the prince removed his shoes and socks. He shook his swaying head and tried to find some order in his thoughts. What was going on? He felt lust pounding in him. He was burning with lust for the gold-en body that knelt before him. He had a bigger cock. He could see that now. Size triumphed. That was what this stuff with guys was all about. Cock worship. He was reeling with a sort of drunken madness, but as long as it lasted, he couldn't will it to pass. He stretched his legs and reveled in his liberation while the prince moved in between them and lowered his head, kneeling before a superior erection.

He felt soft lips moving thrillingly on it. He reached forward and tangled his fingers in the golden hair and raised the face and held it so that he could see his cock lifting against his beauty. The prince looked up with an adorable smile, and the great eyes bathed him in the limpid blue of their acquiescence. He moved his cheek against Rod's conquering masculinity, seeking its caress.

"Jesus," Rod muttered. "Is this what I wanted? Is my cock so great that it can destroy perfection?" For a moment he wanted to save the prince from abject surrender. A sob caught in his throat and stopped his breath. He swallowed hard. "Oh, God. I'm scared. How did we get started on this? You're a man. You're beautiful, but you're a big man like me, with hair on your legs and everything.

It's like fucking every guy I've ever known. I can't pretend you're a girl. This is really homo." He let thick golden hair slip through his fingers and dropped his hands.

The prince placed both his hands around Rod's erection and measured its length with a light-fingered ascent along it. His smile became a dazzled acknowledgment of its supremacy. "Yes, darling. We're both most definitely men, thank heavens. You're an utterly thrilling man. A bit mad, I imagine, but why not? I'm so glad we didn't wait. I wouldn't let myself believe your body was so sublime, but there's no doubt now. Positively blinding. How could I help falling in love with you?"

Rod reached for his elbows and urged him up. The prince rose while Rod let his hands slide down over his body. They came to rest on his hips. The big cock strained up, immense with wanting him, and he was gripped by a compulsion to ease its lustful tension. His mouth opened, and he let his lips and tongue play over it. It leaped up to fill his mouth. The prince uttered a small cry.

"Oh, darling, how heavenly of you. You want it after all. Only a moment, please. I don't want it to end before I've begun. You do it beautifully. What an incredible night. Good heavens. Not yet, darling. Please."

Patrice had ceased to be a quirk. Rod wanted to go on, stirred by the smooth taut power of the flesh thrusting into his mouth and by the surge of excitement he had sent coursing through the fabulous body. He drew back and looked at the big male organ, amazed that his was bigger. "If I'm a homo, I might as well act like one," he said recklessly. "I see why people like to suck cock. It really gets at the heart of things. Amazing. Go on. Fuck my mouth with it." He opened his mouth wide and was filled once more with warm active flesh. Ecstatic cries of protest assured him that he had learned his lessons well. He pulled back with a satisfied smile and exerted pressure on the prince's hips and turned him and looked at the massive flow of his back. He moved his hands down the curves of the buttocks. They quivered under his touch. "My God, a beautiful male ass. All male. There's enough strength there to fell an ox. Pure Michelangelo. Go on. Get whatever you're going to get. I'm pretty interested in that cock. It's a honey."

The prince swung around and opened Rod's mouth with it and ran it over his lips. "Oh, darling. How adorable of you to like it. Yours is going to drive me quite mad. I'll see what there is to help things along."

Rod watched the big body he was going to take move with a long manly stride to a door on the other side of the room. A light switched on. His mind lurched and veered off in a new direction. Love and friendship. That's what it all meant with Patrice. He liked the prince, but he couldn't pretend that this was anything more than a raw sexual encounter. He was naked, locked in a strange room, waiting for a naked man to share pleasures he already knew too much about. One more. And then another? It couldn't be right for him.

Odd shadows played on the bathroom wall. Panic suddenly shook him. He had to escape. He ordered his body to spring up, at least to get him to his feet. His head whirled as he rose slowly. He stood, swaying. He took a step, and his feet seemed to slide away from under him. He landed in a heap on the floor against a chair piled with his clothes.

He shook his head. He supposed he hadn't been asleep very long. Still groggy. He crawled back to the bed on all fours and once more climbed into a sitting position on the edge of it. Trapped.

He was breathing heavily. He looked down with curiosity at his erection, still demanding satisfaction. Why not let it happen just this once with the prince, knowing that there would never be another temptation like him? Their first meeting had been a funny sort of love at first sight; finding each other again by accident was proof that it wasn't something he'd been looking for. No need to panic.

The prince reappeared in the doorway carrying a towel and some other small object. His golden hair was in charming disarray, making him look even younger. Rod's eyes were filled with the splendor of him as he approached. He still hadn't adjusted to his size. He felt as if they ought to be engaged in some athletic contest. What games could two naked athletes play in a bedroom?

He made a dive for Rod, and their bodies were all over each other in an ecstasy of total exposure to each other. Their teeth clashed as their mouths were joined. Rod felt something slick being applied to himself. Their bodies were flung about against each other with mounting urgency.

The prince drew back and spoke breathlessly against Rod's lips. "We're in luck, darling. A very well-appointed household. We're ready for each other. More than ready, I'd say."

Rod looked into a face that was teasingly yielding but still not feminine. They were schoolboys playing dangerous games. "You don't mind using somebody else's towels?"

"I'm a total fraud, darling," the prince admitted with endearing candor. "I'd have walked through that party stark naked to get whatever we needed. I couldn't wait another second for you."

"I keep thinking we're having a wrestling match. That's what we should be doing. The winner would be the first to come."

"It sounds exciting. Later, maybe, if you promise not to wreck the furniture. Right now we seem to be committed to my unmanning."

Rod rolled over and pulled himself up over him. The sight of the magnificent back made his breath catch—so much power to be conquered. He lowered himself and made a tentative thrust between the massive buttocks.

"Please be gentle with me, darling." The prince's voice was suddenly small and helpless. "It *is* awfully big. I've never attempted anything like it before."

Rod drew his hips up and increased the pressure. The prince cried out as his penetration deepened. He waited, letting the prince take it at his own pace. The were slowly joined until the prince encouraged a final lunge, and he was lodged completely within him. The prince cried out again, and they lay still for a moment.

Rod's mind rocked with incredulity. He was having intercourse with the prince, defying all laws of the possible. This wasn't going to be the simple sexual release he had promised himself it would be. He experienced a complex sensation that was a reversal of what was actually happening, as if a wedge were being driven into him that threatened to split him in two.

"I'm going to take you," he warned roughly. "I mean, really take you so that you'll know I've had you. There can't be anything gentle about it."

"No, darling. That was just at the beginning. I don't want you to be gentle now."

"I thought you don't usually do this. Let's look at you." He worked them up to their knees and held his back against his chest. The prince rocked his hips slowly on him in a stunning demonstration of how deeply they were coupled. "You've been fucked a lot, haven't you?"

"Yes, lover. If you must know, by just about anybody who's wanted to, which adds up to a considerable army. It's no great secret. I just wanted you to feel special because you are. I'm madly in love with you. I don't expect you to take that seriously, but you're making me very happy."

Rod placed his hands with deliberation on one part of the prince after another in an effort to absorb the feel of the heroic body—his chest, his abdomen, his buttocks where they were joined, handling him like a precious object, wondering if the sensual thrills offered by smooth naked flesh were worth the conflicts they set up in him—the angry struggle between what he had been taught was right and the right he was establishing for himself, between the dictates of his conscience and the liberties he permitted himself to take with it, between rebellion and the stubborn residue of gentlemanly conformity that remained in him. Panic hovered at the edge of his increasingly passionate involvement with the man in his arms. Had he overlooked an inherent evil in something that felt necessary and good?

The prince pressed down against his thighs and dropped his head back and spoke with his lips against Rod's neck. "Divine. You're made for me, darling. Dear, God, your cock. Your cock, darling. I've never known such a perfect fit. I can lie back in your arms and let myself go. Oh, dear. Perhaps I shouldn't. May I, darling? I've waited so long. Please, darling. Oh, my God." He snatched up the towel and held it against himself while his body was convulsed, and Rod watched his beauty being transfigured by ecstasy. He gripped him close and waited for the spasms to subside. The body went limp, and he felt that he had come as close as he ever could to capturing whatever essence of him he could make his own. "Please don't mind, darling. I couldn't help it. Now I can concentrate on you."

"I don't mind. If you really go for it, I can stay there until you're hard again and ready to come with me."

"If anybody can make it happen again that qui–"

The door opened, and for an instant they were turned to stone. Rod heard a mumble of apology in French and began to breathe again. "Didn't you lock the door?" he whispered fiercely into the prince's ear.

"There's no key. Jacques promised to keep–"

Rod heard a click, and they were spotlighted in harsh overhead light. He was blinded.

"My God. What a splendid sight," a hearty French voice said.

"Let me down, darling," the prince whispered, the words exploding against the corner of Rod's mouth. "I'm too pretty to be ogled by the rabble." They fell forward, and Rod covered him with his body. He heard movement in the room and a growing chorus of voices, ribald, excited, punctuated by bursts of laughter. "*Le grand* Lussigny" and "*l'américain*" kept recurring in the snatches of comment that reached Rod's ears.

"The sons of bitches," he muttered. "What're we going to do?"

"Nothing, darling. Stay in me. If we don't do anything, maybe they'll go away. Jacques swore he'd keep everybody out." Their lips were touching. The prince breathed his words into Rod's mouth.

257

Rod moved a hand to cover the sides of their faces, shielding them from view. The prince moaned down his throat as his body became invisibly active. Every hidden muscle that contained Rod vibrated on him. The voices became lewdly raucous. Questions were called out about the size of Rod's parts.

"I'd like to tell them," the prince murmured. "They may think nothing's happening, but it's the most heavenly ever. You're doing it, darling. You're making me hard again. I can't stand it much longer. I want you to fuck me." His body became more agitated until Rod was obliged to move slightly to his rhythm to hold himself in place. A cheer went up. An obscene chant began urging them on to greater efforts. "Do it, darling," the prince pleaded, biting his lips. "Fuck me. Let them watch. I don't care. I've got a hard-on now. Let them see it."

Rod began to move freely in response to the urgings of the prince's body, only just beginning to recover from shock and to grasp what was happening around him, beginning to feel a murderous loathing for everybody in the room. A hand ran over his buttocks, and he pulled himself to his knees with a roar of rage, bringing the prince up with him.

"You fucking shits," he shouted. "Get the fuck out of here. Don't anybody dare touch me." There were fewer of them than he'd thought, eight or ten at the most, and his mind registered gratefully the fact that he knew none of them. The prince's body was swaying against him, his arms lifted and his fingers running through Rod's hair. His wet mouth moved over the side of Rod's face, and he licked his ear and nose and cheek. With a jolt of horror, Rod realized that the prince was enjoying it, welcoming the opportunity to display his violated body. He slammed an arm against the back of the prince's head and forced him down on all fours and drove hard into him. The prince cried out joyfully. Rod saw a naked youth emerge from the group and climb up over the end of the bed on his knees. The prince reached for him and supported himself on the newcomer's hips and took his cock in his mouth. Rod seized his hair and yanked his head away.

"You bastard. You filthy bastard," he raged. His body was shattered by orgasm, but he was scarcely aware of what had caused the sudden dissolution of his limbs. He knew only that he had somehow been freed from this horror. He wrenched himself brutally from the prince and flung him down and sprang from the bed. He charged through the onlookers, scattering them as he went, and found the bathroom and slammed the door behind him. He washed blindly and dried himself on something and plunged back into the room, prepared to knock down anybody who got in his way.

The group had dwindled to five or six, all naked, all on the bed. Somebody had taken his place on the prince's back. The prince had a cock in his mouth. Other bodies were tangled together in positions that he excluded from his range of vision. His stomach heaved with shame and revulsion. He turned his back on the repellent scene, cursing his stupidity and his loss of control. He had been so deceived by appearances that he had seen sweetness where there was only depravity. He was learning a lesson that he hoped would be seared on his memory, a lesson so ugly that it would be impossible to forget. Queers. They were all vile, degraded, and sex-obsessed. He hoped he never had to speak to another one.

He tried to pull clothes onto his shaking body. Somebody came up behind him and slipped an arm around his waist. He stepped back and swung his fist hard and saw a naked figure reel back and crash to the floor. It released the rage that was seething in him and calmed the violent trembling of his hands. He managed to pull socks over his feet and jam them into his shoes. He shoved his shirt down into his trousers without buttoning it and pulled on his jacket as he rushed for the door. He remembered he had a coat, but he had no intention of looking for it. He saw it on a bench in the entrance hall and snatched it up and hurtled through the front door and tumbled down dark stairs, following them blindly wherever they led him in a passion for escape.

He broke out into a dark narrow street and kept on stumbling forward, half running, rearing away from shadows, steadying himself against buildings. Dimly he became aware of having entered a more populous district and slowed down to a walk. Why was he running? His chest was heaving, and he felt very drunk. He didn't remember being so drunk. His chest was cold. He looked down and saw that his shirt was unbuttoned to his waist. Without stopping he fumbled with the buttons and managed to get some of them fastened. He buttoned his jacket and coat over him. He began to wonder at there being so many people about in the wide well-lit tree-lined street. He'd had the impression that it was very late but guessed he was mistaken. People were walking; people were standing in groups. The presence of people and light made him feel healed, saved from some vague horror that would probably turn out to be a dream as soon as he sobered up. He lurched along the street and was engulfed by a milling crowd. He saw people carrying placards. Laughing faces were turned to him, and he laughed in response. An arm was linked through his, and he was propelled forward. A chant swelled up around him that stirred an unpleasant memory, except that this was friendly and vigorous, not at all unpleasant, something about North Africa that he didn't understand. He was marching. It was fun. Young men and girls fell into ranks around him. It was a party, a celebration. He marched with a will, being forced to follow a reasonably straight course by the press around him and by the arms that supported him on both sides.

Progress slowed, and Rod was restrained when he tried to break through the line in front of him.

"*En avant*," he cried enthusiastically, and the group surged forward briefly before coming to a halt again. He squinted over the heads in front of him and saw the reason for the delay. Helmeted men carrying clubs were advancing on them. The ranks began to waver and disintegrate. There were cries of warning. Somewhere deep in his consciousness he felt a small tremor of alarm, but it was too feeble to be seized by his brain and converted into action.

The air of tumultuous festivity stifled alarm. People were pushing and elbowing all around him. He was borne to and fro, too busy trying to stay on his feet to think about anything else. One of the uniformed men seized him, and he was channeled into a group that was being detached from the rest.

"I'm an American. I'm an American," he kept murmuring politely, making no effort to resist. It wasn't until he was shoved into a dark crowded van that he began to feel that was something was very wrong. There was an excited clamor all around him. Everybody seemed to be talking at once. He couldn't see his neighbors. They pressed on him from both sides. The van lurched into movement, and he was swayed and jostled and bumped between other bodies and the hard seat. Somebody had made a great mistake. He tried to think what to do about it. There was nobody to appeal to, to whom he could state his case. He became aware of a strong stale smell of unwashed clothing. He began to feel as if he had to fight for air. He couldn't stand it much longer. He was suffocating. Get out. That was the thing to do. There was no reason for him to stay. It was a mistake. He tried to rise, but the swaying of the truck immediately jolted him back onto the bench. Somebody beside him muttered a curse. He lifted his head in an effort to reach purer air.

His mind wandered. His tenuous grasp of where he was slipped altogether, and he was simply borne along feeling slightly baffled as he was jostled and bounced to nowhere. When the van stopped at last, he struggled to relate himself to reality, as if he were in fact asleep and caught in some particularly dense dream. When the rear door was thrown open, he could see uniformed men silhouetted against the grim facade of one of Paris' old stone buildings. His fellow passengers were on their feet now, shuffling toward the rear. They were silent, but Rod could feel something new in the air, a tension, a quiet menace. As the van emptied, he managed to pull himself to his feet, but he followed the others with reluctance. Whatever they were here for, it was no concern of his. He must find somebody to explain matters to. This was his only coherent thought as he descended from the van.

He steadied himself when he felt his feet firmly planted on the ground and looked around him. Dark-windowed walls surrounded them. A number of vans similar to the one from which he had just emerged were lined up at one side. One of them rumbled into action as he watched. Figures were moving about in the shadows. Everything blurred and separated before his eyes. He found it very confusing. A command was shouted, and he was aware of movement among his group. Nobody was paying any attention to him. He turned and, making out what appeared to be a gate through which the van was disappearing, he started toward it. He was immediately wedged between two burly men in uniform.

"Gently. Gently," one of them said, not unkindly. "Where do you think you're going?"

"There's no reason for me to be here. I don't know any of those others. I'm an American. I don't know what this is all about." Rod heard himself say all this clearly and intelligibly in the policeman's own tongue.

"He doesn't speak French," one of them explained discouragingly to the other. He went on in carefully spaced syllables, as if speaking to a half-wit, "*All-ez a-vec tes collégues. Compris?*"

His arms were seized from both sides, and he was propelled forward with chilling force. A prickling of dread ran down his spine. He wanted to make an indignant protest, but some deep layer of guilt held him back. There was something he had to hide. Something about money. It surely had nothing to do with his being here and yet an inexplicable guilt was growing in him. He could feel himself turning wary and sly.

"All right, all right," he panted, barely able to remain on his feet under the rough handling of the policemen. "I'm not trying to make any trouble."

"So much the better for you," said one of his escorts.

"So it seems he speaks some French after all," the other said suspiciously.

He was half carried, half dragged across the courtyard to where the others were already being herded through an unmarked door.

"You don't have to hold on to me," Rod tried again to reassure his captors. "I just want to explain to somebody that the whole thing is a mistake."

"You'll have plenty of chance to explain anything you want. Perhaps even some things you don't want, eh?"

Once inside the door they gave him a shove toward a flight of worn stone steps and let him go. He staggered forward and caught the banister and started up. At the top, the stairway gave onto an enormous corridor that seemed to stretch as far as the eye could reach with doors opening off on both sides of it. The floor was made of worn planking that echoed with the tread of many feet. A black-robed lawyer swept by, the bats' wings of his sleeves fluttering menacingly. A pair of policemen flanking a man wearing handcuffs and with bloodstains on the front of his shirt emerged from a door. Policemen in pairs escorted other charges to and fro—a trio of sullen women in shabby finery, a man incongruous in elaborate makeup and sharply tailored suit, a stout man with his face wreathed in dirty bandages. Some sort of freak show, Rod decided sagaciously. The whole world was a fucking freak show. He recoiled from the scene. The night was an endless dream. Small but recurrent shocks jarred his alcoholic torpor. Dread stirred uneasily in him, but he still couldn't relate to his surroundings, so it remained unfocused. The fact that he was alive to some danger without even identifying it made him feel that he was prepared to deal with it. He had already forgotten how he had got here.

Unaware of being guided, he turned off the corridor and entered a large room filled with the harsh light of unshaded bulbs. It contained several battered wooden desks behind which men in sleazy suits were working over papers. People were taking seats on a long bench running along one side of it, and he somehow gathered that he was to join them and did so. He closed his eyes against the light. He wanted a drink. He was sleepy. He could pretend to go to sleep. That would be a smart move, he decided. He slumped against the wall, asleep and awake.

More awake again, he found himself standing in front of a desk behind which two men were seated. He couldn't see their faces. They were bent over what appeared to be a large record book. He hadn't the slightest idea where he was. He looked around him. Policemen. A row of men on a bench. It all looked vaguely familiar. He turned back to the desk. "What?" he said. He had the distinct impression that one of the men asked him something.

"I said I want to see your identity card."

Rod began to fumble through his pockets. They were empty. "I don't think I have it with me. It's at home. With my passport. I'm an American."

"Your name and address."

Rod provided them. He watched as they were inscribed in the book.

"Your means of livelihood?"

Rod opened his mouth and closed it. Fear suddenly clutched at his throat. His mind splintered, casting up fragments of memory. The police. François had warned him. He remembered now. Maybe François had been arrested and had tried to implicate him. The little shit was capable of anything. He remembered he wasn't supposed to be living with Patrice. "Listen. That address I gave you—that's just where I work. I live in a hotel around the corner. You'd better write it down."

"One address is sufficient if you can be reached there. Your means of livelihood?" Their bored repetition of the question seemed a confirmation that they knew the whole story. One side of it. His mouth opened and closed. His legs felt as if they were going to give way. He wasn't going to let François get away with it. He hadn't done anything. Words tumbled from his lips as he hurried to revise the picture.

"I don't know what he's told you, but it's obviously a lot of nonsense. I lent him some money. That's all. I don't know what he wanted it for. He was–François, François Leclerc–he was going to Marseille, and I decided to go with him. Just for the drive. This friend of mine, M. Valmer, wanted to go too. That's all there was to it." He remembered François saying it might be the police following them. If so, they knew about the wild chase around Marseille. He hurried on. "When we were leaving, François thought somebody was following us. All of a sudden he started roaring around town to get rid of them. M. Valmer didn't like the way he was driving and decided to come back on the train. I think somebody shot at us. I'm a painter. I don't know anything about deals with money and all that. I'm perfectly willing to cooperate with you in any way I can, but I don't know anything. Your getting me in here is just a misunderstanding." Rod paused breathlessly. There was a brief silence as the two men looked at each other, not at him. Finally one of them shrugged.

"What do you suppose is the matter with this one?"

"I don't know. It sounds like the *milieu*," said the other. "Perhaps it's a case for the special services."

"*En effet*. But it's not our affair." The official leaned around Rod and gestured.

"I've got to go now," Rod said, satisfied that he had stated his case with clarity and persuasion. He caught a glimpse out of the corner of his eye of a policeman moving in close at his side and went on with a hint of desperation. "You know where you can find me if you want me."

The official bent over his book once more with a sigh. "Monsieur, even Americans are obliged to carry papers," he said. "We must verify your identity. It may take until morning. We'll make you as comfortable as we can." He made a slight dismissive gesture and turned pointedly to his colleague.

"I won't accept this," Rod shouted. The policeman edged closer. His trembling increased. Did anybody know he was here? He couldn't think. They were just checking his identity. That was fair enough. They didn't question his story. He wasn't really being arrested. He put his hand to his forehead and turned from the desk with a spasm like a sob caught deep in his chest. It would help to get some sleep. The policeman fell into step at his side.

Rod leaped aside as the shot was fired. He found himself on his feet looking around dazedly. The pounding of his heart subsided. A dream. Everything was a dream. He moved his head slowly back and forth and blinked his burning eyes. He was still alone in the room where he had been left the night before. The night before? The square of gray light in the window told him it was day. He glanced at his watch and saw that it had stopped. It couldn't be 3:30, morning or afternoon. Before he had time to sit down again, his mind was crowded with memories. They all came back with a rush, simultaneously. Patrice's failure to come home. Lambert and the party. The prince and his disgusting friends. The demonstration or whatever it was that he got mixed up in. The insane "statement" that had led to his being shut up here. There were still a few blanks. Had he done anything worse than the things he remembered? He sank down into the leather armchair in which he had apparently been sleeping.

The first thing to get straight was the period following his arrest. Had he been arrested? If so, how had they picked him out of that crowd? He went over it minute by minute, trying to remember every word he had spoken, every move he had made. He had a clear, vivid memory of his declaration of innocence, though he couldn't re-create the thoughts that had provoked it. What had possessed him to suppose that a couple of policemen making a routine identity check in the middle of the night could know anything about François and the trip to Marseille? They'd said something suspicious. And François. He had warned him that they might be in trouble.

At least he hadn't signed anything. He was sure of that. And if he had mentioned names, they hadn't thought it important enough to ask him to repeat them. The whole interview had, in fact, been so nearly incoherent that he needn't be bound by any of it today. He could dismiss it all as drunken fantasy and nobody could prove otherwise.

Meanwhile, he had to get word to Patrice. He was bound to be home now and worried about him. Why hadn't he done something about their getting a telephone? He would have to send a telegram. Surely they couldn't object to that. He wasn't really under arrest. He hadn't been put in a cell. They hadn't the right to hold him indefinitely.

All the stories he had heard about the lethargic and high-handed methods of the French police came to mind. He pulled himself to his feet again and took his surroundings in more coherently. He seemed to be in a sort of reading room. A table stood in the middle surrounded by chairs. He crossed to a closed door but hesitated before opening it. The thought of facing whatever lay beyond it, of encountering hostility or lack of comprehension made him realize that his head was splitting. There was a foul taste in his mouth. He raised his hand and felt his beard. He must look like hell.

He tried to straighten his coat and discovered that the buttons weren't in the right holes. He unfastened them and found the subsequent layers, jacket and shirt, in similar disarray. He buttoned his shirt properly and tucked it more carefully into his trousers. He shook down his rumpled clothes and felt a bit more presentable. He would demand his rights. They had laws here like anywhere else. He went to the door and pulled it open.

Beyond it, he found a shabby, cluttered office in which a single policeman was sitting behind a desk reading a newspaper, his cap pushed onto the back of his head. He looked up as Rod entered.

"I've got to send a telegram," Rod announced, hoping that his decisive manner would sweep away any obstacles. "It's very important. I've got to let a friend know that I'm all right."

"A telegram?" The policeman shrugged good-humoredly. "Unfortunately, this isn't a telegraph office."

"You can use the telephone."

267

"The telephone." The policeman studied the instrument on the desk before him. "Who would pay for it?"

"I can pay. I think. If I haven't enough, I'll pay later."

"Perhaps. But I don't believe it's covered in the regulations. It sounds irregular." He hunched himself over the desk and looked up at Rod placatingly. "Look, monsieur. M. Gouffron will be here shortly. This is his affair. You will talk to him. He will send the telegram for you. It is not for me to decide."

"But I tell you, this is urgent. I've been gone all night. What will my friends think?" Aware of how disreputable he must look, he advanced slowly to the policeman, trying not to give the impression that he was threatening him. The latter regarded him with an alert but sympathetic eye.

"Listen, monsieur. These things are unpleasant. I regret it. But 15 minutes one way or the other won't make any difference now. Sit down and be patient. That's the only thing you can do if you don't wish to create further difficulties. M. Gouffron will surely be here any minute."

Rod seated himself stiffly upright, trying to suggest in his bearing his disassociation from the whole affair. The least he expected was a browbeating from some self-righteous official who would know nothing about him and who would probably classify him with the rest of the crooks and vagrants that passed before him every day. He remembered that things had been said last night that had given him the idea that François had informed against him. He didn't know what he would do if he were really in trouble. He had to be very sure there was no danger for Patrice in citing him as a witness. He couldn't believe that he had ever taken pride in thinking of himself as a sort of outlaw. Never actively. Never to the point of public defiance. Patrice was a bit to blame for putting his work before every other consideration. Without his implicit sanction, he would never have done some of the things he had done in the last few days. His fists were doubled in his lap. He wanted to smash them down on the desk in front of him. How much longer was he going to have to wait here?

268

As if in answer, the policeman folded his newspaper and pulled his cap forward so that it sat squarely on his head. "I think that's M. Gouffron now," he said. Rod had heard nothing. The policeman rose and pulled down his tunic and settled his belt over his paunch. He went to the door and opened it. A nondescript man in a shabby suit slipped in. A few words were exchanged, which Rod didn't catch, and the policeman withdrew with a salute, closing the door behind him. The newcomer didn't glance at Rod but went to a corner and removed his jacket and hung it on a hook. He put on another, even shabbier, jacket that had been hanging there. He proceeded to the desk the policeman had vacated and sat down. Rod had started to rise but settled back uncertainly. He watched while M. Gouffron read a paper in a folder that lay in front of him, waiting for an opportunity to ask him to send the telegram. After a moment the neat little man pulled on his nose and looked up at Rod and grunted.

"Another American," he said with a touch of incredulity. His eyes were weak behind steel-rimmed spectacles. His gray hair was thin over a freckled skull. "Do you people behave at home the way you do in this country?"

Because this was unwarranted–if he meant Rod's having been picked up in the street with a crowd–his heart constricted with foreboding. M. Gouffron looked down at his paper again. He pulled his nose and cleared his throat.

"Now then. What is this story about one François Leclerc?"

"Nothing," Rod asserted. "I was drunk. I just happened to go to Marseille with him the other day. We had a–well, there wasn't any trouble, really. Just a peculiar incident. I suppose that when I saw policemen, I immediately associated them with that."

M. Gouffron pounced. His weak eyes seemed curiously penetrating as he leaned and said, "So you remember everything you said last night."

Rod's mind was immediately dodging, backtracking, reinforcing his lines of defense. He had apparently given himself away although he didn't quite see how. Either they knew something about François or they didn't. He should probably sham language difficulties. "I remember talking a lot of nonsense," he said, making his French sound labored. "I don't remember what it was all about."

"Yet you were prepared with an explanation for having mentioned Leclerc."

"I had this idea that my being here had something to do with him. It's the sort of association of ideas you have if you're drunk."

"I've never been drunk." M. Gouffron said the word in a way that made Rod wonder whether it was such a good excuse after all. M. Gouffron picked up a pencil and put a fresh piece of paper with the other in the folder. "The names of these friends of yours," he said, poised to write.

"What friends? I hardly know François Leclerc. He was going to Marseille, and this friend of mine and I thought it would be fun to go."

"This M. Valmer is the friend you refer to? His Christian name please."

"Listen. He knows even less about this than I do. There's no point getting him into it."

"Less about what?"

"About nothing really. About why François was going to Marseille."

"Why was he going?"

"He said he had some business. I don't know what. My friend didn't even know that much. He didn't even come back with us."

M. Gouffron sat without moving. The pencil remained poised. He spoke dryly. "Let me remind you that you've told a very odd story. You were followed. You were shot at. Marseille is not the most tranquil city in France, but American tourists aren't usually shot at, even there. This is not a comedy. You would do well to refrain from heroics."

"I don't remember any of that. I must have been thinking of a film I saw recently." He had reached safe ground that he intended to occupy to the end. He remembered nothing.

M. Gouffron let the pencil slip from his grasp and joined the tips of his fingers lightly together and looked at them. "What is your means of livelihood?"

"I'm a painter," he began proudly, although somehow in these surroundings it didn't have quite the ring he would have liked. Painters were notoriously erratic and unstable. Painters often ended up in jail. He went on with some diffidence. "I came over here with a certain sum of money that I've been living on ever since. I'm soon going to have another exhibition that should make enough to keep me for another year or so."

"Yet you have money to lend to people you hardly know?"

"What are you talking about? I don't lend people money." If François had been talking, and they came back to him about that one, he was ready. It hadn't been a loan but an investment—in an unknown project.

"And these dollars? You have of course been changing them legally?" M. Gouffron straightened one finger as Rod began to speak. "Don't bother to say anything. There are always ways to make a little extra. We know them all, and it's very easy to check. You're in order with our tax people?"

"Your tax people? I pay my taxes in the United States. I don't have to pay anything here."

"You earn nothing here? You sell no pictures?"

"No," Rod replied with confidence. He was completely safe on this score. It was a relief to be able to speak openly and truthfully. M. Gouffron gave him a little time to enjoy the sensation. The official picked up his pencil and placed the point on the paper in front of him.

"Let me refresh your memory," he said. "You stated that you lent money to this Leclerc. You said you didn't know what he wanted it for. When people lend money it's not usual for them to demand an explanation of the purpose of the loan. Why did you feel it necessary to emphasize your ignorance?"

"I've told you. I don't lend money."

"You've had no financial dealings with him of any sort?"

"Of any sort? That could include buying him a drink. I think you ought to be more specific." He made a hasty mental note to return the money to his friend at the bank while he prepared himself for a grilling.

271

There was a maddening silence while M. Gouffron stared at the tip of the pencil resting on the paper. "Very well," he said at last. "It's quite evident that you've been engaged in some questionable financial arrangements with M. Leclerc. Whatever they are, your name is now in our files. All your banking and exchange transactions will be closely scrutinized. I see no reason not to warn you of this. Perhaps it will save us all trouble in the future. In a month or so—these things move slowly, but our methods have proved to be effective—you'll be called in by the tax people and the *Office des Changes* to give a complete accounting of your financial dealings since you've been here. If you can satisfy them, that will be the end of the matter about the mysterious M. Valmer than you wish to."

"In a month or so, maybe I won't be here," Rod burst out on the spur of the moment. It filled him with deep unexpected relief to say it. That was one way of getting the hell out of this. He wanted to let out a great shout of protest and helplessness. He thought of being in a place where bombs didn't keep going off in the street, where you weren't bullied by the police, where you weren't locked up for the night because you happened to get caught in a crowd. Yes, where he wasn't always surrounded by queers. They were around at home, but he'd never known any. At home, there were recognizable social signals that told you what was what. He knew who he was there. Home, where you didn't have the responsibility of rewriting the rules, because they were already written. You didn't fall in with petty crooks in America. It helped to remind himself that he had a way out, even though he knew Patrice would never permit him to accept what would amount to defeat. A defeat of what? Home and a good safe job. He'd had a success with part-time work. What was Patrice trying to prove?

"You're thinking of leaving the country?" M. Gouffron asked. "Well, so far we have no grounds for stopping you. There remains the verification of your identity." He pressed a button. The policeman reentered the office and stood beside the desk. Rod had the feeling it was over for the moment. He wouldn't have to send the

272

telegram after all. Once he had talked it all over with Patrice, they'd know how to cope with developments. François was going to be questioned. His head throbbed painfully.

"You will accompany M. Mac-an-teer to his domicile," M. Gouffron instructed the policeman. "Make a note of the numbers of his passport and carte d'identite. The usual routine. That's all. Inspector Lascaux will provide a car." The official turned back to the paper in front of him and began to scribble on it. The policeman looked at Rod and nodded. "Monsieur," he said.

Restored to respectability, Rod didn't want to slink off like a criminal. He rose and held out his hand to M. Gouffron. "Thank you, monsieur. I'm sorry if I've been a trouble to you," he said.

M. Gouffron stopped writing and looked at Rod's hand. The phone rang, and he picked it up and offered his other hand, still holding the pencil, to Rod. He listened for a moment and seemed to come to attention. He gestured Rod back to the chair with his pencil and straightened his tie and smoothed his sparse hair. "Yes, monsieur," he said, bowing at the phone. Of course, monsieur, yes. François Leclerc. Very good, monsieur. Yes, that name figures in the dossier. I understand, monsieur." He closed the folder that lay on the desk in front of him. "You can count on me, monsieur. A pleasure." He bowed to the phone again before hanging up and resumed his air of authority with the policeman. "You will conduct M. Mac–this gentleman to 107. They will know what to do. Give them this." He handed the folder to the policeman.

Rod's heart was pounding uncomfortably again. "What's this all about?" he demanded.

"The affair is out of my hands. You will go, please."

Rod rose again, no longer thinking about making a graceful exit. The policeman preceded him to the door, and they went out into dark deserted corridors and narrow twisting stairs. Nothing resembled anything he remembered from the night before. He supposed he had been transferred to some special section.

They mounted two flights of stairs and followed a corridor around a corner and entered an unmarked door. It gave onto a narrow passage that ran along a sort of screened cell. A waist-high wooden partition was completed by heavy wire mesh that rose to the ceiling. Rod could see men moving around on the other side of it. A shout gathered again in his throat. If they took him in there, he would claw his way out. The policeman took the folder to a slot at the end of the partition and handed it through to a man who glanced at it and held it aloft. Another man came up behind him and took it. All these movements were fragmented by the heavy wire mesh. Rod's muscles were gathered together to resist any attempt to get him inside, while his eyes traveled along the partition looking for an opening in it. He couldn't find one. They had no right to keep him here. M. Gouffron had said it was all over except for the identity check. He was going to start throwing his weight around, demand some written authorization if this went on much longer. He heard a door opening, and he turned. A man wearing a dark raincoat and a felt hat pulled low over his eyes was standing in the doorway Rod had entered. A gangster. He nodded to the policeman and gestured to Rod to come out. Rod did so with alacrity. The man moved away down the corridor, and Rod caught up to him and fell into step beside him.

"What's happening now? Am I getting out of here?"

"Yes. Somebody wants to see you."

"I'm not sure I want to see him. Why should I?"

"Because I have orders to take you to him. A compatriot of yours. I'm doing you a favor."

"Thanks."

They descended stairs in silence and came out into a dingy courtyard where an old black Citroën was waiting. Another man in civilian clothes was at the wheel. Rod's escort gestured him into the backseat and got in with him, and the car rolled forward. Rod took a deep breath of cold morning air. At least he was out. He began to relax. The cold air helped his head. A compatriot? Somebody at the American Embassy who had heard about him and knew his family and wanted to offer help? He didn't need help until he knew what was going on. He wanted to get home to Patrice.

A few glances out the window placed him somewhere around the Palais de Justice. The streets were busy. Judging by the light, he guessed it wasn't much past 9 o'clock. A glimpse of a clock in the street confirmed it–9:30 it said. Patrice would postpone going to work until the last possible moment, wondering about him, assuming he'd spent the night with Nicole. If he were being taken straight home, he'd be in time. Damn not having a telephone.

They drove through traffic, and after a few minutes he saw that they were taking the bridge across to the Ile-St-Louis. They turned onto the quai and passed trees prettily sweeping over the river.

"Stop here," the man beside him ordered. "I'll be only a moment. Monsieur," he said to Rod, letting himself out and holding the door open. They walked half a block before his escort turned his head quickly back and forth along the street and said in a low voice, "In here." They entered an old sagging building and mounted a grand staircase, shabby but elegant in a Parisian way. They stopped in front of a door, and the escort pushed a button.

The door was opened by a big man in slacks and shirt-sleeves. The knot of his tie was pulled down below an unbuttoned collar. He took off glasses as he looked at them.

"Good morning, sir," the escort said.

"Thanks." The man nodded at him and stood aside to admit Rod and closed the door after him. He led the way across a hall into a big room that looked as if nobody lived in it. Pieces of ill-matched furniture stood about in it, but there were no pictures, no homely clutter of objects. A metal office jutted at right angles from one wall. It was the only thing in the room that looked used. Papers littered its surface. Rod took off his coat and put it on the end of a sofa. The big man stopped and faced him.

275

"Mather, as in Cotton," he said as if he had said it thousands of times before. He didn't hold out a hand. "It's Henry, actually. You're Rod. I know quite a lot about you, Rod."

He had a lean lined face and graying hair. A tough character but intelligent, Rod decided. "Nothing surprises me anymore," he said.

"You look a little worse for wear. They don't exactly run a rest home over there, do they? No rough stuff, I hope."

"No. They were polite enough."

"I'm just making some coffee. Would you like to fix yourself up? There's an electric razor in the bathroom if you want to use it. Breakfast? Bacon and eggs?"

"No thanks. I could use a beer if you have some. Actually, I'm in sort of a hurry."

"You can count on an hour, with or without eggs. You might as well try to relax. You're in more trouble than you bargained for."

"Listen, if you'll just tell me what–"

Mather held up a peremptory hand. "Let's have some coffee, and that beer. The bathroom's in there." He pointed at a door and turned and headed off in the opposite direction. Rod watched him go while anger rose and subsided in him. He resigned himself with exasperation to following directions.

He found a modern American-style bathroom, beyond a bedroom, with a toilet beside a glass shower stall. Seeing it made him realize that his bladder was about to burst, and he headed for it gratefully. He washed his face and used the electric razor and found a clean comb. Time for Patrice to give him another haircut. Damn not being able to get to him before he went to work. At least he'd think he knew where he was.

He returned to the big room and found Mather sitting at the desk with an American electric percolator at his side. A glass of beer and a cup were opposite him. Rod picked up the glass and drained it in one swallow.

"It's like that, is it?" Mather said with a brief laugh. "I know the feeling. I'll get you another." He poured coffee and rose and glanced

276

at Rod with a little nod. "You look better. You're a good-looking guy." He left with the glass.

Rod's head reeled as the beer hit his stomach. But then everything began to smooth out and flow freely. He would live. He pulled up a chair to the other side of the desk and drank the hot thin coffee. Better by the minute. Mather returned with another glass of beer and sat and began to fill a pipe. He glanced up at Rod.

"Oh, sorry. Cigarette?" He tossed a pack of American cigarettes across the desk. Rod hadn't smoked for more than a week and took one. Mather lit his pipe and put on his glasses and shuffled through the papers in front of him. "Let's see. We can start with this. I'll want you to sign it."

Rod ran his eyes over the paper that was put before him. It was a statement told in the first person, purportedly by himself. "What's all this about dope," he demanded indignantly. "I don't know anything about it."

"You're learning."

"Yes, but it says here I knew all along."

"That's the way it would look in court. It may not come to that. I still don't know, but we're not in the clear by a long shot. François may have to take the rap. That means you too. We'd look after you both eventually, but it could be a long unpleasant wait."

"François?"

"The same."

"Oh, for God's sake. Who the hell are you?"

"I don't show my credentials in this business. Get that straight. You're here. That must mean I have some pull."

"They were ready to let me go until you got into it. I suppose it was you."

"By tomorrow you'd be back there in a cell. Don't kid yourself about that. You've heard of the CIA? It covers a multitude of sins, but that's close enough for our purposes."

"I'm going to go to the American Embassy about this."

"Go ahead, but it won't get you anywhere. They'll tell you all about me. I'm in business here." Mather reached into a drawer and dropped a crumpled wad of bills onto the desk. Rod stiffened and his scalp prickled as he recognized the money François had given him. "It looks as if Jack Harkins at the bank might be in for a little trouble too. Recognize it? Every one of those has been straightened out and photographed and rolled together again just the way you left them. We're careful. Go ahead. Take it. It's yours. Whatever you do with it, it'll be traced to you. This drug thing is just a cover for something much bigger—I guess you've begun to figure that out for yourself—but we've got to play it straight or the whole operation will come apart at the seams. As far as everybody is concerned, except me, François is just a cheap punk and you are too."

Rod's thoughts were chaotic. Was he being told that he was going to have to think of François as one of the good guys? A hero? "I don't understand how I got into this. Why did I get picked up last night?"

"You were more or less leading a demonstration for Algerian independence. I don't know what possessed you to go into that rigmarole about Marseille. Still, I can't blame you. You didn't know what you'd gotten into. François shouldn't have taken you with him even though he was, in a sense, following instructions. We're interested in recruiting good men. He's had his eye on you. He's impressed by you. He doesn't think your homosexuality is any more of a problem than his is."

"My homosexuality?" It was the last straw. He was a crook and a queer. He felt like overturning the desk on this quiet, keen-voiced tormentor. He stared at him with outrage.

"Oh? Did he get that wrong?" Mather asked.

"He sure as hell did."

"I hope you're telling the truth. I didn't think you looked the type, if there is such a thing. It doesn't matter, but it would make my job a little easier." He leaned forward over the papers for a moment and sucked on his pipe. "You moved back into the Hotel Alabama yesterday."

"Yes. I don't remember why."

"Autosuggestion induced by François, I think. Probably a good idea. We had a man around there in case you turned up. He was supposed to keep an eye on you. He didn't do a very good job." Mather sat back and looked at him. "We can use you. We damn well *have* to use you. I don't know if you're patriotic, but your country needs you, as the saying goes."

"I'm not interested." Ever since he could remember, his father carried on about his responsibilities to his country, which usually turned out to be responsibilities to the family's interests. He was out of all that.

Mather pointed with his pipe stem at the paper facing Rod. "I could nail you with that right now if I wanted to. That is, the French could. You're in our pocket."

"I haven't signed it."

"You will."

Rod's throat felt congested with the shout of protest that had been lodged there since he had woken up this morning. He took a long swallow of beer to clear it. He wasn't going to get dragged into a situation where spies would be watching him, where his telephone, if he had one, or even his mail might be tampered with. There was plenty wrong with the States, but there were certain things you knew couldn't happen there. There weren't many orphans either. Life retained some sort of orderly continuity and progression, developing normally instead of bursting out in strange outcroppings of the unknown and untried. "I'm not sure I'm going to be here much longer," he said.

"You mean Paris? It doesn't matter where you are. We'll find you if we need you. Right now you're signed on for the duration. You have no choice until I've sorted this out. Somebody's playing dirty. We haven't put it all together yet, but it's not funny. We've already got a victim on our hands. Your friend–" he leaned over his papers again. "Patrice Valmer. Correct? He got caught in the cross fire. His body was found yesterday. Shot."

279

Rod's mind was a blank. It suddenly became a roaring tunnel through which he was hurtling. A massive slippage occurred in him, a great ripping and tearing of everything in him, similar to something he remembered happening before, but so violent that it almost knocked him out of his chair. His breath stopped. When he could breathe again, he felt strangely altered, light-headed, detached. He wasn't sure whether he was entering a dream or if everything that had happened until this moment had been a dream. He leaped up and seized something from the desk and hurled it against the wall. There was a crash and a thud. The material world around him was real. He resumed his seat and rubbed his forehead with his fingers.

"Are you all right?" Mather asked.

"All right?" The man's voice had sounded far away. Rod looked up and spoke impatiently. "Of course I'm all right. Why shouldn't I be?"

"No reason. That just happened to be a very expensive camera."

"Oh? Sorry."

"Think nothing of it."

"You got a pen?"

"Sure." Mather handed him one.

Rod signed the paper in front of him and handed it back. Apparently his having to stay here had something to do with that. "I want to go."

"OK. We can take care of the rest of it later. You must be tired. I'd take it easy on the booze for the next couple of days if I were you. You may be in danger." Mather rose and picked up the phone from the desk and put it front of Rod. "Memorize that number. You can call me Cotton to make sure you're talking to the right guy. I want you to keep in touch. I'll have you covered as best I can. Got it now?"

Rod hadn't even seen it yet. He was staring at a celluloid disc with marks on it. "Right," he said. He rose and gathered up his coat and headed for the door. Mather followed him.

"Get some rest. And just remember, I'm trying to get you out of this. Everything you do to cooperate will be in your own interest." He stopped with his hand on the knob of the front door. "You've forgotten your money." He handed it to Rod who stuffed it into his coat pocket. Mather opened the door. "I'm sorry about your friend."

"I don't know who you're talking about." Rod turned abruptly and hurried for the stairs. He ran down them and was out on the quai. He paid no attention to the weather but knew it wasn't raining. He walked rapidly. He felt as if there were a wild beast caged in him somewhere and knew that he must do nothing that might free it. He had to call Nicole to tell her he was back but that he mustn't see her. He'd tell her he was sick. She would want to come to him, but he'd think of something to forestall her. He reached the bridge and turned onto it. He caught a glimpse of a beret on a dark head bobbing among the pedestrians ahead of him. The pattern of hurrying figures shifted, and he caught the swing of a cape. He sped up and weaved his way through the oncoming crowd. When he came abreast of what he could see now was a very young boy, he was beaming.

"I knew you were all right," he exclaimed. "Where've you–" He saw a city dweller's hostile suspicion of strangers come up into the boy's face.

"We don't know each other," he protested in English.

"No. Of course not. I'm sorry. I thought you were–"

It *was* Patrice, of course, and yet somehow it wasn't. Nothing ever quite matched in dreams. Any idiot could see that he was taller and heavier and younger than Patrice, but there was no disguising the eager cheerful sweetness that was beginning to replace hostility as the boy looked him over. His cape was a regular schoolboy's cape. His dark hair was curly.

"Well, I guess we do know each other now," the boy said with a welcoming young grin. "Hello. I'm Georges."

"I'm Henry," Rod said, laughing. He remembered that the address on Gérard's card was on the Ile-St-Louis. "What are you doing over here? Have you been to see Gérard again?"

281

"Gérard? You know Gérard? How amazing. I've just come from there. That's where I live."

"You've gone back to him?" He was prepared for everything to have changed. The wrenching alteration that had taken place in him made it difficult for his to grasp what was happening around him although his head felt quite clear. The boy's voice seemed to reach him from a distance. Dreamlike.

"I don't understand," the boy said. "Have we met before? I don't see how I could forget you."

It was one of Patrice's games, testing him. "Not in this world," he said, playing along with it. "I was just going to have a beer. Do you want to have something with me?"

"Where?"

"Anywhere. There must be a bar along over there somewhere."

"Oh." The boy's grin became cheerfully suggestive. "I hoped you might be going to ask me home with you."

"Why would I do that?" Rod said, trying to make his smile enigmatic.

"I can think of reasons, can't you?"

Something was wrong with time. That explained the differences that puzzled him. Everything would fall into place if he didn't try too hard to make it all fit. "Aren't you awfully young to go home with strange men?"

"I'm almost 17. I'm a man where it matters."

"What makes you think I'm interested?"

"If you weren't, you'd have insulted me by now and left me."

"I wouldn't insult a boy just because he makes a pass at me. You know that."

"Maybe I do. You're sort of peculiar, Henry, but you're awfully handsome. I like you a lot."

"My real name's Rod. My earthling name." He chuckled. "What are you doing today? You aren't working?"

"No. I have to meet my mother later. I have time now."

"Your grandmother. She's coming up from the country to see you?"

"Yes. I'm having lunch with her. That's why I'm not at school right now."

"Your English is excellent. You've got hardly any accent at all."

"I'm supposed to go to the States next year. I've been working on it. I need an American friend to practice with. If you know Gérard, why don't you ever come to see us?"

"Oh, well. You know. It doesn't seem like a good idea."

"I'll tell you a secret." The boy moved closer so that they brushed against each other as they walked. "I come out on my own whenever I can, hoping for something like this to happen. Christian is always having strangers speak to him, but it's never happened to me before. I've always wanted somebody all to myself, somebody I've picked out for myself. You're going to take me home with you, aren't you?"

"Sure. I've been lonely without you. I want to tell you about last night." He decided not to mention Marseille unless the boy did. It didn't seem to fit this particular time sequence.

"I can't wait. Is it far?" He seemed to wriggle with excitement like a puppy.

Rod laughed. "Just off the rue du Bac. We can get a bus along here." They turned off the bridge and headed for a bus stop.

"I have a pretty big you-know and a nice behind. I do everything. You can—is it very bad to say fuck?—you can fuck me if you want."

"That's the way things generally turn out."

"I'll bet you've got a big one."

"It hasn't changed."

"The way you say it, it must be enormous. How exciting. Christian's is the biggest I've ever seen."

"Who's Christian?"

"My friend. He's at Gérard's too."

Competition. Just what he'd suspected. A bus thundered up to them, and they jumped onto the rear platform. It was crowded, and they stayed outside wedged up against each other. The boy's hands stirred on him. One of his hands worked its way under

Rod's coat and found what he was interested in and moved along it. He lifted himself almost to Rod's ear. "It *is* enormous," he whispered delightedly.

"You better wait till we get home," Rod said. Not home, of course. It wouldn't work somehow to go there. The hotel. Surprise him. He was a cheerful presence, largely faceless. He didn't want to scrutinize too closely the confusing differences. In a few minutes they came rattling and lurching to the rue du Bac, and they jumped off. Rod led the way around corners and along narrow streets to the hotel. He found his key hanging on a hook, and they mounted the stairs. When they were nearing his landing, they met the youth who had cruised him the day before. He spoke, and Rod nodded curtly. Mather's man? Let him put it in a report.

He unlocked the door and stood aside to let Georges in and locked the door behind them. The boy remained close to him. When Rod straightened and turned from the door, arms lifted around him, and his head was pulled down for a kiss. He was mildly shocked by the experienced rapaciousness of the young mouth. He shook his coat off and removed the boy's cape and dropped them both on a chair while the kiss continued. A hand ran along his fly. He seized it and broke away and moved the boy to the bed and sat him down beside him on the edge of it. The boy pulled off his beret.

"How come you decided you were queer when you were so young," Rod asked.

"Queer? You mean gay? I guess I've always wanted to be. I'm lucky, don't you think? Some men don't find out until they're married and have children. When did you?"

"When did I what?"

"Find out you were gay."

"Oh, you know me. I've never found out. Except for you—actually, I went to bed with the prince last night, not exactly intentionally, but it happened."

"The prince?"

"You know, Beauty Lussigny."

"You know him? He is beautiful, isn't he? I've had him. That's something we have in common. He's crazy about Christian, but he says Christian's thing is too big. Everybody says that. You should see it. He finally found a boy who wasn't afraid of it just the other day."

"Good for him, but you haven't answered my question."

"About being gay? I don't know. Gérard expects us to be, and I like it." He slipped a hand along the inside of Rod's thigh. "Now that this is happening, I can see what it would be like to have one person to care about. You're so handsome. I think I'm going to fall in love with you."

"Can you come back later?"

"You mean today? I don't see how I can. Maybe I could get out of lunch with my mother."

"I thought it was your grandmother. Never mind. I wouldn't want you to do that. Can't you come back afterward? I want you to spend the night with me. Here. We don't have to go home."

"You're so exciting. It doesn't matter where. Maybe I can think of an excuse, something to do with my mother. They wouldn't find out right away. It'll cause a horrible row, but it would be worth it for a night with you."

"I'm thinking of going to the States soon myself. I'll marry Nicole. Naturally, I want you to come with me."

"You're amazing. We haven't even made love together. You mean you want to keep me?"

"Well, we have the money. I'll help you find a job. That shouldn't be a problem."

"I'm all mixed up. Don't you want me to get undressed?"

"Sure. Go ahead. You'll come back later? There's something you could help me do." He thought about home. Something to do with his pictures? He didn't want to think about it now.

"I'll see what I can arrange if you really want me to." The boy rose.

285

Rod stared at the floor. He was tired. Sleep. It was nice having company. He took off his shoes and socks. He looked up just as the boy was pulling his legs out of his trousers. Funny catching him so young. A sturdy body but overgrown in an adolescent way. He couldn't believe he had been this young when he had repulsed the advances of the senior at college. The boy turned to fold his trousers over a chair. A plump round bottom. He returned to the bed in a few quick paces and dropped down beside Rod and nudged his arm. Rod put it around him.

"Do you like me?" He took Rod's hand and put it on his erection. It's pretty big, isn't it? Christian says it's still growing."

"It seems to have grown quite a lot recently."

"I'm cold with nothing on. I want to be in bed with you. We can keep each other warm." He began to busy himself with Rod's clothes. He took his jacket off and hung it on the end of the bed. He unbuttoned his shirt.

"You don't seem surprised about going to New York," Rod said to the floor, "but I've been thinking about it. It's been wonderful here, and I know I should work full time, but it's not that simple. I don't guess anybody can really get away from where they come from. That means having a job and making money and getting married and all the rest of it. When I'm a success in New York, then I can really make my own rules." He felt his shirt being removed and shifted his arms to cooperate. When he was being threatened, going back to the States seemed reasonable, perhaps necessary, but putting it into words made it sound like quitting. Patrice hated for him to think that way. Patrice believed in him, believed in his ability to triumph over all the odds. "I don't know," he added. "Maybe I'm just tired. When I get rested up I'll probably be ready to carry on the battle here. There may be problems. We have a lot to talk about."

"What a terrific body." The boy's voice still sounded curiously distant. "I'd go anywhere in the world with you." He was pushed back flat on the bed, and the boy knelt over him and went to work on his trousers. "Oh, Rod. How amazing. Christian may be bigger, but this is more exciting somehow. Wait till I make it all the way hard."

Rod lay with his eyes closed while the rest of his clothes were removed, and the boy performed his effective tricks. It was soothing to be with him again, but the beast still prowled. Something was wrong. Hadn't they gone beyond these technical exercises?

"There," the distant voice exclaimed. "It's all ready to take me. I hope that's what you're going to do."

The boy stretched out and offered his mouth to be kissed again. Rod obliged. It was all right this time. The expected generous delight. Rod pulled away. "It wasn't good with the prince, in case you're wondering. It was exciting at first, but then it turned into an orgy—we were at a party—I was disgusted by it. Still, you're not exactly a quirk anymore. I can be tempted. I won't let myself be taken by surprise in the future."

"If you mean you won't want other boys, that's fine with me. I want to be the best lover you've ever had. Where do you keep what you use?"

"I don't know. Do we have some in the bag? I'll look."

"No. Don't move. You mean the bag over there? Just a second." The boy sprang up and was back in a moment. Rod felt himself being efficiently prepared. "What a cock. I've dreamed of something like this happening. A handsome naked boy I found for myself about to make love to me. Now."

Rod moved to the bidding of the indistinct voice. He remembered his resolution as he was rushing from the party, but he hadn't meant it to include his boy. He shifted into his customary position and gripped a strangely ample body and drove into it swiftly as he was accustomed to do.

"Oh, God, you're hurting me," the boy cried out. "It hurts. No. Go on. Hurt me."

"What is it?" The beast was clawing at the cage, rattling the bars to be free. He got a precarious grip on violence and lay on the boy, trembling slightly. "I'm sorry. I don't want to hurt you."

"I love it. Oh, Rod, it's so exciting." His voice altered with astonishment as he repeated the name. "Rod? I remember now. I'll bet I know who you are. Are you a painter? Do you have a girl? You must be Patrice's American."

"Who did you think I was?"

"How amazing. Now you've both had me. Did he tell you? That's something else we have in common."

"What're you talking about?" His hearing had cleared. The boy's voice was loud and taunting in his ears.

"Last week, when he came to see us. He had us both, Christian and me. And we had him. I told you. He's the first boy Christian ever had that way. He was fabulous."

Rod looked down at the head on the pillow and saw an unknown evil child, lips parted with depraved remembered pleasure. How had he gotten here? His head seemed to split in two, separating him from his controls. The cage collapsed. The beast sprang free. He wrenched himself from the boy and lifted himself and struck with all his force. His fist smashed deceit and corruption. His tears began to flow. There was a cry and a brief struggle. He swung both fists in quick succession, and the body subsided. His fists flailed. Blood spurted. He was blinded by tears. He grunted with his exertions while his fists continued to pound soft flesh. A tooth fell from the battered mouth. Chest and stomach became a target for his blows. He felt bone snap. He struck a glancing blow to the groin, and the body jerked up and lay lifeless and inert. Patrice was dead. He deserved to die. Deception and betrayal. He thought he saw an eye glittering at him through an ooze of blood.

He scrambled up and backed away and hit the wall. He slid down on it and let out a pent-up shout. He huddled on the floor with his head back, and the shout rose to a scream. It broke off, and he slumped over and stared at his bloody hands. He shouted again and continued to shout. He realized that his mouth was forming words.

"Help. Murder." It roared out over the city. "Help. Murder," as if he were the victim. He heard rapid footsteps in the hall. He shouted again. Someone was hammering on the door. Gérard? His voice choked on tears, and his shout came out as a drowning rasp. "Help. Murder." Let them take him. He had had enough.

The body on the bed stirred.

"Yes, I understand, but I see no need to do it in this way." Nicole was seated on the sofa that she hadn't seen since her first afternoon with Rod. She sat stiff and upright as if resisting its associations. "You make it seem like a film or a charade."

The American called Mather paced in front of the fireplace. He stopped and hitched up his trousers and faced her. They had talked several times on the telephone, but this was their first meeting. "I guess it does sound kind of melodramatic, but I'm hoping the place will force him to accept reality. Your being here too. I can't make up my mind how much he's really off his rocker and how much is playacting."

"No. Not playacting. Not Rod. He is the most true man I have ever known."

"Yeah, well, he's a lucky guy to have you. You haven't seen him since all this happened. He still says he killed Valmer. I don't know if he means it literally or in some sort of symbolic way. He hasn't been here since I told him the kid was dead. They lived together for six months or so. If he still thinks he killed him after he's seen the place, I'll know we're in trouble."

"But you see, you're mistaken. He worked here. He talked about moving in, but he hadn't decided until the last time I talked to him, the day before he went away. He lived at the hotel where—" Nicole's voice trailed off, and she dropped her eyes.

"That's what he told you? Interesting. He's not the simplest guy I've ever met. He's been living here, all right. He took a room at the hotel again the day he got back at Marseille."

"But it's impossible. I don't understand. He's been *living* here?"

289

"That's right. Since the beginning of November." Nicole remained silent, looking at her nails with a perplexed frown. Mather went on, "Listen, Miss–Do you object to Nicole? It's easier than all that de la business. There are certain things in this situation I've got to speak plainly about. I'm sorry if it upsets you."

"No. I understand. The boy he–the boy at the hotel–it was sexual?"

"They were both naked, but there's more to it than that. According to one of my men, who's a declared homosexual, Rod more or less admitted that the thing with Valmer wasn't just friendship. We've checked his movements pretty carefully to make sure he's clean as far as our interests are concerned. The evening he came back from Marseille, he went to an all-male party. While there he went to bed with a fellow called Lussigny-Forbain. There are more than half a dozen witnesses–apparently some sort of an orgy. There's a pattern of violence that suggests he's gotten into something he doesn't know how to handle. Have you had any reason to suspect it might be a problem?"

Nicole gave her head a small distracted shake. "No. Lussigny-Forbain. How odd."

"I don't know how much to make of it. Guys fooling around. Drunk. Funny things can happen. How would you say things stand between you and Rod after all this?"

Nicole straightened her shoulders and faced the American squarely. "I don't see how that can be any concern of yours. What do you want? Why don't you leave him alone and let him work it out for himself?"

"Well, we know what would happen to him if I did that. You can't go around bashing teenage youngsters without having trouble with the law. Luckily, I had my people at the hotel. They took over before anybody knew what had happened. So far, Rod's name doesn't figure in any of the official reports. If the kid dies, of course, there won't be much I can do. He's still on the critical list. The doctors are worried about a kidney complication, but they think he'll pull through. There's a fellow called Thillier, the boy's guardian, who seems to be out for Rod's blood, but there's nothing he can do without bringing it all out in the open. I don't think he wants that any more than we do."

"It's all so horrible. I just can't believe it. It has nothing to do with Rod as I know him."

"Sex does funny things to people. Temporary insanity. If you'd seen him in the last ten days, you'd know the defense could make a pretty strong case with that line."

"But the trip to Marseille. That had nothing to do with sex."

"No, that was a straight business deal. You've probably guessed that I'm not interested in that. A two-bit dope operation. There's something else involved. When it all seemed to be blowing up, I didn't know where the chips were going to fall. Now that we've got it sorted out, I think we're OK. Valmer's murder is the only piece that doesn't fit. I suspect it's not supposed to. I've discovered a connection with a very highly placed individual on the French side. I think somebody may have recognized Valmer and jumped to the wrong conclusions. A private account settled. Tough luck."

A brief shudder contracted Nicole's body. She took a deep breath and lifted her head. "He doesn't know I am here?"

"I've been of two minds about that. There's the shock value of finding you here unexpectedly, but on the other hand I'm not sure just how much shock he can take. I've dropped your name into the conversation pretty frequently. It's hard to judge what his reaction is. I think he's so riddled with guilt that he doesn't dare count on you."

"He apparently has much to feel guilty about."

"It's piling up. You intend to be rough on him?"

"I? Why should I be? We were very deeply in love with each other ten days ago. I know nothing that makes me think it has changed. Whatever has happened with Patrice Valmer, what we have is not in my imagination. Parties and orgies—as you say, men sometimes do things that women can never understand. The only thing that troubles me is the boy at the hotel—the violence—but there must be more to that story than we know."

"I wish I had a wife like you. You're planning to marry him?"

"You ask questions that I find insolent. Why should I answer you? Who are you? What do you want with Rod? Why shouldn't we see each other in our own way instead of letting you use me for some game you're playing?"

"It's a pretty serious game. If you knew more about it, you might want to play it with me." He ran a hand over his face and glanced at his watch and shoved his hands into his pockets. "He should be here any minute. Let's not forget that if it hadn't been for me, our friend Rod wouldn't have had ten days of expert care and attention. He'd have been in a French jail. He's had a total breakdown, but I think he's coming out of it. I'm not running a benevolent society for the protection of deranged Americans. I've got a job to do, and I think he can be useful. If he can't be—well, I'm a busy man, and I have just so many trump cards. I can't afford to throw them away on risks that aren't worth taking. That may sound callous, but I want you to understand my position."

"What do you want him to do?"

"It's a bit soon to go into that. First, I want you two to sort things out for yourselves. If what you decide fits into a scheme that looks profitable to me, all well and good. Otherwise—it may be unpleasant for Rod, but it won't be the end of the world."

"But is that really fair? Shouldn't you make it clear what the choices are?"

A tight little smile appeared on Mather's weathered face. "I've planted a few seeds in the last few days. We'll see if they germinate. We want to make people feel that they're volunteers. I've found that the wrong kind of coercion doesn't pay."

"But you will warn him if you decide he's a risk not worth taking?"

Mather considered for a moment. "OK. I'll do that. I like the guy. He's—"

There was a knock on the door. They exchanged a quick look of warning and surmise before Mather moved around the sofa toward the door. Nicole sat without moving, her hands clasped to control the slight tremor in them. She heard the door open, Rod's voice, footsteps. She rose and turned with a faint smile to face him as he entered the room.

His penetrating eyes slid past her, and he stood absorbing the feel of the place. "Hello," he said. He had to force the greeting out.

"Hello, my dearest," she said quietly.

He moved quickly to the easel and removed the canvas that was standing on it and put it on the floor with the others, facing the wall. He straightened and stood staring out of the big studio window without seeing anything. The clothes Mather had brought him for this outing, his best jacket and slacks, made him feel overdressed for home. "Monkey?" he called. He turned his head and spoke over his shoulder in the general direction of Mather. "I know he's not here." He had been badly mixed up about Patrice. He had started to get it straight in his mind a day or two ago. Patrice had never come back from Marseille. Being here reminded him of the long afternoon's wait for him. They said he was dead, but Rod wasn't entirely convinced of it. They might be holding him somewhere as part of the plot. "Is he dead?" he demanded.

"I'm afraid so. He was killed."

"I didn't do it. I know I thought I did, but I didn't. I wanted to kill him."

"Is that what it was all about?" Mather asked sharply. "Did you think the boy at the hotel was Patrice?"

"Yes. It was Patrice. Why else did he come to the hotel? We talked about things only Patrice knew about. Then somehow it wasn't Patrice. I don't understand it any more than you do."

"Illusion," Mather said with the satisfaction of a man disposing of a problem. "You were exhausted and overwrought. I'd just told you that Patrice was dead. It's perfectly understandable. I'm glad we've got it straight finally. I'll run along and leave you two in peace."

Rod whirled around to him. "You don't want me to go with you?" He glanced again at Nicole. She was looking at him with tears silently rolling down her face. What was she doing here? Their dream of marriage was ended. What could he say to her? She must loathe him.

293

"I think we can get along without each other for a day or two," Mather said. "The telephone's there if you want me."

"The telephone?"

Mather pointed at the instrument on a table at the end of the room. "I had it put in a few days ago."

"Aren't you taking a lot for granted? What right had you to put a telephone in a place that doesn't belong to either of us?"

"I've been known to take liberties from time to time. As a matter of fact, you're wrong. The place belongs to you. Patrice left it to you. The will has to be probated or whatever they call it here. Meanwhile, I've arranged with the management to let you stay here if you want to. You can sell it if you go. It's worth quite a lot of money. The management is ready to give you $20,000. You could probably get more if you wait."

"He's really dead," Rod said, speaking to himself. Tears came into his eyes, and he turned quickly back to the window and saw now, blurred but known in minute detail, the walls and roofs and chimneys that it framed. He had studied it all thousands of times while the power Patrice had nurtured in him flowed out to shape paint on canvas. He had stood watching, as now, the late-afternoon light deepen into wedges of dark shadow, knowing that his boy would soon be here, lifting his spirits when they were down, bright and saucy with praise, eager to feed him and care for him, offering him his body for whatever pleasure he could find in it, selfless and undemanding. He had given so little in return, and now it was too late to make amends. Patrice was gone. No more pretending. No more hope. Would he ever be able to work again? He had to. Patrice had left him a parting gift of time, laid a burden of obligation on him. He had to prove that his boy hadn't misjudged him. "You're my life." The last whispered words came back to him, and he gasped with the sudden pain of loss.

He was aware of sounds behind him, a few murmured words, movement, the sound of a door closing. The floor creaked close beside him. Nicole? All of his body stiffened with the shame and guilt she stirred in him.

294

"Can't I help, my dearest?" she asked gently.

"How?" His voice was hoarse. He was barely able to get the word out.

"In any way I can. Perhaps it would help to talk to me."

"How much do you know about all this?"

"That man, Mr. Mather, I think he's told me everything, but only bare facts, without the meaning they must have for you."

Rod slowly turned toward her and found her standing only a few feet from him. Her tears were gone, and she looked at him with love and solicitude. He couldn't bear it. He had an impulse to hit her and drive her away once and for all. His eyes couldn't meet hers. "You mean you expect me to justify myself?" he asked roughly.

"No, darling. Only explain a little more perhaps. Was Patrice very bad to you?"

His eyes lifted and looked into hers. "No. He was wonderful."

"But you said you wanted to kill him."

"I was nearly mad. That boy—the one I beat up—he said they'd been to bed together, and I went over the deep end. Isn't that enough? Do you want to be in love with a madman?"

"I know you're more sensitive to life than most people. If you were very badly hurt, I understand that it would drive you nearly mad. Were you and Patrice lovers?"

Something in him balked at the word, but he found that he was past caring about appearances. "Yes, in a way. Ever since you've known me. The sex part was mostly doing things, letting him do things because they made him so happy. He was bound to want a real lover sooner or later. I'd stared to fall in love with him. I suppose that's why I felt I had to kill him."

"My poor darling. How terrible for you. Does it help to know that I think I can understand, or doesn't it matter anymore?"

"You ask *me* that? You don't know all of it. I've been to bed with Beauty Lussigny. Do you want a man who wants boys?"

"If he also wants a girl, that's probably more important. Life is full of adjustments—usually later, as one goes along. It might be better to make some of them right at the start. All the time when there was Patrice, you also made me very happy. We shouldn't forget that. If you would hold me, you would know the answer."

He took a quick step to her and put his arms around her. She moved in against him. "Oh, God. I was so damn happy." He choked on the words. Remembered sweetness and tenderness unhinged him. He was suddenly clinging to her, his whole body torn by sobs. She got him to the sofa and let him down on it, and he buried his head in her lap while all his agony was wrenched from him in great gasping sobs. She held his head and stroked his hair and soothed him. As torment subsided, he felt her love and was eased by it, but he was not yet able to draw it into himself. The magic and wonder he had known with her was gone forever; her acceptance of him was frightening. Why was she so confident that she knew who he was? She was still thinking in terms of a lifetime, but his mind could no longer encompass the concept. His sense of time remained badly dislocated. Fragments. There was still one fragment that had to be weighed and examined before he could hope to be intact. The thought of it agitated him and brought his shattered body upright. He sat on the edge of the sofa, creating distance between them, and kneaded his forehead with trembling fingers.

"Some man you've got on your hands," he said dully.

"Very precious to me, my dearest."

"What are we going to do?"

"I don't think we need worry about that yet. You're still recovering from a terrible ordeal. Let's think only of simple things—like whether you'd like me to go out and get us something to eat or would rather come home with me."

"No. I'm not hungry. I need a day or two before I can start functioning right again."

"But I can't leave you here alone, dearest."

"You have to. I'm not here yet. Have I talked to you about New York? I get mixed up. I talked to somebody about it. My idea was to go back to my old job so we could get married. What would you think of that?"

296

"Didn't you hate the job?"

"Not when I was doing it. It could be worse. I've got to make a living. I've failed here. Patrice wouldn't let me face it, and now he's made it even more difficult by getting himself killed. This place. I have his money. I don't see how I can help giving it another try for his sake."

"That man Mather worries me. What does he want you to do?"

"I'm not sure. I think he wants me to go back, but he hasn't actually said so. On the contrary, he keeps warning me of the trouble I'll be in if I try to leave. It seems that kid might still–" His body was seized by a spasm. His face was contorted. His hands doubled into fists. He took a breath that was a gasp. The spasm passed. "Oh, God, it's all so horrible."

"Try not to think about it. Think of Patrice. I think you're right. I think you must go on with the work he believed in, that I believe in. You couldn't be happy with me or anybody else if you go back to something you hate."

"Yes, I've thought of that. But what if I never paint another picture? I don't think I ever will."

"That will pass when you feel better."

"It might," he agreed, thinking of what he was going to do as soon as she left. He rose, feeling overdressed again in his working surroundings. Maybe if he got out of these clothes, he would capture some sense of life resuming. "You should go. You're wonderful to have come. I don't like you to see me when I'm like this."

"Don't be foolish, darling. If we can comfort each other, that's what we're here for. I can't bear to think of your being here by yourself."

"Don't worry. It's good for me to get used to the fact that he won't be coming back. I'll probably be fine tomorrow." He turned. She stood in front of him. He reached out for her again and held her and knew that it was too soon. He wanted her still but not with the blazing intensity he wanted somebody else. They exchanged a kiss that to his relief she kept chaste and affectionate. They released each other, and she gathered up her bag and a light coat, and they moved to the door.

"Very well, dearest. At least you have a telephone now. That's a comfort. Mr. Mather gave me the number. I won't bother you, but please call when you feel like talking. For what it's worth, I love you very dearly."

"It's worth everything. I don't deserve it, but I'll try." He wanted her to go. What could he say to her if he didn't know how he could live with himself, let alone anybody else?

The instant he had closed the door behind her, he shed his jacket and started pulling off his tie as he returned to the living room. His thoughts flew to the prince. His body was burning with a need for the prince's body. His need had suddenly lit his disjointed consciousness a few days ago, and his mind had been clearing ever since. It was a simple reality around that he could reassemble his thoughts. Something appalling had happened to Patrice. Nicole had become a terrible question mark from which he shrank. His work, the future, whatever Mather had been trying to communicate to him—they all lay outside his power to control them. His body's need fell within the possible. The prince had marked him in some way he couldn't quite reconstruct. He had to repeat the experience to learn everything he could from it. He knew he had never felt anything like it with Patrice. He loved Patrice; he could never love the prince. He remembered a moment of revulsion against all queers, but he didn't know what had prompted it. If he were one of them, he would have to think again. Patrice was the most wonderful person he had ever known, but physical need had come slowly. His need for the prince had apparently remained in him since he had first grappled with his body. Holding Nicole briefly had told him that he might need her again. What did it mean? He couldn't start living again until he had finally penetrated this mystery in himself. The never-ending discovery of self—a life force, the only hope of salvation.

He continued to shed his clothes until he stood naked by the sofa. Thoughts of the prince had aroused him. He looked down at himself and wished he remembered the prince's erection more clearly; it was the key that would unlock the mystery. He wanted to see it standing up for him again, choosing him unequivocally, stretching out with desire for him. He had not yet adjusted to having such thoughts and found them bizarre, perhaps even shameful, but he welcomed their healing power; they were prodding him back to the reality he had sought to flee. Had Patrice turned him into a cock worshiper?

He dropped onto the sofa, and his body was racked again with silent sobs. "Oh, God," he gasped when he had them under control. "Why, monkey?" He spoke aloud to the presence he felt vividly all around him. He had wanted to kill him, but it was a comforting presence. Patrice's infidelity still jarred–it had been a definitive reversion, not a haphazard relapse, an abandonment of all the values he had chosen for himself, a failure–but he would encourage him to be unfaithful every day if he would come back. What would life be without him? That was what he was going to have to find out.

He reached for his jacket and pulled the prince's card out of his wallet and went to the new instrument and dialed the number. His heart began to beat rapidly with anticipation. He recognized the charming voice as soon as he heard it and felt himself lifting into full erection.

"Hello. Phil? Thank God you're home."

"Phil? No. Can it possibly be? How heavenly. Nicole said you weren't well. How are you?"

"Better. I've got to see you. I called as soon as I could."

"How sweet of you, darling. That's the best news I've had in months. I was afraid you were displeased with me. I wouldn't blame you if you had been. However, we can talk about that later. When shall we meet?"

Rod hesitated, feeling suddenly ridiculous. He didn't know how to court a man. "Now? I mean soon? I suppose you're busy."

"I have a drinks date in half an hour and a dinner later. I'll cancel everything and be with you in ten minutes. Will that do, darling?"

"Wonderful. You don't know what it means to me."

"And to me. You've turned me quite giddy again. Will we be seeing each other with nothing on?"

"I haven't got anything on right now. Well, I've got a hard-on to be exact. If you want to make a night of it, you might bring some wine and anything to eat you have around the house. I've just got back." He gave him the address.

"I'll bring heaps. Considering the size of it, that cock must need lots of nourishment."

Rod laughed. He hadn't laughed since the last time he had seen the prince. In fact, he couldn't remember much laughter for some time. A tough, lean, and bleak period. Doubtless what he'd come here for—to learn that life was grim. "You should see it. If you don't hurry, I'm going to jerk myself off."

"Don't, darling. If nothing else, I'm a perfect antidote to masturbation. I'll be right there."

Rod hung up with another burst of laughter and went about gathering up his clothes with a renewed little spring in his step. Life wasn't all solemn drudgery. Hadn't he once thought he was happy here? He went back to the bedroom and put things away. One of Mather's henchmen had evidently been here; everything had been left in order. There were gaps on hooks and shelves where Patrice's things had been. That was all right; things didn't matter. Patrice was still here. Rod could hear his merry laughter as he started to put on a dressing gown and then tossed it aside. Patrice knew that Rod didn't want to cover up for the prince.

He returned to the living room, but he avoided the studio area. He would make himself whole again and then discover what was left for his work. He stepped into the bathroom-kitchen to make sure that everything was clean and tidy. He took towels back to the bedroom and checked to see if the essential product was where he expected it to be. Mather's men were certainly models of efficiency.

He heard the knock on the door before he expected it, and his heart bounced up with welcome. He strode down the corridor, eager to be swept up once more in the raw, liberating excitement that dominated his memory of the other time. He opened the door and closed it after the prince stepped inside. The prince dropped a hamper at his feet, and they were in each other's arms. Rod ran his hands over expensive cloth, exulting in the bulk of the magnificent body that he would make his for a little while. They kissed deeply and broke apart with laughter. Rod looked into the limpid blue of the prince's gentle eyes while his fingers worked down over the buttons of his shirt. "My turn to undress you," he said.

He hesitated an instant before he pulled the shirt open and reached for the fly, finding it very nearly inconceivable as he proceeded that he had the right—that it was expected of him—to open his friend's pants and free the startlingly big cock that thrust out into his hands. He dropped down and ran his tongue along the underside of it. He had done this the other time, but his memory of it was dim; he was sharply conscious of what he was doing now. He felt knotted muscle beneath infinitely delicate skin. He listened with satisfaction to the delighted cries he provoked as he opened his mouth to receive it. The prince was struggling to get out of his shoes, and Rod offered a hand to help. He pulled trousers and shorts down to the floor, and the prince stepped closer. Jacket, tie, and shirt fell around him. Rod coiled his arms around sturdy thighs and hoisted slightly, testing the weight he could bring crashing down on him. A thought of the wrestling match he had proposed crossed his mind; it would be an even contest.

He raised himself to the lifting angle of the muscular flesh in his mouth and felt explosive strength gather in it. The prince's cries became a rhythmic accompaniment to the pressures of his caressing tongue. Hands fluttered over his face in light-fingered encouragement. He was stirring his friend to a passion of wanting him, taking total control of a man's desire and a man's ecstasy. The need to dominate some area of his life was appeased. His groin ached with the response of his own straining erection. He drew his head back and looked at the hard shaft of flesh that he had nursed into rampant potency and remembered that his was bigger.

He sprang up with breathless triumphant laughter and took a step back and stood with his hips thrown forward and his thumbs resting on his thighs, proudly offering it for comparison.

The prince's eyes were on it. "Good heavens, darling. Bigger and better than ever. And I'm not exactly a midget, am I? We're quite sinfully gorgeous together."

"Yeah," he said, surveying the great golden body, astonished that their nakedness and the candidly lustful display of their erections, even what he'd just been doing with the prince's, should seem so natural and inevitable. Nothing challenged or threatened him. "I could stand here gawking all night," he exclaimed. "Come on." He sprang into action, helping the prince snatch up his scattered clothes, and they hurried back to the bedroom. They dropped the clothes and headed for the bed. Rod seized the prince's wrists as they reached it and faced him for further appraisal. The aristocratic beauty of the head required no comment; it was there for all the world to marvel at, although the tension of desire in the wide blue eyes was thrillingly for him. The similarity of their physiques—matching height and weight (although the prince's smooth, burnished full-blown flesh made him look heavier), matching shoulders, matching hand spans (although the prince's hands were beautiful), down to the nearly matching cocks—contained a residue of uneasiness until he recognized the uneasy delight of equality. They were equals; neither could be responsible for the other. He fell back on the bed and pulled the prince down on top of him. He let out an exultant shout. "Oh, God. Your body all over me. I'm about to come. Quickly, sweetheart."

They made love to each other with their mouths and had quick simultaneous orgasms and lay together with their bodies loosely entwined.

"Yeah," Rod said with the prince's tongue running around the corner of his mouth. Now we can roll along with it and have it all."

"I feel as if I'd been struck by lightning. For somebody who more or less *doesn't*, you're a revelation," the prince said.

"I'm a novice, but it's awfully easy to let myself go with you."

"I'm stunned. I mean, when I was flinging myself at you, I did seem to rather bounce off."

"I didn't know anything then. I didn't even know I like to suck cock. I want to tell you. You know Patrice Valmer, don't you?"

"Gérard's Patrice? Of course. An utter sweetie. I was quite mad about him in my inconstant fashion once upon a time."

Rod could talk about Patrice at last and knew that his need to do so was as great as his need for the prince's body. His throat tightened. His vision dimmed. He took a long shuddering breath of release. "I've wanted to talk to you about him. I can't with anybody else." He told him about their odd life together. He told him how it had ended.

"Good God," the prince exclaimed. "You mean, just the other day? When we were together? How ghastly for you. You must've made him very happy even when you were holding back. It's hard for me to imagine. I've never had any doubt about what I wanted in bed."

"If he'd had a body like yours, it might not have taken me so long to figure it out. It took you to show me what it was all about. I'm still finding out. I have to."

"I'm so glad it's me, darling."

"It's you, all right. Come up here and sit the way you were when you first let me look at you." He ran his hands indolently over all the magnificent body as the prince lifted himself and straddled him and settled lightly on his stomach. Rod brushed his fingers through crisp golden curls and held the soft sex in the palm of his hand so that he could see it. "Fabulous. I can look at all of you now. The other night I couldn't take my eyes off this. It's pretty damned impressive even when it isn't hard. If I ran into you in a shower, I'd definitely want to see how big it could get. I've never thought about that with anybody before. Do you know a kid called Christian? I think he lives with Thillier."

"Oh, dear. I do believe I'm blushing. Christian and his incredible giant cock?" "Is it twice as big as mine?" Rod asked, thinking of something he had once said to Patrice.

"Really, darling, let's remain within the limits of possibility. It's bigger certainly. The biggest I've ever seen. Why do you want to know? I'm sure he'd be delighted to show you if you asked."

"No. I just wondered. Patrice knew him."

"Patrice knew everybody, and everybody loved Patrice."

"I'm not surprised, but I had the impression he was rather ashamed of what he'd been before we got together."

"Oh, well, the atmosphere at Gérard's is fairly bizarre. Nobody's allowed in the house who isn't prepared to perform in public, and he can't bear for any of his boys to be turned down, not that anybody often wants to. It's a socialist dictatorship. Hardly the thing for a sensitive growing boy. I wasn't surprised when I heard he'd walked out. Somebody told me they'd seen you together. You must be the only person he ever lived with on his own, in his own way."

"Yes, I am." He understood now. Patrice had done it for him, to win his way back into Thillier's good graces. He remembered how odd he'd been when he'd come home that evening. He must have been sick with guilt if he had enjoyed it. Poor baby. "If he—he'd be pleased that this has happened with us. He wanted me to have boys."

"Really? Did he want to get you away from Nicole?"

"No. I think he thought I needed girls on the side. He thought I was queerer than I'd admit."

"Are you?"

"What would you say?"

"I'd say you've admitted to quite a lot with me, darling. Cock sucking among men *is* generally considered a bit peculiar."

They burst out laughing together. "I guess it is, but I also want to fuck you–*and* girls."

"Perhaps you just have a nice healthy interest in sex."

"I hope that's it. I don't see why I shouldn't have sex with anybody I feel something special about. You. I can't believe there'll be many others. I don't think I'll ever be promiscuous like you."

"Touché, darling. Have you forgiven me for the other night?

"I know you behaved outrageously, but it's all pretty hazy. Forget it. I want you. I'm glad there's nobody else around for you to want. Look at it now, sweetheart." He moved his hand secretly, insinuatingly along silken skin and watched with fascination as the contours of the prince's burgeoning erection grew more and more imposing. "It's so heavy. It's enormous already, and it isn't really hard yet. It's about time for you to offer to bring it up here to me. This time I'll accept, even though it's something guys who like girls don't do. You are beautiful. Sex rampant. Being with you is so marvelously physical. I've never been so excited and relaxed at the same time. Now, sweetheart, I want to feel it getting hard in my mouth." He put his hands on the back of the prince's thighs and drew him up until knees were gripping his shoulders. Rod punched the pillow to make himself comfortable. The head of the prince's cock was resting on the side of his neck. He lifted it and drew it into his mouth and felt it surge up, swell hugely, harden. After a few moments he released it and let it swing up and stand commandingly in front of him. He laughed. There's no denying it. A girl couldn't give me a thrill like that. All of it wanting me. That's what I like to see." He put a finger on its base and prodded it gently, making it sway with heavy rigidity against his face. He looked up at the prince around it. "I wish I could have it with my mouth when I'm fucking you."

The prince smiled down at him. "You can, darling."

"Really? How?"

"How lovely. I still have things to show you. My wee cock is quite long enough for that trick." He dropped forward and slid down Rod's body, scooping up Rod's erection between his thighs as he went. When their eyes were level, they met and gloated over each other. Their mouths opened, and their tongues played over their lips. The prince fell away onto his back and rolled Rod up on top of him.

Much later, when their bodies were no longer joined, Rod slipped away to the bathroom. In a few minutes the prince joined him, trailing a towel. "Here you are, darling. What bizarre sanitary arrangements."

Rod turned from the sink, drying himself. When the prince reached him, he laid his fingers lightly on the side of Rod's face and fixed him with his wide blue eyes. "All yours at last. What utter heaven. Is it good for you, darling?"

"More than that. You're untying all the knots. I think you may be making it possible for me to go on living. The other night I remember being shocked by it happening with two such big masculine guys as if doing it with a girlish boy made it more normal. I don't understand it all yet, but I guess if you like it with a guy, any guy, that's that. You somehow make me feel it's perfectly natural. Man to man, doing fabulous things with our bodies that we could never do with a girl. Narcissus, maybe, but dammit, discovering that my cock can hold its head up in such awe-inspiring company does give me a thrill. We both take what we want. Neither of us is giving in to the other. There's nothing very feminine about either of us. That's all part of it, I think, part of what makes it so right and—and so damn *satisfying*. We understand men's orgasms and how cocks work. We've come four times together, and we still have a long way to go. I'll probably have more to tell you in the morning if you're interested."

The prince leaned forward and kissed him lingeringly on the mouth, and Rod stepped closer and held the big body against him and felt its power under his exploring hands. The prince drew back with his angelic smile. "Why don't you go peep into that hamper and see if there's anything you like? I'll splash about for a moment in this adorable tub. If the evening's just beginning, we should snatch a moment for nourishment."

Rod did as suggested and found an assortment of exotic groceries–tinned duck and foie gras and smoked eel and other delica-
cies. He was even more impressed by the wine, some bottles of
overwhelmingly distinguished Burgundies, plus a bottle of the most
expensive cognac in the world. It figured. He couldn't even pick up
a boy who wasn't a luxury item. His destiny guided him to the rich.
Why fight it? Life had gotten completely out of control because of
money troubles. Twenty-thousand dollars was hardly a fortune, but
he would have done almost anything for it two weeks ago.

Their meal was an erotic banquet. They ate it reclining on
the sofa, shifting constantly as they sought new visual and tac-
tile thrills in the interplay of their bodies. They fed each other.
They drank wine from each other's mouths. The prince's in-
ventive abandon created a world of sensuality into which Rod
gratefully retreated. He wallowed in rich food and voluptuous
rose-gold flesh.

The night passed in fitful drowsing and renewed outbursts of desire. They turned the light out when dawn was beginning to turn
the room gray. They slept heavily and awoke in late morning and
again reached out for each other. Eventually, Rod made coffee, feeling vividly alive and almost complete again. The fragments were
knitting together. He supposed that everybody was made up of fragments. If you could make them fit and mesh you became an acceptable human being. Everything was turning out as he had
hoped it would; his desire for a male body was no longer a source
of conflict but a recognized element of his nature. He had no more
secrets from himself. That must be a good start for probing the rid-
dles that still surrounded him. When the prince joined him in the
kitchen, he used Rod's toothbrush.

"Don't I remember something about your not liking to use other
people's towels?" Rod asked.

"Other people. You're not other people, darling. I'm not at all
sure I haven't got your teeth in my mouth. The least I can do is
brush them."

They drank coffee and splashed around together in the tub. Rod lay back with his legs draped over the prince's and looked at him through lowered lids. "I remember your saying I was mad. I was. Literally. It had started when I met you, and you didn't help. I can't say that now. You're curing me. I hope you don't mind being used as therapy."

"I know it's something like that, darling. I'm so glad I could be here when you needed me. Does that mean it's time for me to go?"

Rod grasped his knees. "Oh, no. Please. I want to be with you all day and all night. Maybe tomorrow I'll be able to face real life."

"I doubt very much that I will be if real life doesn't include you, but I always feel like that when I'm with somebody I adore. Not that anything like this could happen more than once or twice in a lifetime. Still, I survive. I'd better make some phone calls if I'm going to be out of circulation for another 24 hours."

They climbed out of the tub and dried each other and completed their morning toilet by shaving each other amid wild bursts of laughter. "That's the sexiest thing I've ever done in my life," the prince said as they ended in each other's arms.

The prince made his phone calls. It didn't occur to either of them to put on any clothes. Rod called Nicole and was able to assure her convincingly that he was much better and arranged to see her the next day. He hung up and turned to find the prince watching him from the armchair, a slightly troubled look in his peaceful eyes. Rod went to him and dropped to his knees in front of him and parted his legs to move in between them. The prince ran his fingers through Rod's hair.

"She hasn't told you her secret, has she?"

"Not that I know of. Has she a secret, Beauty? I said that was a silly name, but I don't know what else I *can* call you. That's what you are. Beauty."

"It's my secret too. She has to tell you sooner or later. What would you think of me if you discovered I'd known it all along? I don't feel right not telling you. I don't understand her. It's really very naughty."

308

"This is getting interesting. I always felt there was something mysterious about her."

"A rather foolish little mystery. She's my wife."

Rod stared at him. "Your what?"

"She's *madame la princesse*. We're married."

"I don't believe it."

"I don't blame you. It wasn't much of a marriage, as marriages go. Still, there it is. It's all to do with a tiresome old story about a will and a rather tidy bit of lolly that I couldn't touch until I was married. I was in quite serious trouble, thanks to my usual folly. Prison gates yawned. The only way out was marriage, and Nicole obliged. We always assumed that we'd do something about it when the time came, but it hasn't proved as simple as that."

"When was all this?"

"Years ago. Seven, to be exact. We were infants."

"How old are you now?"

"I was afraid you'd ask eventually. I'm 28."

"I'm about to be 27. You look much younger."

He looked up at the prince's face. The small shock passed, and he burst out laughing. "Nicole's two husbands." He lifted himself and sat on the prince's knees, his legs spread, facing him. "I must say, she has marvelous taste," he said in a voice that trembled with laughter.

"I always thought she had," the prince agreed, responding to Rod's blatant invitation. Within seconds, the superior erection had lifted vigorously between them. Rod gripped the prince's shoulders and let himself fall back at arm's length so that his erection slapped against his belly. The prince took possession of it again. "Are you still mad about it?" Rod demanded, the laughter bubbling in his throat. "Of course you are. We're mad about each other, but it can't go on forever. I want to hear more about this marriage."

You pick the most peculiar time for a serious conversation."

Rod leaned forward and rested his forehead on the prince's so that their noses touched. "Don't stop. I love what you're doing. Did you ever sleep with her?"

"Once. I went to bed with her boy, and he insisted that we should all get together. I didn't expect anything much to come of it, but it was rather sweet."

"And how does she expect to marry me if she's already married to you?"

"That's the question. She'd better not try it here. The Vatican and all that. If you do it in the States, I'm sure nobody will pay any attention. As I remember, she somehow managed to keep her passport in her maiden name. Can you imagine that I would make trouble? Of course, if you become very famous and have dozens of families, like Picasso, you'd be in the soup. But you'll die eventually, and your children can fight it out."

"Do many people know?"

"Not a soul except the drones who took care of the will."

"Then that leaves us. We seem to have worked things out very nicely for ourselves." He rubbed noses with the prince and watched him deliciously manipulate them both, holding them against each other in a way that emphasized Rod's supremacy. "God, yes. Me first? Now." He lifted himself hastily and uttered a cry as the prince took charge of his orgasm. He dropped to his knees again and bowed his head in time to receive the prince's ejaculation. He swallowed it gratefully and sank down with his head in the prince's lap, his cheek resting against the subsiding erection. Something slipped into place in his mind. He could marry Nicole now. He had let himself go completely with his male lover, but the prince hadn't come between him and his girl. All his deepest instincts were attuned to what Nicole could offer him—stability, children, the labels that would make it possible to live in the world he knew and felt at home in. There would be boys (he accepted it tranquilly), but she understood about that; she had been to bed with the prince.

The more he knew about her, the more sure he was that they would be good together as soon as they had told each other everything. They had been living in a sort of dream before, but dreams didn't help with everyday reality. She was a flesh-and-blood girl, not a fantasy of delicate ladylike perfection. She had certainly been exposed to his weaknesses and seemed to have come to terms with them. Best of all, he was beginning to think they could have fun together. He would marry Nicole. He lifted his head and looked up at the prince who was lovingly stroking his hair.

"Maybe it *will* go on forever. Why try to pin it down? I'm going to marry Nicole. I mean, I finally know it. I've just realized how important it is, thanks to you. I love you madly, Phil beauty." He sprang up and reached for the prince's hands and pulled him to his feet.

"There's some less exciting therapy you can help me through." He slipped an arm around the prince's slim waist and started for the studio end of the room. He ran his hand down over the rich flow of the buttocks in motion. He moved it up along the muscles of the back and felt the light swing of the wide shoulders. He dropped his arm again to the waist and stopped and turned to him and held him close. He lifted a hand and traced the hard formation of jaw and cheekbone with his fingers and marveled at the exquisite modeling of the straight nose and full disciplined mouth. He felt the wide-set blue eyes gentle on him.

"I was terrified at first when you looked at me like that," the prince said, "but I'm not anymore. The menace is gone, if it was ever there. I do believe you approve of me."

Rod laughed at the understatement. "I'll say. I told you—you're too perfect for art, but we'll see. I'm trying to say something. I don't know how to thank you for—for so many things. I'll be grateful for the rest of my life." He ran his hand over the thick golden hair and tangled his fingers in it and held his head, still hungry to possess all of him. "You've taken me on a sort of trip of—of recovery, convalescence, of *dis*covery. I feel as if there were about ten times more of me than there was before, ten times more to cope with. You've let me carry on about myself. You've been patient. You haven't laughed at me. You've been as perfect as you look. That's why it's difficult to thank you."

"I don't think we need to start thanking each other, darling. I have no problems. I'm having a glorious time with somebody I adore. I *am* in love with you, much more than I realized or thought possible. If it had happened five years ago, we *would* have a problem. As it is, I'm as happy as a lark because I see no reason why it shouldn't go on forever. Not necessarily like this, but everything else. Knowing you. Knowing Nicole. Bless you, my dearest darling."

They hugged each other. Rod gave the big behind a loving little slap, and they broke apart. He was on edge as he got out his drawing materials. He wasn't sure he was ready for this, but for the first time since his collapse, he felt able to risk a try. Progress. The prince moved with almost blinding radiance into the light in the center of the work area.

"What am I supposed to do?" he asked.

Rod chuckled nervously. "Just stand there and look gorgeous. It won't require any effort." He looked, trying to find form and structure beneath the surface splendor. His hand began to move hesitantly, waiting to feel the current that flowed from his eyes when he was working well. It wasn't there. He was looking at his subject with the eye of a lover, not an artist. So be it. He would draw a beautiful man that he wanted. He began to work more confidently. By the third try, something was coming through, his eye functioning more accurately. He could do good work without the intense concentrated effort of his whole being that Patrice had expected of him. He began again. A bell rang. He ignored the sound as a tiresome distraction until he remembered that he had a telephone and muttered "Damn" as he put down his pad.

"Just a second. Stay there," he said as he started across the room. He picked up the phone and said "Hello."

"Hi there. Cotton. Just wanted to check in. How goes it?"

All his nerves were immediately in an excruciating tangle. "Pretty good," he snapped. If Mather had news that could destroy his life, he would surely get it out quickly. Each passing second calmed him. "How's the kid?" he managed with only normal concern.

"OK. The doctors are talking about an operation, but they're not sure he's up to it. They're going to let it ride for another day or two."

"I hope to God they're as good as you say they are."

"Don't worry about that. How's the prince? Everything going smoothly? No violence? Don't forget you've been—"

"Goddamn you," he blurted through clenched teeth. He thought of the things he had said to the prince on the phone, and his cheeks were burning. "You said you were going to leave me in peace."

"So long as it's peace, I'm all for it. I don't want you to do anything that'll throw you off balance again. I thought the prince was—"

"I don't care what you thought, damn you. Leave me alone." He slammed down the phone and seized the wire and ripped it from the wall. He was seething with outrage and terror. His knees began to tremble. He couldn't take it—the spying, the tapped telephone (everything taped for posterity?), not being able to have a friend here without everybody knowing. Doctors? An operation? Was Mather trying to drive him crazy again? Why should he wait around for the kid to—. Police. Jail. His stomach seemed to turn to water. All the carefully assembled fragments were about to fall apart. He wasn't going to go to jail for a kid he'd never really seen. He hadn't been born tough enough to survive it. He doubled over and tore at his hair and pounded his head with his fists. He felt the prince's arms around him. He straightened and flung himself against his friend and was held in a strong embrace. He was trembling all over. His breath came in gasps. Get out, his mind dinned at him. Go home. Get out. Home was safety. Outwit Mather. Leave everything and walk out. Go to the airport and go. No one could touch him at home. Get out.

The strong arms around him and his mind's premise of escape calmed him. At least there was no more telephone. He kissed the prince's shoulder and shook his head and lifted it. "I'm sorry, darling. Thank you. I'm all right."

"Are you sure, darling?" They held each other's faces and looked intently into each other's eyes. "You frightened me. What is it?"

"Don't ask me to go into it now. I'll tell you later. Actually, it has less to do with me than you'd think from the way I'm acting. Let's knock off the art class. I need a drink. There's plenty of brandy left.

I put everything in the kitchen. Would you get me something, darling? My dearest darling, as you so rightly put it."

The prince drew his mouth to his and kissed it softly and left him. Rod didn't see him go. Monkey? He didn't say it aloud although he still felt Patrice's presence around him everywhere. He didn't want to be caught talking to himself. He walked slowly to the chair beside the fireplace where his boy always sat and looked down at it. Patrice wouldn't want him to go through any more of this. He was quitting. He had probably lost his single-minded determination to triumph in his uncompromising vocation; he had discovered so much more of himself that required satisfaction. He would go back to a job, but he would regain control of his life. Patrice's encouragement had been a goad driving him to excel himself always, confining him to the impossible. The impossible had seemed possible with Patrice; it never would again. They had lived through their heroic period together. Even Patrice had failed. His passionate attachment to an ideal that had found expression in his undivided love for a stray American painter must have shattered and died that afternoon at Thillier's. Perhaps he had wanted to die with it. He had failed, as everyone who set his sights too high was bound to fail. With a little shrinking of his heart that brought tears to his eyes, Rod told himself that he must never let himself be driven to extremes. Come to terms with the possible. Get out. Never again lose his control over events.

I've tried, goddamnit, he silently addressed the rebellious spirit that struggled to retain contact with the beloved presence. His birth had unfitted him to be anything more than a dilettante. A rich boy couldn't learn how to be a poor boy. He turned from the chair and took a few quick strides into the room and veered off toward the prince as he emerged from the kitchen carrying two glasses. They met near the easel, and the prince handed him a glass. They put their arms around each other. They stood with their bodies brushing against each other.

"I put water with it. Is that all right?" Do you want to lie down?"

"Not here. I'd rather you didn't leave me for quite so long for the time being. Will you help me, darling? I promise there's no danger involved, even though it may sound sort of weird. I've decided to go back to New York as soon as possible. In the next couple of days. People may try to stop me. I'm being watched. It makes it difficult to get anything done."

"How exciting, darling. Are you a spy?" The tranquil beauty of the prince's face was undisturbed.

Rod edged closer to him. "Insanely enough, I think somebody wants me to be. Don't worry. I'm not going to play. I want to get my pictures home. There's been an offer for this place. You and Nicole can help me get it all squared away. I should maybe just go and let her follow when everything's organized. You said you wanted to go to the States. Why don't you come too?"

The prince lit up with a boyish excitement Rod hadn't seen in him before. The joyous innocence of it made his beauty almost unbearable. "What a heavenly idea. I will."

"You mean it?"

"Of course." They both laughed rather breathlessly. Their hands strayed eagerly over each other. "Will you teach me how to behave like a nice normal American?"

"If you promise to seduce me every now and then. There's nothing un-American about that. You can be my best man at your wife's wedding. That should make it official." They laughed some more. This was what life would be like when he got back where he belonged. Fun with Nicole. Fun with his friends. The freedom he had thought he was finding here but which only money, after all, could buy. Yet there was something here, a strangely coherent but elusive view of life that had shattered the rigid moral precepts he had grown up with. Right and wrong, good and bad, normal and abnormal—they all seemed to melt into each other and overlap in people's lives here. It had troubled him deeply at times, but it didn't seem to do anybody harm. There was freedom in it, something he wanted to take with him while he went on trying to get everything straight in his mind. He would never get anything straight until he freed himself from Mather. He gripped a caressing hand. "I want to get out of here. We don't have to worry about anything today. I'll get down to business tomorrow. I'll let Nicole know I'm with you. I mean, I hope that's where I'll be. Will you take me home with you?"

"Oh, darling, will I ever." They drained their glasses and got rid of them on the nearest table, freeing their hands for their bodies' pleasure. "If you're being followed, you couldn't have found a better accomplice. Circumstances have obliged me to find ways of getting in and out of my building that nobody would believe. We'll fool them. I have some lovely toys to show you. We've eaten off each other's tummies. I might find something that'll lead us to wilder flights of fancy. I know. I have a golden suit—solid gold, if you please—more like trappings really, bits and pieces that fit on me here and there like a ceremonial elephant. An outrageous codpiece and a scandalous bit that goes down my behind. Seductive is hardly the word for it. I'll put it all on and see if you can get me out of it."

"That's the idea. Games for depraved children. A treasure hunt, and I get all the prizes. Except that I have the impression that you want me. I'll be interested to see how you get this into a codpiece. Let's go." Rod glanced around him and suddenly felt as if all the strains of the last months were gathering and intensifying in him until they seemed as confining and tangible as shackles. The strain of trying to be what he and Patrice had wanted him to be. He turned abruptly from the prince's caressing hands. "Let's go," he repeated in an altered voice, harsh and peremptory. "I never want to see this place again."

A final communication was received in the obscure office outside Washington:

BIRD HAS FLOWN. PLAN 2 NOW OPERATIVE. WATCH MARITAL DEVELOPMENTS. WEDDING PLANNED WITH NICOLE LUSSIGNY-FORBAIN, ALIAS DE LA VENDRAYE. MARRIED. NOT DIVORCED. BIGAMY WILL PROVIDE CONVENIENT CONTROL. ALSO BOYS. APPLY CAREFULLY AS INDICATED. SEE MY 748. A NEAT PACKAGE. MAKE THE MOST OF IT. COTTON.

316

alyson
books

A FRAGILE CIRCLE, *by Mark Senak.* The story of a man's love for his friends, his partner, and himself set against the backdrop of the AIDS epidemic.

B-BOY BLUES, *by James Earl Hardy.* A seriously sexy, fiercely funny black-on-black love story. A walk on the wild side turns into more than Mitchell Crawford ever expected. An Alyson best-seller you shouldn't miss.

2ND TIME AROUND, *by James Earl Hardy.* The seriously sexy, fiercely funny sequel to the best-selling *B-Boy Blues.* Raheim Rivers (a.k.a. "Pooquie") and Mitchell Crawford (a.k.a. "Little Bit") are back—back in love, back together, and back to stirring up the hip-hop community and the rest of New York.

DESMOND, *by Ulysses G. Dietz.* When gay vampire Desmond falls in love with a human man, his dark world will be forever changed.

THE GOOD LIFE, *by Gordon Merrick.* In 1943 a high-society murder case drew international attention for its irresistible combination of violent crime, scandalous sex, and enormous wealth. Gordon Merrick and Charles Hulse put their own fictional stamp on the story, and an entertaining romp through the lives of rich young gay men emerges. "Beautifully visual writing," says *The Washington Blade.*

JOCKS, *by Dan Woog.* An intriguing look at America's gay male jocks as the locker-room closet opens up. Is there life after coming out to your teammates? Is there life before coming out? This collection of more than 25 inspiring real-life stories digs deeply into two of America's twin obsessions: sports and sex.

LOVE BEWTEEN MEN: ENHANCING INTIMACY AND KEEPING YOUR RE-LATIONSHIP ALIVE, *by Rik Isensee.* The only step-by-step self-help book specifically geared toward gay men in relationships.

MY FIRST TIME, *edited by Jack Hart.* A fascinating collection of true stories by men across the country, describing their first same-sex encounters. This is an intriguing look at just how gay men begin the process of exploring their sexuality.

THE PRESIDENT'S SON, by Krandall Kraus. "President Marshall's son is gay. The president, who is beginning a tough battle for reelection, knows it but can't handle it. *The President's Son* is a delicious, oh-so-thinly-veiled tale of a political empire gone insane. A great read," according to Marvin Shaw in *The Advocate.*

These books and other Alyson titles are available at your local bookstore.
If you can't find a book listed above or would like more information,
please visit our home page on the World Wide Web at **www.alyson.com**.